3 -

Dave Mason
The Making of a Man

The last baseball hero retired in 1951
Will Dave be the next hero? Will he be the man?

JOHN DE RUSSY MORELL

Order this book online at www.trafford.com/07-2298
or email orders@trafford.com

Most Trafford titles are also available at major online book retailers.

Note for Librarians: A cataloguing record for this book is available from Library and Archives Canada at www.collectionscanada.ca/amicus/index-e.html

Printed in Victoria, BC, Canada.

ISBN: 978-1-4251-5230-7

We at Trafford believe that it is the responsibility of us all, as both individuals and corporations, to make choices that are environmentally and socially sound. You, in turn, are supporting this responsible conduct each time you purchase a Trafford book, or make use of our publishing services. To find out how you are helping, please visit www.trafford.com/responsiblepublishing.html

Our mission is to efficiently provide the world's finest, most comprehensive book publishing service, enabling every author to experience success. To find out how to publish your book, your way, and have it available worldwide, visit us online at www.trafford.com/10510

www.trafford.com

North America & international
toll-free: 1 888 232 4444 (USA & Canada)
phone: 250 383 6864 • fax: 250 383 6804 • email: info@trafford.com

The United Kingdom & Europe
phone: +44 (0)1865 722 113 • local rate: 0845 230 9601
facsimile: +44 (0)1865 722 868 • email: info.uk@trafford.com

10 9 8 7 6 5 4 3 2

DAVE MASON: *The Making of a Man*

is respectfully dedicated to the memory of
my late mother Francis De Russy Gordon
a beautiful Christian lady

and to

every high school student
who is struggling with school work,
relations with their fellow students
and or athletic performance,

in the hope that this book
will inspire them to improve in all areas of life

PART ONE

PALO ALTO, CALIFORNIA

May 4, 1945

Chapter One

Palo Alto High School Baseball Field

Palo Alto, California

4:45 PM May 4, 1945

DAVE MASON IS standing on the pitcher's mound of the Palo Alto High baseball diamond. It is the first half of the ninth inning of a game with San Jose High School. If Dave can get three batters out without a hit, he will have pitched his first no-hit game. The score is Palo Alto 2 and San Jose 0.

Dave's journey to this day started six years ago. While on a church picnic he was playing catch with a friend when an older man walked up to him and asked Dave to throw the ball again. He did, and the ball had a sinking drop to it. The man asked Dave to show him how he held the ball. Dave showed him the sinker ball grip. "How did you learn that grip," the man asked. "I read it in a book," Dave replied. The man told Dave he had a natural sinker ball and if he developed good control he could be a good pitcher. The man gave Dave a description of the target he should build. He said, "You should throw balls at it every day."

The target had a frame within a frame that created slots large enough for a baseball to pass through on the inside and outside of the plate. The man said, "You have to be able to locate your pitches on the inside and outside edge of the plate. If you don't have good control, batters will wait you out instead of swinging at your sinker.

Make the slots a bit larger than the plate, because umpires are not perfect. That will provide larger slots to aim for." Then the man was gone. The boys never did learn his name. A rumor started that it was Ty Cobb, who lived in Atherton, but no one knew for sure.

As the years went by, Dave practiced almost daily pitching to the target. He was a fan of the San Francisco Sea Lions of the Pacific Coast League. The Sea Lions had sent Vic Marko to the New York Dukes of the American League. During World War II most players on the Sea Lions Club were former major league players who were over-age or could not pass the physical for military service. Dave's favorite player was Bob Royce a pitcher who had perfected a slider that made batters hit ground balls to infielders and fly balls to outfielders that were caught in the big outfield of Sea Lions Stadium. Dave even adopted the windup and over arm pitching style of Bob Royce.

Dave started his playing career in the Palo Alto Junior Baseball League. Later he graduated to American Legion baseball at the age of 14. In high school, the baseball team was at the bottom of the barrel of Palo Alto High School (Paly High), sports teams. In the spring, the best athletes were on the swimming team that had a record 63 dual meet wins without loss in 1945. The track team contested for the league championship yearly, and had not lost a duel meet for some years. During his high school career, Dave had a low earned run average of 2.00 but had only 10 wins to his credit. Dave allowed a high number of hits per game but few earned runs. He had pitched in 29 games in three years. The problem was poor defense. A "ground ball" pitcher must have good defense or the ground balls become hits instead of outs. In a game against Half Moon Bay High School in 1943, the team committed 15 errors. That's difficult to do in the seven inning games high school teams played.

The first batter steps into the batter's box and Dave throws the sinker. The batter hits the ball into the ground on a line to Dave, who throws him out. The next batter takes a strike

Then he fouls off the next pitch. It's now no balls and two strikes on the batter. Looking for the sinker, the batter swings way under a rising fast ball, and Dave has an infrequent strike out. Two down, one batter away from the no-hitter! The next batter takes the sinker first pitch low for a ball. On the next pitch, the batter, looking for the sinker, swings too soon. The count is now one ball and one strike. Dave thinks he may have the batter lulled into the idea that Dave is not going to take a chance on a sinker and another error in the field. The team has made two in the game, which resulted in the only San Jose threat to score. Dave throws the sinker, the batter over swings, and the count is one ball and two strikes. Dave thinks the batter is really confused now. The next pitch is an inside sinker that handcuffs the batter and sinks into the strike zone for a called strike three! The game is over and the no hit game is history! The team carries Dave off the field.

In the stands following the game, Luke Devore, the West Coast scout for the New York Dukes of the American League, was seen congratulating George Mason and his wife, the parents of Dave. Luke had been following Dave's career since he was a first year high school pitcher. The Dukes liked "ground ball" pitchers because the team always had an excellent defense and played in a stadium with a large outfield. The center field in Dukes' stadium was called "The big pasture."

The Mason Residence
512 Coleridge Avenue
Palo Alto, California
6:15 PM May 4, 1945

During dinner this evening, there was no talk of the game or base-ball. It was the usual talk of the war and other subjects. Dave did much of the talking and asking questions. He was always the slowest eater, and since the family had a formal dinner, served in courses by the cook, the rest of the family had to wait for Dave to finish before dessert could be served. Dave's sister Pam was the most aggravated. She wanted to eat and leave the table.

The discussion this evening was about the war, specifically the war in Europe. "General Eisenhower reports surrender in Holland, North Germany and Denmark," the headline read in the afternoon

Palo Alto Times. Dave's father George was president of Peninsula Newspapers, Inc. the firm that owned the Times and two other newspapers on the San Francisco peninsula. Dave's mother Ann was a newshound, camping by the radio while she knitted for the Red Cross. Since the invasion of Europe, she had kept a map showing exactly where the front lines were. During these evening dinners Dave and Pam were receiving an education they could not obtain anywhere else. Dave asked his dad how long after the Germans surrendered it would take to defeat the Japanese. George Mason's reply was, "Two years to invade and conquer Japan." Although Dave had just turned 17 in April, his interest was whether he would he be serving in the armed forces before the war was over.

After dinner, George asked Dave to come to the upstairs master bedroom at eight o' clock so he could talk to him. George and Dave sat in chairs looking out over the spacious back yard of the Mason home. George said he wanted Dave to know what Luke Devore had said to him after the game. He said, "The Dukes will make a formal contract offer to you following high school commencement." George asked Dave if he had any second thoughts regarding what he had previously decided about a contract with the Dukes.

Early in the baseball season, when it became obvious that the Dukes were interested in signing Dave to a contract upon his graduation, George had done considerable study of what Dave would face as a young baseball player in the Dukes' farm system. A friend

George knew well had a son, Jim who was an outstanding baseball player in high school before the war. He had signed with the St. Louis Cardinals and played his first season in 1940 as a member of the Midland City Cardinals in Alabama, a member of the Mid South League. In baseball classification it was a D league, the lowest of the minor leagues. Jim had endured the bad food, long bus rides and the oppressive heat and humidity of the south to play very well and probably would have been promoted to a C or B league team in 1941 if the event at Pearl Harbor had not occurred.

Jim's father was an executive of the Pacific Steamship Lines, so he urged Jim to immediately join the Navy. He did, and was sent to

UCLA for possible pre-officer qualifications in the V-12 program. Later, he served in the Pacific. After the war Jim attended Stanford on the G.I. Bill that paid for college attendance. He played intramural and Palo Alto City League softball.

As the result of Jim's experience, George recommended Dave not sign a professional contract. Dave had decided the time was not right and he was not ready for professional baseball. Also, he had to think about probable service in the armed forces. His choice for some time had been the Navy. He was interested being an aircraft mechanic.

Because Dave was 17, his dad would have to sign for him to enlist in the Navy. George had advised Dave early in the year that to enlist as a very young high school graduate with no skills would mean he would be swabbing decks and chipping paint. George said Dave needed to acquire a skill through training. Dave had developed an interest in airplanes and had taken three years of auto mechanics shop in high school, so he said he would like to learn about aircraft engines. George found the Samuel Gompers Trade School located in the Mission District of San Francisco. The school had a summer course in aircraft engines. George said they would visit the school soon after high school commencement.

Throughout high school, Dave had little interest in school work and academics. His interests were sports, working at the family ranch on Black Mountain and the Navy. He had studied the Blue Jacket's Manual, the Navy's instruction book for new recruits, stem to stern. He had to be tutored to pass geometry and spent one summer in a reading school at Stanford University. Dave read no books, only newspapers, particularly the sports pages.

Dave was friendly and had a good personality around friends and people he knew, but was shy around strangers and girls. He had an inferiority complex, partly because he had suffered from a bad case of acne during his early years in high school. His sister Pam was always reminding him of it. So Dave had almost no social activity with girls. He went to only two dances during his three years at Paly High. Dave did not build his confidence by being successful with girls. He built his confidence on the baseball field. During his junior year, George sent Dave to Dr. Montgomery, a dermatologist located in San Francisco for treatment. "Monty" gave Dave extensive x-ray treatments that cleared up his face and back but would later cause skin problems for Dave. "Monty" was a long-time friend of George Mason and would not charge for the treatments. George had helped him out of a difficult situation in the past for which he was very grateful.

6:15 PM May 7 1945

VICTORY! This was the headline on the front page of the Palo Alto Times. Germany had surrendered unconditionally. The report had been made at General Eisenhower's headquarters at Reims, France. The next day, May 8th, was designated VE Day. The end of the European war brought a conclusion to that part of the bloodiest and costliest war in human history. The end came after five years, eight months and six days of strife that spread over the whole world.

At the Mason dinner table, the main subject again was how long it will take us to defeat Japan. As George Mason, had previously said, it would take at least two years to invade and occupy Japan. He thought the Japanese would be fanatical in defending their country. Dave asked his father how much more training he would need after Samuel Gompers before he would sign for him to enlist in the Navy. George said, "I'll investigate that and let you know."

During Dave's senior year he had study hall during the first period of the day. Students could study in the library instead of the study hall classroom if they desired. Dave decided to study there because his friend Geary was studying there with his girl friend Anne, a sophomore. Anne's friend Earlene, also a sophomore studied with the group. Later, they were all in danger of being sent back to the classroom because of Earlene's laughter. Dave became friendly with Earlene, as he now felt less inferior because of the improvement of his skin.

As the time of graduation approached, Dave wanted to attend the Senior Prom. He asked Earlene, and she accepted, and with Geary and Anne they had a great prom.

Chapter Two

Samuel Gompers Trade School

2800 Mission Street

San Francisco, California

11:00 AM June 21, 1945

A WEEK AFTER commencement, George and Dave traveled to San Francisco by car to visit Samuel Gompers Trade School so Dave could sign up for summer school. George encouraged Dave to take one or two additional courses besides aircraft engines. The school counselor also encouraged this. But Dave, thinking about time for baseball, declined. He knew he would have to ride the train and two streetcars to get to the school. This would take time out of each day, so Dave registered for only the course in aircraft engines, a class held in the afternoon.

Riding in the car on the way home from San Francisco, Dave thought about his immediate future. Being a senior member of the Redwood City Post 105 American Legion team, he hoped their season would continue as it had started. The team had won three games without defeat, and Dave had pitched two of the wins. He wanted the team to make the playoffs so team members would be seriously considered by professional baseball scouts. Because of the war and restricted travel, the playoffs would only be regional, but they would attract scouts.

Living in the area covered by Palo Alto High School, Dave had to try out for the Palo Alto Post 52 American Legion team when he was 14. However, at that age he did not have much velocity on his fast ball, partly because of his "string bean" stature of 6′ 2″ and 160 pounds. The coaches were not convinced Dave could win games with his sinker ball pitching. It may have been because the coaches knew the team would not have a good defensive infield. Dave did not make the team.

This allowed him to try out for the Redwood City team. Dave knew this team would have better players because the baseball teams at Sequoia High School in Redwood City were consistently very good. Dave made the team, but not because of his pitching, but his hitting. At the age of 14, he was a good contact hitter who hit to all fields. It was ironic because Dave's father had founded the Palo Alto American Legion Post.

Dave started thinking about the high school baccalaureate service. He had been affected by the message of The Rev. Marvin Stewart, pastor of the Methodist Church. Dave had attended Presbyterian Sunday school through the ninth grade. His teacher, Marshall Verillo, during the junior high years, was very good. He was the son of Dave's barber, Victor. Marshall sold advertising for the Palo Alto Times.

At the time, Dave was not excited about religion. He had not heard the message of salvation in Sunday school. He and his sister Pam had heard it from Elsie, one of the Mason's cooks. She was a member of the Seventh Day Adventist Church. Dave would learn later that the Palo Alto First Presbyterian Church had a liberal interpretation of theology. Dave and Pam had heard that the high school youth group featured folk dancing. They were not interested in folk dancing, so they wanted to drop out. Their dad did not object. George Mason had been a member of the Presbyterian Church because his best friend and fellow American Legion member, George Whistler, was the pastor. Born and raised in Massachusetts, George Mason grew up in the Congregational Church. He would later become a member and leader of the Palo Alto Congregational Church.

Dave had been thinking about looking for a different church since graduation. Then, while getting a hair cut in Vic Verillo's chair, Dave asked if there was another Presbyterian Church in the area. Vic suggested Dave visit the Menlo Park Presbyterian Church, located in the town just north of Palo Alto. Dave thought he would do that on Sunday.

Dave was also thinking he should ask Earlene for a date. They had enjoyed the senior prom. Summer dances were being held at the Community Center on Friday evenings, so he decided he would ask Earlene to one of the dances.

Menlo Park Presbyterian Church
716 Santa Cruz Avenue
Menlo Park, California
11:00 AM June 24 1945

Dave was attending his first church service in four years. The last service he had attended was Youth Day at the First Presbyterian Church in Palo Alto. He remembered it, because the pastor preached two sermons. There was one for the young people and one for the adults. It had been a long service.

The pastor of the Menlo Park church was The Rev. Don Emerson Hall. He was a young man who had graduated from seminary just a year ago. The subject of his sermon this Sunday was Ephesians 2: 8-13. Verse 8 reads "For by grace are ye saved through faith; and that not of yourselves: it is the gift of God." Verse 9 said, "Not of works, lest any man should boast." (In 1949 most churches used the King James translation of the Bible).

Since this was all new to Dave, he was glued to what Hall was saying. Dave realized he would have to get his Bible out and read it. It was one he had been given during a Sunday school graduation years ago.

The congregation attending the service appeared to be about 100 by Dave's estimate. He thought it was a nice small church. It was called "The Church of the Pioneers." Dave decided he would return.

The Mason Residence
6:30 PM June 25, 1945

During the Monday evening dinner, the family discussion was about the long battle for Okinawa. It had been a very bloody battle. There had been 12,500 American deaths and 36,000 wounded, making it the highest toll of any Pacific campaign. Among the dead was General Simon Bolivar Buckner, commander of the 10th Army. This battle was just an indication of what the toll might be in the invasion of the main Japanese Islands.

Sequoia High School Baseball Field
Redwood City, California
1:30 PM June 26, 1945

During this practice of his American Legion team, Dave pitched batting practice. The players always wanted Dave to pitch batting practice because he got the ball over the plate. No pitches were wasted.

The team was still undefeated, having won five games. Dave had pitched three of the wins and played right field in the other games. He was hitting well, leading the team in batting average. Catcher Bruce Boyd Katcher, called B.B., it really was his name, was supplying the power with home runs and doubles. He was a typical big catcher, but he could run. In Dave's estimation, he was the best professional prospect on the team.

Early in Dave's American Legion baseball career, a coach had told him he had a great opportunity to pitch inside because of his control. If you can pitch inside, the batter can't get the fat part of the bat on the ball. Also, it tends to drive the batter away from the plate so he can't reach outside pitches. Dave followed this advice with good success. Although he wanted batters to hit his sinker the less bat they put on the ball the better.

After practice, Dave asked some teammates to join him for bowling. Dave did this quite often as his response to his teammates barbs about him being a Palo Alto High School Viking. All the other team members were from Sequoia High and Palo Alto and Sequoia were heated rivals.

Dave was a very good bowler. The same gift he had developed in pitching a ball where he wanted it to go gave him the same control of a bowling ball. A veteran bowler had demonstrated to Dave how to make the ball curve to make strikes. Dave had bowled two 300 games since starting to bowl at the age of 13. Most important, Dave enjoyed bowling, and it kept him active when he was not playing baseball. Dave also learned he could make money by challenging bowlers to games for money stakes. Many experienced bowlers were very willing to engage a young high school boy in games until they learned how good Dave was on the lanes. In time, bowling would help him in some financial negotiations. It was something he couldn't imagine at this time.

The Mason Residence
6:30 PM June 26, 1945

When the family sat down to dinner, the subject discussed was the signing of the World Security Charter establishing the United Nations. The meeting in San Francisco was attended by representatives of fifty nations. Dave asked his dad, "Will this organization work better than the League of Nations?" His dad replied, "It will work better because the U.S. will be a member. Our Congress would not approve membership in the League because Congress was dominated by isolationists. The big test will be whether the organization can stop one country from attacking another." The world would find out soon enough.

The family did not interrupt dinner for anything except the radio program Fibber McGee and Molly on Tuesday evening. On that night a radio was moved into the dining room and all listened and laughed at McGee and his group of characters: The Great Gildersleeve, The Old Timer, Teeny, Ole Olsen, Mr. Wimple and others.

Samuel Gompers Trade School
3:30 PM July 13, 1945

It was Friday afternoon. Dave had completed two weeks of summer school and was very interested in the course in aircraft engines. He was beginning to learn how to study, something he had not learned in high school. He did his studying on the train trip to and from San Francisco. At Samuel Gompers, Dave had met John, who became a friend. He was a member of a well known San Francisco family. One day, while riding the Mission street car, Dave did not ask the conductor for the transfer he needed for the Third Street car. He returned to get the transfer, but the conductor wouldn't give it to him since he didn't ask for it upon boarding. John talked to the conductor and came back with Dave's transfer.

On the trip home to Palo Alto each afternoon, Dave was able to ride a train that made few stops. It reduced the trip time to 50 minutes. He used the time to study. His Dad's continuous encouragement to do the important things first was working.

Palo Alto City Baseball Park
5:15 PM July 13, 1945

In the first playoff game against Palo Alto Post 52 Dave had pitched a win, although he gave up nine hits and three runs. He had done better in the batting department, getting three hits and driving in three runs. Redwood City won the game 8 to 3.

In today's game the team's fast ball pitcher, Willie "Dizzy" Dean, pitched a shutout, and Redwood City defeated Santa Clara Post 419, 6 to 0.Dave continued his hitting while playing right field. He had two hits and two runs batted in.

After the game a baseball scout came up to Dave and said, "You should give up pitching and concentrate on hitting and playing the outfield." Dave's reply was, "If I play professional baseball, it will be as a pitcher."

The Mason Residence
7:30 PM July 17, 1945

Dave and his dad were again in the upstairs master bedroom for a talk. George said he had done some research on future educational options for Dave. He said, "To have any opportunity to serve in aviation you need more training before you enlist in the Navy."

"I have found two schools that would train you as a mechanic and prepare you to obtain Civil Aeronautics Administration (CAA) licenses to work on aircraft engines and the aircraft themselves. The first is Cal Aero Tech, located in Glendale. It offers a two year course that would ensure that you would earn the licenses and the school would provide experience working on engines and aircraft. The second choice is California Polytechnic College, (Cal Poly) located in San Luis Obispo. The college offers the same course as Cal Aero plus a B.S. degree in aeronautical engineering. While Cal Poly has been primarily a Navy training school during the war, the college had a full sports program before the war, including a baseball team."

Dave almost immediately chose Cal Poly. George agreed that Cal Poly was the best choice. He gave Dave the Cal Poly course handbook that Dave would study for many hours. He didn't learn until he had read the catalog that Cal Poly students were all men, no coeds. However, because of Dave's history of relations with girls, he didn't give it another thought.

Indian Bowl
735 Emerson Street
Palo Alto, California
8:00 PM July 18, 1945

Dave was a substitute member of the Palo Alto Times team in the summer Service League. The league was made up of service business firms in Palo Alto. Filling in for a vacationing regular, Dave bowled the high average of 178 for the team. Because of summer school and baseball, he had not bowled much during the summer, but as the score showed he had not lost his touch. Dave really liked to bowl. It stirred his competitiveness, but he could relax while bowling. He had thought that bowling could be an alternate to baseball as a sport to compete in while he was young and as a good activity as he aged. It would be an important activity in Dave's future.

Palo Alto City Baseball Field
1:30 PM July 21, 1945

San Jose Post 89 and Redwood City Post 105 were the teams ready to play the final game of the regional playoffs. San Jose had come through the lower bracket in the double elimination playoff. They had lost one game. Redwood City was undefeated. If the Redwoods won the game, they would be the regional champs. If San Jose won, it would require a second game. Dave would be the pitcher for Redwood City.

The date with Earlene that Dave had thought about had finally happened the previous evening when they attended the dance at the Community Center. After the dance they had gone to Piers Dairy for peach milk shakes. Dave had invited Earlene to attend the baseball game, and she was there with her friend Anne.

The game was played on a beautiful sunny day with no wind. For five innings it was a pitcher's duel, with no runs scored. Dave had allowed two hits but no San Jose runner had reached second base. The San Jose pitcher, a big fast ball chucker, had allowed only three hits and no runner past second base.

In the top of the fifth, with the bottom of the Redwood City batting order due up, the Redwood fans were not optimistic. Then shortstop Billy Winn, batting number eight, singled to left field. Dave was up next and laid down a perfect bunt along the third base line that died halfway to third. There were now two men on and no outs. The lead off batter, second baseman Jimmy Stone, sacrificed the runners to second and third respectively. Right fielder Don James struck out for the first out. Center fielder Fred Wood popped out to short. There were two outs and the clean up batter B.B. Katcher coming up. The first pitch was a ball, low. The next pitch, a fastball, was a bit high, but over the plate, and B.B. got all of it for a home run. It gave Redwood City a 3-0 lead. The next batter, third baseman Sam Slade, flied out to left field, to end the inning.

In the bottom of the fifth, Dave threw five pitches and got three ground ball outs. The Redwoods went out one-two-three in the top of the sixth. In the bottom of the inning. Dave got two ground outs and one short fly ball out to left field.

Dave was up in the top of the seventh inning. Although he was still working on becoming a switch hitter, he batted right-handed in games. With the count one strike and one ball, Dave singled to left field. A sacrifice and Dave was on second, with one out. Right fielder James singled to right and Dave scored. The next two batters were outs, so at the end of six and a half innings, it was Redwood City 4 and San Jose 0. Dave had to get just three outs, and Redwood City would be regional champs. (All games were seven innings).

The first batter fouled out to B. B. Katcher. The next batter grounded to short. Dave threw the next batter a rising fast ball that he hit into center field for the last out. Redwood City Post 105 was the Regional Champions of American Legion Baseball. The final score was 4 to 0.

The baseball scout who had advised Dave to concentrate on hitting did not talk to him after the game. Earlene and Anne congratulated Dave following the game. Dave felt very good.

Menlo Park Presbyterian Church
11:00 AM July 22, 1945

The next day, Dave was attending the worship service at Menlo Park Presbyterian Church. The sermon by Rev. Hall was from Luke, Chapter 10, verses 25 through 37. It was the parable of the Good Samaritan. Rev. Hall challenged the congregation to be good Samaritans, to help people who are obviously in trouble or pain.

Island of Tinian
American Held Marianas
2:45 AM August 6, 1945

A heavily loaded B-29 bomber, the Enola Gay, rolled down the coral runway. It carried the first atomic bomb. Its destination was the city of Hiroshima, Japan. Later, as the Enola Gay flew at more than 31,000 feet, the city of Hiroshima lay below. At 8:15 AM the bomb bay doors opened, and the bomb dropped. First Lieutenant Morris R. Jeppson, who was monitoring the electrical circuits, had started a count on when the bomb should explode. 40…41…42…Jeppson stopped the count. He thought the bomb might be a dud. At that instant the world went purple in a flash. The tail gunner, Bob Caron, experienced his eyes closing involuntarily behind his goggles. He thought he had been blinded. Caron had been looking at an explosion which had become a ball of fire 1800 feet across, with a temperature at its center of 100 million degrees. Hiroshima was a missing city.

Dave and his family heard about the bomb via radio. The secret of the Manhattan project was told. Plants had been built in Richland, Washington and Oak Ridge, Tennessee to make the bomb. These were new cities built by the government where none had previously existed. Each plant had built part of the bomb. The workers didn't know what they were building and that was how the secret was kept.

The family also learned about the first test of an atomic explosion on July 16, 1945 at a remote area of the Alamogordo, New Mexico Air Base. All members of the family were amazed at this development in the war. "Will Japan surrender?" That was Dave's first question. His dad was not sure. If they did it would mean much in the lives of many Americans both in and not yet in the armed forces. Everyone was waiting and hoping Japan would surrender. George Mason read from the family Bible and led prayers for the end of the war.

Japan did not surrender. With no surrender, President Truman authorized a second bomb to be dropped. It was exploded over Nagasaki on August 9, 1945. The Japanese Cabinet voted to surrender. The surrender was approved by the Emperor. Unknown to the world, a group of Japanese Army officers who opposed the surrender were attempting to stop it. While the effort to surrender played out in Japan, Dave and his family waited with anticipation. Again this would mean much to Dave and the lives of many Americans.

Aboard the Southern Pacific Coaster Departing Los Angeles Union Station 8:30 AM August 10, 1945

Brandon Jouker pronounced Jolker, but usually called Joker by most people, was on his way home to northern California. Brandon was born and raised in Yreka, the first city south of the Oregon-California border. Highway 99 ran through the center of town. The family was supported by Yreka Garage and Service, an independent repair garage and a Tide Water Associated gas station. Brandon was interested in anything mechanical or electrical and wanted to learn how any device functioned. His mother never had to call a repairman for any appliance in the home because Brandon could fix anything. He learned about cars and logging trucks from his dad. He started working in the garage at the age of 13.

A member of the Yreka High School class of 1943, Brandon joined the Navy soon after graduation. In the Navy he learned about radios and electronics. He had been a C average student in high school primarily because he wasn't interested in most of the subjects he was required to take. During the war he had not thought about attending college, but a friend changed his mind. Bill, a fellow radio man, had wanted to become a Navy aviator.

The first step was to attend a refresher course to qualify for preflight school. Bill wrote to Brandon about the college where he was taking the refresher course. It was California Polytechnic, a college Brandon had never heard of. Bill said Cal Poly had some interesting courses, like Agricultural Engineering. Bill had learned that admission to the college only required a high school diploma. Bill encouraged Brandon to check it out when he was discharged.

Brandon had been discharged two days ago in San Diego. While buying his train ticket home, he learned the train would run right past California Polytechnic College. He decided he would stop off and find out what he could about this college.

As the result of talking to a Cal Poly advisor, Brandon decided he would try Agricultural Engineering. It appeared to offer a student with mechanical interest and ability an opportunity to earn a degree. It also appeared to be the least difficult of the engineering courses. He applied for his G.I. Bill benefits, which would pay all of his college fees and a small living allowance. He could tell his dad, who expected him to return to Yreka to work in the garage, that by attending college he would be better prepared to run the business. He would return to the college during the first week in September to enroll.

Upon returning home, Brandon told his parents what he planned to do. His mother supported him. His father, looking forward to having Brandon's help in the garage, was not so happy. Brandon didn't say so, but he really wanted to live in a larger city where there would be interesting new machines to work on.

Brandon had always been one to play tricks on people, and he continued this during his time in the Navy. The word soon got around, "Beware Brandon." His last name fit him very well.

Samuel Gompers Trade School
4:00 PM August 14, 1945

It had been a normal school day, but with much discussion about the possible end of the war. At 4:00 PM, Pacific War Time, President Truman announced by radio that Japan had surrendered unconditionally and the Emperor was announcing the surrender by radio. It would be the first time a Japanese Emperor had addressed the Japanese people. To Dave, it meant he would not have to serve in the Navy and could get on with his education and maybe play some baseball. To the thousands of men of the Army, Marines and Navy, it was like a death sentence being lifted, because they would not be involved in the invasion of Japan. General George Marshall, Chief of Staff of the Army had estimated 250,000 army deaths in an invasion. This did not include Navy aircraft crews or ship crew deaths as the result of the kamikazes.

Mr. Jacobs, Dave's instructor, who lived in Palo Alto, told Dave he could ride home with him. He said, "The street cars would be mobbed and traffic bad in San Francisco." Upon reaching home, Dave rode his bike to downtown Palo Alto to watch the biggest celebration he had ever seen in his quiet town.

Del Mar Club
Aptos, California
1:30 PM August 20, 1945

During the war years the Del Mar Club had offered family memberships for a very reasonable fee. George Mason had bought one. The Del Mar Club was a hotel located high on the Aptos cliffs south of Santa Cruz. The club offered dinner, dancing and was featuring Hal Pruden and his Band. Pruden was a fast playing pianist. His band had just completed a date in the Mural room of the St. Francis Hotel in San Francisco.

The club had a private beach below the cliffs. It had everything you could want at the beach, including dressing rooms and a snack bar. During the war, many Navy blimps patrolled the Pacific Ocean in search of Japanese submarines. The blimps were based at Moffett Field in Sunnyvale. Also, there was a small base above the cliffs south of Aptos. With no more subs to look for the Navy boys spent their time cruising above the beaches in the blimps and using their high powered binoculars, they looked at girls.

Dave and the family were here at the Del Mar Club for a week before both Dave and Pam departed for college. Later in the week, Tommy Dorsey and the band came to stay for a couple of nights before playing for a dance at the Coconut Grove, the dance hall on the beach at Santa Cruz. On Sunday the family had gone to Carmel for the day and had lunch at The Carmel Valley Ranch. On the trip back to Aptos, they picked up a couple of service men. They had gone to the dance in Santa Cruz and said it was packed. The war was over, most people had plenty of money, and now they wanted to spend it.

Chapter Three

U.S. Highway 101

10 Miles South of Paso Robles, California

3:30 PM August 29, 1945

JILL GARBER WAS driving back to school at San Luis Obispo Junior College. She would be starting her second year next week. Jill had grown up on a cattle ranch near a small town in the San Joaquin Valley. When she had reached the age of 13 she had come to dislike life on the ranch and the cowboys who dominated the town. In high school, through reading, she became interested in life in the city, away from cows, their smell and flies. Jill was an intelligent girl but not much interested in school work. Her grades were not good enough to get her admitted to a four year college.

The alternative was a junior college, but what junior college? Jill's parents wanted her to attend a college in the valley, in Fresno or Modesto. Jill wanted to get completely away from the agricultural and cattle country of the San Joaquin Valley. Jill had learned from a girlfriend who had a brother in the Navy that there were more than 500 Navy trainees at California Polytechnic College in San Luis Obispo. She had also learned that San Luis Obispo had a small junior college. Jill thought San Luis Obispo J.C. could be her ticket out of the valley.

Jill was a member of the high school class of 1944. With the war on, few men were in college, so a place where there were Navy boys sounded good to Jill. Following a visit to San Luis Obispo with her parents, they agreed that she could attend San Luis Obispo J.C. for at least one year. The second year would depend on her grades. The Garber's wanted Jill to be able to transfer to a four year college, preferably one in the valley.

Jill had flourished in San Luis Obispo. She liked the people and the town. She had some dates with Navy boys after attending dances at Cal Poly. She loved the beach at Avila. Jill was an attractive blonde with a friendly personality. When she decided she wanted something, she was intense in her effort to be successful.

Jill's grades during her freshman year were good, and her parents agreed to her returning to San Luis Obispo for the second year. In the fall of 1945 the war was over and civilian students were returning to Cal Poly. There had been only about 80 civilian students enrolled in the college during the war. 500 Naval trainees were still there, although half would leave in early September.

Jill had gone home for the summer to a job in the regional county library. Her parents gave her one of the ranch cars, a 1941 Ford coupe, with the understanding that she would use the money earned during the summer to pay for the operation of the car. In 1945, cars were scarce because none had been produced since 1942. Jill was looking forward to another year in San Luis Obispo. She had heard that civilian boys would be back in school this year, including the war veterans. Also, the Navy boys were still there.

Southern Pacific Depot
Palo Alto, California
9:00 AM September 8, 1945

Dave's parents had always encouraged him to be independent; and he liked that. When it came time for Dave to go to college, his parents didn't take him. They put him on the Southern Pacific's Daylight, known as the most beautiful train in the world in its orange, red, silver and black color scheme. The train ran on a fast schedule and would make stops only at San Jose and Salinas. Just before arriving in San Luis Obispo, the train would round the horseshoe curve on the south side of the Cuesta grade.

PART TWO

CALIFORNIA POLYTECHNIC COLLEGE

SEPTEMBER 8, 1945

Chapter Four

Southern Pacific Depot

Santa Rosa Street

San Luis Obispo, California

1:30 PM September 8, 1945

DAVE HAD JUST arrived in San Luis Obispo. He took a taxi to travel to the Cal Poly campus. During the ride, the first surprising scene was soldiers lined up around the block for a Saturday afternoon movie. The cabbie said there were 30,000 troops at Camp San Luis Obispo. It was the 104th Infantry Division, nicknamed the Timberwolves. The Division was just home from Europe. The Timberwolves had landed in France on September 7, 1944 and fought throughout the European campaign until they met up with the Russian Army at Pretzsch, Germany on April 16, 1945.

The next surprise was seeing Packard Clipper taxi cabs lined up across the street from the movie theatre. The cabbie said the destination of many trips with soldiers was Los Angeles, so a big, heavy car was needed.

Arriving on campus, Dave found Jespersen Dormitory where he had been assigned. It would be his college home for four years. Finding his room located on the first floor, he learned his roommate was Jim Olson a redhead from Sonora, California, a small town at the base of the Sierra Nevada Mountains. Jim had attended summer school and had gone home during the quarter break.

One of the first students Dave met was Wes Witten. He was also an Aero major who had an upstairs room in Jespersen Dorm. His roommate was Hal, a sophomore chicken farming major. They were called "feather merchants." Wes was a country boy off a farm in Riverdale, a small town southwest of Fresno. He was 17 like Dave, but as Dave soon learned, he was a smart country boy. Wes had graduated from high school at the age of 16. He would be a life-long friend.

Greyhound Bus Depot
Monterey Street
San Luis Obispo, California
4:00 PM September 8, 1945

Brandon Jouker had just gotten off the bus that had brought him from Yreka. He asked at the ticket counter how he could get out to Cal Poly? He was told the cheapest way was to walk south on Monterey Street to the dead end and get a little green bus. It would take him right to the campus for 15 cents.

Arriving at Jespersen Dormitory, where he had been assigned, he met his roommate, Lester Prince. Lester was a very serious electrical engineering student who had graduated from high school in June at the age of 17. Could these two very different personalities co-exist as roommates? Only time would tell.

Jespersen Dormitory
College Avenue
Cal Poly
12:30 AM September 9, 1945

In his first night in the dorm room, Dave was wakened by an over powering noise that sounded like the world was coming to an end. He jumped out of bed and went to the window to see what it was. He saw a freight train charging by the campus on the way up to the Cuesta grade. It was powered by at least three engines, two on the front and one on the rear. They were Cab Forward steam engines, a Southern Pacific design that only S.P. used. When it woke Dave up, it had sounded like the train was coming right through his room.

Cal Poly
9:00 AM September 9, 1945

Dave was walking around the campus to learn where buildings and classroom were located. Sunday dinner was served at noon and the cafeteria did not serve a meal in the evening. Dave would go into town to eat supper.

After Dave had returned from town, Jim Olson arrived. He told Dave the classes he had taken during the summer. He described the celebration in downtown San Luis Obispo on VJ Day. The soldiers in town were particularly happy because they wouldn't have to participate in an invasion of Japan.

Administration Building
California Polytechnic College
9:00 AM September 10, 1945

Students were lined up to register for the fall quarter. There were 150 students to waiting to register. Included, were 56 veterans of the war registering for college under the G.I. Bill of Rights. These were veterans discharged before the war ended. 1945 high school graduates like Dave made up the balance of the registrants. They, like Dave were fortunate that the war had ended and they could go on to college immediately after high school graduation.

The educational philosophy of Dr. Julian McPhee, the President of Cal Poly, was the belief that many young people did not excel in high school because they had no interest in the subjects they were required to study. If a young man became interested in the subjects being studied, he was likely to improve his scholastic performance. Dr. McPhee wanted to give any student who had earned a high school diploma the opportunity to enter college and not be on immediate probation as required by some California state colleges.

To develop immediate interest, Cal Poly students start taking classes in their major during the freshman year. Called the "upside-down" system, it contrasted with the conventional lower and upper divisions in most colleges. There, students were required to take subjects unrelated to their major in their freshman and sophomore years. No major subject classes were taken until the junior year. At some universities, grade performance in the lower division could determine whether a student would qualify for his desired major.

Dave Mason was a very typical student that President McPhee talked about. Would he be a "Poster Boy" for McPhee? Only time would tell.

Civilian students were the minority at Cal Poly in September, 1945. 500 Naval aviation aspirants taking a refresher course prior to attending the pre-flight program were still at the college. In early September this number was cut in half. Many trainees dropped out of the program because it required a two year commitment to the Navy even if they did not qualify for flight training.

The cost of a college education was relatively low in 1945 and the cost of attending Cal Poly was likely the lowest of all California State Colleges. From the May, 1945 College Bulletin, "a student entering California Polytechnic with the expectation of completing a school year should expect to expend from $425 to $460 for the necessities of food, shelter, books, fees, laundry, medical care, and essential clothing. The average student's budget for three quarters would look like this."

Dormitory room @ 8.00 per month	$ 72.00
Meals @ 33.00 per month	279.00
Laundry @ $2.00 per month	18.00
Incidentals	65.00
Total	$452.00

Dave had been saving money ever since he was born. He first had a small bank that he put his pennies in. During high school summers he added to the savings via income from working at the Sutter Packing Company, the local cannery. He had also earned a fair amount of money in bowling via stakes for head to head games. By the fall of 1945 he had about $2,500 in a savings account and war bonds. He would pay all his college fees from these funds

Dave's courses for the fall quarter would be as follows:

Aero Engine Theory
Physical Education
Machine Shop
Aero Construction Theory
Aero Construction Shop
Welding Shop
Aero Engine Shop
Engineering Drafting Theory
Mathematics (Bonehead)
Physics (Bonehead)

All Cal Poly engineering courses included welding and machine shop. It was the Cal Poly emphasis on a practical education and learn-by-doing.

Monterey & Chorro Streets
San Luis Obispo, California
1:30 PM September 11, 1945

George Mason had given Dave a book on the California Missions. This gave him the history on the beginning of the town of San Luis Obispo. Father Junipero Serra founded the Mission San Luis Obispo de Tolosa on September 1, 1772. It was named for Saint Luis, Bishop of Toulouse, France. The Mission, located near the Valley of the Bears, where the Spaniards had found such a large population of bears they were able to keep other missions from near starvation by hunting the bears and sending the meat to the other missions.

Many friendly Native Americans lived in the area surrounding the Mission. This was the main reason Father Serra chose this location for the Mission. However, south of the Mission were tribes that were not friendly and were determined to drive the white men out of the area. They began shooting burning arrows into the dry tinder buildings of the Mission that would quickly spread to other buildings causing considerable damage and setbacks for the missionaries.

Recalling the fire resistant Spanish tile roofs of their homeland, the missionaries began to manufacture red clay tiles. The red clay, mined from pits, was spread over wooden models to be dried in the sun. Then they were baked in a kiln. These were the first roof tiles made in California. They would be used on all future mission buildings and become an architectural feature associated with California.

The town of San Luis Obispo sprung up around the Mission and is one of California's oldest communities. In the late 1890s, the old mission town grew into a full-fledged city with the arrival of the Southern Pacific Railroad. Daily trips from San Francisco began in 1894 and by 1901 trains were running through to Los Angeles. In the future Dave would learn that the city had a unique history.

Dave had gone to into town to find the Presbyterian Church and the bowling lanes. He learned that transportation to town was via a little green bus called the "green hornet." On Tuesday afternoon, the day after registration he ventured into town.

He found the Presbyterian Church at 981 Marsh Street. It was named the Old Stone Church, built of blue granite quarried at Bishop Peak and completed in 1905. Sunday school started at 9:30 AM and the church worship service at 11:00. The Minister was Frederick J. Hart. Dave had continued to attend services at the Menlo Park Presbyterian Church throughout the summer. While he had made no decision about joining the church he had enjoyed the sermons of Rev. Hall. He decided he would try out a Sunday school class. Afterward he could return to the campus in time for Sunday dinner. Then he was off to find the bowling lanes. Since Dave did not have a map of the city he had to ask how to find the El Camino Bowl located at 1115 Santa Rosa Street.

At the bowing lanes, Dave asked about league teams that he might join. He was advised that fall leagues were just forming and suggested he get a team of Cal Poly students together and the lanes manager would help him find a sponsor. Dave said he would work on that possibility.

On the bus ride back to the campus Dave was thinking how he could continue to practice pitching. He couldn't bring his pitching target from home, so he had to find a replacement. He would investigate the possibility of building a new target here at the college. It would be an opportunity to learn-by-doing.

Football Stadium Cal Poly 8:00 PM September 15, 1945

Football had returned to Cal Poly after a two year absence during the War. The team was composed primarily of Navel Trainees with a few civilian freshmen. The first game opponent was Fresno State College. Cal Poly's small football stadium was overrun with soldiers from Camp San Luis Obispo. The soldiers hadn't seen a football game in two or three years. The crowd was reported to be 5,000. The game was typical for the first game of the season, with lots mistakes and the game ended in a 6 to 6 tie.

Cal Poly football before the War was nothing outstanding. The teams in 1940 and 41 had a combined record of 10 wins and 7 losses. When the Navel Trainees came to Cal Poly in 1943, a number of well known college football players were on campus. However, no games could be scheduled, so there was no team.

In the early 1950's, after many years of losing teams, Coach Roy Hughes came to Cal Poly from a very successful program at Menlo Junior College located near Stanford University. In 1953, Cal Poly had an undefeated team that was the highest scoring college team in the country, including the big football powers. Unfortunately, there were no bowls or play-offs for small college teams in those days.

Tragedy would strike the Mustangs in 1960. Following an afternoon came with Bowling Green State College in Toledo, Ohio, the airplane carrying the team home crashed on take off and burned. Sixteen team members, the student manager, a member of the Mustang Booster's Club and four others perished that October day. Of 48 persons aboard the plane, 22 were injured, some gravely.

In the fall of 2006 Mustang Memorial Plaza was dedicated as a memorial to those who lost their life in that tragedy. The plaza is located at the south end of the newly renovated Alex G. Spanos Stadium. The football field itself is named Mustang Memorial Field.

Recovery to the football program came in 1980 when Cal Poly won the Division II National Championship in an upset. The team's star running back had been injured and could not play.

More than half of the students who occupied Jespersen dormitory were veterans, age 21 or over. A number of these students had found the bars on Monetary Street and liked to tip a few beers along with the many soldiers still at Camp San Luis Obispo. On this night when many of the soldiers had gone to the football game, the students had plenty of room in the Monterey Street watering holes. A number of these students returned to the dorm in "three sheets to the wind" condition. At least two students upon opening the door to their room were drenched with water from above. Where had the water come from and how did it get there?

The next morning an inspection by the half drowned students revealed nothing. All that remained was water on the floor. It was just the first of a number of unexplained incidents in Jespersen.

Presbyterian Church
981 Marsh Street
San Luis Obispo, California
9:30 AM September 16, 1945

Dave had ridden the green hornet to town so he could attend Sunday school. He attended an adult class made up primarily of couples in their thirties and forties. Dave was by far the youngest member. The teacher was Wendell Strong, a high school history teacher. His background in history would be a big plus in the class studies. The current study was in the 2nd book of Samuel. David had become King of Judah, but it would take seven years before he was King of both Judah and Israel.

Snow White Creamery
888 Monterey Street
San Luis Obispo, California
5:30 PM September 16, 1945

This was the second trip Dave had made into town today. As he stepped off the bus he noticed a big commotion a block away on Monterey Street, the town's main street. A Military Police (M.P.) "paddy wagon" was in the middle of the street and the M.P.s were trying to put a soldier into the wagon. The soldier was obviously very drunk. Every time he was thrown into the wagon he popped out again. Finally, he was thrown in followed by a tear gas grenade tossed by an M.P. and he didn't come out again. He was hauled off to the stockade.

Because there were soldiers stationed at Camp San Luis Obispo all through the war, the main street of town had become filled with bars to cater to the troops. It would be more than a year after the camp closed before the downtown would return to normal and girls and ladies would be seen on the streets during evenings.

Dave walked to the Snow White Creamery, the most popular college hang out in town. The creamery made their own ice cream and employed Cal Poly dairy students to produce it. It was more opportunities for students to learn-by-doing.

After supper, Dave walked the three blocks to the Fremont Theatre with the intention to see the movie. He was greeted by a lineup of soldiers extending around the block. He decided to go bowling instead.

Even without his ball, Dave bowled three games and averaged 205. A young fellow who was watching Dave came up to him just as he finished the third game and asked if he would like a little competition. Dave said, "Sure." He hadn't had any head to head competition for some time. Such contests always involved money. This one would be a three game series for $10.00.The young man introduced himself as Les Towne. The first two games were close with Les one pin ahead. Then in the last game, Dave bowled a 270 and took the $10.00.

Afterwards Dave learned that Les was a San Luis Obispo native, who had graduated from high school in 1943 and joined the Navy. He had been discharged a few weeks ago and was planning to attend Cal Poly starting in January. Les had worked on heating and air conditioning equipment on ships and wanted to take Air Conditioning. Les had, like Dave started bowling at a young age.

Dave asked Les if he had ever bowled on a league team. Les said, "I bowled on a team in high school but none since." Dave said, "I talked to the lanes clerk about a Cal Poly team in a league and he said the lanes manager could likely get a sponsor. Would you be interested in bowling on a Cal Poly team?" Les said he would. Dave and Les exchanged telephone numbers and Dave promised to call and schedule a time to bowl again so Les could have an opportunity to win his money back. "That's great Dave."

Chapter Five

Jespersen Dormitory

7:30 PM September 24, 1945

DAVE HAD BEEN designing a new pitching target. It was to be made of steel tubing and angle steel. It was now completed.

After a couple of welding shops, Dave thought he might be able to make the target as a shop project. He took the design to his welding instructor who had some suggestions for improvement. Following a welding demonstration by Dave, his instructor gave his approval for Dave to weld the target during class time. It was a demonstration of learn-by-doing.

Then Dave had to find a location to set up the target so he wouldn't have to chase baseballs all over the lot. He had brought his bag of 20 balls with him. The tennis courts were close to Jespersen Dorm, so he would try pitching there when the target was completed.

Pitchers run to get and keep their legs in shape, the leg push off being an important function of the pitching motion. So Dave ran around the football stadium that was next to the dorm. Running on the grass was easy on the feet.

Snow White Creamery
12:00 noon September 27, 1945

Dave, Jim and John had come to town for lunch. They were sitting in a booth in the back of the creamery. Soon, two girls walked in and took a booth in front. One of the girls was Jill Garber. She was sitting with her back to the front looking to the back of the creamery. She was looking at Dave between the people in between. She liked what she saw, including his big smile. Although she didn't let on she said to herself, I've got to find out who he is.

Jespersen Dormitory
12:00 midnight September 19, 1945

Some of the students returning to their rooms received a shock when they grabbed the door knob to their room. No wires could be found, so some students used a handkerchief to insulate their hand to get their door opened. They still couldn't find any wires, so they all went to bed. In the morning, many were talking about the shock they had received. They were trying to figure out how it was done, but they didn't have a clue. This after the water bombs two weeks ago. Who was doing this and what would be next?

Presbyterian Church
9:30 AM September 30. 1945

Dave was attending the Sunday school class for the third time. The lesson today covered the capture of Jerusalem, the fortress of Zion, by David and his men. The city would he known to this day as the City of David.

Tennis Courts
Behind Heron Hall & Jespersen Dormitory
Cal Poly
6:30 AM October 1, 1945

Dave was pitching balls at his newly completed target. He had measured the correct distance from pitcher's mound to home plate, and was throwing easy to get his arm in shape for real pitching practice. Since he did not have an elevated mound to throw from like he had built at home, he was thinking how he could elevate his pitching location. Maybe he could find some carpet that would serve the purpose. He threw his standard 100 pitches, picking up the balls after each 20 pitches. As the mornings got colder he might consider pitching in the late afternoon. At this time of year, he thought pitching every other day would be a good schedule.

Dave liked the mornings as he was a morning person. He had started to study in the early morning, taking his books to the dorm lounge. He felt more awake and better able to absorb information in the morning when he was not tired.

He had finally written a letter to Earlene to tell her what college life was like. He did not receive a reply, so it was the only letter he wrote.

Snow White Creamery
8:00 PM October 3, 1945

Jill went to the creamery to ask if anyone knew who the fellow was with the big smile. He was tall and slim with light brown hair. Because there were so many new Cal Poly students, the waitresses hadn't learned all their names. So they couldn't help. They suggested she come back in about two weeks and maybe someone would know by then. Jill left disappointed.

College Avenue
Cal Poly
7:30 PM October 9, 1945

The few upper classmen had started to "haze" the freshmen. The number odds were on the side of the freshmen about 10 to 1. Some seniors had taken freshmen for rides miles out of town and let them out to walk back to the campus. The freshmen had first responded by revising the big 'P' on the hill behind the campus into an F for freshman. This was all done under the leadership of class president, Reginald "Boston" Murphy. He was from Boston and had the accent. He was called Boston or Reggie.

Tonight the freshman were painting the avenue FROSH with white slaked lime, a by-product of the acetylene generator behind the welding shop. Dave had suggested the source. The next morning the upper classmen were embarrassed again.

On a Saturday, Dave, Jim and Bill, another Jespersen dweller had gone to town for an early movie at the Obispo Theatre where double feature B movies were shown. They were walking to the bus stop when Tom Dean, a fellow Aero student and senior class President pulled up and asked if they would like a ride back to the campus? Being naive about being taken for a ride, they willingly got in the car. However, it was soon obvious they were not headed back to the campus. They were let out some four or five miles out of town and had a long walk back to the dorm.

Boston had become the hero of the freshmen when he foiled such a ride by the same Tom Dean. When Boston had been let out of the car, he climbed on the old style spare tire mounted on the back bumper and rode back to town. When Tom stopped the car at a stop light, Boston got off the tire and walked past the car, resulting in Tom and his senior mates doing a double take and wondering if they were seeing things. So much for college high jinx.

Snow White Creamery
9:45 PM October 12, 1945

Jill was back in less than two weeks after a Friday night show. This time one of the waitresses had a first name. It was Dave and he is a bowler. "I heard him talking about a bowling team." Jill thanked her and off she went to the El Camino Bowl. At the bowling lanes, Jill asked the manager if he knew of a bowler named Dave. "Yes" he said, "two or three of them." Jill said, "This Dave is tall and slim and has a big smile" "Oh, that's Dave Mason," the manager said. "He bowls on the Cal Poly team in the Club League. They bowl on Tuesday night at 7:30." Jill thanked him.

El Camino Bowl
1115 Santa Rosa Street
San Luis Obispo, California
7:00 PM October 16, 1945

Jill had asked her apartment mate, Gwen, to go with her to watch the bowling, and of course Dave. They arrived at 7:00, before the bowlers, so their arrival would not be noticed. When the Cal Poly bowlers started warming up, Jill pointed out Dave to Gwen. Jill said, "It looks like he's the captain of the team." The girls watched Dave and the Cal Poly team, win their match and saw that Dave was a very good bowler. Jill wasn't ready to introduce herself to Dave, so she had to figure out how to get an introduction.

Presbyterian Church
9:30 AM November 4, 1945

The adult Sunday school class had a new member. Helen had returned after attending Cosmetology College in Santa Barbara. Helen had taught Sunday school while she was in high school. She was tall and very attractive. Dave decided during the class to ask her for a date.

In the study of 2nd Samuel, David's kingship was secure as far as God was concerned, but he had to fight to secure it against men. David battles constantly against the Philistines, Moabites, Edomites and Ammonites. This period of wars suggested the continuous need for God's people to battle God's enemies to preserve the promise of God's blessings.

After class, it was off to catch the green hornet bus back to the campus for Sunday dinner. He would spend the afternoon studying.

On Friday, Dave had seen Helen in the Snow White Creamery. She had come there for lunch with co-workers. He asked her for a movie date, but she was dated up. She was obviously a popular girl. He vowed to ask again.

Jill was reading the Sunday newspaper, and read that Cal Poly would have the first dance of the year with the New Collegians, the college dance band, supplying the music. She asked Gwen, her apartment mate to go with her in hopes Dave would attend and she could meet him. Gwen said, "I'll see if Ken will take us." Ken was Gwen's boyfriend, a J.C. student who lived in San Luis Obispo with his parents.

Aero Engine Shop
University Drive
Cal Poly
10:15 AM November 14, 1945

The students in Dave's engine shop class were having a shop clean up for a fall open house. Dave saw some round pieces of metal in a box and thought they were scrap. He proceeded to dump them into the trash. Soon, Ray Mantz, the instructor, noticed them and all heck broke loose. When Mr. Mantz got excited, he would rock back and forth on the balls of his feet. He wanted to know who threw his lathe mandrels in the trash. Dave owned up and got a good "reaming." He now knew what mandrels looked like.

The engine shop had a test stand where engines were run up and had simulated problems so students could learn the symptoms and the cure. Students graduated to this training when they were juniors. Freshmen learned to work on engines by taking them apart and putting them back together in the correct order. The big problem in 1945 was the lack of modern engines. The shop had not received any engines since the start of the war. Soon, surplus engines, and airplanes from the Air Force and Navy would be received. Dave's particular interest was engines, so he looked forward to working on modern engines.

Crandall Gym
College Avenue
Cal Poly
8:00 PM November 17, 1945

Gwen's boyfriend, Ken, had agreed to take her to the dance and

Jill could ride along. When they arrived at Crandall Gym where the dance was being held, the stag line was long and deep. If Jill just wanted to dance, she wouldn't have to sit out any numbers. About 30 minutes later, Dave entered the gym with another fellow. Jill was beside herself. Now, she thought, if he will just ask me to dance! Jill had danced with a number of students before Dave arrived, but now she turned down a fellow who looked like a cowboy. Jill had learned there were a few cowboy students at Cal Poly, but they were in the minority. Dave had come to the dance mainly to listen to the music. He liked dance music and was familiar with most of the dance bands and their music.

Jill started looking at Dave in hopes he would notice and ask her for a dance. Finally, he started across the floor, but seemed headed for some other girl. Then he changed direction and walked straight to Jill and said, "May I have this dance?" She could hardly contain herself, but was able to get out a calm yes. Dave started right out asking her questions. What was her name? Was she from San Luis Obispo? She had to provide many answers before she could ask one question. Jill did ask his name, even though she knew his first name. They danced three dances. Then a fast number started, and Dave said, "I'll sit this one out, but I'll be back." He did return and he and Jill danced the rest of the evening. He got her phone number and Jill introduced Dave to Gwen and Ken.

On the way to her apartment Jill was excited. Being attracted to a boy via looks was one thing, but to learn he was an interesting fellow was something else! When they were in their apartment, Jill told Gwen that Dave was an engineering student and his home was in Palo Alto. Jill said, "He is definitely not a cowboy." That made them both laugh.

Dave thought Jill was an attractive, down to earth girl, but he reserved judgment until he knew her better.

Presbyterian Church
9:30 AM November 18, 1945

In 2nd Samuel Chapter 11, verses 2 through 5, David commits adultery with Bathsheba. Then he makes it worse in his attempt to cover it up. He then sends Uriah, Bathsheba's husband, back to the army with orders to put him in the front lines where the fighting is the fiercest. Uriah is killed. How would God react to this? Dave thought the next lesson would be most interesting.

Following the class, Dave asked Helen to the Cal Poly Christmas dance and she accepted.

Chapter Six

Aboard The Daylight

San Luis Obispo, California

2:00 PM November 21, 1945

DAVE WAS ON his way home for Thanksgiving. The streamlined Daylight had a storied history. Inaugurated in 1937, it was a new train in bight colors of red, orange and black. Even the steam engine was streamlined and painted in the train's color scheme. It was like no other train and brought on statements of "Where's the circus."

Dave settled down to enjoy the trip and the scenery. Dave planned to attend the annual football game between Palo Alto High and rival Sequoia of Redwood City on Thanksgiving Day. For the first time the game would be played in Stanford Stadium.

Dave was met by his dad and mother in Palo Alto. Upon reaching the family home and entering the back yard, Dave received a big welcome from Sarge and Pudge, the Mason's father and son cocker spaniels.

On Thanksgiving Day morning Dave joined his best high school friend, Geary, Geary's girl friend Anne, and Geary's parents to attend the football game. Geary's dad was still in the Navy. The game ended in a 10 to 10 tie.

Aboard The Coaster
Southern Pacific Railroad
7:30 PM November 25, 1945

Dave was returning to the campus on the Southern Pacific Coaster. The Coaster coasted down the coast. It was so slow it was said the train stopped at railroad crossings to let the cars go by. When Dave boarded, the train was full of soldiers returning to Fort Ord in Monterey. When the soldiers left the train at Salinas, Dave had a seat to himself. First it was too hot, the seats were hard, and as the night wore on it got cold. The ordeal finally ended in San Luis Obispo at 2:30 AM.

Jespersen Dormitory
8:00 PM November 26, 1945

Dave was talking to Jill on the dorm pay phone. He asked her how her Thanksgiving was and related his long train trip back to San Luis Obispo. Dave asked Jill for a movie date for Saturday night and said he could meet her some place downtown. She accepted the date and said she would come to the Dorm and pick him up. Okay, Dave thought, you can't beat that, but he knew he would get ribbed by his dorm buddies if they saw her picking him up. Jill said she would pick Dave up at 6:45 for the 7:15 movie at the Fremont. The movie was The Harvey Girls staring Judy Garland and Ray Bolger. Dave said he would be waiting in front of the dorm. A quick pick up would minimize the chances of being seen.

Snow White Creamery
9:50 PM December 1, 1950

Jill had picked up Dave with no other students in view, at least that he could see. The movie included the Movietone News and a Tom and Jerry cartoon. Following the movie, they had walked to the Snow White. When the waitress came to take their order she said, "I'm glad you two got together." Jill immediately blushed and Dave asked, "What did she mean by that?" So Jill had to tell him the story. When she finished, Dave said, "I'm flattered. I've never had a girl do that even in grammar school." They both laughed.

They were getting to know each other and when Dave learned of Jill's dislike of the cattle ranch life and cowboys, he decided not to say anything about the Mason ranch or his interest in horseback riding. They had some more good laughs together. It was a good evening.

Presbyterian Church
9:30 AM December 2, 1945

Wendell Strong opened the class by saying, "Since a number of you were absent last Sunday because of Thanksgiving, we reviewed what we had studied in 2nd Samuel and we didn't continue the study. I didn't want those who were absent to miss the next important part of this scripture."

In the lesson today, the death of Uriah, Bathsheba's husband, is reported to David. When Bathsheba learns of her husband's death, she mourns for him. After the mourning period, David has Bathsheba brought to his house and he marries her.

The class had a lively discussion about David's actions. Many questioned what God would do to David. Others had suggestions of what God should do to David. Wendell Strong said, "Next week we will search for answers."

Later that afternoon, Dave returned to town and the El Camino Bowl. He had agreed to meet Les Towne and a friend to bowl. They bowled for a dollar a game and $5.00 for the series. Dave won $2.00 on games and the $5.00 on the series. He bowled a high game of 260 and 1376 for an average of 172 for the eight games. Les took the rest of the game money and lost the series by two pins. An observer told Dave he could be a professional bowler if he concentrated on it. Dave said. "I'm a baseball player and I don't know what the future of professional bowling is. I do know baseball has a good future."

Following bowling, Dave walked to the Snow White to have supper before returning to the dorm to study. On the bus trip back to the campus, Dave thought about what he would do about the Christmas dance date he had with Helen and how he would tell Jill. After all, he had just met Jill, and having a date would indicate to Jill that he was a popular fellow. He had heard about a Saturday night dance in Pismo Beach, a town ten miles south of San Luis Obispo. Maybe he could take Jill there before the Christmas dance. Since Dave had little experience with girls and dates, this was all new to him.

On Monday, Dave asked around and learned that the dance at Pismo Beach was in the Rendezvous Ballroom and a live band played. Dave decided to ask Jill to go Saturday night.

When Dave called and asked Jill about the dance she said, "Sure, I've been there, and the music is good."

Tennis Courts
Cal Poly
6:30 AM December 5, 1945

Dave was pitching baseballs at the target from an improvised pitching mound made of some carpet scraps. It was lower than the real thing, but it was better than pitching from the flat surface of the court.

Dave was about half way through the 100 pitches he made regularly, when Captain R.R. Bell, the baseball coach, arrived to watch from a distance. Sam Crawford, a sophomore who lived in Chase Hall where Captain Bell and his wife lived, had told the Captain about this fellow who threw baseballs at a target on the tennis courts. He said he looked familiar, but hadn't asked his name. The Captain had to see for himself. He watched silently, observing 7 out of 10 pitches finding the slots on the inside and outside of the target strike zone. The Captain had not heard about Dave because he had not talked about his pitching accomplishments since coming to Cal Poly. It was the Mason philosophy, encouraged by George Mason, that members of the family would not promote themselves or the family. Dave's dad had told Dave, "The word will eventually get out about your pitching, and if it doesn't, you can surprise people when the baseball season starts."

When Dave had completed his 100 pitches, the Captain introduced himself to Dave and asked about the pitches he threw. Dave said, "I'm a sinker ball pitcher with a change up and my fast ball rises. My velocity is still not up to what I would like it to be, but I think it is increasing as my weight increases. "Have you played a position when you're not pitching," the Captain asked. "Yes, I have played right field and some first base. I'm a singles hitter without much power. I hope to improve my power with added weight."

The Captain asked Dave "Did you play other than high school baseball?" "Yes, I started in American Legion baseball when I was 14. My team is Redwood City Post 105. The Captain encouraged Dave and told him about the best baseball pitcher he had coached at Cal Poly.

Thornton Lee was a pitcher on the Cal Poly baseball team in the late twenties and early thirties. He signed a contract with the Cleveland Indians organization of the American League. Lee made his major league debut on September 19, 1933. In his first four years he appeared in 102 games, winning 12 and losing 17. On December 10, 1936 Thornton Lee was traded as a part of a 3-team trade by the Cleveland Indians to the Chicago White Sox. With the White Sox, Lee had his best years. Over 11 years he appeared in 261 games, won 106 and lost 104. Lee was an All-Star selection in 1941 and 45.

The Captain said, "I look forward to having you as a member of our baseball team."

"Thank you," Dave said.

In the cafeteria that evening, Captain Bell saw Sam Crawford and said the name of the fellow pitching baseballs on the tennis court is Dave Mason. He said he played for the American Legion team in Redwood City. Isn't that your home town Sam?" "That's where I've seen him. I was a score keeper for American Legion and Sequoia High School baseball games. But it's been more than a year since I've seen him. He was a good pitcher for the American Legion team. He made batters hit balls to infielders for outs. I heard he pitched a no-hitter in a high school game." "Thank you Sam."

The Rendezvous Ballroom Pismo Beach, California 10:00 PM December 8, 1945

The dance was great. The music was good and Dave had even tried a little jitterbug. He and Jill were having a good time and Dave was feeling more comfortable with Jill. After the dance they stopped at the Tower Café for hamburgers and coffee.

Then Dave proceeded to tell Jill about the Cal Poly Christmas dance. Jill said, "I read about it but I wasn't thinking about it." Jill said, "I understand." "When will you be going home for Christmas Jill?" "I will leave after classes on the 19th." "Dave said, "For the next 10 days I'll be cramming for and taking finals. Let's try to take in a movie Sunday evening, December 16. That would give me a break in the finals ordeal. Before I forget, please give me your home telephone number so I can call you during the Christmas vacation." "Oh Dave, you are such a doll!"

So the ordeal of telling Jill about the Cal Poly Christmas dance was not an ordeal after all.

Presbyterian Church 9:30 AM December 9, 1945

In the lesson today, the Lord sends Nathan, the prophet, to David. Nathan tells the story of two men in a town, one rich and the other poor. The rich man had many sheep and cattle, but the poor man had only on little ewe lamb he had raised and it grew up with his children. A traveler came to the rich man but he refrained from taking one of his own sheep to prepare a meal for the traveler. Instead, he took the ewe lamb from the poor man and prepared it for the traveler.

"And David's anger was greatly kindled against the man; and he said to Nathan, As the Lord liveith, the man that hath done this thing shall surely die: And he shall restore the lamb fourfold, because he did this thing, and because he had no pity. And Nathan said to David, Thou art the man."

As the result of his sins, Nathan tells David that the sword will never depart from his house. The Lord will take your wives and give them to your neighbor, and he shall lie with them in public. You did it secretly, but I will do it before all Israel.

That was the end of today's lesson. Next week the class would learn of David's response.

Jespersen Dormitory
7:00 PM December 12, 1945

It was cram for final exams time, something new to Dave. Many students did nominal studying during the quarter then studied intensely in preparation for taking final exams. This was partly brought on by the large percentage of a course grade being dependent on the final. Dave had done much studying during the quarter, limiting his "goof off" time and trips to town. He had bowled one night or afternoon a week and did not see a show every week. However, he was still studying hard for finals. He would study until 9:30 or 10:00 in the evening go to sleep and get up at 5:00 AM to study more.

Finals in aero construction theory, math and physics were the most challenging for Dave. His summer study in aircraft engines had helped him do well in engine theory and shop. In the shop he was very interested in the test run-ups of engines, learning what their problems were. He was looking forward to his junior and senior years when he would be trouble shooting engine problems.

Crandall Gymnasium
9:00 PM December 15, 1945

It was the night of the Christmas Dance. Dave had worked hard to find "wheels" to be able to pick up Helen. He finally learned that Jack, a fellow aero student who had a Model A Ford with a rumble seat, had a date and would let Dave and Helen ride in the rumble seat. Fortunately, it was not a cold evening and Helen brought a hair net to save her hair do.

The Collegians were in great form, playing all those big band tunes of the forties. Dave learned that Helen loved to jitterbug and Dave was not good at it. He decided he would have to learn.

Over hamburgers and coffee at the Tower Café, the foursome talked about Cal Poly having no coeds. The girls thought it was great, the boys weren't so sure. It did leave lots of time for study. Dave would learn later why Cal Poly had no coeds. Helen said, "I would have gone away to college if Cal Poly had been coed. With all those Navy fellows out there and now the veterans, why leave?"

Presbyterian Church
9:30 AM December 16, 1945

In the lesson today, David reacts to what Nathan has told him. "... David said unto Nathan, I have sinned against the Lord. And Nathan said unto David, The Lord also hath put away thy sin; thou shalt not die."

Wendell stopped the lesson at this point. He wanted to emphasize, what had happened. He asked, "Does anyone know?" One of the lady members of the class said, "It is God's forgiveness." "That's correct. It is one of the most important truths of our faith. Most non-Christians do not understand it. In fact too many Christians don't understand or practice it."

This resulted in a lively class discussion. Some questioned forgiveness. Wendell Strong read from Luke Chapter 17, verses 2 and 4. "Take heed to yourselves: If thy brother trespass against thee, rebuke him; and if he repents, forgive him. And if he trespass against thee seven times in a day, and seven times in a day turn again to thee, saying, repent, I repent; thou shalt forgive him." Wendell Strong said, "All of us should remember this scripture."

"So we have seen in our lesson today that God has forgiven David because he repented. God still has issues with David that we will study next week."

This was all new to Dave, but it was very interesting to him. He would be on Christmas vacation for the next two weeks, so he would have to read his Bible to keep up with the class.

Southern Pacific Depot San Luis Obispo, California 12:53 PM December 20, 1945

Dave was about to board the Daylight for the ride home for Christmas. He had taken his last final exam that morning and thought he did well. He would know when he returned following the holidays and picked up his grades.

Dave was looking forward to seeing his sister Pam. She would be home for Christmas from the University of Colorado. Absence had given Dave a better feeling about his sister. They had been close during grammar school years but that had ended in high school. Pam had been critical of Dave because of his acne and poor school grades.

Dave also hoped to see some Stanford basketball games while at home. During junior high years Dave had accompanied his mother Ann to most all Stanford games in the small cramped basketball court that featured spectators sitting two feet from the out of bounds lines.

George Mason was not a basketball fan, so Dave was able to see the games from the "press box" which was just a roped off section of the stands. The highlight of those years was the 1941-42 National Championship team that featured a starting five, each of whom stood 6′ 0″ or taller. Jim Pollard, who would play many years in the NBA and Howie Dalmar were the stars of the team. Center Ed Voss at 6′ 6″ was a "big man" in those days.

After the slow climb over the Cuesta grade and through the tunnels with a helper engine, the train sped along with none of the delays experienced by Amtrak trains of today. Freight trains waited on sidings for the Daylight to pass. Up through the Salinas valley, the lettuce capital of the world and then it was Gilroy, the garlic capital and soon into the Santa Clara Valley, the prune capital, a fertile valley that also produced apricots, peaches and plums.

San Jose was the last stop before Palo Alto. Then it was through the small towns of Santa Clara, Sunnyvale and Mountain View, towns that would become cities in the era of Silicone Valley. Dave thought about Moffett Field, where the huge hanger had been built as the

West Coast base of the ill-fated Navy dirigibles, Akron and Macon. It had served the many Navy blimps of the submarine patrol during the War. Both the Dirigibles had crashed in bad weather one over the Atlantic and one over the Pacific ocean. It signaled a poor future for that type of airship. Its death came with the firry crash of the German dirigible Hindenburg in 1937.

Soon Palo Alto was called by the conductor, and Dave grabbed his bag and headed for the vestibule. George and Ann were at the station to meet Dave with a warm welcome. Pam had not arrived from Colorado yet. Dave and his parents would travel to Oakland to greet Pam when her train arrived the next day. At the Mason home, Dave received another big greeting from Sarge and Pudge.

The threesome would have dinner at Motley's restaurant on University Avenue, saving a dinner at Rickey's, the area's most popular eatery, until Pam's arrival. Dave, who still had a hollow leg, and was just starting to gain some weight, always looked forward to eating at Rickey's where the food was served smorgasbord style.

At dinner, one of Dave's first questions of his dad was, "When can we go to the ranch?" George said, "Some day after Christmas." Dave ate one of his favorite entrees, Halibut for dinner. He said," The Cal Poly cafeteria does not serve much fish."

That night Dave enjoyed sleeping in his own bed instead of a steel bunk.

Chapter Seven

Oakland Mole

San Francisco Bay

Oakland, California

9:30 AM December 21, 1945

WITH GEORGE MASON driving the family 1940 Ford, he Ann and Dave had arrived at the Ferry Terminal in San Francisco. They had taken a ferry boat to the Oakland Mole located on the east shore of San Francisco Bay. The Mole was the Western terminal of all Southern Pacific cross country trains. Here under the great train shed that covered eight tracks, they waited for Pam's train from Denver.

Pam was met with hugs and kisses. A ride on the ferry to San Francisco and then in the family Ford, brought them home where Pam was greeted by Sarge and Pudge.

The family enjoyed Christmas. Then Dave and George were off to the ranch on the Thursday following Christmas. On the drive up the Page Mill Road, George asked Dave if he was satisfied with his first quarter of college. Dave said, "I'll be better able to answer that question when I receive my grades. However, I think I did okay. I do like college. The classes are small and going to college with the veterans is a plus."

"During the next quarter I will not bowl on a team and spend more time studying and. progressing in my Bible study. I must prepare for the time that baseball will require starting in March." George asked Dave if he had any regrets about not starting a professional career in baseball. Dave replied, "No dad, I was not ready for pro ball, either from a baseball performance standpoint or from the requirements of the non-baseball life of bus travel and poor food. I'm sure I would not have gained the weight I have on a minor league meals allowance. I am almost up to 170 pounds."

Arriving at the first gate to the ranch road, Dave did his usual task of opening and closing the gate. Two gates later they approached the gate to Black Mountain Ranch. The ranch was George Mason's pride and joy. It had been a 40 minute drive. They drove to the barn and were greeted by the ranch dogs, all German Shepherds, including Dave's dog Roundup. They were greeted by the ranch foreman, Steve, a bachelor who managed the ranch by himself.

The ranch of 240 acres plus leased acreage brought it up to 1,000 acres, mostly cattle grazing land. The ranch buildings were on the mountain ridge that led to the Peak of Black Mountain at 3,000 feet. Cultivated fields of oat hay were also on the ridge. A small ranch house looked out over the Santa Clara Valley, and on a clear day you could see San Francisco. The Black Mountain Ranch was a cattle ranch featuring registered white face Hereford cattle. Horses, dogs and cats completed the animal population. George Mason sold cattle to the Liddicoat Meat Market in Palo Alto on a regular basis. The land included a canyon that dropped a thousand feet to the headwaters of Stevens Creek, the largest creek in the County. The cattle herd spent most of the year in the canyon.

Dave's early interest in the ranch was in horseback riding that led to learning how to herd cattle and driving the tractor. He had learned to drive a car on trips to and from the ranch. A driving tour of the canyon and the ranch ridge in George Mason's "Buckskin" a Chevrolet station wagon of buckskin color completed the trip.

On the trip home, Dave asked his dad about the future of the ranch. "Will you be able to keep it?" George said, "I hope to keep it at least until you learn what your future will be and whether you can assume the task of managing it." "That sounds good," Dave replied.

The Mason Residence
5:35 PM December 25, 1945

Dave had finally gotten his call through to Jill. She sounded surprised that he had called as he said he would. They had a good conversation about Christmas and being at home. Dave said, "I'll call you when I return to San Luis." "Have a good New Years Dave." "You too," said Dave.

Menlo Park Presbyterian Church
11:00 AM December 30, 1945

Dave was attending a worship service for the first time since summer. The sermon today by Rev Hall, was on the continuing story of the birth of Jesus.

The Mason Residence
5:00 PM January 1, 1946

Dave and Ann had been listening to the radio broadcast of the Rose Bowl Game. Alabama had defeated USC 34 to 14. Nineteen year old Harry Gilmer of Alabama had been the star of the game because of his successful passing.

Aboard the Southern Pacific Daylight
Near San Jose, California
9: 30 AM January 2, 1946

Dave had decided during his trip home for Christmas he would return on the Daylight and not endure another trip on the Coaster. If he met his goal of having a car by the start of college next fall, this would be his next to last trip on the train.

He thought about his first months in college. He was looking forward to learning what his grades were for the first quarter. He thought he did okay but knew he could do better. A high point of the fall had been the success of the Cal Poly bowling team that bowled in the Club League. Led by Dave and Les Towne, the team had won the league title. Dave's average of 255 led the team. The team's success had sparked interest from many Poly students. So Dave's decision not to bowl on the team in the Winter League would not be a problem. With baseball starting in March, Dave needed to concentrate on school work during the winter quarter. He also planned to step up his running in preparation for baseball, while continuing to practice his control by pitching to the target. He had taken his Bible with him on the train and spent considerable time in study.

Arriving in San Luis Obispo, he took a cab to the campus. The cab driver reported that many new students were arriving to take advantage of the G.I. Bill. He was recently discharged from the army and had never thought of going to college but now with the financial aid, he was looking into it.

After dropping his suitcase off in this room, he walked to the campus post office to get his grades. The result was encouraging to Dave. Three B and seven C grades gave him almost a C+ average. Not bad for a student who would be on probation at any other State College. He vowed to do better in the coming quarter.

Crandall Gymnasium
1:30 PM January 3, 1946

Registration for the Winter Quarter was a far cry from the one hundred-fifty students who registered in the Administration Building in September. Tables were set up in the Gym, and it was obvious the student body had increased many fold. Dave's courses for the Winter Quarter included the following:

Aero Engine Theory
Physical Education
Machine Shop
Aero Construction Theory
Aero Construction Shop
Welding Shop

Aero Engine Shop
Engineering Drafting Theory
Health Education
Mathematics (Bonehead)
Physics (Bonehead)

Dave returned to the dorm following registration to be greeted by Jim Olson and a friend from Sonora, Chuck Ryer. The most important feature of Chuck's arrival was he had a car. Having wheels would eliminate some rides on the green hornet and allow travel out-of-town. Chuck's car was a 1932 Ford Model B with a V8 engine and a transmission with a home made modification that provided over-drive. It had speed on the level that would startle other drivers.

While Jim and Chuck were registering, Dave went to the pay phone and called Jill. There was no answer. He would call again later.

Following Jim and Chuck's return the three of them piled into Huck's car and drove to a truck stop restaurant south of town. Dave and Jim had visited the truck stop when riding with others. Margo, the waitress was friendly to the boys as she was to the truck drivers. She drew customers.

When they returned to the dorm, Dave called Jill again and she answered. "How was the rest of your vacation after our phone conversation?" Jill said "Fine, but I'm glad to be back so I can see a fellow named Dave. When can I see you?" Dave said," Let me consult my social calendar." They both laughed. "There is nothing on my calendar. How about driving out here about six o' clock and we'll go to the Snow White to eat and then to a show?" "I'll be there at 6:00." "I'll be waiting."

Snow White Creamery
6:30 PM January 3, 1946

At the Snow White they talked about Christmas and their vacations. Dave was still hesitant to talk about the ranch so he didn't say anything about his ranch visit.

Dave told Jill he would be carrying a large class load this quarter so he could take a light one next quarter. Also, he would not bowl on the Cal Poly team this quarter. "I'm doing this so I will have time for baseball next quarter." "Are you a baseball player?" "Yes," said Dave. "I pitch baseballs." "Oh my" said Jill, "I have a nice boy friend who is a baseball player. Can I come and watch you play?" "Sure you can," said Dave, and they both laughed.

"Since I don't start classes until Monday Jill, I would like to see lots of you this weekend." "I think that can be arranged." "I invite you to have dinner with me tomorrow night and then go to the dance in Pismo on Saturday night. Then we could wind up the weekend with a show Sunday night. How does that sound?" "That sounds wonderful Dave." "Now Jill, shall we be off to the show?"

The movie, Blood on the Sun with James Cagney was different and on the way to the dorm they had to discuss it to really understand it. Jill had started the practice of driving into the dorm parking lot for their good night kiss. This limited the possibility of having an audience. "What time should I pick up tomorrow night?" "How about between 6:00 and 6:15." "I'll be here." "Good night Jill." "Good Night Dave."

Tower Café
8:30 PM January 4, 1946

Jill had been late picking Dave up because her mother had called just as she was leaving her apartment. Thelma, a girl friend of Jill's had just won a scholarship that would allow her to attend Fresno State College. She was attending Modesto Junior College and would graduate in June. As Jill explained to Dave, it was another strong hint that her parents wanted Jill to transfer to Fresno State next fall. "I don't want to go to Fresno State or any other college," Jill said when they had been seated. Dave asked if she had ever thought of becoming an airline stewardess? "I've never thought about it Dave. I just don't enjoy school work that much and I definitely don't want to attend Fresno State." Dave was not sure what the requirements were, but thought Jill would be a good stewardess. "Let me get the address of United Airlines, and then you can write for information. I think it's worth looking into." "That sounds interesting. Thank you Dave."

They lingered over their desert, and didn't leave the restaurant until almost 10:00 PM. When they were in Jill's car, Jill said, "Let's go for a drive." Dave said, "You're the driver, so carry on." Jill drove north on Hiegera Street and then to Monterey where she continued north. Just before leaving town she started up a hill. Dave had heard that this hill was the favorite place for necker's. It was called "Necker's Nob." Dave couldn't resist asking where they were going. Jill was silent until they arrived at the top of the hill and parked. They looked out over the lights of the city, and Jill said, "Isn't it beautiful Dave." "Yes it is." "I came up here Dave so I can get more than a good night kiss in the parking lot." "Jill, I think you should sit on my lap so we can have togetherness and I can kiss you easier." Jill was there in an instant.

"I think you are a romantic Jill." "I don't know Dave. What is a romantic?" "My understanding is that two people do things for each other that are unusual and out of the ordinary in showing affection for each other. An example is what my dad did during the year our family lived in Carmel. Our house was just two blocks from the beach. The street that ran along the side of the house dead ended in a parking area where you could park and look out to sea. After dinner, dad would take mother in the car, park there and watch the sunset" He did many things like that." "I understand what you mean, but I haven't witnessed anything like that. I think the kind of place I grew up in did not lend itself to being romantic. It was too rough and tumble, if you know what I mean." "Yes, I think so." ... It was midnight when Jill drove into the dorm parking lot and they kissed good night.

Presbyterian Church
9:30 AM January 6, 1946

During Dave's absence, the study of 2nd Samuel had progressed to the birth of David's son Solomon. The life of David's child born of Bathsheba had been taken by the Lord. Now, Solomon has been born to David and Bathsheba. Another son, Absalom was rebelling.

El Camino Bowl
2:30 PM January 6, 1946

Dave had returned to town after Sunday dinner to bowl with Les Towne. He had asked Jill to meet him in the Snow White at 5:00 PM for an early supper followed by a show. Upon meeting Les Towne, Les said, "I haven't seen much of you lately Dave. Is that blonde keeping you busy" "Oh, you know about her?" "Oh yes, we saw she and her friend when they came to watch you bowl back in October. We didn't know then she was here to watch you, but the word gets around, Dave." They both laughed.

Dave didn't bowl too well and Les took some of his money back from Dave. "I think you're rusty Dave." "Yes. I probably am. And I won't have much time to lose the rust this quarter. I'm taking a big load so I can lighten up for baseball next quarter." Dave had told Les that he was a baseball pitcher. "I'm sure the blonde takes up some of your bowling time too Dave." They laughed again.

Snow White Creamery
4:45 PM January 6, 1946

Dave had arrived early from his bowling with Les Towne and had taken the back booth. The waitress came with the water, saying, "Where's your blonde?" "Oh, who is that?" said Dave." "You know who." Dave responded, "I think she just might be here soon." The waitress smiled.

Dave was thinking about the dance at Pismo last night. He thought he was becoming a good dancer. He even danced the fast numbers.

Then Jill arrived. She had no more than sat down, than Jim, Chuck and Wes came in the door. Spying Dave, they headed for the back booth looking for a first time introduction to Dave's girl. Dave introduced each to Jill saying, "This is my roommate Jim. He comes from a small town too, Sonora, and Chuck is from the same place. Wes is from the valley too. All of you meet Jill Garber. Now isn't she a doll?"

They all agreed, as Jill blushed. Recovering, Jill asked Wes, "Where do you live in the valley?" "My home is in Riverdale, about 25 miles southwest of Fresno. And you?" "I live near Hopeton, ever heard of it?" "No." "It's a big place northeast of Merced in the cattle country." "Nice to meet you all," said Jill. "Now I know who Dave is talking about." In unison they said, "So do we." They all laughed.

The movie was State Fair starring Dana Andrews, Jeanne Crain and Dick Haymes. It was a happy musical, a good way to end a good weekend. Tomorrow, it would be back to the books.

During the next three weeks, about all Dave did was study. He did attend Sunday school and had one date each week with Jill. He also scheduled time for pitching to his target.

Crandall Gym
8:40 PM January 25, 1946

This weekend Dave had wanted to do something different since he had been studying so much. He compromised his schedule by not studying Friday night and attended the basketball game with Jim and Chuck. The Cal Poly team was too late in trying to make up a schedule of college games so they entered the San Luis Obispo City League. The team was undefeated, having won five games. Tonight they were playing the Octanes, the number two team in the league. It wasn't much of a contest, the Mustangs winning 57 to 29. But it was a fun night out with the boys.

After the game, they walked to the dorm with Bill Baker, a member of the basketball team. He was a senior, having attended Cal Poly before the war. He and his family were living in the Jespersen Dorm apartment and he was serving as superintendent.

Dave asked Baker if the feud between the Music and Athletic Departments was real or planned by the participants. He said, "They assure everyone its real, but I'm not convinced. He did say the Music, Athletic and Journalism departments competed for students to participate in their extra curricula activities.

Returning to the dorm, Dave Jim and Chick traveled in Chuck's car to the truck stop to eat and visit Margo.

Until tonight, Dave had restricted his nights out to Saturday night with Jill. Dave was keeping up with his heavy class load, but it took lots of study. He had continued his running on the football turf and pitching to his target. Tomorrow night would be a special one at the Rendezvous Ballroom in Pismo Beach. The Dick Jurgens band would be playing. The Jurgens band was a fixture at the Clearmont Hotel, located in the hills behind Oakland. The band was on a tour of college campuses. The band couldn't work out a date at Cal Poly, so they made one in Pismo. The next night they would play for a dance at University of California at Santa Barbara. A big crowd was expected at the Rendezvous Saturday night.

Rendezvous Ballroom
Pismo Beach, California
10:00 PM January 26, 1946

It was intermission at the ballroom. Jill and Dave had gone outside to get some air and walk around Pismo Beach. The crowd for the dance featuring the Dick Jurgens band was huge and real dancing was difficult. Dave and Jill spent much of their time close to the bandstand so they had some room to move, and they could watch and listen to the band. Jurgens music that was tailored for the hotel dinner dancing crowd was very danceable.

Dave and Jill stopped to watch the bingo players. Most were senior citizens. Dave and Jill decided they were there because they didn't have anything else to do. Maybe they got excited about the chance to win.

Stopping at the Tower Café for something to eat on the way home, Jill talked again about what she might do when the school year was over and she had her Associate of Arts degree. She had written to United Airlines about the requirements for being a stewardess. Dave had obtained the address for her. Jill's parents were still encouraging her to attend Fresno State next year.

After saying goodnight to Jill Dave was able to turn the lights on when he entered his room because Jim had gone home for the weekend. Dave undressed and started to climb into the upper bunk, he grabbed bed frame and received the shock of his life. It almost put him on his rear end. He quickly let go and sat on the floor for a minute. The he looked under the bed. In the far corner he saw a small black object that looked like a small automobile battery. Wires were connected to the bed frame. Dave wondered, how did this battery get into my room and under the bed? To get into bed I've got to disconnect the wires from the bed frame. I'll get a towel to use as an insulator and pull the wires from the bed frame. And that's what he did and went to bed.

In the morning, Dave lay in bed trying to figure out how the battery was placed under the bed and by whom.

He retraced his movements the afternoon and evening before Jill came to pick him up. The one time he had left the room was when he went to take a shower. Did I lock the door? I must not have. It was very seldom that Jim and I were in the shower at the same time, so we didn't usually lock the door. That must have been the time. Now who put it in the room? Dave had no clue. He would hide the battery so it couldn't be retrieved.

I might even leave the door unlocked and observe from Ken's room across the hall. Dave had heard about some students being shocked last year when they gripped their door knobs. He wondered if they were connected with his bed shock.

Chapter Eight

Classroom

University Drive

Cal Poly

10:30 AM February 5, 1946

DAVE WAS ATTENDING a Health Education class, one of the non-major courses required by all to earn a degree in any major at Cal Poly. The course was miss-named because it was about relationships between men and women or you could call it sex education. The instructor was Frank Diller, who was primarily a history teacher.

During the class, a student asked Diller, "Why doesn't Cal Poly have coeds like the other State Colleges?" Diller related that in 1929, with the start of the depression, the State Legislature and Governor C. C. Young barred women from enrolling or studying at Cal Poly, after 1930. This action eliminated the need to improve the women's dormitory and maintain the household arts curriculum. The San Luis Obispo PTA, the County Superintendent of Schools, and the city superintendent all petitioned the legislature to reinstate women students, but to no avail.

Cal Poly Baseball Field
Cal Poly
4:00 PM March 1 1946

Captain R. R. Bell had called for the first turn-out on this Friday, to primarily learn how many baseball players he would have for this year's team. George Adams, Luis Martinez, and Art Milroy, Poly lettermen from pre-war teams greeted the Captain. 15 new players who in pre war days would be called freshman also turned out.

Initially, it appeared there would be a four man pitching staff, including Dave. However, a dose of bad luck hit the team when one left school, another quit the team, and the most experienced pitcher came down with a sore arm. This left Dave as the only pitcher with experience at any level. George Adams, an experienced outfielder volunteered to pitch which gave the team a two man staff.

It was soon obvious that Dave had great control. The team members wanted Dave to throw batting practice because he got the ball over the plate. There were no wasted pitches. His teammates soon learned that Dave was also a good hitter. Dave was developing some power in his hitting aided by his weight gain of at least eight pounds since arriving at college. He was continuing to develop as a switch hitter. He spent much of his batting practice time batting left handed.

El Camino Bowl
8:05 PM March 3, 1946

Dave was teaching Jill how to bowl. She had been after him to teach her so she could bowl with him. He had not bowled all month, sticking to his study schedule. He finally agreed to Jill's request on this Sunday evening. Jill was a good student, and made some good progress.

After bowling, it was still early, so Jill asked, "can we go up the hill?" Dave said, "Sure." When they arrived, Jill sat on Dave's lap.

They were silent for a while as they looked out over the lights of the city. Then Jill said, "Gwen is going home to Paso Robles for her birthday next weekend. I invite you to come to dinner…,bring your protection, and you can stay over night." Dave was thinking, Oh, that's nice; I get a home cooked dinner. Then he realized what she had said after the pause. If Jill could have seen his face she would have seen a very red one. After some silence, Dave blurted out, "Please explain yourself." "Oh Dave I've heard good and bad about sex. I want to find out for myself with a nice fellow instead of some guy who is trying to get into my pants." So far in his few months of attending church and Sunday school he had not heard any teaching of being celibate while single, a belief of the Presbyterian Church. His response was practical. "First, Jill, I'm a virgin" "Me too." "I have not been any where near having sex with a girl. I would hardly know what to do. You would not get a good evaluation from me. I'm inexperienced. Since you are the same, we might not be able to do anything." They both laughed. "Seriously Jill I think we have a very good relationship for two young people who have known each other for only four months. We've had lots of fun and laughs which is good. To introduce sex into our relationship could ruin it. Also, I have more than three years of difficult engineering school ahead of me. I'm in no position to make a commitment to you."

"Yes Jill, I will come to dinner, you can put your records on and we'll dance and neck. Then you can take me to the dorm, and we will both sleep well." "Oh Dave, for a 17 year old boy, you are so mature." "The boys in the dorm would call me crazy or at least naive, but I believe what I said. Now, let me romance you."

Jill's Apartment
Johnson Avenue
San Luis Obispo, California
7:45 PM March 9, 1946

Dave and Jill had finished a nice dinner. It included meatloaf, mashed potatoes and carrots. They had cupcakes for desert. Dave helped Jill clear off the table and was selecting records to play for dancing. Jill turned the lights down low and they danced in their private dance hall. They worked on dancing some fast numbers so they wouldn't have to sit them out in the future. Jill served Dave his ginger ale and she drank a coke. They finished the evening with Jill on Dave's lap and some more romancing.

When Jill took Dave to the dorm, he said, "Jill, I had a wonderful time tonight. The dinner was delicious, the music and dancing was the best, and I will sleep very well tonight. I hope you will too." "I will Dave, good night."

In bed, Dave thought about the evening and his relationship with Jill. From the beginning, Jill had been the aggressor. She had the car, so she was in control of where they went that was not planned. Dave was quite willing to let her do this because of his lack of experience with girls. However he was proud and reassured of himself in the way he handled Jill's invitation to sleep over. He felt good about all of it.

Cal Poly Baseball Field
5:00 PM March 13, 1946

With the first game of the season ten days away, the team was having an inter-squad game with umpires, just like a real game. Dave was pitching for the Green Team against the probable starters on the Gold Team. Coach Bell wanted the starters to hit against the best pitching. He asked Dave to throw mainly fast balls and change ups, the pitches they would see the most of in games. Since Dave did not throw a curve ball, the starters would not get experience hitting that pitch.

Even though the velocity on Dave's fastball was not up to what he would like, his rising fast ball had batters swinging under the ball. Dave showed a good change up that fooled a number of batters. The game had little hitting and ended with the score Green 3 and Gold 2. Hitting would be a problem. Dave was the best hitter of the day, hitting two singles and a double. The game confirmed that more batting practice was needed.

Crandall Gymnasium
9:00 PM March 22, 1946

It was billed as the Baseball Prance, the dance sponsored by the Freshman Class. The advertisement on the back of "Boston" Murphy's car read, Leave the old bat at home and bring your curves Friday, March 22. Jill and Dave were there. Jill had encouraged Gwen to get Ken to bring her, and he did. Ken was considering registering at Cal Poly next fall, after one year at J.C.

Dave commented to Jill that there were more local "curves" at this dance than those who attended last fall. Jill though it was because there were more eligible men at Cal Poly now. The word gets around. The collegians were getting better. They played some of Les Brown's best numbers and played very danceable music. Three fellow aero students were members of the band. Following the dance, Jill and Dave met Gwen and Ken at the Tower Café for hamburgers and coffee.

Deuel Dormitory
College Avenue
Cal Poly
10:00 AM March 23, 1946

Dave and other students had emerged from the dorm to go to town for a late breakfast or just to get some sunshine. In front of Deuel dorm were two police cars and a crowd of students. A San Luis Obispo girl, Nancy, drove a Crosley automobile. It was smaller than the original VW "Bug." It was powered by a very small engine that sounded like the engine in your grandmother's Maytag washing machine. The car was so light, it encouraged students to pick it up and place it on the sidewalk when they saw it parked in downtown San Luis Obispo.

Nancy had driven the Crosley to the campus the night before to attend the Baseball Prance. She parked the car on College Avenue near Deuel dorm. It being late in the month, many students had run out of money, so they had not gone to town. They had time on their hands.

When they spotted the Crosley a group of students decided they should do something with the car. Four or five students picked up the car, took it up the front steps of Deuel dorm and placed it on the front porch. The porch had a four foot wall, except where the steps were located. After the car had been placed on the porch, one would have to look very closely to see just the top of the car over the wall.

When Nancy walked up College Avenue following the dance, she found no car. This morning, students were carrying the car down the steps of Deuel dorm while the two policemen looked on.

Baseball Field
U.C. Santa Barbara
Santa Barbara, California
2:30 PM April 6 1946

The first game of the season was scheduled for March 22 with Santa Barbara at Cal Poly. But it was rained out. The second game against Jose State was also washed away.

The season was finally starting today against the Gauchos in Santa Barbara. Playing on a baseball diamond with a dirt infield, the Mustangs with an infield composed of Jack Crowe, Tom Chambers, Chuck Dean and Louis Martinez, were doing a good job. Dave was making the Gaucho batters beat the ball into the ground for outs.

At the start of the eighth inning Dave had a shutout having allowed only two hits. He had knocked in one of the four runs for the Mustangs hitting a double in the fifth inning. In the Santa Barbara half of the eighth inning, an error, a sacrifice and a "Texas League" hit into right field yielded two runs, but that's all they got. Dave pitched a shut out in the ninth inning for a 4 to 2 win. It was Dave's first college baseball win.

Following the game, two girls, Joan and June, Palo Alto High School classmates of Dave's came and talked to him.

Returning to the campus, Dave found his grades for the Winter Quarter in his mail box. Already walking on air because of this pitching win, Dave found he had just missed a B average by one grade point! He was very happy with his progress and he set a goal to make the B average during the spring quarter. It would mean a minimum of movies and bowling because of the time devoted to baseball, but Dave was determined to get the B average.

Classroom
University Drive
Cal Poly
2:00 PM April 9, 1946

Dave had registered for a course in California History to fulfill some of the history requirements for his degree. It was a one unit course, meeting just once per week. It fit Dave's light class load this quarter. The instructor, Victor Hathaway, had a good reputation. It was said he acted out history.

The first message Victor gave the class was that all tests would be unannounced. He said, "The beach at Avila is too inviting in the spring. It makes too many students absent from class. Cut the class at your peril."

"Our first study will cover San Luis Obispo, one of California's oldest cities. This should build your interest in the history of other parts of the state. He related the start of the town which Dave had learned from the book his dad had given him. In the late 1800s, three German born brothers, Bernard, Henry and A.Z. Sinsheimer came to town. They established Sinsheimer Brothers Mercantile, and had a building built at 849 Monterey Street. The building, an elaborate example of 19th century architecture, used locally manufactured brick and had six pairs of elongated French entranced doors. The building survives today as a working retail store.

The brothers started the town gas company, initially manufacturing gas by roasting coal and capturing the fumes. The gas was piped all over town.

In 1919, A.Z Sinsheimer was elected Mayor of San Luis Obispo. One of his goals was to preserve San Luis Obispo as the last frontier town in the west. The city street lights were still gas fired in the late 1930s. Cal Poly Students were employed to ride their bicycles around town and light the lamps. In 1939 a new Mayor was elected and the street lights were eventually converted to electricity.

Barber Shop Anderson Hotel Monterey Street San Luis Obispo, California 10:00 AM April 20, 1946

Dave had come to town to get a hair cut from Gill. Walking to the barber shop, Dave noticed that young ladies were shopping. This was six months after the army camp had closed and girls were now being seen downtown.

Leaving the barber shop, Dave walked to the drug store. He needed to buy some items. Waiting to pay for his purchases, an elderly man was trying to find his money to pay for what he needed. It appeared the "old timer" didn't have enough money. Dave asked the cashier, "How much is needed?" She said, "One dollar." "Here it is," said Dave. The old timer protested, but Dave said, "It's my good deed for the day." The old timer thanked him.

When Dave emerged from the store the old timer was waiting. He thanked Dave again. "Are you a Cal Poly student?" "Yes I am and I'm heading for the bus to return to the campus." "What's your name?" "Dave." "I'm Sam." "I'm glad to know you Sam." "The old timer asked if he could walk with Dave because he was heading for the green hornet too. "You sure can," said Dave.

Sitting on the bench waiting for the bus, the old timer pointed to Sinsheimer's store and asked Dave if he knew the history of Monterey Street and highway 101?" Dave said he didn't know that story. "Well, I worked for the city in street maintenance for many years. When the state wanted to move highway 101 from Monterey to Higuera Street Mayor Sinsheimer fought the move. It would mean 101 would not run in front of his store. Also, the state would no longer pay for any of the maintenance on Monterey Street. The city would have to pay for all of it. I didn't see it, but there was a report that Mayor Sinsheimer sat out in front of his store and cried the day highway was rerouted. "I hadn't heard that story Sam."

Southern Pacific Depot
1:30 PM April 27, 1946

The Queen was arriving! Encouraged by John Dillon, a member of the baseball team and an officer of Poly Royal, members of the team including Dave had come to the station to help welcome the Poly Royal Queen, Patricia Munchhof, a co-ed attending San Jose State College.

Poly Royal was, a Country Fair on a College Campus. It was held over a week end in April of each year. It had been started in 1933 as an open house, and to publicize the college. Since Cal Poly was all men, a queen was needed. The best place to find a queen of college age was from one of the other California State Colleges. Four San Luis Obispo girls were selected to be Poly Royal Princesses. Another reason for Dave's attendance was that Helen had told him some time ago that she had been selected as one of the princesses.

Poly Royal included all of a typical country fair, including agricultural exhibits and open houses in all the college departments. The Aero Department had obtained war surplus aircraft to aid students in learning about modern aircraft and engines. The planes would be run up for visitors who came to the new Aero Hanger on the Cal Poly air strip.

The big events of Poly Royal, the thirteenth, included a Friday night Country Fair Dance, a Rodeo and the Coronation Ball during which the queen would be crowned. The baseball team would play the San Luis Obispo Merchants on Saturday afternoon.

Cal Poly Baseball Field
3:30 PM April 27, 1946

It was the first half of the ninth inning. Poly was leading the San Luis

Obispo Merchants by a score of 10 to 3. It had been a hitting game for Dave. He had hit two doubles and a single driving in four runs. The Merchants had hit nine singles, mostly through the infield. Singles along with an error had scored the Merchant's three runs in the fifth inning. While Dave allowed lots of hits he kept the runners on second and third for the rest of the game. In the ninth inning Dave wanted to end the game quickly. The game had lasted too long. He threw five fast balls and got two fly outs and one foul to Henry Wilkler, the Mustangs' rolly polly catcher. The game was over.

This was Dave's fifth win of the season. He had not lost a game and had pitched five complete games. The team had five wins and one loss. Dave had walked only three batters in 45 innings of pitching.

Jill had watched the game, just the second she had been able to see. That evening Jill and Dave made a good looking couple at the Coronation Ball. Dave pointed out Helen to Jill. Jill had never met Helen. She said, "She is attractive and tall, so I'm not surprised you dated her." "Only once, and I was turned down once when she already had a date. She is a popular girl."

Dave and Jill danced the night away, standing during some numbers to watch and listen to the Collegians. After the dance, at the Tower Café, Dave said he would have to study tomorrow afternoon and evening, so he wouldn't be going to the rodeo.

Chapter Nine

Tower Café

Broad & Higuera Streets

San Luis Obispo, California

1:15 AM May 12, 1946

JILL AND DAVE had danced at Pismo and were having their after dance hamburgers and coffee. Jill had received a reply from United Airlines giving the requirements for becoming a stewardess. Besides height and weight standards, which Jill would have no problem meeting, the girl had to be 21 and unmarried. Two years of college was the minimum educational requirement or two years experience in some kind of public contact work. A telephone company customer relations position was given as an example. At the present time United was not hiring stewardess because of the slow growth of business. It was suggested that Jill seek a public relations job following completion of her Associate of Arts degree. That would give her an excellent opportunity of being hired when the company started recruiting stewardess again.

Jill had called the Pacific Bell office to inquire about a customer relations job. She was asked to complete and submit an application form that they would mail to her. If the application looked good, she would be called for an interview when there was an opening. They did expect to be hiring at least one person by the first of July.

Dave said, "That sounds great Jill. I would like you to stay in San Luis Obispo." "I'm glad you feel that way Dave." They laughed, both knowing how they felt about each other.

Cal Poly Baseball Field
San Jose State at Cal Poly
4:45 PM May 17, 1946

Dave was standing on the pitchers mound, ready to pitch to the first batter in the top of the ninth inning. If he could get three outs without allowing a run, he would have a 5-0 shutout. The first batter choked up to bunt, but Dave had thrown a fast ball that rose and The batter missed for a strike. Dave threw a sinker and the batter grounded out to short stop. The next batter took a called strike on a sinker. He hit the next pitch in the air that catcher Henry Wilker caught just behind the plate. The batter had hit a change up. The last batter watched two sinkers nick the plate on the inside and then the outside for strikes. Dave threw the batter a rising fast ball that he swung at with a home run swing, but all he got was air. Dave had completed the shut out.

The game was a good ending to the season. The team had won 14 and lost 3 games for a good season. Dave was 8-1, pitching 81 innings, and had an ERA of 1.89. He had walked only 4 batters. Dave hit .451 and developed some power, hitting 5 doubles and 2 home runs. He was second on the team in runs batted in (RBIs), driving in 23 runs.

Dave was not excited about next season. There would be a new coach. The baseball field was to be torn up and a new diamond constructed. This would require playing a number of home games at the high school. When his parents visited during spring break Dave's dad had advised him, "Your education is the most important endeavor now." He was not optimistic about the future of the aircraft industry that was in the doldrums following the war, and the airlines still required big government subsidies. George Mason encouraged Dave to continue to improve his school work. He extended a carrot to Dave by mentioning that Dave could earn a master's degree in engineering from a University like Stanford if he did well at Cal Poly. That was a new idea for Dave to think about, particularly with his dad's support.

The visit of Dave's parents allowed them to meet Jill, the girl he had been talking about. They were weary because of Dave's limited involvement with girls. After watching the baseball game, George and Ann Mason returned to their room in the Anderson Hotel. They had invited Dave and Jill to dinner at Mattie's in Pismo Beach. It was the area's best restaurant.

George Mason drove to the dorm to pick up Dave and then returned to the hotel to pick up Ann. From there they drove to Jill's apartment to pick her up. Dave brought her out to the car where she met Dave's mother and father. Dave had advised his dad about Jill's dislike of the ranch life and wanting to get away from the San Joaquin Valley. He suggested little talk of the Mason ranch. They had a good dinner and George and Ann seemed to like Jill. Jill told about her interest in becoming an airline stewardess. However it would be at least nine months before she could qualify because she had to be 21. Also United and other airlines were not hiring now because of slow business growth.

After Jill was taken home, both Ann and George said they liked Jill. They complemented Dave on developing a relationship with a girl, something he had not done in high school. Dave was glad they approved, although he had been sure they would. In saying good night to Jill, Dave said, "With cram week coming up, I must stay in my room and study after my parents leave in the morning. How about coming out to get me tomorrow evening about 9:30 and we can go to the Tower Café for hamburgers" "I think that can be arranged. I'll talk with the chauffer." They laughed again. Jill said, "I like your parents. They are very nice." "Thank you Jill. I'll see you tomorrow night. Goodnight." With a kiss, Dave was gone.

Coffee Shop
Anderson Hotel
Monterey and Morro Streets
San Luis Obispo, California
7:30 AM May 18, 1946

Dave and his dad were having breakfast. Dave's dad had just told him that Mr. Jacobs, his instructor at Samuels Gompers Trade School, had obtained a job for him at Pan American Airways for the summer as a mechanic's helper. "That's great dad. I have learned that two Cal Poly grads worked their way up to flight engineer at Pan Am." When do you expect to come home?" "I'm not sure yet, but I will stay through June 5th for Jill's graduation. Her parents are coming, so I'll get to meet them. I'll let you know as soon as I determine when I can leave." Then George Mason said, "It's time to go Dave, we have a long drive. Study hard for those exams. "I will dad."

Tower Café
10:00 PM May 18, 1946

Jill had driven to the dorm to pick up Dave for their late night snack. Jill reported she had been scheduled for an interview at Pacific Bell on Monday afternoon. "That's good news Jill; I just hope you can stay in town. I'll be gone this summer, but the time will go fast. Do you know yet how long your parents will be in town?" "Not yet. My mother said she would call me this weekend." "Please let me know as soon as you find out so I can make a train reservation for my trip home." "I will Dave." "Now, it's been a long day, please take me to the dorm."

Jespersen Dormitory
1:30 PM May 31, 1946

Finals were over and Dave was starting to pack for the trip home. Dave's dad had sent him a trunk to fill with the items he had collected in nine months of school. He would check the trunk on his train ticket. He had a Thursday, June 6th reservation on the Daylight.

Jim Olson doubted he or Chuck would return next year. It was Dave's opinion that Jim had enrolled at Cal Poly for the summer session because he was 18 and his dad thought the draft board would be less likely to call him if he was in college. The draft having ended, the college need was gone. Dave was sorry because he liked Jim and his friend Chuck. Dave said he would try to visit them during the summer.

Jim would stay in Sonora and open an auto repair garage. Chuck Ryer would later lose his life in a lumber mill accident.

Snow White Creamery
10:00 PM May 31, 1946

Dave and Jill had planned a big weekend, their last for the next three months. They watched a movie tonight and would attend the Pismo dance tomorrow night. Sunday afternoon they planned to bowl and Jill would cook dinner that night. It would be a nice conclusion to their seven month relationship.

Dave encouraged Jill to date other fellows during the summer if she found some she liked. Dave said he would be too busy with work, American Legion baseball and bowling. Also, he didn't know any girls in Palo Alto that he could ask for a date. Jill indicated she would be particular about dating any fellow.

Jespersen Dormitory
10:30 AM June 1, 1946

Dave was satisfied with his life during the past three months. He had a good feeling about school work and expected to make his B average. He had received important assistance from two fellow students, both veterans, in improving his math. He had improved his drafting practice, something that had been weak even though he took a year of drafting in high school.

Following the conclusion of baseball season, Dave was awarded his Block P. During the Block P initiation at the county park, Dave had been thrown in the creek and drank his first beer. It was bitter, so Dave was a "tea totaled" like his dad.

Dave had really enjoyed the Sunday school class and the study of David from the Old Testament. However, he looked forward to attending church and an adult class at Menlo Park Presbyterian Church during the coming summer.

Cal Poly had changed during Dave's freshman year. From 150 students in September to over 800 by year end.125 houses had arrived to form Vets Village for married veterans. It was just the beginning of even greater growth to come.

San Luis Obispo Junior College
San Luis Drive
San Luis Obispo, California
9:00 PM June 5, 1946

Dave was sitting with Jill's parents, watching diplomas being awarded to the graduating students. Following the ceremony Jill, Dave and Jill's parents went to the Tower Café. Jill was so happy to be finished with college and she had a job!

Jill had done well in her interview at Pacific Bell. Unfortunately a telephone operator wanted to transfer to customer service even though it paid less, so she could eliminate shift work. Since both she and Jill were equal in the company's evaluation, the company employee got the job. However the customer service supervisor was impressed enough with Jill to send her application and interview record to the Santa Barbara office for future consideration.

Within a week Jill received a call from Santa Barbara, requesting she come for an interview. Her interview was very good and she was hired to start on July 1, 1946. She would be scheduled for training during the last week in June in Pacific Bell's training facility in Los Angeles.

When Jill advised her mother about her job, her mother said, "That's good." Jill's parents had become resigned to the fact that Jill would not attend a four year college. You can come with us on our vacation in La Jolla, located north of San Diego. It was a favorite vacation spot of the Garber's. The family had vacationed there in the past. They would stop in Santa Barbara and help Jill find an apartment then drive to the hotel in La Jolla. They would send Jill to Los Angeles by train, for her training, then pick her up at its conclusion, and take her to San Luis Obispo so she could move to Santa Barbara.

Dave was happy that Jill would be as close as Santa Barbara. San Luis would have been better, but it would help him spend more time studying and improving his grades.

Jill's Apartment
10:30 PM June 5, 1946

Jill and Dave had ridden with Jill's parents to her apartment. Once there Jill was in no hurry to take Dave to the dorm. Gwen had gone home for the summer so they had the apartment to themselves. Jill put on some records and they danced and talked about what the summer would hold for each of them. Jill said, "My parents, particularly my dad, were very impressed with you Dave. They both said you have good manners. They complemented me on my selection."
"That's great Jill. Now let's turn the lights down and you can sit on my lap so I can give you some loving. It will be the last time for a while. I do plan to visit you in August before I return to the campus to register for the fall quarter."

Jill thought she knew how Dave would react, so she said, "I don't know if I will have a couch that will fit you. I'll see if my interior decorator can come up with one so you can stay in my apartment and save money." Dave fooled her and just laughed, so she joined him, and they both laughed.

Later Jill took Dave to the dorm and they said their good night and good by. "Send me you address and phone number as soon as you have them Jill. I'm giving you this pack of penny post cards, already addressed, so you can send me a short note each week. If you want to say something you don't want the postman to read then write a letter." "I will. Goodbye Dave." "Goodbye. Jill."

Approaching the Cuesta Grade
Aboard the Daylight
San Luis Obispo County, California
1:50 PM June 6, 1946

Dave was on his last college trip on the Daylight. For the next three years he knew he would have a car to drive home. It had been a most interesting and satisfying year. He was happy about his big improvement in school work, a good baseball season, and a girl friend, his first in years. He couldn't have asked for more. He did look forward to the summer, particularly attending church and Sunday school at Menlo Park Presbyterian Church. He thought he was close to making a decision about church membership. He concluded that his decision to attend Cal Poly had been a good one. Then Dave closed his eyes and took a nap.

Chapter Ten

Football Stadium

Cal Poly

2:30 PM June 3, 1949

THREE YEARS HAD passed since that June, 1946 day when Dave was on his way home for summer vacation following his freshman year at Cal Poly. Now it was commencement time.

Dave Mason sat in the warm sunlight among his fellow college graduates. It was the day of college graduation, the reward for four years of hard work and study. Dave reflected on his opportunity to attend college with the veterans of World War II, many of whom had been there only because of the educational benefits of the G.I. Bill of Rights. This was certainly the best investment our country had ever made in its people. Thinking back over the last three years, Dave thought about the summer of 1946. He began attending Sunday school and worship at Menlo Park Presbyterian Church. Don Emerson Hall was still preaching his interesting sermons. A college age Sunday school class had been formed that included students attending Stanford. At a breakfast meeting of men of the church Dave heard the speaker say that many non-Christians have better behavior than do Christians. However, they have not made a decision to accept Christ and join the church. Dave thought he was a good person with good behavior. He decided then and there to accept Jesus Christ and join the church. Following four weekly church membership classes, Dave was accepted into the membership of the Menlo Park Presbyterian Church. Dave, along with the other new members in the membership class were welcomed into membership during a Sunday worship service.

Dave had started working at Pan American World Airways, driving to the San Francisco Airport each day. Looking for a book on the history of Pan American in the Palo Alto Library, Dave stumbled upon a book, entitled The Man Nobody Knows. It was a book about Jesus written in 1925 by Bruce Barton, an advertising man. It had opened Dave's interest in the life of Jesus that would result in a continuing study of the Lord throughout Dave's life. The first chapter of the book, entitled The Leader, describes the rejection of Jesus and his disciples by the people of En-Gannim, a Samaritan village for an overnight stay as found in Luke Chapter 9, verses 52 and 53. The reaction of Jesus to his disciples' request to bring fire down from heaven to burn up the village was described in layman's language. This first chapter also gave the probable thoughts of Jesus as he led his band of followers to another village.

The next big event of the summer was the purchase of Dave's first car. It was a 1933 Chevrolet coupe with a rumble seat. He painted it blue and installed blue fabric inside. The rumble seat cushions had been painted red! The car was called the blue beetle.

The Redwood City Post 105 American League baseball team had made it to the national playoffs in Omaha, Nebraska. The team progressed to a semi-final game, but the team lost. Willie "Dizzy" Dean was the losing pitcher. However, it was lack of hitting that lost the game. Dave had won all his starts during the playoffs and was getting more attention from baseball scouts.

In Late August of 1946 Dave had driven to Santa Barbara to spend the week end with Jill as he had promised. Dave told Jill he had lived in Santa Barbara for four years, from age two to six. He had always liked the town. They had a great time together after a three month absence including two afternoons at the beach.

For the first time they talked seriously about church. Jill said she and her brothers had attended Sunday school in a small community church. It was a church in which her father's parents had been charter members. She had dropped out after the eighth grade. Jill had not developed any interest in religion. The church had become more of a community center for social events. Her parents did not attend church regularly but participated in pot luck dinners and a monthly dance held in the church social hall.

Dave told Jill he had attended Presbyterian Sunday school through the ninth grade. Then he dropped out. He had started to attend the Menlo Park Presbyterian Church before he started Cal Poly and as Jill knew he was attending Sunday school at the San Luis Obispo Presbyterian Church when they met. Dave reported that he had joined the Menlo Park Presbyterian Church in July. At this time in her life, Jill said religion still did not hold much interest for her. Dave said he went through three years of not even thinking about church.

Dave took Jill to El Paseo for dinner. El Paseo was a well known Mexican restaurant that was popular when Dave lived in Santa Barbara. Dave said he would return in September for the weekend of the football game between Cal Poly and U.C. Santa Barbara. They planned monthly trips for a weekend together, alternating the driving. Dave gave Jill more penny post cards that he had pre-addressed. Dave thanked Jill for her post card messages she had sent him through the summer. She wrote one letter, telling about a man in his forties who started stalking her. The company reported him to the police and he was stopped.

Jill told Dave, "One of the many things I like about you Dave, is you always do what you have promised. That means a lot to me." "Thank you Jill. It is something my dad impressed upon me to the point that if I don't do something I have promised, I feel guilty."

When Dave returned to the campus he was amazed at the number of new students. Bunks had been set up in Crandall Gym to provide temporary lodging for the many veterans arriving to take advantage of the G.I. Bill and gain a college education. Dave had a new roommate, Chester, a dairy major. Dave had moved to the southwest corner room in Jespersen Dorm.

Now that he had a car he could attend the Sunday worship service at the Presbyterian Church as well as Sunday school. The car enabled him to return to the campus for noon dinner. Dave enjoyed the sermons of The Rev. Frederick J. Hart, the pastor. Dave was slowly growing in his faith,

Dave invited Jill to attend Poly Royal in April, 1947 and they had a good weekend. In May, Jill had been hired by United Air Lines as a stewardess. She was assigned to Denver and not working flights to the West Coast. Jill and Dave used their post card system of communication with a very occasional phone call to keep in touch.

In the fall of 1947 Dave was surprised to learn he had been appointed assistant dormitory superintendent by Herman Tanzmier a member of the faculty. Tanzmier was serving as the dormitory superintendent. Dave had been in Tanzmier's bonehead physics class so he knew Dave. He must have been impressed with Dave to appoint a 19 year old non-veteran to be the assistant in a Dorm full of veterans, two to five years older. He may have been influenced by Captain Bell, who was superintendent of all dormitories.

The perks of the position included free dorm rent and an upstairs room with a bathroom. When Chuck, the student who had been the previous assistant's roommate returned to the dorm, he was a bit taken back that this Kid was the new assistant and his room mate. The previous assistant had been a student who was almost 40. Chuck was 23 or 24.

Following the summer of 1947, Dave vowed to become more social, attend dances and try to meet and date other girls. Jill had been his only girl friend since grammar school. Dave re-read the book How to Win Friends and Influence People by Dale Carnegie. His dad had given him the book while he was in high school. He attended Cal Poly dances and the dances at the Rendezvous Ballroom in Pismo Beach. As the result of spending time at the beach at Avila, Dave had met some girls, although many were in high school; "robbing the cradle" Dave called it. He was spoiled by having a girl friend his own age.

Dave had met Sadie at the beach before he danced with her at the Rendezvous. This led to dates for the Saturday night dance. Her home was just a couple of blocks from the ballroom. In those years well known performers came to the ballroom on one night stands. Included were The Nat King Cole Trio, Frankie Lane and Alvino Ray. A band Sadie and Dave liked was Shep Fields. The band played a lilting style of music, something like the Champaign Music of Lawrence Welk. Shep Fields played a great arrangement of A Slow Boat to China, a popular song of the day.

Dave and Sadie also enjoyed Cal Poly basketball games and dances. One was a Sadie Hawkins dance.

During Christmas vacation in 1947, George Mason asked Dave if he would go with him to the Congregational Church to hear a visiting pastor from Scotland? He would be speaking about missionaries. Dave said he would. George Mason had been raised in the Congregational church in South Amherst, Massachusetts. He had joined the Presbyterian Church in the 1920s because his best friend and fellow Legionnaire was the Pastor. When George Whistler left the ministry, George Mason dropped his membership and had not held membership in any church until he joined the Palo Alto Congregational Church in 1947.

The Rev. D. K. McKenzie spoke about the missionaries sent to China by the London Missionary Society who were members of the Scottish Congregational Church. One, Eric Liddell, intrigued Dave because he was an athlete, a track man who ran the sprints and the 400 meters. He also was an outstanding Rugby player. Before each race and game Eric shook hands with his competitors. Because he would not run on Sunday in the 1924 Olympics, he would not compete in the 100 meters, his best event. Instead he would run the 400 meters, thought to be too long a race for him. Surprising everyone, he won the race and the Gold Medal. He also won a Bronze Medal in the 200 meters.

The son of China missionaries, Eric returned to China as a missionary following ordination in the Scottish Congregational Church. In 1980 Eric Liddell would be the main character in the Academy Award winning movie Chariots of Fire. Dave decided to use the example of Eric Liddell as a guide in his life. Eric Liddell had died in a Japanese internment camp in February, 1945 at the age of 43.

As the result of learning about Eric Liddell's practice of greeting and shaking hands with his competitors in races, Dave started greeting opposing players before baseball games in 1948. It was a practice he would continue throughout his baseball career.

In his senior year, Dave had decided to seek an opportunity in the airline industry, working towards entering the field of air freight. He thought it had a good future spurred by the start of Flying Tiger Lines and Slick, both air freight carriers. Dave was writing his thesis on The Loading and Stowage of Air Freight. The thesis was a Cal Poly requirement that helped many graduates' secure good positions in their field because it demonstrated writing and research skills.

Just after Christmas of 1948, Jill called and said she was working a flight to San Francisco the next day. Would Dave meet her at the airport? Dave did and took her home. They talked until 2:00 AM. They had not been together since Jill's three day visit to San Luis Obispo in June. Jill reported she would be working a flight to San Francisco starting in January. She said, "The turnover in stewardesses was so great that her seniority would allow her to change her base to San Francisco by next June. Do you know yet where you will be following graduation?" "I don't know because of baseball possibilities. The next six months will be critical to my future, on the baseball field and in the classroom. If I had my choice I would be in Palo Alto or close-by." Dave took Jill to the airport the next afternoon and hoped to see her in June.

In January, 1949 Dave had attended a meeting of the Aviation Section of the Society of Automotive Engineers (SAE), in Los Angeles. Dave had joined the student chapter of SAE as soon as it was established on campus. During this meeting he learned about consulting engineering for the first time. Following the meeting, he talked with one of the consultants who had made a presentation. He asked how a young engineer could get into consulting engineering. He was advised to earn a master's degree in mechanical engineering that would give him opportunities in the heating, ventilating and air conditioning field. The master's degree would also widen his opportunities in other areas. Dave though back to what his Dad had said about striving for entry to Stanford to earn a master's degree.

In 1949, some Cal Poly friends invited Dave to Newman Club meetings. The Catholic youth group met at the Mission. One of the girls who attended was Sheila who he had met at the beach. Dave was known as the boy with the big smile. Dave and Sheila became good friends and became wave jumpers at Avila beach. She was Dave's date at the Senior Prom in 1949.

The 1949 Poly Royal Chairman was Larry, a fellow aero student and resident of Jespersen dorm. Dave was selected to escort one of the Poly Royal Princesses.

In March, 1949, Dave had attended the wedding of Helen to Bruce, one of Dave's friends who lived in Jespersen dorm. On the day of the wedding, Bruce had parked his car in front of the dorm, an invitation to fix it so it wouldn't run. With Wes, Dave removed the distributor rotor, thus disabling the car. Following the wedding ceremony, Dave received a "dirty" look from Alan, the 14 year old brother of Bruce. Bruce had done the same fix to Dave's car. So they exchanged rotors.

Throughout his college years, Dave had kept up his bowling, usually bowling with Les Towne on Sunday afternoon. Les provided a good challenge for Dave because he was a good bowler. Les had remained on the Cal Poly bowling team during his four years of college.

Local bowling observers had told Dave he could compete in the newly started professional bowling tour now appearing on TV. Dave kept it in mind as an alternate to baseball.

Les Towne was also sitting with the graduates on this day. He would receive his degree in Heating and Air Conditioning. Les would leave his San Luis Obispo home soon for a job with a Phoenix, Arizona air conditioning firm. Arizona was in the forefront of the air conditioning expansion because of the desert temperatures.

Even though Dave had no intention of working in the maintenance field, his instructors in engines and aircraft construction convinced him to take the examinations for his engine and aircraft mechanics licenses. He did and passed both written and the shop tests. The licenses would have an impact on Dave's life in the not too distance future.

Dave had demonstrated a surprising ability to trouble shoot aircraft engines. He developed an "ear" in which he could tell from listening to an engine run, what the probable problem was. However, Dave's experience working at Pan American during the summer of 1946, had convinced him that he did not want to work in the maintenance field and the path to being a flight engineer was just too long.

At Cal Poly, the 1947 baseball season had been a down year in which Dave's record was 6 wins and 3 losses. As the 1947 season wound down, Dave learned that a new summer baseball league of college and amateur players had been formed at cities of state and small private colleges. Players could return home for the summer, play baseball for the home team and take classes at the local college if desired. It was named the National Amateur Baseball Association (NABA). Since the Palo Alto area did not have a team, Dave decided to stay in San Luis Obispo and play for the San Luis Obispo Missions. This allowed Dave to take summer courses that would lighten his load during baseball seasons.

He played baseball and attended summer school in the summer of 1947 and 48. In 1948 Dave led the team with his pitching and hitting to the National Championship of NABA. This resulted in more interest by major league scouts. Also Luke Devore of the New York Dukes was still following Dave.

Dave had started two practices that were important to his baseball performance. First, he wanted to know how many pitches he was making in a game. Starting his junior season, he asked his friend Wes to count pitches with a mechanical number counter. Push a button and the counter adds one number and shows the total as all times. For a pitcher who depended on control this was important. It was part of what Dave called pitching efficiency. Following each game Dave divided the number of pitches by the number of outs. The result was his pitching efficiency or PE. If it took 100 pitches in a 9 inning game, his PE was 100 divided by 27 which = 3.7. So it took an average of 3.7 pitches to get one out. Dave's goal was a PE of 3.

At the same time, Dave started having his pitches charted. He wanted to know which pitches were hit for hits and which were outs. It also helped Dave to know the strength and weaknesses of conference team players who he would face a number of times each season. Dave needed someone who knew the difference between a fast ball and a slider to do the charting. He asked Jack Crowe a fellow aero student, to sit behind home plate during home games and do the charting. Jack had played first base on the 1946 Poly team but hadn't played after the 1946 season. Dave asked reserve players to do the counting and charting during games away from Poly.

As the 1949 college baseball season wound down, Dave was the subject of great interest from scouts of major league teams that had good defense and a large home stadium outfield. This was thought to be the requirements of a sinker ball pitcher to be successful in the majors. A few scouts were of the opinion that Dave's future in professional baseball was in the outfield because of his hitting. Dave was a disciplined batter who seldom struck out and would accept walks. His power had increased with his weight.

A scout for the Boston Red Sox thought he saw a potential new Babe Ruth in Dave. It would be ironic as the "Bean Towners" had not lived down the sale of the Babe to the New York Yankees in 1920. As many baseball fans Know, Babe Ruth started his baseball career as a pitcher and was twice a 20 game winner. The so called "curse" on the Boston team would last for many years to come. Boston would lose World Series Championships through unusual plays and errors.

Dave ended his college career with a record of 31 wins and 5 losses. He had pitched a two hit shutout in a game against Stanford at the Indian's sunken diamond in his senior year. In 312 innings pitched during college, Dave walked only 18 batters.

By their agreement, Dave had referred all baseball interest of scouts and proposed contracts to his dad. George Mason was an experienced negotiator and if contract offers were made, George would negotiate.

In 1942 the federal government planned to place an aircraft warning beacon on the top of Black Mountain near the Mason ranch. The power and telephone lines for the automatic beacon would have to run across the Mason property. The preferred route, which was the lowest cost to the government, would run the lines in front of the Mason ranch house, thus cluttering the view. George insisted that the lines be run around the back of the property, out of view of the house. Also, he wanted the lines to provide power and telephone service for the ranch. Heating, cooking and lighting was currently done with wood, coal oil and Coleman lamps.

Over a six months period, negotiations dragged on. Finally, the government gave in and George had won another negotiation.

George Mason received five contract offers for Dave's baseball future. Four from major league teams and one from the San Francisco Sea Lions of the Pacific Coast League, a minor league, just below the majors. The Pacific Coast League (PCL), had been campaigning to be raised to major league status and become a third major league. All but one team was independent. They had no working agreement with a major league team.

Walter Dent, an Importer/Exporter, had purchased the Sea Lions in 1945. The team had been successfully operated for many years by developing players and selling them to major league teams for players and cash. The Sea Lions had the most modern stadium in the league with a large outfield. A home run hit in Sea Lions Stadium was a real home run. Many fly balls caught in the outfield would have been home runs in other PCL parks.

Dent had upgraded San Francisco baseball. The club house had been rebuilt and travel changed from train to airplane. This changed a trip to Seattle from an overnight 17-1/2 hour trip to one of 4 hours. Dent had also raised salaries to closely match those of young major league players.

Luke Devore of the New York Dukes made the best money offer. The Dukes offered a $25,000 bonus to sign and a starting salary of $6,000 per year. It would qualify Dave as a bonus player and the team would be required to carry him on their major league roster. Dave did not want the pressure of being a bonus player.

The Sea Lions' manager Drew "Tub" Warren had been a major

league catcher and knew pitchers and pitching. Warren had been aware of Dave as the result of his American Legion baseball. He had invited Dave to work out with the Sea Lions during the summer of 1945.

The Sea Lions offered Dave a $5,000 bonus and $4,000 for the balance of the 1949 season, about four months. Since the bonus was under $6,000, Dave would not be subject to a major league draft at the end of the season. Compared to the million dollar bonuses of today, it seems puny. However consider this: in 1949 the average income of Americans was a little less than $3,000. You could buy a house for $7,500. Gasoline was 17 cents per gallon and a movie ticket 60 cents. Dave had decided to sign with the San Francisco Sea Lions.

George Mason had done his research well and learned that baseball had changed a provision of the reserve clause in the standard contract. It allowed a minor league team to pay to a player being sold, a percentage of the player's sale price to a major league team. The major leagues had agreed to the change, thinking it would restrain young high priced players from making higher salary demands in their early years in the majors. The change had been kept quiet though, and George was fortunate to learn about it.

When George introduced the percentage provision of a potential sale, he started high, suggesting a 35% cut to Dave if he was sold to a major league team. Dent countered with a sliding scale that would drop year by year. His proposal was 30% the first year, declining by 5% each year. Dent doubted that there would be a sale in the first year since Dave would only play for four months of the 1949 season. George countered with a 30% start, but only a 3% drop each year. Dent filially agreed and George Mason had won another negotiation contest.

Dave was happy to be starting his professional baseball career on the West Coast, close to home. George had one other provision that could not be part of the contract and was handled in another fashion that we will learn about in the near future.

To top it off, Jill had advised Dave she would be based in San Francisco by June 1. She would be living in Burlingame with two other stewardesses.

The reminiscing over, Dave turned his attention to the commencement program. Fellow aero student Eldon Price presented the class gift. It was the corner stone for the War Memorial Student Union Building, then in the planning stage. Dr. John L. Lounsbury, Superintendent of San Bernardino Valley College was the Commencement speaker.

An honorary Bachelors Degree was awarded to Charles B. Voorhis, 77. He is the father of former Congressman Jerry Voorhis who gave the 157 acre San Dimas campus to Cal Poly in 1938.

Dave was about to step to the platform to receive his diploma. He did reflect on his decision to attend Cal Poly. He decided it had been the best decision he had made in his young life. George and Ann Mason watched with parental pride as Dave accepted his diploma from Dr. Julian McPhee.

From bonehead courses to a degree in aeronautical engineering was an outstanding achievement. In the fall of 1945, if odds had been offered on Dave earning this degree they would have been at least 100 to 1.Dave had become a "Poster Boy" for Cal Poly and the educational philosophy of Dr.McPhee.

The recessional was Pomp and Chivalry played by the Cal Poly band, directed by Eddie Jay, who had helped Dave conquer the mysteries of calculus.

The members of the class of 1949, the largest in history, would be the first large group that would start building a reputation for Cal Poly, particularly in engineering. During Dave's years, when he told someone he was an engineering student at Cal Poly, the typical response was, "Oh, Cal Tech." California Institute of Technology known as Cal Tech, was considered second only to Massachusetts Institute of Technology, (MIT) in engineering. When a person said Cal Tech, Dave didn't correct them.

Now fast forward to August, 2006 and the U.S. News & World Report's Guidebook of America's Best Colleges. For the fourteenth year in a row, Cal Poly, now California State Polytechnic University was rated the best public-master's university in the West. The interest by students who wanted to attend Cal Poly was overwhelming.

Applications for the 2006 fall quarter totaled 30,786, almost twice the number of the student body.

The College of Engineering was ranked as the number two program at a public school behind only the U.S. Military and Naval Academes. Aerospace Engineering, formerly Aero, was ranked number three at a public university. Cal Poly's engineering graduates have established great records in the working world of engineering.

During dinner with his parents, Dave signed his first baseball contract with Walter Dent himself representing the San Francisco Sea Lions. The next phase of Dave's life would be another challenge.

PART THREE

SAN FRANCISCO, CALIFORNIA

JUNE 6, 1949

Chapter Eleven

Brice Terrace

2230 Bryant Street

San Francisco, California

10:30 AM June 6, 1949

DAVE AND HIS mother Ann had driven to the apartment Ann had rented for him. It was located near Sea Lions Stadium. She knew Dave would have little time between graduation and having to report to the Sea Lions who would be playing out-of-town. Dave was to report to the team in Seattle on Monday, June 14.

Dave liked the apartment and he unloaded the basic needs they had brought in the family Ford. One of Dave's first priorities was to buy a new car, but that would have to wait until he and the team returned to San Francisco.

During the drive back to Palo Alto Dave asked his mother what the news was from his sister Pam. Ann said, "As you know she will finish college at the end of summer. The fellow Pam initially called "Smitty" is now Jim Smith. He is more than the pal she called him when she first wrote. I think she's in love." "That's interesting," Dave said.

Jill had advised Dave to call her apartment when he was home to learn what her flight schedule was. Dave called Sunday and was advised by Jane, one of Jill's apartment mates, that Jill would return the next day on flight 1224 at 3:00 PM. Dave thanked Jane and said he would meet the flight.

The flight was 35 minutes late because of a late departure from Denver, so Dave read the San Francisco Chronicle sports page while he waited. The Sea Lions record was 35 wins and 46 losses. It put the team 11 games under .500. The team didn't appear to have a pitcher who could be called an ace. As the time for flight arrival neared, Dave thought about Jill's warning when he met her at Christmas time. She could not kiss him in public while she was wearing her uniform. They had to wait until they were in a car.

Dave walked to the arrival gate out on the tarmac and watched the Douglas DC-6 pull up to the gate. The movable stairs were rolled to the plane and the door opened. Passengers streamed down the stairs and across the tarmac to the gate. Dave waited for the last passenger to deplane and then a wait for the crew. Jill came into sight appeared surprised and waved. She looked very attractive in her uniform. Jill came through the gate, gave Dave her suitcase and her hand and they walked to the parking lot, talking a mile a minute. Once in Jill's car they kissed and hugged for at least fifteen minutes.

Dave followed Jill's car to her apartment in Burlingame and Dave met Sally, the second stewardess who lived with Jill. She was preparing for a 6:00 PM flight to Salt Lake City. Dave and Jill went to dinner and had a good reunion. Dave gave Jill the Sea Lions' schedule and Jill told Dave the flight she was assigned to. She was now a lead stewardess and would soon be flying to Chicago. The longer flights would mean she would have more time between flights at home. They talked about doing San Francisco, including the Top of The Mark, the world famous lounge at the top of the Mark Hopkins Hotel on Nob Hill.

In Jill's apartment, Dave said, "Jill, come sit on my lap like you did on the hill." Jill was there in a flash. "Jill Garber, I love you." "Oh Dave, I've loved you for so long, but you had to say it first." "I know but I didn't want to say it until I could do something to back it up. My future is developing so we can start talking about our future. What do you want to do now as a stewardess?" "I want to bid on the Hawaii trips. I would accept a Hawaii flight even if I'm not the lead stewardess, although with two years plus of seniority, I'm quite senior." In 1949 the average longevity of a stewardess was 18 months because marriage required their resignation. "Those would be interesting flights," said Dave.

"What would you like to do when you couldn't be a stewardess any longer?" "You mean if I was married?" "Yes. I'm not proposing, but we can talk about what will result in a good marriage."

"We get along so well Dave it's a quality I have admired in my parents. They seldom argued and if they had conflicts, they settled them in private. That is one of the qualities of our relationship that has sustained me during our separations."

"To answer your question; I have become interested in our food preparation at United and have visited the kitchen in Denver a number of times. I have talked to the dietitian there and asked what training is required to qualify as a dietitian. She said, "With my Associate of Arts Degree I could take courses while I'm working that would earn my qualifications. It would take maybe two years. I asked if such classes were offered at a college in San Francisco, and she said yes; at San Francisco State College. While doing that I'm sure I could get a job in reservations. I've known stewardesses in Denver who have done that after marriage. Evidently, there is turnover in that work too." "That sounds great Jill, particularly becoming a dietitian. You know how I like to eat." They both laughed.

Dave said, "It's time I should go. I'm moving into my apartment tomorrow and I hope to have a telephone by Friday. As soon as I have the number I'll call. Let's see," Dave said, looking at Jill's schedule, "You will be back Sunday afternoon." "That's right." "Okay, I'll be there to meet you."

Menlo Park Presbyterian Church
716 Santa Cruz Avenue
Menlo Park, California
11:00 AM June 12, 1949

Dave was attending worship here for the first time since Christmas, 1948. It was good to be back. Dave enjoyed the music of the choir.

The pastor, Don Emerson Hall preached on Matthew 6:19-21, lay up your treasures in heaven.

Dave took notes and later wrote this summary of the sermon.

* Christian work ethic often produces wealth.

* What we do with the wealth is the test of where our treasures are located.

* Do we use our treasures to help people in need and to fulfill the great commission, to make disciples of all nations?

* Where a person's money is located, is where the person's heart is.

The sermon reminded Dave of the trial weekly money pledge that those in his membership class were asked to make and contribute during the four weeks of the class. It had helped him start giving the tithe, ten percent of his income. It wasn't much at the time, but it got him started and he had continued, even contributing ten percent of his bowling winnings. In 1985 a board game called Generosity became very popular in the Christian community. The game was won by the player who laid up the most treasures in heaven.

One of Dave's first priorities was to bring Jill to a worship service. Her agreement with him on church would be critical to his asking her to marry him.

Departing the church, he asked the for a suggested Presbyterian Church in San Francisco near his apartment. He knew he would only be able to attend Sunday school because of the Sunday game schedule. The First Presbyterian Church was suggested. Dave would visit there as soon as he returned from a trip to Seattle.

Rickey's
4219 El Camino Real
Palo Alto, California
7:30 PM June 12, 1949

Dave and Jill were having dinner at Dave's favorite restaurant. As a young boy with a "hollow leg," he looked forward to the smorgasbord style feast at Rickey's. It was Jill's first visit.

They were talking more about their future. Dave had explained why he had applied to Stanford for acceptance in a master's degree program in mechanical engineering. He said it would give him more options for employment in the San Francisco Bay area no matter what happened in baseball. Jill asked how a player progressed to a major league team. "In my case, a major league team would have to purchase me from the Sea Lions, probably for cash and players. The negative about the major leagues is all the teams are in the East or Middle West. I spent a month in New York and Connecticut when I was 9 years old, and the summer weather was hot and humid, not like California.

Jill asked, "Dave, do you want to have children?" "Oh yes at least three maybe four." "Oh Dave, if you had asked me the same question I would have said the same thing. We are so compatible."

Benjamin Franklin Hotel
1930 Fifth Avenue
Seattle Washington
7:30 AM June 14, 1949

Dave was having breakfast. He had flown to Seattle yesterday afternoon, arriving at the hotel at 6:00 PM. The Sea Lions had played a game with the Yakima Bears last night. The Yakima team was the Sea Lions' farm team in the Western International League. Manager Tub Warren walked into the coffee shop, spotted Dave, and came to his table. He welcomed Dave and said, "We can use some good pitching." Dave said, "I'll do my best." Warren said, "The team will leave for tonight's game at 3:00 PM. The bus will be out in front" "I'll be there."

After breakfast Dave walked around Seattle, and shopped at Fredericks & Nelsons department store for a gift for Jill. She liked bracelets and Dave bought a beautiful bracelet with an Indian design.

In the afternoon Dave waited until most of the players were on the bus. Then he climbed aboard. The first player to talk to him was

Orval Overwall, a seldom used pitcher who had been a member of the Sea Lions since 1940. Oscar's greeting was, "Hi rookie." That's all he said. Later in the season Dave and Oscar would have an unusual connection.

Sick's Seattle Stadium
Rainier Avenue at McClellan Street
Seattle, Washington
San Francisco at Seattle
5:35 PM June 14, 1949

Dave was running in the outfield, something he had not done for two weeks. When he completed his running he warmed up by throwing 50 easy pitches to Bill Parks. Parks was a veteran catcher who had major league experience. After that he shagged balls in the outfield. The additional provision of Dave's signing the contract with the Sea Lions was that he could take batting practice with the position players. This was agreed upon in a letter from Manager Drew Warren.

When Dave came to the batting cage, he was asked by one of the position players what he was doing there. Dave replied, "I'm here to work on my hitting." About that time manager Tub Warren came to the cage and told the position players, "I forgot to tell you that Mason will take batting practice with you every day." So Dave would continue to take the same batting practice as the position players.

Dave sat in the dugout and watched Seattle win the game 6 to 4. After the game, Manager Warren asked catcher Bill Parks how Dave looked during his warm up. Parks said, "He has a good sinker. I think he can pitch in a few days." Tub Warren then told Dave he would pitch the second game of the Sunday doubleheader. It would be a seven inning game. "This will give you the week to get ready," said Tub.

On the bus ride to the stadium, Dave had seen a sign, Rainier Bowl. He needed to do some bowling. He didn't have his ball, but he would still come tomorrow morning and bowl a few games. He hadn't done any for at least three weeks.

Rainier Bowl
1000 Rainier Avenue
Seattle Washington
9:00 AM June 19, 1949

Dave had taken a taxi to the bowling lanes at a time when he thought lanes would be available. After bowling three games, he watched the other bowlers in action. The best was a young man in his thirties. After watching him bowl a number of games, Dave approached him, asking if he would like some competition. "Sure," he said, "How much a game?" Dave said, "How about $5.00 per game and $20.00 for a three game series?" "You're on." "My name is Dave." "I'm Sam."

They did some good bowling. Sam took two of the three games and the series, winning $25.00 of Dave's money. Dave had asked Sam, "What do you do for a living that allows you to bowl in the morning?" "I'm a cook at the Hong Kong Cafe located in the International District. I work nights, so I can bowl in the daytime. And you?" "I'm a rookie baseball player, here with the San Francisco Sea Lions." "Oh, I take my family to the baseball games on Sunday. Will you be playing on Sunday?" "Yes, I will pitch the second game, my first in professional baseball." "That's interesting Dave, What's your last name?" "Mason." "Good, I'll tell my boys. They are 10 and 8 and baseball nuts. "Thanks for bowling with me Sam." "It was my pleasure Dave. Come to the Hong Kong Café some time and ask for Sam Wong." "Thank you Sam."

Sick's Seattle Stadium
4:30 PM June 19, 1949

It was the bottom of the seventh inning. The Sea Lions held a 4 to 0 lead. Dave had allowed only four hits, struck out one and issued no walks. 12 outs had been via ground balls to infielders. Just three more outs and Dave would have a shut out in his first professional game.(The second game of Sunday doubleheaders was 7 innings). The first batter fouled off the first pitch. The second pitch, a sinker, was hit to the short stop who threw him out. The second batter took the first pitch for a strike. He hit the next pitch to the second baseman who threw him out. Two down. The next batter swung at the first pitch, a change. The batter was way out in front of the pitch for a swinging strike. The next pitch, a sinker was hit to Dave who ran half way to first and tossed the runner out. Game over, and Dave had pitched a shut out. He had also walked, hit a single and scored two runs.

After the game Dave received many slaps on the back and hand shakes. In the visitors clubhouse Dave went around and thanked each of his infielders for their error-less play. It was a great start for Dave even though the team lost the week's series five games to two. As soon as he returned to the hotel, he called Jill to tell her the good news.

Dave's Apartment
8:00 AM June 20, 1949

Dave was leaving on a shopping trip for what he needed in his apartment. It would include a TV set. While TV was in its infancy, his mother, ever the sports fan, had decided to purchase a set in 1948 to watch wrestling. Dave had seen TV for the first time at the 1939 San Francisco Worlds Fair on Treasure Island. He decided at the time it will be great to see all the sports games on TV. However, that day was still a long way off. Dave also needed to buy food and staples. He would wait until later in the week to shop for a new car.

Lavell Chevrolet
1700 Van Ness Avenue
San Francisco, California
2:15 PM June 23, 1949

Dave had decided that Lavell Chevrolet had the best deal on the car he wanted. Also, they appeared to be boosters of the Sea Lions with posters promoting their radio broadcasts of the games. Dave was buying a Chevrolet Fleetline two door sedan, model 1552. It was blue, naturally. A condition of the sale had been to take Dave's Blue Beetle off his hands. He hadn't asked for any trade-in amount, he just didn't want the task of disposing it. However, they had given him a $25.00 trade in. Dave was writing a check for the full amount. The salesman said the car would be ready next Monday morning. Dave thanked him and went to his apartment satisfied.

Dave and Jill had talked by telephone on Monday and planned their night on the town for Saturday night. The ball game would be in the afternoon that day. Dave invited Jill to attend the game and sit with the player's wives. She said she wouldn't be able to do that because of a stewardess meeting. She would meet Dave at his apartment following the game where she could change her clothes. Jill was interested in learning what kind of ladies married baseball players but that would have to wait. Dave was looking forward to the evening. He was just sorry he wouldn't have his new car.

Sea Lions Stadium
2350 16th at Bryant Street
San Francisco, California
Portland at San Francisco
8:30 PM June 24, 1949

Playing in his first home game, Dave was involved in a pitcher's duel through five innings. The score was 1-1. Dave had set the Beavers down in the first half of the sixth inning on just six pitches, all ground ball infield outs. The Sea Lions' lead off batter Del Hoffman walked to open the bottom of the sixth inning. He was sacrificed to second by short stop Les Short. Catcher Jim Jarvis struck out. That brought Dave to bat. Dave fouled off the first pitch. The second was a ball. The pitcher, following the usual approach to get pitchers out, fed Dave a fast ball. Pitchers are notoriously late swingers. Dave was not late, he crushed the ball, and it cleared the left field fence with plenty to spare. Sea Lions 2, Portland 1.

Dave retired the next nine batters without allowing a base runner. Dave had won his second game with pitching and hitting and the Sea Lions were looking up! During this game Dave had started his past practice of facing the infielders and giving a thumb up when they made a good play. He was starting to bond with his fielders who were so important to his pitching. The position players liked Dave's fast work which minimized their standing around.

When Dave arrived the next day for the Saturday afternoon game, manager Tub Warren asked to see Dave in his office. Warren said, "I haven't been counting your pitches, but I know you make fewer in a game than any of our other pitchers. Would you be willing to try pitching on three days rest?" "Sure, I'd like to try it."

Dave said, "I had planned to talk to you about having my pitches counted. In college I had a fellow student do it with a mechanical counter." "That's not a problem. I'll have a utility player do it" "Also, I had my pitches charted. I had a fellow who was our first baseman my first year do it. He didn't play after that one year and he knew the difference between the pitches." "Let's talk about that later Dave. I will schedule you to pitch next Tuesday on three days rest. We'll watch you closely and you must tell me if there are any problems. Don't hide them." "I agree," Dave said.

Top of the Mark
Mark Hopkins Hotel
1 Nob Hill
California & Mason Streets
San Francisco, California
6:00 PM June 25, 1949

Dave and Jill had been given a window table looking out over San Francisco Bay. The fog was starting to roll in beyond the Golden Gate Bridge. Jill ordered a glass of wine. Dave, still a tea totaled ordered ginger ale.

Soon after they were seated, Dave gave Jill the bracelet he had purchased in Seattle. She loved it because she had none with an Indian design. Jill was beaming, and while Dave thought she was attractive, for the first time Dave thought she looked beautiful.

Dave had made reservations for dinner in the Mural Room of the Saint Francis Hotel. Dinner would be followed by dancing to Freddy

Martin's Band. The vocalist was Merv Griffin.

Mural Room
St. Francis Hotel
335 Powell Street
San Francisco, California
8:00 PM June 25, 1949

Dave and Jill were seated for dinner at a table near the bandstand. Jill asked, "How did you arrange this Dave?" "I didn't, I just asked for a table not too far away from the music." They enjoyed, a fine dinner and the band was ready to play.

When the music started Dave said, "May I have this dance Miss Garber?" "Yes you may Mr. Mason" The both laughed. The first tune was Room Full of Roses, a number made popular by Sammy Kay and his swing and sway music. Later Merv Griffin sang Galway Bay, a Bing Crosby favorite. Dave even danced some fast numbers. They danced until midnight, when they were ready to head for home. Dave would be continuing on to Palo Alto after he followed Jill home. He was having breakfast with his dad in the morning. He just hadn't had time to talk with him since the day of college commencement.

Montley's Restaurant
179 University Avenue
Palo Alto, California
7:30 AM June 26, 1949

Dave and his dad were having breakfast and catching up. Dave described his trip to Seattle and the past week. "Needless to say, baseball could only be better if the team was winning more often. We have another week at home and then we go to Hollywood for a week." Dave asked if there was any mail for him. He was waiting for an answer from Stanford about his application for the master's program. George said he had seen nothing. He thought a decision could come any day now.

George asked Dave how he was handling cash since his bank account was in the Palo Alto Branch of American Trust Company. In 1949 about the only place to cash a check was at your bank. Few stores or businesses would cash a check unless they knew you very well. "I suggest you buy a small safe that you can keep in your apartment. Buy one you can chain to something so it can't be carried off. You can keep a supply of cash in the safe and won't have go to the bank or carry lots of cash." There were no credit cards in 1949. The department stores had charge cards, but the balance had to paid each month.

George said, "When you have time, I encourage you to join a service club." George had been a member of Rotary for many years. "As a young man, just starting out, I suggest you consider Junior Chamber of Commerce or Kiwanis. Junior Chamber is more business oriented and Kiwanis concentrates on helping children young people and their communities. Dallas Trent has been a Kiwanian for many years." Dallas was George Mason's first associate in the purchase of the Palo Alto Times in 1919. He served as editor for many years. "I will look into that when I return from the trip to Hollywood."

"I'm getting serious about my relationship with Jill. We have started to talk about the things we need to agree on before I make any proposal. So far we agree on everything we have talked about. The next subject will be religion. I think I mentioned previously that Jill was raised in a community church Sunday school. The church was more community club than a church. She says she is just not interested in religion. When the baseball season is over I want to bring Jill to worship services at Menlo Park Presbyterian Church. We need to agree on this subject because of how it would affect children and our relationship in the marriage." "You are very smart to discuss this subject Dave."

Dave said, "Tomorrow I will pick up my new Chevrolet." "I'm glad to hear that, if only for safety sake." "Now dad, I must be on my way to the baseball stadium. Thank you for breakfast."

Sea Lions Stadium
Portland at San Francisco
4:00 PM June 26, 1949

Dave sat in the dugout and watched the Sea Lions win the first game of the double header 6-4, insuring they would win the series even if they lost the second game. There seemed to be a new spirit on the team as described by some of the veteran players. The Sea Lions did lose the nightcap, but the team looked improved winning the series 5 games to 2. However, they were still one spot above the cellar.

Lavell Chevrolet
9:00 AM June 27, 1949

Sales manager Bill Fox knocked on Larry Lavell's open door and got an immediate "Come in Bill." "Did you know that Dave Mason, the Sea Lions rookie pitcher bought a car from us last week? No, I hadn't noticed." "He will be in this morning to pick up the car and I wondered if your might want your picture taken with him? Right now he is a new local baseball hero." "That's a great idea, Bill. Let's think about placing it in a newspaper ad." "That's a good idea Bill if he approves." "Let me know when he arrives." "I'll do that."

Lavell Chevrolet
11:00 AM June 27, 1949

Dave had arrived to pick up his new Chevrolet and turn in the blue beetle. The salesman and sales manager Bill Fox were completing the paper work for Dave to sign. Bill asked Dave if they could take his picture with Larry Lavell, owner of the dealership. "Sure," said Dave. Larry came to the showroom and met Dave. He said he was a big baseball fan and the dealership had sponsored the Sea Lions' radio broadcasts for a number of years. Dave said, "I noticed that when I was here last week." The picture of Dave and Larry was taken by Bill Fox. Larry asked, "Would it be okay if we used the picture in our newspaper advertisement? Dave said it was okay. "I did buy the car here."

Larry asked Dave, "At some time in the future would you be interested in making a personal appearance here in our showroom? We would have you autograph baseballs and give them out to kids." "Well, I don't know how valuable my autograph is, but yes, I would be willing to talk about doing that. It should be discussed with my dad, George Mason." Dave gave Larry George Mason's card. "Thank you Dave, we will be in touch with you. Now, I know you will enjoy your new Chevrolet." "Thank you," said Dave.

Dave drove his new car to his apartment. It was like driving a dream after three years of driving the blue beetle.

Sports Center
3333 Mission Street
San Francisco, California
1:15 PM June 27, 1949

Dave was bowling with his ball for the first time in more than a month. He was a little rusty, so he bowled more than three games. He thought, I must do more bowling. It relaxes me so much and if I don't keep my game up I can't challenge anyone for money.

Sea Lions Stadium
Los Angeles at San Francisco
9:45 PM June 28, 1949

The Los Angeles Angels were perennial PCL champs. As the farm club of the Chicago Cubs, they had lots of young talent. This was supplemented by players who excelled in the PCL, but were busts with the Cubs and returned to play with the Angels. The Angeles had a terrible start this season, and were in the league cellar, just below the Sea Lions.

The game was over and the Sea Lions had won the first game of the series. Dave pitched another shut out even though he allowed eight hits. Three double plays cut off any potential runs. The Sea Lions scored four runs in the first inning, so Dave could pitch his game, getting batters to hit the ball to infielders. Dave hit a single and drove in two runs. There was no more scoring after the first inning and the Sea Lions won the game 4-0.

Dave's Apartment
10:00 AM June 29, 1949

Dave had done some Bible study this morning for the first time since his move from college. Besides locating a Presbyterian Church where he could attend adult Sunday school, Dave though he would try to locate a church nearby that had a Sunday evening worship service. It would be the only way he could hear sermons during baseball season.

Jill called and invited Dave to dinner at her apartment on Sunday night. Jane had invited her friend, a United Airlines flight engineer. "You two should have something in common. Jill said, Come as soon as you can after the games. Please call me when you leave your apartment." "I'll be there in my new blue car." "That right, you got your car today." "Yes I did and it drives like a dream." "Oh, I want a ride." "Your wish is my command," and they both laughed. "I'll see you on Sunday Jill."

Dave decided the First Presbyterian Church located on the corner of Sacramento Street and Van Ness Avenue would be the closest Presbyterian Church. He visited and learned the church had an adult Sunday school class that met at 9:30 AM. That would allow time for Dave to get to the stadium for Sunday games. Locating a church for Sunday evening worship would take more time.

Dave's Apartment
9:00 AM July 1, 1949

Dave had called Jill with an invitation in mind. He asked, "Would you like to attend our game tomorrow afternoon?" "I wondered if you were going to ask me to watch you pitch?" "Oh, you know?" "Sure, I read the sports page now." The both laughed. "After the game I invite you to have dinner with me and then attend a show of your choice."

"Sure Dave that sounds like a fun afternoon and evening." "Okay, I'll leave your ticket in will call. You will be sitting in the wives box, a very good seat." "Will there be wives of players attending?" "Yes, likely more than at a night game." Jill said, "That will be interesting. I've wondered what kinds of girls marry baseball players." "Now you can find out. I'll see you about a half hour after the game. Just wait in your seat." "Thank you Dave."

After winning the opening game of the series on Tuesday, the Sea Lions lost the games on Wednesday and Thursday evening 5-3 and 7-2 respectively. The Lions were not getting timely hits with men on base. Dave hoped the team would rebound tonight with a win.

Sea Lions Stadium
10:16 PM July 1, 1949

Veteran pitcher Al Armer had pitched a good game shutting out the Angles through seven innings. He allowed two runs in the eighth inning but was able pitch a complete game.

Dino Reselli and Mike Roc hit home runs to power the Lions offense for a 4-2 win. It tied the series at 2-2.

Chapter Twelve

Sea Lions Stadium

Los Angeles at San Francisco

3:15 PM July 2, 1949

IT WAS THE top of the fourth inning and the Sea Lions were leading 4 to 0. Dave had shut out the Angels with ground balls and fly ball outs. He had allowed just two hits. Dave had continued his hot hitting, with a single and an RBI. The first Angel batter of the inning singled to center field. The next batter swung away and hit into a double play. The next batter fouled out to the catcher for the final out of the inning. There was no more scoring until the top of the eighth inning when Los Angeles scratched out an unearned run on a single, a walk and an error. The score was now Sea Lions 4 and L.A.1.

In the bottom of the eighth, the Sea Lions loaded the bases with one out. The catcher, Bill Parks, struck out. That brought Dave up. Batting right handed, Dave took a strike on the outside corner of the plate. Dave hit the next pitch, a fast ball, right on the fat of the bat and there was no doubt the ball was going out of the stadium for a grand slam home run. Dave was mobbed by his teammates. That's the way the game ended, the Sea Lions winning 8 to 1.

When Jill had arrived at the wives box she found her seat in a row of empty seats. At first the others in the box ignored her. Finally, Fern, one of the older wives turned around and asked, "Who are you?" Jill thought by her body language that she was saying "what are you doing in our box?" Jill gave her name and said, "I'm a friend of Dave Mason." "Oh" the wife said, "The rookie pitcher." Then she turned around and said no more and no one else talked to Jill. It appears this wife is the leader of the group. The other wives are watching her. Jill quietly watched the game through seven and a half innings. She wanted to yell when Dave made good pitches, but decided she would not draw attention to herself. When the Sea Lions loaded the bases in the eighth inning, the wives and Jill got excited. Then when Dave hit the grand slam home run, Jill was not restrained. She was so excited she almost fell over the seat and the older wife in front of her. Still none of the wives said anything to Jill.

Finally Lisa May, the young wife of the second baseman Billy, got up from her seat two rows down and sat down next to Jill. This got her a dirty look from Fern. Lisa introduced herself, but didn't say more.

When the game was over Lisa asked Jill to go to the ladies room with her. She told Jill the older wives rule the group and don't make it easy for new wives or girl friends. Lisa said, "I would prefer not to sit in the wives box, but I have no choice. When we go back out we will sit in an empty box away from the others." "Thank you Lisa. Dave told me to stay in my seat and he would come and get me." "That's okay Dave will see where we're sitting."

Dave soon arrived with Billy May. Lisa introduced Jill to her husband. She said, "Jill was getting 'the business' from Fern, if you know what I mean." Billy made a face and said, "That's for the birds." Dave said, "I think we should go Jill, we have a dinner reservation." "I'll see you tomorrow Billy." "Goodbye Dave."

On the way to their cars Dave asked Jill what that was all about. Jill said, "The wives are ruled by Fern, an older wife who asked me who I was and with her body language asked why I was sitting in their box. Then she gave me the silent treatment. She is evidently the leader of the group because they were all looking at her to determine if any one else should talk to me. After you hit the home run Lisa came and sat next to me and got a dirty look from Fern." Lisa said the wives treat new wives and girl friends like rookie players used to be treated and I guess still are in the major leagues. Jill told Dave about Lisa asking Jill to go to the ladies room with her and what she said. "If that's the kind of girls these wives are I don't want to sit in the wives box again." Dave said, "I'll talk to Billy and find out what this is all about. Now let's forget about it and enjoy our evening."

Omar Khayyam's
196 O'Farrell at Powell Street
San Francisco, California
7:30 PM July 2, 1949

Dave had brought Jill to this unique, well known restaurant for a different kind of dinner. They planned to see the movie Ma and Pa Kettle at the Orpheum Theater following dinner. Jill and Dave ordered different entrées so they could compare. Both were very good. They enjoyed the atmosphere. "I forgot to check your schedule, but you are usually home on Mondays aren't you." "Yes, I'm always flying on Sunday." "Okay, if you are home on Monday, the 11th, I invite you to go to the Black Mountain Ranch to see it." "Oh, the ranch you wouldn't tell me about for so long." "That's the one. If you agree, I will see what kind of a ranch girl you are by having you open the three gates on the road to the ranch." "Well, I might surprise you. Sure, I accept your invitation." "Great."

Dave paid the check and when the waiter brought his change, Dave counted it and it was too much. A mistake had been made. Dave called the waiter back and explained the incorrect change. He gave $9.55 to the waiter to correct the amount. The waiter thanked Dave profusely.

Returning to Dave's apartment, he gave Jill some romancing. She departed for home about midnight. Dave was looking forward to Sunday school tomorrow morning.

First Presbyterian Church
1751 Sacramento Street
San Francisco, California
9:30 AM July 3, 1949

Dave had just entered the classroom where the adult Sunday school class was held. The teacher, Dr. Charles Milligan, advised the class, "We have a new member today. Please give us your name and tell us about yourself." "My name is Dave and I'm a member of Menlo Park Presbyterian Church. I'm working in San Francisco this summer through September." "Thank you Dave welcome. Our class is a bit small today because of the so called summer slump, which actually means members are on vacation. Our study is in the book of Acts, and we are starting the 15th chapter today."

The lesson covered the great controversy over whether Gentiles had to be circumcised to be saved. The apostles and elders called a meeting in Jerusalem to consider the issue. The Pharisees insisted that Gentiles be circumcised and keep the laws of Moses. The Apostle Peter rose and demanded to be heard. Peter's statement was that it is only by the grace of God that we Jews are saved, and we are no different from the Gentiles.

Dr. Milligan appeared to be a knowledgeable Bible teacher and Dave found the lesson very interesting. He decided he would return.

Sea Lions Stadium
Los Angeles at San Francisco, Doubleheader
3:15 PM July 3, 1949

The Sea Lions were losing the first game of the double header 3 to 2. The Lions were coning to bat in the bottom of the seventh inning. The top of the batting order would hopefully produce some runs. Lead off man Billy May singled to left field. Bill Vaughn struck out. Dino Reselli singled to right field. Two men were on base with one out. Mike Roc was intentionally walked to load the bases. Del Hoffman, the next batter was called back and Dave was announced as a pinch hitter. It was his first pinch hitting opportunity. With the count 2-2, Dave hit a single to left field, scoring two runs for a 4-3 lead. With runners on first and second, and still one out, would the Sea Lions break the game open? Right fielder Ray Chess hit a double play ball to the shortstop who tossed to second for the force out on Dave, but he took out the second baseman with a hard slide, so he couldn't make the relay to first. Two out, runners on first and third. Shortstop Les Short singled to right field, scoring Roc. The Lions now led 5 to 3. Bill Parks stuck out to end the inning.

Los Angeles would score one run in the eighth, making the final score 5 to 4. Dave's pinch hit and slide to break up the double play were critical. The Angles won the second game 6 to 3. With the Monday 4th of July doubleheader coming up, the Sea Lions led in the series 4 games to 3.

In the clubhouse Dave asked Billy May if he would be at home about six o'clock. "I want to call you." "Yes I'll be there Dave."

Dave made his call to Billy to learn about the wives and Fern. Billy gave him the scoop. "It's not a good situation Dave but I don't think it will change as long as Fern's husband is on the team." Dave would tell Jill the story later.

Jill's Apartment
Primrose Road
Burlingame, California
7:45 PM July 3, 1949

Arriving at Jill's apartment, Dave presented her with a dozen red roses. He met Jane and her friend Woody. Jane was a stunning blonde who looked older than Jill, maybe 24 or 25. Dave would learn later that Jane was a Stanford graduate who worked for a San Francisco public relations firm for three years. She didn't like it because the business was so male dominated. She had been a United Airlines stewardess for about 18 months.

Woody Block introduced himself and said he had been called "Chip" for obvious reasons. Dave said, "I like Woody." Woody was not only a flight engineer for United, as Jill had told Dave, but was the head trainer of flight engineers. Dave and Woody would meet in the future and Dave would hear the interesting story of Woody's start in aviation. Also, he would learn about Woody's war experiences.

The two couples had an evening of good food and conversation. Jill and Jane were good cooks. When it was time to leave, Dave asked Jill if she would like to take in a movie Tuesday night. "Sounds good," Jill said. "Okay, I'll call you after the games tomorrow." After a good night kiss, Dave was on his way home.

Sea Lions Stadium
Los Angeles at San Francisco, Doubleheader
6:15 PM July 4, 1949

The Sea Lions played two good games and won both games of the 4th of July Doubleheader, to win the series 6 games to 3. It put some distance between the Sea Lions and the Angels in the race for the league cellar. The Sea Lions' record was now 48 wins and 56 losses. They were in seventh place, 2-1/2 games out of sixth.

Kiwanis Meeting
Fairmont Hotel
California and Mason Streets
San Francisco, California
12:00 noon July 5, 1949

Dave was following his dad's suggestion that he consider Kiwanis and Junior Chamber of Commerce as a service club to join. Today he was attending the meeting of The Kiwanis Club of San Francisco. After introducing himself, he was asked if he was a Kiwanis member. Dave said, "No, I'm here to learn about your club." Dave was asked to sign the guest register and was told he would be the club's guest for lunch. "Oh, thank you." Dave was led to a seat at one of the tables and was introduced to the members at the table. The member who would introduce guests came to the table and asked Dave some questions. The Club President Kenneth called the meeting to order. Following the Flag salute and singing of God Bless America, a member gave the invocation.

Guests were then introduced, starting with visiting Kiwanis members. Dave was introduced as one who was attending to learn about the club and could be a prospective member. "He is a pitcher for the San Francisco Sea Lions," a member said. "He has won four games without a loss," and everyone cheered. Dave liked the meeting and was particularly interested in the two high school students who were president and vice president of the Washington High School Key Club. The Key Club program as reported by the president sounded interesting. Dave was surprised that the Key Club members were attending the meeting during summer vacation.

Programs supporting children were reported by committee chairmen. The club was planning a big fund raising auction to be held in October.

The program speaker was from the Port of San Francisco. He described the economic impact of the Port on the City. It was an interesting talk.

Dave was given a Kiwanis membership packet and encouraged to return. Dave liked the Kiwanis Club, but would withhold his decision on joining until he visited the Junior Chamber. They met on Wednesday, so he would do that when he returned from Hollywood next week.

The Broadway Theater
Broadway Avenue
Burlingame, California
7:30 PM July 5, 1949

The movie was Any Number Can Play with a great cast that included Clark Gable, Alexis Smith, Wendell Corey and Audrey Trotter. It was an entertaining show, with good acting, something you don't always see today. Since Dave would leave early the next day on the trip to Hollywood, they made it an early night.

After the movie Jill said, "I'll treat you to an ice cream Sunday at Dairy Queen Dave." While they enjoyed their sundaes Dave told Jill about the wives and Fern as told to him by Billy May. "Fern's husband Orval Overwall is a little used veteran pitcher who has been with the Sea Lions for nine years. He has been a member of the team longer than any other player. He had three good years for the Chicago White Sox before the war. Billy thinks he is 38 or 39. They have never had any children so Fern has nothing to do but boss the wives around. She evidently decides who sits where in the box. She is very intimidating and in the past has scared off some wives from sitting in the box. Their husbands have asked for tickets in the stands. Since Orval is an easy going likeable guy, Fern wares the pants in that family. Some players have questioned why the team keeps Orval."

"Billy said, even though she is only 20, Lisa is not afraid of Fern and let her know it when they came to the team at the end of last season. She just ignores Fern which makes Fern mad."

"When you want to attend the next game I'll get you a ticket in another box. Maybe Lisa can sit with you." "That's too bad Dave." "Yes, but that's life Jill."

The next morning the Sea Lions had flown into the Burbank airport and were bused to the Roosevelt Hotel in Hollywood. At 3:30 in the afternoon the players took a bus to Gilmore Stadium for warm up and batting practice.

Gilmore Stadium
Hollywood, California
San Francisco at Hollywood
8:30 PM July 6, 1949

Dave had been thinking about the practice of Eric Liddell before his races. He would shake hands with all competitors, and on the Rugby pitch he did the same before the game started. How could Dave do something similar? Dave had been with the team for three weeks. He decided he could now do something. Before the game he sought out the young players on the Stars team.

The first was Gordon Enson, who had played for the University of California Bears. Cal Poly had played Cal in San Luis Obispo, although Dave had not pitched. Enson won the game with a three run home run. So he and Enson had something to talk about. Enson had been signed by the New York Dukes after his junior year. The Dukes sent him to Hollywood where he was not a local hero. It would give him experience in dealing with big city baseball media. Dave asked Enson how he liked Hollywood. He said it was different than any place he had ever lived. He hadn't decided if he liked it or not. Dave said, "Good luck except when you play us." Enson laughed.

The Hollywood Stars were leading the Pacific Coast League, so this game would be Dave's biggest challenge in his young profession baseball career. Through the first three innings, he was doing fine, allowing just one hit and no runs. However, the "Twinks" pitcher had matched Dave's performance, allowing two hits and no runs. In the top half of the fourth inning, the Sea Lions got two men aboard on first and second with two out and Dave coming to bat. The Stars pitcher threw Dave nothing but fast balls, the typical strategy when facing pitchers. Dave fouled off two pitches, but could not get wood on another pitch, a strike on the outside corner of the plate. It was a good pitch, as Dave commented later.

The pitchers dueled through the eighth inning, each allowing a run. As the ninth inning started the score was 1 to 1, with the Lions coming up. The lead off batter, Les Short, singled to right and was sacrificed to second. Second baseman, Billy May then hit a long single to left center field, and Short scored. The Sea Lions now led 2 to 1.

In the bottom half of the ninth, the first batter tried to wait Dave out by looking at the first three pitches. The count was now two strikes and a ball. The batter waited again, and Dave struck him out looking with a fast ball. The next batter had a different strategy. He swung at the first pitch and flied out to short center. One more out to go and Gordon Enson was coming to the plate. The first two pitches were sinkers, a strike and a ball. The next pitch was a fast ball that Enson swung at and missed. The count was now 1 and 2. What would Enson expect on the next pitch? Dave thought a sinker. Dave threw a super change up and Enson swung way out in front of the pitch and the game was over. Dave had won his fifth game 2 to 1.

The next morning a number of the players including Dave toured the Twentieth Century Fox studios. They saw Shirley Temple's bungalow, preserved by the studio. They also watched a movie being filmed on a sound stage. The next day, Dave and some of the team went on a tour of the homes of movie stars. While these homes are plush and gigantic, the tour guide said, "They are shacks compared to the homes of the twenties, before the depression and income tax."

Back at the hotel, Dave bought some cards to send to Jill. He planned to send her a personal card when he was on a road trip.

Gilmore Stadium
San Francisco at Hollywood
4:05 PM July 9, 1949

After the Sea Lions' win on Wednesday, Hollywood won Thursday night 10 to 2 and 6 to 3 Friday. Today's game is in the top of the eighth inning. The Sea Lions are trailing 5 to 4. Dino Reselli leads off with a single to centerfield. Mike Roc fouls out to the catcher. Del Hoffman singles to left. With two on and one out, Ray Chess walks to fill the bases. On the first pitch, shortstop Less Short bunts to the pitcher and Reselli scores on the suicide squeeze. The other runners held their bases. The score is now a 5 to 5 tie, with runners on first and second and still one out. Catcher Jim Jarvis was due up. He is called back and Dave is announced as a pinch hitter.

Before pitching to Dave, the Hollywood catcher had a conference with his pitcher on the mound. Sending a pitcher up to pinch hit must mean he can hit. They decided not to offer him fast balls. He gets two curves, one for a strike and one for a ball. On the next pitch, a slider, Dave ripped a line drive into left field scoring Hoffman. The Sea Lions now led 6-5 and they had runners on first and second and still one out. Billy May struck out and Bill Vaughn flied out to centerfield to end the Lions rally. In the middle of the eighth inning, the Sea Lions lead 6-5.

The Sea Lions had a one run lead to protect. Al Armer, a left handed pitcher came on to face the left handed batters coming to the plate for Hollywood. Armer pitched a shut out inning for the Lions.

In the ninth inning the Sea Lions put two runners aboard, but couldn't get them home. Hollywood was coming up in the bottom of the ninth inning with the Sea Lions still leading 6-5.

The Stars wasted no time getting a runner on second with one out and rookie Gordon Enson coming to bat. He fouled off two pitches and took a ball for a 1-2 count. He hit the next pitch over the left field fence for a two run home run that won the ball game 7-6. The Lions pitching had failed in the clutch.

The win gave Hollywood a 3-1 lead in the series. The Sea Lions would have to sweep tomorrow's doubleheader to just get a tie in the series.

Hollywood Palladium
6215 W. Sunset Boulevard
Hollywood, California
10:00 PM July 9, 1949

Following the Saturday afternoon game, tickets to the Hollywood Palladium were offered to any team member who wanted to go there in the evening. Les Brown and his Band of Renown were playing for dancing. The Palladium was a famous dance hall that featured the best of the dance bands. Dave had heard about it, but had never been there. He liked Les Brown's music, so he wanted to go just to listen to the band. Del Hoffman, the club's confirmed bachelor who was always looking for attractive ladies, was the only other player who wanted to go.

The Palladium was crowded, this being a Saturday night. A big crowd stood at the bandstand, just listening and watching the band. Dave listened and watched as the band played Bizet Has His Day and Butch Stone sang the novelty number A Good Man is Hard to Find.

Dave was asked to dance by a good looking blonde who was standing near him by the bandstand. He asked her some questions, but got vague answers. She didn't know he was a baseball player. Del danced most of the night with a succession of girls, but he only danced one group of numbers with each partner. He was really playing the field. Del was an excellent dancer as the girls soon noticed, so he got no turn downs for dances. Del and Dave departed about midnight.

Gilmore Stadium
San Francisco at Hollywood, Doubleheader
4:20 PM July 10, 1949

The Sea Lions lost the first game 7-2, giving up five runs in the first inning. The Hollywood baseball scribes had been flabbergasted when Dave was announced as the pitcher for the seven inning game today. Pitching with only three days rest, was not considered good for a young pitcher.

Dave was not as sharp as he was on Wednesday, but he and the team made is easier by scoring early to reduce the stress. In the first inning the Sea Lions batted around, capped by Dave's base clearing double, for a 5-0 lead. Dave fed the batters a steady diet of sinkers and while they got eight hits, only two runs scored. By then the Sea Lions had added three more runs and won the game 8 to 2. Dave had a single to go with his first inning double. Hollywood won the series 4-2, but the Sea Lions were playing better.

The Page Mill Road
A Mile before the First Ranch Gate
Santa Clara County, California
1:40 PM July 11, 1949

Dave had picked up Jill before lunch and they had driven to the Stanford campus where they had lunch in the Stanford Union. It was Jill's first visit to the campus. She was amazed at how large it was, and she hadn't seen all of it yet. After lunch they had driven up the winding Page Mill Road and were now approaching the first gate to the ranch. On the way up the road, Dave explained his Dad's interest in cattle raising that had started when he was a cowboy on the Bloomfield Ranch of Henry Miller near Gilroy back in the early 1900s. He was earning money so he could enter Stanford University. Later when his dad left Stanford to take a job as advertising manager for a real estate firm in Fresno, he started cattle raising on the side. Eventually he bought a ranch in the Merced area. In 1940 George bought the Black Mountain Ranch, giving him something he liked to do that gave him relief from the pressure of running a newspaper firm.

When Dave and Jill arrived at the barn, they were greeted by the ranch dogs including Dave's German shepherd dog Roundup. They saw the horses and took a trip down the road to the green canyon that included the headwaters of Stevens creek, the largest in the county. Jill agreed the scenery was beautiful and since she didn't see any cows, she seemed interested in the ranch.

When they returned from the canyon, Dave drove to the ranch house and they looked out over the San Francisco Peninsula and the Bay. They could almost see San Francisco.

On the way back to the Page Mill Road Jill opened the gates as she had done on the way up with no problem. She did ask Dave what his attraction to the ranch was. He said, "I wanted to drive the tractor and ride the horses. It also gave me a place to learn to drive a car."

In 1942 and 43 when the family went to Palm Springs during spring school break, I stayed here, and batched. I rode the horse Capt. down to the canyon, camped out over night and worked in the blue clay mine on Stevens Creek. We made many items out of the blue clay. Later, Dad would let me drive to and from the ranch before I had a license and I could drive around the ranch. It was a great place for boys to experience the out doors in a rural setting. When I was a youngster I lived in Hollywood for 18 months, it was all paved streets in the city. Then we moved to rural Meiners Oaks near Ojai that had no side walks and was a great place for kids. That's my attraction."

"Oh we have friends who have orange groves and raise horses near Ojai. You have never told me about living in Hollywood and Ojai" "That right, Jill. Those were my 'kid' years. I'll tell you about it some time. Now, what kind of food would you like to eat for dinner?"

"I'd like Chinese food. Is there a good Chinese restaurant in Palo Alto?" "There sure is. Let's stop by the house and then go get our Chinese dinner at the Golden Dragon." "That sounds good, Dave."

At the Mason home Dave said they were going to the Golden Dragon for Chinese food. While Jill was cleaning up, Dave's dad told him he had talked twice with Larry Lavell about you making personal appearances at his dealership. Lavell has agreed to $50.00 per hour for up to 1-1/2 hours. After 1-1/2 hours the fee would be $10.00 for every half hour additional. They want you to plan on one and half hours to start. You will earn $75.00 for the appearance." "That's great dad." George said, "Bill Fox will work out a schedule with you. I suggest you call him tomorrow." "I certainly will."

Then Dave and Jill were then off to have Chinese food at the Golden Dragon.

Chamber of Commerce
333 Pine Street
San Francisco, California
12:00 noon July 13, 1949

Dave was attending the Junior Chamber of Commerce meeting to compare it with Kiwanis. His notoriety was spreading and he was recognized almost immediately upon entering the meeting room. The members put on a big rush to get Dave to join. They were much more aggressive than the Kiwanians. It was a good meeting with a good speaker, so Dave would have to think about which club he would join.

Dave didn't have to call Bill Fox. Upon returning to his apartment, Bill called, saying "He was calling to set up a schedule for your appearance. Could you make an appearance Friday during the noon hour from 11:30 to 1:00? "Yes I can," said Dave. "That's fine," Bill said. "We will supply baseballs for you to sign. Since time is short would you agree on a verbal contract for the fee of $75.00?" "I agree. I will plan to arrive at 11:15." Bill said, "I'll see you then."

Dave was on the phone talking to Jill. She would be on a flight to Chicago on Saturday, so he wouldn't see her until Monday. He would call her Sunday evening and suggest they go to dinner some place on the peninsula. "In San Francisco I'm being recognized almost every place I go." "Poor boy," said Jill. Dave laughed and Jill joined in. "I'm glad you can laugh at yourself Dave." "Thanks Jill. I will pick you up at 5:30 on Monday. "I'll be ready to go."

Dave was reflecting on the sudden attention he was getting. He was being recognized often in San Francisco. He was having a difficult time handling it and keeping in mind what his dad had always told him about not promoting himself and or the family. "Don't tell you friends that you dad owns the town newspaper or that the family has a ranch." Dave was particularly concerned about his relationship with his teammates. After all, he was a rookie, and shouldn't be so much in the limelight. He thought back to the meeting he attended at the Palo Alto Congregational Church in 1947. He thought he needed to learn more, if he could, about Eric Liddell. He decided he would go to the Public library in the morning before he went to Lavell, and look for information about Eric.

Sea Lions Stadium
Seattle at San Francisco
5:00 PM July 14, 1949

When Dave entered the clubhouse, he was asked to see manager Warren in his office. Tub advised Dave that he had someone to chart pitches during home games. "I haven't solved the problem of having it done on the road, but I'm working on it." "That's great," said Dave. "During home games Sam Hammuck will do the job. Sam is an old timer who pitched in the low miners years ago and then for semi-pro teams around San Francisco. His wife died two years ago, so he comes to just about all the home games. I made a deal with him for free tickets to the games, a seat behind home plate, in exchange for charting pitches. I'm going to have all pitchers charted and see how it helps. I've asked Sam to come to the clubhouse before the game on Saturday so you can explain the chart to him. He knows all the pitches, and probably some we don't know, so that won't be a problem." "That sounds great," said Dave.

The Seattle Rainiers were in town and the Sea Lions had won the first game of the series on Wednesday, 6 to 4. Dave was pitching tonight, following another three day rest. The Rainiers came out choking up on the bat to try and place the sinker pitch where there was no infielder. After one batter had singled between third and shortstop, Dave had a conference with catcher Jim Jarvis. He suggested more fast balls, since they want to choke up. Jim agreed. The next two batters watched while Dave threw four fast balls and two changeups for outs. The final batter gave up the choke and grounded out to second on a sinker.

There was no score through three and a half innings. In the bottom of the third the Sea Lions scored two runs. They added three in the fourth for a 5 to 0 lead. Dave allowed six hits, but just one run because the infield turned three double plays and the Sea Lions won 5 to 1. It was the first time this season the team had won two games in a row.

San Francisco Public Library
Civic Center Plaza
San Francisco, California
10:00 AM July 15, 1949

Dave found four books on Eric Liddell that provided a more comprehensive description of the athlete turned missionary. Interviews with people who knew Eric were very revealing. They reported Eric was not pious and gave examples. An example was during the time when Eric was answering a group of inquirers about the spiritual quality of his running. With a grin he informed them, "I really don't like to lose." Another told about life in the Japanese internment camp.

Then Dave found what he was really looking for. Returning from his Olympic victories Eric Liddell was mobbed by the British people who had longed for a hero following the death and sadness of World War I. Following the graduation exercises at Edinburgh University, during which Eric was awarded a Bachelor of Science degree, he was cheered by the audience. Then he was then carried by the students to the steps of St.Giles the medieval church, where a speech was called for. Eric said, "In the dust of defeat as well as in the laurels of victory there is a glory to be found if one has done his best. Those who had done their best and did not achieve victory were owed as much honor as those who received honors for winning."

In a column in the Edinburgh University magazine, the writer said, "Success in athletics sufficient to turn the head of any ordinary man has left Liddell absolutely unspoiled. His modesty is genuine and unaffected. He has taken his victories in stride and never made a fuss. What can be said better of any student who has left the fame of his university fairer than he found it. His grateful alma mater is proud to recognize and praise Eric Henry Liddell."

Dave decided his idea of seeking out the rookie players on each opponent's team to encourage them was a good response.

Lavell Chevrolet
12:15 PM July 15, 1949

Dave was sitting at a table in the Lavell showroom signing baseballs for the kids lined up with mothers. When Dave had arrived at the dealership at 11:15 he saw at least 20 people lined up in front of the table. He was amazed! When Sales Manager Bill Fox greeted him, saying, "I'm not surprised. He said, "We received many phone calls about your appearance, wanting to know how long you would be in the show room."

Dave was having fun talking with the kids and signing baseballs. The advertisement of Dave's appearance said the first 25 kids under the age of 18 would receive balls. Dave also talked to the mothers about driving a Chevrolet. He said, "I've owned two in my life time, and they are the best. I'm driving a new Fleetline that I bought here at Lavell Chevrolet." A couple of mothers talked with salesmen and said they would bring their husband in to look. When Dave departed the table, Bill Fox and Larry Lavell were beaming and thanking Dave. Bill handed Dave his check. Dave said, "It was fun and I hope it helped you sell some Chevy's." Bill Fox said, "I'll be calling again for another appearance." "That's good," said Dave.

Coffee Shop
St. Francis Hotel
7:30 AM July16, 1949

Dave and Woody were sitting in a booth and had ordered their breakfasts. Woody said, "Dave, you are becoming a celebrity." "I don't know about that, but I am recognized in San Francisco almost everywhere I go. I'm going to suggest to Jill that we have our dates on the Peninsula where I'm not recognized so much." "How long have you known Jill?" "Almost four years now. But during two of those years we didn't see much of each other because she was based in Denver and I was still in college. We met in San Luis Obispo where she was attending Junior college and I was a freshman at Cal Poly."

Dave said, "Jane is a stunning girl, how did you meet her?" "That was my opinion when I first saw her on a flight about a year ago. I was doing a check ride on a flight engineer. I asked her for her telephone number before the flight ended, and she willingly gave it to me. She told me later that I looked older than she and that's what she was looking for. She had turned down dates from younger fellows" "I'd say Jane is 24 or 25." "She is 25, Dave almost 26." "I would guess you are 28 or 29." "You are a good judge of age. I'm 28, soon to be 29."

"Tell me just what you do in flight engineering." "My title is director of flight engineering training. This includes training new ones and maintaining the proficiency of regular crew members." "When I took the job, I did so with the proviso that I could work at least one trip per month as a crew flight engineer so I could keep up with problems and my proficiency. In the long haul I don't see flight engineering enduring. In the not too distant future we will enter the jet age and engines will not require monitoring like piston engines do. Also, flight and flight controls will become more automatic, resulting in the air lines pushing to reduce the number of crew members. I'm taking every opportunity to learn about jet engines and will attend all the schools I can to become competent on jets".

"I may even have to join a Navy reserve outfit to gain operation experience on jet engines. It's the only place you can get that experience now." "You were in the Navy?" "Yes, that's where I became a flight engineer on Coronado Flying Boats."

"Have you ever thought of becoming a consultant in your field?" "No I haven't. I don't know anything about consulting." "In January of my senior year in college, I attended a meeting of the SAE aviation section in Los Angeles. I was a member of our student chapter of SAE. I heard consultants talk about aircraft and their problems. I was so interested I talked with one of the consultants after the meeting. I asked how a young engineer with a degree in aeronautical engineering could get into consulting. He suggested I get a master's degree in mechanical engineering that would give me opportunities to get a job with a consulting engineering firm. That's why I have applied to Stanford to earn a master's degree.

"The consultants who spoke during the meeting had engineering degrees, but their expertise came from long experience with manufacturers and or airlines. It's something you might want to keep in mind Woody." "It is certainly a new idea to me Dave. Thank you. And now I must get to my meeting on the latest CAA regulations for flight and flight engineers." "I have enjoyed our talk Woody lets do it again." "I'm all for it Dave."

First Presbyterian Church
9:30 AM July 17, 1949

Dave was attending the adult Sunday school class for the second time. The teacher, Dr. Milligan, introduced Dave to those who had been absent when Dave had attended two Sundays ago. This time he was introduced with his first and last name. Dave had given only his first name last time.

One of the class members had told Dr. Milligan that Dave would not be attending last week because he was Dave Mason, a pitcher for the San Francisco Sea Lions and they were playing in Hollywood today. This resulted in some surprised expressions from members of the class when they learned about Dave. Dr. Milligan suggested to the members of the class, that if and when Dave returned, he be treated as just one the class, nothing more. Since Dave did not give us his last name two weeks ago, I think that's the way he would like it. Agreed? The class members all agreed. Today, Dave was received as just another class member.

Today the class was starting chapter 16 of Acts. Paul and Barnabas had separated and Timothy had joined Paul and Silas. They traveled through Galatia and Philippi where they met Lydia and were put in prison.

After the class Dave talked to Dr. Milligan. He said, "Since I read the book The Man Nobody Knows, I have wanted to study the life of Jesus. Do you know of a chronological listing of scriptures that I could use in such a study?." "Yes I do, Dave. I can bring you a listing. And I know of the book by Bruce Barton." "Thank you, I will be gone the next two Sundays, but I will return."

Dave's Apartment
7:35 PM July17, 1949

After winning the first two games in the series, Seattle had won on Friday night and Saturday afternoon. The Sea Lions won the first game on Sunday 6-4, but lost the night cap 3-1, so the series ended in a 3-3 tie.

Dave had called his mother. He said he would be leaving soon to come to the house for the evening. "I would like to have breakfast with dad in the morning and I invite you to have lunch with me" "Oh, that sounds nice, Dave. You can tell me all about the team. I'm sure your dad will be glad to have breakfast with you. I'll see you when you arrive."

The Mason Residence
10:15 PM July 17, 1949

Dave's mother was still up and welcomed him with a hug. "I didn't want to tell you on the phone, but you have a letter from Stanford on the hall table. Dave went to the table, picked up the envelope and tore it open. Dave said, "Great, I've been accepted! I will be required to take some undergraduate courses, but I'm in. Registration is in late September." "Congratulations Dave," his mother said.

Unknown to Dave or his dad, the acceptance committee had done a special investigation of Dave's performance and character while at Cal Poly to be sure there was no appearance of favoritism. This because George Mason was a Trustee of Stanford University

Dave was up early the next morning so he could tell his dad about the Stanford acceptance. George Mason gave Dave a big hug and said, "I'm very proud of you Dave. You have worked hard and improved since you graduated from high school." "Thank you dad. Your encouragement has been a big factor." "Now. George said, "Let's go have breakfast. You drive so I can ride in your new car. You can drop me at the office afterwards." George Mason liked Dave's car. He was glad he had a safer car than the blue beetle

Dave gave his dad a report on his appearance at Lavell Chevrolet and his attending meetings of Kiwanis and Junior Chamber of Commerce. "I have decided to join Kiwanis, mainly because of their Key Club program for high school students. I will be a member of the Kiwanis Club of San Francisco. The club meets in the Fairmont Hotel.

"I'm glad you have done that Dave. It will allow you to meet good people. How long will you be here today?" "I'm taking mother to lunch." "Great, she will appreciate that." "This evening I'm taking Jill to dinner in the Benjamin Franklin Hotel in San Mateo." "Now, please take me to my office." The Peninsula Newspapers office was no longer in a house behind the newspaper building. It had been the office for many years and was painted Southern Pacific "outhouse brown." as George Mason described it. His office interior had a western motif. His autograph book was the walls of the office. Signatures on knotty pine boards lining the walls included some famous people.

Gulliver's Restaurant
1800 El Camino Real
Menlo Park, California
12:15 PM July 18, 1949

Dave and his mother were talking baseball. Ann said, "I have just about talked your father into taking me to a game. It will be a Saturday or Sunday game, one when we can see you pitch." Dave said, "It will be a while, because we are in Oakland this week and then we travel to San Diego."

Dave asked when Pam would be finished with college. Ann said, "By the third week in August. Then she will come home." "What will she do?" "I don't know. Jim Smith does not have a job yet, so she doesn't know where he will be working. I think she will want to go where Jim finds a job."

Benjamin Franklin Hotel
50 E. 3rd Avenue
San Mateo, California
8:00 PM July 18, 1949

Jill and Dave were having dinner in the hotel dinning room. This was the airlines hotel for transient flight crews. It was the closest good hotel with enough rooms to handle the crews of all the airlines that flew into San Francisco International Airport. No one recognized Dave, so they dined with no one looking or pointing.

Dave told Jill he had found a Presbyterian Church where he could attend Sunday school at 9:30 and get to the stadium in time for Sundays games. The teacher is Dr. Charles Milligan, who I was told by one of the class members, is a prominent obstetrics and gynecology (OB-GYN) doctor in San Francisco. He is a very good teacher. When baseball season is over, I invite you Jill to attend church with me at the Menlo Park Presbyterian Church when you are in town." "Dave, I am willing to see what it offers." "That's all I ask."

After dinner they returned to Jill's empty apartment. Jane and Sally were on flights. Dave immediately said, sit on me lap Jill." They did some intimate necking. Dave departed at midnight for his apartment.

Chapter Thirteen

Oakland Oaks Ball Park

San Pablo Avenue

Emeryville, California

San Francisco at Oakland

8:40 PM July 19, 1949

DAVE WAS FACING the biggest early inning challenge he had faced in pro baseball. Oakland has loaded the bases on a single, an error and a walk, with no outs, and the cleanup batter coming to the plate. Dave needed a strike out. So he threw two fast balls for strikes, then a change up and the over eager batter swung early and went down swinging. The next batter took a sinker and a fast ball for a one ball, one strike count. Dave then threw his best sinker, and the batter hit to the second baseman Billy May, who started the double play. Dave had escaped the inning with no runs scored.

Dave gave up nine hits tonight, but only two runs. Meanwhile the Sea Lions scored four runs, one run at a time in the fifth, sixth, seventh, and eighth innings. Dave hit a double, and scored one of the runs. It was a good start in the series with the rival Oakland Oaks.

Oakland Oaks Ball Park San Francisco at Oakland 10:00 PM July 20, 1949

The Sea Lions got off to a good start in the second game with the Oakland Oaks by scoring two runs in the first inning. They lost the lead in the fifth inning when the Oaks scored four runs and chased Lester Schultz, the Sea Lions starting pitcher. Cal, C.C. Chuker came on in relief and did a good job, not allowing any runs through the eighth inning.

In the top of the ninth, the Sea Lions' leadoff batter, Billy May singled to right field. Bill Vaughn walked. With two men on and no outs, the Sea Lions appeared to have a rally going. However, Roselli struck out and Mike Roc grounded out to first base, while May and Vaughn moved to second and third. With two out Dave was called by Tub Warren to pinch hit. Batting left handed, Dave took a strike and a ball. He fouled off the next pitch. That made the count one ball and two strikes. He fouled off a change. The count was still one and two. The next pitch was a curve ball that hung just a bit. Dave hit it high over the right filed fence for a three run home run. It made the score Sea Lions 5 Oaks 4. Ray Chess flied out to center field. Now, the Sea Lions had to protect the one run lead.

C.C. Chuker was still pitching. The first batter walked. The next batter, tried to bunt, but fouled out to catcher Parks. The next batter fouled off two pitches, then hit a double play ball to May at second base who started the twin killing that killed the Oaks. The final score was Sea Lions 5 Oaks 4. Dave got the big hit and batted in three runs.

The Oakland Times Tribune

The sports page had the following headline.

Rookie Pitcher Turns Hitter and Blasts the Oaks

He is the rookie pitching sensation of the San Francisco Sea Lions with a record of 8-0 in eight compete games. He is also an outstanding hitter with power. In his third pinch hitting roll, Dave Mason hit a

310 foot home run that cleared the right field fence by at least 20 feet to defeat the Oaks last night. Mason, a natural right hander, started switch hitting in high school. His hitting and power batting left handed have improved over the past two years, we are told. It looked very good last night.

The Oaks will see more of Mason on Saturday when he takes the mound in his second start in the series and ninth of the season since joining the Sea Lions in mid June. He came off the campus of California Polytechnic College, a small college in San Luis Obispo.

University of California Campus
Berkeley, California
11:00 AM July 21, 1949

On this Thursday morning Dave and Billy May, Dave's roommate on the road, had taken a taxi to the campus for a walking tour. Billy was a young player, who had just turned 21, the same age as Dave. Billy and his wife Lisa were from Redding located in Northern California. They were high school sweethearts and married soon after Billy signed with the Sea Lions in 1946.

He played his first year for the Yakima Bears of the Western International League, was the league's most valuable player and was promoted to Salt Lake City the following year. Billy played well for Salt Lake and he joined the Sea Lions at the end of the 1948 season. In this year's spring training he won the second base job and has been one of the better players on the improving Sea Lions. He was batting just above .300 and had made few errors in the field.

Billy had good grades in high school and if he hadn't been a very good baseball player he would have gone to college, most likely the University of California. His father is a Cal alumni.

Dave and Billy went up in the Campanile and had lunch in the Student Union. The campus was full of veterans going to college on the G.I. Bill of Rights. Dave told Billy how the veterans had helped him earn a degree in engineering. They returned to the hotel after lunch, ready to go to the ball park.

Emeryville Lanes
San Pablo Avenue
Emeryville, California
11:00 AM July 22, 1949

The team had lost the Thursday night game 6 to 3. Dave asked Billy May to go bowling with him. Dave had brought his ball on this trip. Billy was not an experienced bowler, so Dave gave him some pointers and Billy improved with each game. It was a good way to spend time on the road.

Oakland Oaks Ball Park
San Francisco at Oakland
4:15 PM July 23, 1949

This had been an unusual game. The score was tied three times at 1-1, 2-2, and 3-3. Dave's pitch location was not the best today and he had allowed seven hits through seven innings. Two double plays had helped keep the score tied. In the top half of the seventh, the Sea Lions had loaded the bases on two walks and an error. Catcher Jim Jarvis struck out for the first out. This brought Dave to the plate. If there had been an open base, the Oaks would have given Dave a free pass to first. But with no place to put him, he had to be pitched to.

Dave took a ball and a strike. The next pitch was a slider that didn't slide very far and Dave hit it for a double, giving the Lions a 5 to 3 lead. Dave was on second with one out. Billy May hit the first pitch he saw for a single scoring Dave for a 6 to 3 lead. Bill Vaughn popped out to end the inning.

Over the next three innings Dave threw 32 pitches, retiring nine batters without any hits to win the game 6-3. He had allowed seven hits, struck out one, and walked one batter. Dave had one hit, a double that drove in two runs. He also scored a run. It was Dave's ninth win. The win gave the Sea Lions a 2-1 lead in the series.

Jill was due home from a flight, so Dave called her when he returned to the hotel. Before he could say anything, Jill said, "And that rookie pitching sensation of the San Francisco Sea Lions, Dave Mason, did it again tonight folks, defeating the Oakland Oaks for his ninth win with no losses. He also hit a double, driving in two runs and scoring one." Dave said, "You're hired to be my press agent." They both laughed. Dave said, "You could get a job as a baseball reporter. Forget about being a dietitian." "Tonight was the first time I could listen to the whole game without interruption because I was here alone. I got so excited and was yelling so loud during the big inning that I hope I don't get any complaints" "Jill, you're becoming a real baseball fan." "You betcha." "Let's see, will you be back Sunday night? " "Yes I will." "Okay, I'll call when I get to my apartment." "I'll look forward to hearing your voice, Dave." "I love you, Jill." "I love you too." "Good night Jill."

Oakland Oaks Ball Park
San Francisco at Oakland, Doubleheader
5:20 PM July 24, 1949

The double header was over and the Sea Lions had split the games, winning the first, but losing the short game. The Lions got a 3-3 tie in the series. It was another positive sign of improvement. The next series in San Diego would tell if the team was going to continue to improve.

Dave's Apartment
8:00 PM July 24, 1949

Dave called Jill and almost before he said hello, Jill said, "Thank you for the beautiful roses. They arrived this afternoon. You are so considerate Dave." "I'm romancing you Jill." "I love it Dave." Then they made plans to drive to Santa Cruz tomorrow to spend the day. They both looked forward to it. Dave said he would pick her up about 8:00 in the morning.

Near Los Gatos, California
9:15 AM July 25, 1949

As they approached Los Gatos, Dave told Jill, "This is where I was born, 'The Cats.' However, I only lived here for two years. Then my mother and I moved to Santa Barbara. You remember my telling you that I lived there for four years." "Yes, I remember you telling me that when I was living in Santa Barbara. It seems like ages ago Dave." "Yes it does," said Dave.

"What are we going to do in Santa Cruz besides getting some beach time?" First, we are going to drive to Aptos, a small town south of Santa Cruz, to the Del Mar Club." "Sounds fancy, tell me more." "In 1944 the club was offering family memberships for a reduced fee and my Dad bought one. The club is a hotel with dining room and lounge, located high on the cliff above the beach with a great view of the ocean. They have a private beach below with everything you would want including dressing rooms and a snack bar. Our family came here in August of 1945 just after the war ended for a week's vacation before my sister and I went off to college. It was a great week. Tommy Dorsey's band stayed at the club for a few days before playing for a dance at the Coconut Grove, the dance hall on the Santa Cruz beach."

We can have lunch at the snack bar at the beach, get some sun then it's your choice. We can go to the Santa Cruz boardwalk, go on rides walk some beaches or anything else you want to do. Then, we'll drive to Boulder Creek and beyond to a restaurant where a stream runs through the dining room. There is no other place like it." "Oh Dave you know of so many nice places to take your girl." "And you are my girl, aren't you?" They laughed.

The Del Mar Club Beach
Aptos, California
3:30 PM July 25, 1949

Jill and Dave had lunch at the beach club snack bar. They put on their bathing suits and relaxed in the sun. Later Dave challenged Jill to a swim in the ocean. "Will it be cold Dave?" "Probably, but lets find out." The water was not too bad, the Japanese current having its effect on the California beaches. They jumped some waves and then went back to their lounges on the beach. Dave had not seen Jill in a bathing suit since his visit to Santa Barbara three years ago. Boy, he thought, has she matured. She just looks great! I am so fortunate.

Later they drove to Santa Cruz and walked the boardwalk. Dave pointed out the Coconut Grove dance hall above the penny arcade. They drove through the beautiful forest along highway 9 to the Brookdale Lodge where they had a delicious dinner while they listened to the babbling brook that ran through the dining room. "It has been a lovely day Dave. I'd like to spend the rest of my life enjoying such days with you," "I know, Jill. Let's keep progressing in the important things we need to consider to make sure our life together would be good and forever. Also, that our children will have the benefit of parents who love each other and who, like your parents are very compatible." "I agree." They drove home to Palo Alto, where Jill was to stay overnight.

Lane Field
12th & Broadway Streets
San Diego, California
San Francisco at San Diego
9:00 PM July 27, 1949

The team had flown in to town at 10:30 AM, a great advantage over a 17 hour trip on the train. This would be the Padres first look at Dave Mason, who would be the starting pitcher tonight. San Diego's big slugger Luke Jackson was terrorizing PCL pitchers.

Dave started the game with two sharp innings, throwing only 17 pitches to get six outs. The Sea Lions scratched out a run in the third inning and Dave had a no-hitter through five innings. His sinker was doing just what it was designed to do making batters hit the ball into the ground to infielders. Even Luke Jackson had no success.

In the bottom of the sixth, the same Luke Jackson hit a single to right field, ending the no-hitter. But Luke was wiped out with a double play. In the seventh the Lions got another run on a single, a sacrifice, a steal of third and a deep fly out to center field, allowing the runner on third to tag and score. In the next three innings Dave threw 28 pitches, retiring nine batters in a row for a one hit 2-0 win. Dave had won his 10th game with no losses

Dave did not get a hit tonight, a Padre accomplishment. It was only the third game in which he had gone hitless. After the game Dave made his regular visit with his infielders, thanking them for their errorless play. Also he complemented those who had produced the runs. Orval Overwall talked to Dave for the second time since he joined the team in Seattle. He said, "Nice game rookie."

Following the after the game meal in the coffee shop, Dave and Billy May went to their room. Soon the phone range, Billy answered, and said, "For you Dave." It was Jill, gushing about his pitching. She had listened to the game and had worried about every pitch Dave made. They had a good conversation. She said she wanted to call before she flew out to Chicago tomorrow. "Thank you, Jill. Have a good flight."

Fleet Bowling Lanes
2550 Market Street
San Diego, California
1:30 PM July 29, 1949

Billy May and Dave were bowling again. Billy suggested it. They had a good time doing something other than playing baseball. Dave did well without his ball and with little recent bowling. With everything he was doing, he had little time for bowling. He would have to wait until the baseball season was over to bowl at least once a week. Dave planned to move back to the family home when the season ended.

The Sea Lions Flight
20,000 Feet over Monterey, California
10:15 PM July 31, 1949

The team was in a happy mood. They had won their first series of the season 4-3. Dave had won the seven inning game today allowing one run, while the Lions battered the Padre pitching for 10 runs. Winning the game clinched the series.

At the end of July the team's record was 60 wins and 69 losses. They were 2-1/2 games out of sixth place in the league. The Sea Lions were improving though. Dave was 11-0. He had an earned run average (ERA) of .149 runs per 9 inning game. It was almost no runs per game! He had walked only three batters in 85 innings. Dave was hitting .357 and had hit three doubles and two home runs. Could August be better?

Chapter Fourteen

Dave's Apartment

7:00 AM August 1, 1949

DAVE HAD RETURNED to his apartment last night following the flight home from San Diego. He had called Jill and they talked for at least twenty minutes. Dave asked her for a dinner date Monday evening. Dave had learned about a new restaurant he wanted to experience. He had a personal appearance scheduled for 6:30 to 8:00 PM at Lavell Chevrolet. So it would be a late date. Jill said. "That's okay Dave I'll see you when you get here." The appearance was his first of two this week, the other on Friday.

Dave planned to bowl today, probably after lunch. He needed to work on his bowling.

Sports Center
1:30 PM August 1, 1949

After bowling three games, Dave was trying some trick shots he had been taught by a professional trick shot bowler. When Dave appeared to be about done, a young fellow walked up to Dave and asked if he would like to bowl for some stakes. "Sure," said Dave. They agreed on $10.00 a game and $20.00 for the series. Dave thought, this fellow must be good or he has lots of money. They bowled the three games in which Dave took thirty dollars and the series, for a total of $50.00. The young fellow went away without much comment.

Dave thought he was surprised that he lost. Maybe he only saw Dave trying the trick shots.

Portola House Restaurant
Just off the Portola Road
Portola Valley, California
9:30 PM August 1, 1949

Jill and Dave were enjoying coffee following their delicious dinner. The restaurant was in an old house of Spanish design. Dining was by very low lights and candle light. The restaurant was owned by Frances Frank who was a well known San Francisco chef. He prepared each meal and came to the diner's table when it was served. He wanted to be sure it met the diner's expectations. Dave had learned about the place from Del Hoffman, the Sea Lions third baseman and the club's confirmed bachelor. Del brought his best girl friend here for a romantic dinner.

Dave had described his day to Jill starting with bowling and the money he had won. He described his appearance at Lavell Chevrolet where the line up of kids and parents was longer than last time. He had made more money as the result of these two events than he would earn playing a day of baseball. He had another date at Lavell for Friday from 11:30 to 1:00 PM. "What do you plan to do with all this money Dave." "First I want to buy a house or duplex, a place I can live during the off season. If the folks sell the family home, I would like them to live in one apartment and I would rent out the other while I'm playing baseball. Also, I have a dream, not yet a plan, to own an engineering company. It all takes money Jill."

"Will you be back Thursday night Jill I haven't looked at your schedule?" "No I'm taking back to back trips Tuesday-Wednesday and Thursday-Friday so I can attend your game on Saturday and Sunday school with you on Sunday." "Oh, that's great Jill."

Kiwanis Club Meeting 12:00 noon August 2, 1949

Dave had arrived early so he could give the Secretary his application for membership. He also wanted to avoid a big response when he walked into the room. He had been recognized on the sidewalk, as well as in the lobby of the Hotel.

The speaker today was a representative of "Save the Cable Cars." The group was opposing the plan of the Municipal Railway to eliminate the cable cars and replace them with busses. It was interesting. After the meeting, many of the members came up to Dave and thanked him for joining.

Sea Lions Stadium Sacramento at San Francisco 9:35 PM August 4, 1949

Dave had walked into the club house in the early afternoon and was greeted by at least three baseball writers and a radio sportscaster. They said they were here to talk about the interview you said you would give after you won 10 games. That's correct gentlemen, but I didn't say when I would grant it. I will give the interview some time before Saturday. Between now and then, I will decide who I will interview me. Now gentlemen, I have to get my uniform on.

It was the first half of the eighth inning. Dave had changed his strategy for this game, with the team at home and the Sacramento lineup light on power hitters. With the big outfield, fly balls hit off of Dave's rising fast ball could be easy outs. It had worked out that way. Of the first 15 outs, 10 were fly balls to the outfield. Since his plan was working, he didn't change. Dave had given up five hits and walked no batter. The Solons had scratched a run from a single, sacrifice and an error for its one and only run. The Sea Lions had gone to work early, getting four runs in the first inning. Dave singled, knocking in a run for an RBI. The score was 4-1. Dave threw five fast balls and two change ups and the three batters were gone in the eighth. He would also pitch a perfect ninth inning, throwing only six pitches. After the game, Dave gave his first thanks to his outfielders who caught 15 fly balls tonight. But he didn't overlook the infielders.

Lavell Chevrolet
2:10 PM August 5, 1949

The mid-day appearance was overwhelming. There were so many kids and mothers in the showroom that Bill Fox had asked Dave if he could stay for another half hour. Dave agreed. A big cheer went when it was announced. Dave couldn't even begin to count the crowd.

At 1:00, Dan White, the young baseball writer for the San Francisco Times entered the show room. He was by far the youngest writer who followed the Sea Lions. The Times was one of the smaller papers in town, but had a young aggressive news staff. Because of their size and flexibility, their reporters had scooped the big dailies a number of time recently. At 1:30 PM Dave walked out of the show room, to the office of Bill Fox. Dan followed him. At the office door he saw Dan and Dan didn't beat around the bush. He asked Dave for an exclusive interview. Dave had liked Dan who was always friendly and courteous. Dave thought, if I give Dan an exclusive interview, I won't have to give another one for now. "When would you like to do it, Dan?" "Can we do it right now? "Okay, let me talk to Bill Fox for a few minutes and then we can go sit in my car and do it." "Great," said Dan. Dave asked Bill if he would talk to Larry and find out if there are two seats available in his Sea Lions box for the doubleheader on Sunday. My girl friend does not want to sit in the wives box and Lisa May would sit with her. "Sure," said Bill. "Call me tomorrow." "Thank you Bill."

Seated in Dave's car Dan started off with basic questions, so Dave knew he was prepared.

Q "You are not a fast ball power pitcher or one who has a curve ball or 'breaking' pitch. How did you get the chance to pitch as a young baseball player?"

A "At first I didn't. When I tried out for my American Legion Team in my home area of Palo Alto, the coaches and the manager didn't think I had enough velocity on my sinker, let alone my fast ball to make it as a pitcher. I almost made it as a hitter, but I was only 14, tall and skinny with little power, so I didn't make the team. This allowed me to go to the Redwood City Post team for a tryout. I made the team because of my hitting. It was a blessing because the players were much better. I pitched in just a few games that first year and played some right field. The second year I became the second starting pitcher because I was able to get batters out."

Q "Because you are a sinker ball pitcher, poor defense hurt your win-loss record in high school. Was this frustrating to you?"

A "I knew Palo Alto High School had poor baseball teams because of the outstanding swimming and track teams that took the good athletes. In 1943 I watched our team make 15 errors in a game with Half Moon Bay. I was a sophomore and didn't play in the game. So, I knew what to expect when I started pitching. It was a good lesson in not letting errors affect my pitching and to appreciate good fielding."

Q "I have heard that you started pitching baseballs at a target when you were 10 or 11 years old. Is that true?"

A "Yes, I started when I was 11. I threw 100 balls five days each week when I wasn't playing baseball. I cut it down to every other day during the season. Also the target was not just the outline of the strike zone. It was a target with slots on the inside and outside of the strike zone, so I could learn control on both sides of the plate."

Q "Do you think all that practice developed your arm and wrist strength so you can pitch on three days rest?"

A "It likely has something to do with it. I do believe the Lord gave me a strong flexible arm. I don't have to exert myself to throw hard. My arm seems to act like a sling shot."

Q "You mention The Lord. Are you a practicing Christian?"

A "The short answer is yes. I am a member of the Menlo Park Presbyterian Church. I have adopted the life of Eric Liddell as a role model. Eric won the 400 meters at the 1924 Olympics and was an outstanding Rugby player. He returned to China where he was born as a missionary. He died in a Japanese internment camp during the War."

Q "Is your practice of talking with young players on opposing teams before games something you learned from Eric Liddell?"

A "Yes, before races Eric would shake hands with all the runners. In Rugby games, Eric was noted for picking up players who had been knocked down, if it didn't affect his play. But I'm like Eric. When the game starts I'm a fierce competitor. Eric was asked if he was satisfied with the bronze medal he won in the 200 meter race in the 1924 Olympics. He said was he was disappointed because he lost the race. I don't like to lose a game."

Q "When you came to the Sea Lions I understand you requested the opportunity to take batting practice with the position players. Why did you do that?"

A "To be a good hitter you must work on it continuously. I want to be a good hitter so I won't be lifted for a pinch hitter in late innings. Also, a good hitting pitcher can help himself and his team. In hitting, you must be able to recognize the pitch and react. You can only do that with practice and seeing lots of pitches."

Q "You have a degree in aeronautical engineering. I understand you have applied to Stanford to start a master's degree program in engineering. How will this affect your baseball career?"

A "Baseball can be a fleeting, short time profession. Even a long time ball player is still young when baseball is over. I want to be prepared for any eventuality in baseball and prepare myself for life after baseball. If I continue in baseball, I will attend college in the off season."

Q "You are developing another career in these personal appearances. What do you see in the future?"

A "This is all new to me, so I can't answer that question. It's fun to talk with the kids and give them a baseball. The appearances have come about because of baseball."

Q "Do you think the Sea Lions can improve their position in the PCL and rise out of the lower division of the league?"

A "I think we can do better than we have. Some timely hits would do wonders for us."

Q "How has the attention of baseball fans and others in the city affected you life?

A "It hasn't been a problem. I can go for a short drive to my home where I'm the local boy, so it's not a problem."

"Thank you for you time Dave." "You're very welcome Dan."

Dave's Apartment
9:00 AM August 6, 1949

Jill was calling. She had arrived home very late last night because of an hour delay in the departure of her flight from Chicago. During the delay many of the businessmen spent the time in the airport bar, so they were a wild bunch on the flight. Jill was exhausted by the time she returned to her apartment. She gave Dave a funny description of the passenger's antics. She said, "we earned our pay last night!' "It sounds like it," Dave said. "I was calling to see if you would like to double date with Jane and Woody tonight? They want to go to Rickey's. Jane had been there when she was at Stanford, but Woody hasn't." "Sure, that would be great. I suggest we stay over night in Palo Alto."

"Okay, I'll make reservations and see you here after the game."

Just before Dave departed for the ball park he called Bill Fox. Bill said, "Larry would be happy to have your girl friend and Lisa May sit in our box on Sunday. What name should I put the tickets under in will call?" "Jill Garber Bill, and please thank Larry." "I'll do it Dave."

Sea Lions Stadium
Sacramento at San Francisco
11:00 AM August 6, 1949

When Dave entered the clubhouse he was met by Stanton S. First who was the dean of the San Francisco baseball writers. Dave could tell that Stan First was in a tizzy because he had a very red face. First's motto was "First will be first." First said, "I've read the interview by Dan White in the Times." First wanted to know why Dave gave his first interview to that young kid White? Dave replied, "I gave the interview to Dan because he came to me and asked for it. He was aggressive and came to see me during my appearance at Lavell Chevrolet." That made First even more exasperated and his face redden again. Dave asked, "Weren't you once a young aggressive reporter who obtained good interviews because you asked for them?" "You bet I was, and I was the best." First did not have a problem flaunting his ego. "Remember Stan, I said on Thursday that I would grant the interview before today. I have and I gave it to the reporter who came and asked for it." "Well, I'm not happy about it Dave. Seniority should have some consideration." "I'm sorry you feel that way Stan. Now I must get ready for the game."

Dave told Billy May he had two seats in Larry Lavell's box for the doubleheader tomorrow. "Please ask Lisa if she will sit with Jill." "I'm sure she will Dave." "Okay I'll call you to confirm it this evening."

Rickey's
8:15 PM August 6, 1949

The Sea Lions won the game today 6 to 3, giving them a 4-2 lead in the series. Dave drove to Jill's apartment after the game and they met Jane and Woody at Rickey's. They were enjoying their dinner. Woody commented, "Dave this smorgasbord could be habit forming." "Yes it could. When I was a teenager and had a hollow leg, I could eat all I could get down, and never gain a pound. But I can't anymore."

As they departed the restaurant Woody asked Dave if he could have breakfast with him on Monday morning in the Sir Francis Drake Hotel. "Sure, what time." How about 7:30?" "Could we make it 7:00? I will get less attention at that time." "That's fine. I'll meet you in the coffee shop."

On the drive to the Mason home, Dave told Jill about her seat in Larry Lavell's box for the games tomorrow. "Lisa May will join you. Pick up your tickets from will call. They are under your name. Lisa will meet you at the will call window at 1:15." "Oh thank you Dave, I would still have attended, but I didn't look forward to sitting in the wives box.

First Presbyterian Church
9:30 AM August 7, 1949

Dave introduced Jill to the class. Dr. Milligan welcomed her. The study in Acts had progressed to the 18th chapter in Dave's absence. Paul had left Athens and traveled to Corinth, where he met Aquila and Priscilla who were tent makers like Paul. He stayed and worked with them. On the Sabbath, Paul spoke in the synagogue, trying to win over both Jews and Greeks to the Kingdom of God.

Following the class, Dr. Milligan gave Dave the chronological listing of scriptures that covered the life of Jesus. With this, Dave would start his study of the ministry of Jesus.

On the way to the stadium, Jill said, "You need to expand on that lesson for me Dave. Please keep that in mind." "I sure will." "Let's plan a study time." After arriving at the Sea Lions stadium, Jill drove to Dave's apartment to change her clothes, eat lunch and return to the stadium for the double header.

Sea Lions Stadium
Sacramento at San Francisco, Doubleheader
3:35 PM August 7, 1949

It was the last half of the eighth inning of the first game. The Sea Lions trailed the Solons 4-2. Billy May led off with a single. Bill Vaughn was walked. Dino Roselli singled and May scored. It made the score Sacramento 4, Sea Lions 3. Mike Roc struck out. With one out and Roselli on second base, Del Hoffman grounded out to first base and Vaughn went to third. Now there were two outs.

Dave was called to pinch hit. This would be the fourth time. He had two hits as a pinch hitter. Dave went after the first pitch, batting left against the right handed Sacramento pitcher. He hit a screaming line drive down the first base line that rattled around in the right field corner. Dave could see the right fielder chasing the ball, as he rounded first base, so he kept going to third and was in, standing up. The score was now tied, 4 to 4 and Les Short, the weakest hitter on the team was coming to bat.

Manager Warren had no other decent short stop so he didn't call for another pinch hitter. Les fouled off the first pitch. On the second he golfed a low pitch over the left field wall giving the Lions a 6-4 lead. That's the way the game ended.

In the second game C.C. Chuker pitched a shut out for a 4-0 win and the Sea Lions won the series 6 games to 2. It was the best series of the season for the Lions.

Next week San Diego and Luke Jackson were coming to town.

After the games Jill and Dave picked up hamburgers, and took them to his apartment. They watched the Fred Waring TV show and Jill sat on Dave's lap for some loving. He took her home early so she could get a good night's sleep for her flight tomorrow. She would be gone tomorrow and Tuesday.

Coffee Shop
Sir Francis Drake Hotel
450 Powell Street
San Francisco, California
7:00 AM August 8, 1949

Dave met Woody in the coffee shop and they were led to a booth. Woody said, "I hear you are making personal appearances at the Chevrolet dealership where you bought your car." "Yes, the owner Larry Lavell, is a baseball fan and the dealership has sponsored the Sea Lions radio broadcasts for some time. There have been lots of kids in the showroom to get baseballs. I hope it has resulted in some sales. The idea is that the kids will bring the parents in and they will look and possibly buy. I'm limited on evening appearances so it has been mainly mothers with the kids." Dave asked, "Are you attending another meeting here today?" "Yes, the CAA is in the process of writing new regulations for cockpit procedures and I need to know how they will affect flight engineers."

"During our previous breakfast, you mentioned you may join a Navy reserve unit to get experience in jet engines. Where would you do this? "There is a squadron at Alameda, however, I might have to join one in San Diego." "Was your Navy service in the Pacific?" "Yes, the Coronado flying boat was developed by Consolidated to be a long range patrol aircraft for the Pacific because of the distances. However, the Consolidated PBY and Martin PBM became the primary patrol craft. Because of its payload the Coronado became primarily a transport plane for personnel and cargo. My Coronado was based at Espiritu Santo, located in the southern Solomon Islands for some time in the early part of the war. It was when we were fighting to take Guadalcanal. Our flights were to and from Pearl Harbor, San Diego and Brisbane, Australia. In all the miles we flew we saw a Japanese plane only once and that was enough."

"We were returning to our base when a single carrier patrol plane spotted us and attacked. We fought it off for a while, but it got one of the engines. The Jap was at the end of his range so he broke off the attack and it was then a question of whether we could make it to Espiritu on three engines. We were about forty-five minutes out. Soon we lost a second engine, so we started reducing our weight by throwing everything we could out of the plane. We were losing altitude and at thirty minutes out our radio operator started sending a mayday call, giving our position. I nursed those two engines, well beyond what I could expect, but they kept us in the air until we were within fifteen minutes of our base and the pilot set it down while we still had power. A crash boat was on the scene in ten minutes and it towed us to our base.

It was quite an experience and afterwards I went to talk to the Chaplin. I was raised in the Methodist Church but had never joined the church. The Chaplin was Methodist and we had a long talk. I felt we were kept aloft by something more than those engines. At that point in my life I became a Christian. After the war I joined the Methodist Church in which I had grown up. I have told you this story because Jane tells me you are a member of the Menlo Park Presbyterian Church." "That's right Woody." "Jane was raised in the Episcopal Church, but said she attended church at Menlo Park at times while she was attending Stanford." "That was quite an experience Woody. Are you and Jane getting serious?" "Yes, I think we will make a decision in a few months." That sounds great."

"Are you looking forward to starting your master's degree work?" "Yes, I have an appointment next Monday to meet with an advisor to discuss my courses." "How long will it take you to complete the master's study?" "That will depend on baseball. If I took classes year around, it would take two years.

"I've enjoyed our talk, Woody. Have a good meeting." "Thank you, Dave."

Kiwanis Club Meeting
12:00 noon August 9, 1949

Dave was interested in the Key Club sponsored by the club. He asked the sponsored youth chairman when school would start and when the Key Club had meetings? He advised that school would start September 6, the day after Labor Day. Their regular meetings are held after school on the third Wednesday. They have some special meetings on Saturday morning. "I would like to attend a Saturday morning meeting some time. Please let me know when one will be held." There was also a report on the activities of the club in support of children.

President Kenneth introduced the program speaker who was from the San Francisco Chamber of Commerce. He talked about post war business development in San Francisco.

Sea Lions Stadium
San Diego at San Francisco
9:00 PM August 9, 1949

This was the second look the hard hitting San Diego Padres had at Dave's pitching. He had beaten them twice in San Diego last month. Early in this game, Dave had to deal with the first hit batter situation in a game in which he was pitching. He had watched it in other games and had considered how he would respond. It was one of baseball's unwritten rules. When a batter on your team was hit with a pitch, you retaliated by hitting the opposing pitcher or their best hitter.

In the second inning, Dino Roselli hit a huge home run over the center field fence, a 450 foot blast. The Lions led 1-0. The San Diego pitcher was really upset, and when Dino came to bat again, the first pitch, an inside fast ball hit him on the arm. The San Diego pitcher must have forgotten he would be batting in the next inning. Dave had decided if he had to hit a batter he would aim for the batter's legs. When the pitcher came up with one man on base, and no outs, fans may have wondered what would happen. Dave's first pitch hit the Padre chucker in the leg, actually in the knee because he turned on the ball. He limped to first. He didn't have to run because Dave struck out one batter and got the other two on fly balls.

In the next inning the San Diego pitcher was ineffective, maybe because of the knee. He was relieved after giving up two hits and a walk. Hitting a batter is sometimes not the best strategy. The Sea

Lions scored a run to take a 2-1 lead.

The game continued as a tight pitcher's battle. In the seventh inning, the first San Diego batter beat out a slow roller to third. Luke Jackson was the next batter. After fouling off three pitches, with the count 2-2, Jackson hit a ball that just cleared the right field fence. It was a change up that Jackson measured just right. It was only the second home run hit off Dave. The two runs made the score 3-2 for the Padres. The Sea Lions could not mount a rally and Dave lost his first game.

In the clubhouse, Dave thanked every player who had played in the game for their effort. Dave never said, "You can't win them all" because he thought that was a negative statement.

One of the baseball writers asked Dave, "What are your thoughts about the game?" Dave said, "It was bad, I lost.

Dave's Apartment
8:00 AM August 10, 1949

Dave's project for today is to find a local church that has a Sunday evening service so he can hear a weekly sermon. He had saved his newspapers so he could study the church page in the Saturday edition. He found a couple of churches to visit.

Jill called about 9:00. She wanted to plan time for Dave to talk about the Sunday school lesson. They decided on tomorrow morning at 11:00 in Jill's apartment. Jill said, "I will serve lunch." Dave replied, "Do I dress for lunch?" "Sure," said Jill. "Wear your swimming trunks." "I just might do that." They laughed. "I'll see you in the morning Jill."

Sea Lions Stadium
San Diego at San Francisco
5:56 PM August 10, 1949

San Diego won the game, blasting two Lion pitchers for a 7-2 win.

Jill's Apartment
11:00 AM August 11, 1949

Dave arrived with his Bible and a book on Paul. He was prepared to be a teacher of the Bible for the first time.

Dave asked Jill if she knew who Paul was. "Yes I think so." "Well, let's review. At one time Paul was a Pharisees and a Rabbi. He persecuted the followers of Jesus. Angered at the spread of the church, in spite of his efforts of opposition, he prepared an expedition to Damascus where he had heard many Christians were hiding from the persecution in Jerusalem. Approaching the city, Paul was blinded and Jesus spoke to him. The result was complete surrender to the Lord. Paul asked what the Lord would have him do. He was told to go into the city, and he would be told what he must do."

"In the 18th Chapter of Acts, Paul is on his second Missionary Journey. He has arrived in Corinth from Athens, Greece. With a population of some 650,000, Corinth was a major city of Greece. It was favorably situated for both land and sea trade. Looking for the street where the tentmakers were located Paul met Aquila and Priscilla, fellow tentmakers. Aquila was a Jewish refugee who had left Rome when Emperor Claudius put a ban upon all Jews. Aquila was glad to have extra help and, because Paul was a Jew, Priscilla gave him lodging in their home. Through Paul, Aquila and Priscilla became disciples of Jesus. That is as far as lesson went Sunday. Now I'm going to continue a bit more in this chapter."

"Paul spoke in the synagogue every Sabbath, trying to convince all that Jesus was the Messiah. When he was opposed, Paul said, 'If you are lost, you yourselves must take the blame for it. I am not responsible. From now on I will go to the Gentiles.' "Paul then went to live in the home of Titus Justus, a Gentile. His house was next to the synagogue. Crispus, the leader of the synagogue, believed in the Lord, he and his family; and many other people in Corinth heard the message, believed, and were baptized."

Jill asked, "Just what did people have to believe to be a disciple?" "They had to believe that Jesus died on the cross and shed his blood to have their sins taken away. As John 3:16 states, 'For God so loved the world that He gave His only begotten Son, that whoever believeth in him should not perish but have everlasting life.' It required faith. Just like you have faith that your car will start in the morning when you depart for a drive to the airport." "Dave, What I remember about my Sunday school lessons was a focus on God not Jesus." "Dave said, "That is not unusual in a non-evangelical church. "I think we have done enough for today. I'm hungry." "Oh you men, you're always thinking about your stomach."

Following a nice lunch served by Jill, Dave departed for his apartment. Having no real knowledge of what Jill's community church taught, Dave thought, I'll just have to start with the basics.

Sea Lions Stadium
San Diego at San Francisco
9:35 PM August 11, 1949

C.C. Chucker was the starting pitcher in this game and he pitched well through the seventh inning. In the eighth he lost his control and walked the first two batters. Then he had to face Luke Jackson. Jackson hit the first pitch on a line drive so hard that it hit the right field fence and bounced back toward the infield. Billy May fielded the ball and held Jackson to a single. The runner on second scored, making the score 3-2 for San Diego. C.C. got the next batter on a strike out. Then the Padres pulled off a double steal, and both runners were safe when the pitch was almost wild. San Diego had one out and runners on second and third. On a 2-2 count the batter popped out to catcher Parks. With first base open, C.C pitched carefully to the next batter. The count was 3-2, when the batter hit a pitch off the end of his bat down the first base line, just past first baseman Mike Roc. The runner on third scored easily, and the runner on second was waived in by the third base coach. However, Mike Roc ran the ball down and fired a perfect throw to catcher Parks who tagged the sliding runner out. That ended the inning with San Diego leading 4-2.

The Sea Lions went out 1-2-3 in the eighth, and San Diego didn't add anything to their lead in the ninth, so it was up to the Sea Lions to overcome the two run lead in the bottom of the ninth.

Lead off batter Billy May singled. Bill Vaughn walked. Dino Reselli hit a slow roller to the first baseman, advancing the runners. There was one out and runners on second and third. First baseman Mike Roc popped out to shortstop. Dave was called to pinch hit. With Dave coming to bat, the San Diego manager "Slick" James, wanted to change from a lefty to a right handed pitcher. Dave, a switch hitter would bat left, his weaker side. Dave was a natural right handed batter.

However Dave crossed James up by coming to the plate batting right handed. With the count 2-1, Dave hit a line drive down the third base line all the way to the fence for a stand up double. Two runs scored, making it a tie game again 4-4. With two out, it was now up to Ray Chess. On a 2-2 count, Ray hit a single into short right field. Off with the pitch, Dave was given the go sign by Tub Warren, coaching at third. Dave made a great fade away slide to the outside of the plate, tagging it with his hand as he slid by. SAFE was the call, and the Sea Lions had won the game 5-4!

In the clubhouse, all the writers crowded around Dave's locker and started firing questions. Dave held up his hand and said, no questions until you talk to Ray Chess. He got the winning hit. Dan White had been the only writer to go to Ray's locker, so he had almost an interview with Ray. Then, all the other writers came following Dave's suggestion, with one exception. Who might that be? Well, of course it was Stanley First. He had looked over at Ray's locker and seen White there talking to Ray, and First must be First. So Stan stood by Dave's locker while he took his uniform off so he could be the first to ask Dave a question.

When the writers all returned to Dave's locker, Stan First asked the first question. "Did you anticipate Tub giving you the go sign when you rounded third base?" "No, I didn't anticipate because the play was behind me and if you do that you might over run the sign. I was just running hard and looking for the sign." One of the other writers asked, "Have you practiced that slide Dave?" "Since I had no spring practice, I haven't practiced sliding since college. I knew I had to get away from the catcher, so I went outside and reached for the plate." There were other questions, so Dave didn't leave the ball park until almost 11:00 PM.

Lavell Chevrolet
11:30 AM August 12, 1949

Dave was doing another appearance in the showroom with lots of kids and mothers lined up for baseballs. Dave had asked Bill Fox if he could take some time towards the end of the appearance to talk with adults who came with their children about buying a Chevrolet. Bill said, "Sure, and we want to talk to you about something else when you are done." "Great."

Just after 1:30 Dave entered the office of Sales Manager Bill Fox. "How did it go Dave?"

"I think I have a couple of people ready to buy. I turned them over to salesmen." "That sounds good Dave. It's close to what I want to talk to you about. Would you be interested in appearing in one of our newspaper advertisements? If you agree, we would contact your dad and work out the details." "Yes I would do that." "Good." Also, I want you to think about doing a radio commercial for us." "Well, I don't know how well qualified I am to do that, but I'll think about it." "We would have the radio people work with you. I think you would do well. You would have to join the broadcaster's union and you would be paid a union scale plus a fee for doing the ad. Think about it and we will consider that after we do the newspaper ad."

Sea Lions Stadium
San Diego at San Francisco
2:15 PM August 13, 1949

San Diego had won the Friday night game 6-3. Luke Jackson had put on a hitting show that included a double and two home runs. One of the homers was to dead center field that traveled 450 feet. After the second homer Dave, sitting in the dugout said, "I hope he goes to the 'bigs' next season so we won't have to face him."

Pitching in the first game after a loss is always critical for a pitcher. No matter what his record is, a loss is a threat to his confidence. His performance in the next game will tell how much the loss affected him. Dave had faced the situation many times before, particularly during high school games when he would pitch well, but lose the game because of poor defense and or hitting. But this was his first in professional baseball.

Working quickly, as was his practice, Dave sailed through the first three innings without allowing a hit. Because he threw the sinker pitch most of the time, the catcher only needed to signal the location of the pitch, so little time was taken between pitches. A signal from the catcher would change the pitch to a change or a fast ball. The Padres were hitting the ball on the ground to infielders with a few fly balls to the outfield. At the end of three innings there was no score.

In the top of the fourth inning, San Diego ended the no-hitter with a single, but the runner died on first.

In the Lions half, catcher Bill Parks singled. Dave was up next. What would manager Tub Warren have Dave do? San Diego didn't really believe Dave would bunt to sacrifice the runner. Catchers don't run well and Dave had done little bunting. On the first pitch, Dave didn't show bunt. On the second, he bunted down the third base line. The ball went about twenty feet and died. The third baseman had no chance and both runners were safe. Billy May hit the first pitch down the third base line for a double. Parks scored easily and Dave, showing good speed, scored from first with a good slide. It gave the Sea Lions a 2-0 lead. The Lions added a run in the seventh to make the score 3-0. Dave allowed just five hits and won his 13th game. He had won number 13 on August 13.

In the clubhouse, all Dave's teammates were thanked for their good play. The win put the Sea Lions just 1-1/2 games out of sixth place.

First Presbyterian Church
9:30 AM August 14, 1949

The study today was continuing in Chapter 18 of Acts. When the Jews opposed Paul, who had been speaking in the synagogue, he protested by shaking the dust from his clothes and saying, "Your blood be upon your own heads; I am clean: from henceforth I will go unto the Gentiles." Paul departed to the house of Justus, a man who worshiped God. His house was next to the synagogue. "And Crispus, the chief ruler of the synagogue, believed on the Lord with all his house; and many of the Corinthians hearing believed, and were baptized."

Sea Lions Stadium
San Diego at San Francisco Doubleheader
6:05 PM August 14, 1949

The Sea Lions had won the first game 5-3, making the nightcap the deciding game for the series win. The veteran Padre pitcher, Clinton "Ace" Parker, threw his crafty junk ball pitches at the Lions batters and they got only three hits and one run for a 4-1 loss so San Diego won the series 4-3.

Temple Baptist Church
3355 19th Street
San Francisco, California
7:00 PM August 14, 1949

Dave had found the church through their advertisement on the religion page of the San Francisco Chronicle. He was attending the evening worship service to hear a sermon. He hadn't heard one for two months.

The subject of the sermon was the unforgivable sin. The scripture was Matthew 12:30-32. "He that is not with me is against me; and he that gathereth not with me scattereth abroad. Wherefore I say unto you, All manner of sin and blasphemy shall be forgiven unto men; but the blasphemy against the Holy Ghost shall not be forgiven unto men. And whosoever speaketh a word against the Son of man, it shall be forgiven him; but whosoever speaketh against the Holy Ghost, it shall not be forgiven him, neither in this world, neither in the world to come."

Dave thought the scripture covered the subject very well.

Chapter Fifteen

Dave's Apartment

9:00 AM August 15, 1949

JILL CALLED WHILE Dave was engrossed in his Bible study. On her lay-over in Chicago, a San Francisco based stewardess asked Jill if she had been to Carmel. Jill had heard about the small artist town that was becoming popular with tourists, but said she hadn't been there. Jill asked Dave, "Could we drive there and do the trip in a day?" "We sure can. I'll pick you up in an hour." "Thank you Dave."

Restaurant
Pebble Beach Golf Club
Carmel California
12:30 PM August 15, 1949

The view from the restaurant was the golf course and the ocean beyond. Jill and Dave had a nice drive to Monterey and then to Pebble Beach. After lunch they would drive into Carmel. During the drive Dave told Jill about the year his family lived in Carmel. "I'll show where we lived." "Why did your family leave Palo Alto for a year?" "Bill, my older brother, had been sent to boarding high school in Arizona to finish high school because he had school problems. He had finished and now needed to get a job. Dad didn't want to be obligated to any employer in Palo Alto who would give Bill a job. So he decided to move the family for a year. Bill got a job with the Ford dealer as soon as the family arrived in town. One of his jobs was to travel to San Francisco to pick up cars and drive them back to Carmel for customer delivery. In a few months he was hired by a San Francisco dealer and moved there."

"In 1937, Carmel was a quiet artist's town. On any day of the week few cars traveled the main street. On Saturday, my sister Pam and I would walk to town and pick up copies of the Carmel Cymbal newspaper to sell. The Cymbal was a high class newspaper printed on heavy paper in a tabloid format. We got two cents for every paper we sold."

After lunch Dave drove into Carmel and down Scenic Road that ran along the beach cliffs, then to the corner of Carmelo Street and 12th Avenue. The house the family lived in that year of 1937-38 is on that corner just two blocks from the beach. "We had a great summer at the beach in 1937 and we all liked Carmel. Dad commuted to Palo Alto on the Southern Pacific Del Monte train. He did set up an office a couple of blocks from the house. It was a house called Hedge Gate. I'm sure it's still there."

Later they looked through the Carmel shops and art galleries. They had dinner in the dining room of the La Plya Hotel on Camino Real.

On the return trip, Dave was driving on Highway 101 between Gilroy and San Jose. The Highway was three lanes wide. A north and south bound lane and a passing lane in the middle. It was called the "suicide lane" because cars would use it to pass going north and south. It was an invitation to head-on collisions. Driving north, Dave saw a car trying to enter the traffic flow from a side street without success. There were just too many cars. Seeing no car in the center passing lane, Dave changed lanes so the car could enter the north bound traffic. Jill said, "Dave, you are so considerate. Few drivers would have done that." It's the Eric Liddell influence Jill. He set a challenging example for one's life. I attempt to follow it."

Wrigley Field
42nd Place & Avalon Boulevard.
Los Angeles, California
San Francisco at Los Angeles
9:15 PM August 16, 1949

This was Dave's first look at Wrigley Field, built in 1935 at a cost of $1.3 million by William Wrigley, the chewing gum king. He had bought the ball club two years after buying Catalina Island. The stadium was the only one in the Pacific Coast League with a double deck. The field had turned out to be a hitter's paradise. The power alleys were 345 feet to the fence slanted towards the playing field.

The Los Angeles Angels had developed a number of power hitters. However some were never able to hit major league pitching. Lew Novikoff, "The Mad Russian," was an example. In 1940, Lew led the PCL, batting .363 and hitting 41 home runs. In four years with the Cubs, he hit .300 one year, but never hit more than 7 home runs. He spent the first part of the 1946 season with the Philadelphia Phillies appearing in only 17 games. Then it was back to the PCL, where he joined the Seattle Rainiers and played for three seasons.

In the game tonight, hitting was the order of the evening for the Sea Lions. In the first inning, they had batted around, scoring five runs. Dave hit a two run home run over the left field fence at 350 feet. Now, in the eighth inning it was Lions 7 Angeles 1. That's the way it ended. Dave allowed seven hits, struck out two and walked no batter. It was Dave's win number 14.

Avalon Lanes
3802 Avalon Boulevard
Los Angeles, California
1:15 PM August 17, 1949

Dave and Billy May were bowling in this gigantic bowling facility. There were 30 lanes and even at this time of day, many of them were occupied. Dave brought his ball on this trip, thinking there might not be much to do in downtown Los Angeles.

Dave and Billy bowled three games. Dave bowled a 245 average. Dave told Billy, "I must bowl more if I'm going to bowl on a team in Palo Alto in the off season. Billy said, "You are doing fine, Dave. I'll never catch up with you on the lanes."

Wrigley Field
San Francisco at Los Angeles
2:45 PM August 18, 1949

Dave had come to the ball park early for an interview. He had limited granting interviews because he didn't want to receive too much individual publicity. He was still a rookie. Because this was Los Angeles, the league's largest market, Dave was encouraged by the Sea Lions management to grant an interview with Sam Pittsher, a baseball writer for the Los Angeles Tribune.

Dave met Sam in the visitor's club house. He indicated they could use the manager's office for the interview.

Q "The biggest question about you is how you are able to pitch on three days rest and still excel?"

A "First, I don't throw as many pitches in a game as most pitchers do. Also, I have taken very good care of my arm. Since I have a natural sinker ball pitch, I was advised not to throw a curve ball because it puts more strain on your arm. Starting when I was 11 years old, I have thrown a lot of pitches, practicing control and then pitching for my high school and American Legion teams. In my first year in college I pitched a college season and then an American Legion season. Then two years of National Armature Baseball Association (NABA) baseball. So I pitched more innings than the typical college pitcher."

Q "Part of your answer raises my next question. Besides the sinker pitch that you use extensively, what are your other pitches?"

A "I have a rising fast ball and a change up. My fast ball is not one that I can throw past a batter. I don't have that much velocity on it. I depend on the rising movement. My change is an important pitch because it's a big change from both the sinker that is thrown at just below fast ball speed and the fast ball. I have worked to improve my change, so I can throw it at a lower speed."

Q "Have you always been a fast worker on the mound?"

A "Yes I have always wanted to reduce the time between pitches. It helps that a majority of my pitches are sinkers, so signaling by the catcher is only for location most of the time. I have always thought a rapidly played game was a benefit for the position players. They do less standing around. It keeps them more alert. When I wasn't pitching I played right field and some first base in high school, American Legion and college baseball. I didn't like standing around, waiting for the next pitch."

Q "You seem to have a different approach to pitching that most pitchers?"

A "I'm not sure about that. Most pitchers just want to get batters out. Because I'm what most call a control pitcher, my objective is to get the most outs with the fewest pitches possible. I call it pitching efficiency. One of my objectives is to throw first pitch strikes. That puts the pitcher in control of the situation."

Q "Some baseball people say because you are a graduate engineer, you think in a technical manner."

A "I don't think my engineering has that much to do with it. I have always thought about pitching efficiency, even when I was a high school and American Legion pitcher."

Q "You mention your American Legion baseball experience often. How important was it in your development?"

A "It was very important because the competition was higher than high school baseball. Also, unlike high school, I was a member of a team with a very good defense, a critical quality for a sinker ball pitcher. It gave me confidence that I could win games."

Q "You are hitting .351, a very high average for a pitcher. How do you explain the hitting? Most pitchers are not good hitters."

A "No matter what position you play, to be a good hitter you must be interested in the art of hitting. I really think it is an art and a very difficult one to master. It requires continued practice for good coordination and to be able to recognize pitches. I like to hit, so I work on it all the time, taking daily batting practice with the position players."

Q "I understand you were a contact hitter in your early years. How has that changed?"

A "As a boy, I was tall and skinny. I tried to add weight, but I wasn't able to, until I started college. Then, with maturity I gained 25 pounds over four years. I had plenty of height to handle it and I kept active in the off season. As I gained weight, I developed more power, but still retained my pitch selectivity."

Q "I'm told you are a bowler and a very good one."

A "Yes I like to bowl. I started as a young boy. It requires some of the same hand to eye coordination that pitching requires. It also is something that relaxes me. When the season is over I plan to bowl on a team in a Palo Alto league."

Q "It has been reported you turned down a large signing bonus offered by the New York Dukes to sign with the Sea Lions. What was you reason for doing so?"

A "I wanted to stay on the West Coast to play in good weather. Also, I didn't want to have the pressure of being a bonus player. I think it was a good decision."

Thank you for your time Dave. "You're welcome."

Dave watched from the dugout as the Sea Lions defeated the Angels 6-2 for the third win in the series. The win gave the Sea Lions a three game winning streak.

Biltmore Hotel
506 South Grand Avenue
Los Angeles, California
12:15 PM August 19, 1949

Dave was making up at the big Kiwanis Club of Los Angeles. Initially he was not recognized, but as soon as he put his visitor's badge on at least one member knew who he was. Upon being introduced it was announced that Dave would be pitching against the hometown Angeles on Saturday. Members were encouraged to attend the game and root for the Angeles.

Reports were given on the club's ongoing programs for the benefit of children. The chairman of the Human and Spiritual services committee reported on a program to identify children who had no father at home. These children were referred to an organization that provided volunteer acting fathers. Outings and special programs were being planned for the children. Dave estimated the attendance at 150 members.

Avalon Lanes
10:00 AM August 19, 1949

Dave had decided to bowl again this morning before going to the ball park. He needed the practice. Like ski bums who either worked nights at a ski resort or worked as an instructor, there were BBs, bowling bums. They had a night job, and spent the day hanging around lanes to promote games with unsuspecting amateur bowlers for money.

A BB came up to Dave and asked if he would like to bowl three games for money. Dave has just started to bowl, so the BB didn't know Dave's competence. They bowled three games, and Dave took all the money, $30.00. That built up Dave's confidence in his bowling.

Wrigley Field
San Francisco at Los Angeles
4:20 PM August 20, 1949

Wrigley Field was living up to its reputation as a hitter's park. The Sea Lions had produced three runs before Dave came to bat in the first inning. With Les Short and Bill Parks on base and one out, Dave worked the count to 2-2, and hit a double into the left field power ally, knocking in two runs. Billy May singled Dave home for a 6-0 leas before the Angels came to bat.

Dave allowed four hits in the first four innings, but no runs. In the fifth inning, Dave achieved a perfect inning. He made three pitches and the three batters each hit the first pitch for an out. Three pitches for three outs. Except for an unearned run in the eighth, Dave had shut down the Angeles for win number 15. The Sea Lions now had a 4 to 1 lead in the series.

Dance Hall
Santa Monica Pier
Santa Monica California
9:30 PM August 20, 1949

Dave had asked Billy if he would like to go with him to see and hear Bob Wills and the Texas Playboys. Billy didn't like country music so he declined. Dave then asked Del Hoffman, who had gone to the Palladium with him. Del said he would go. He wasn't a country music fan either, but anywhere there were females, he was eager to be there. They would also check out a band that played in the Aragon Ballroom some place on the Santa Monica beach. Dave didn't know anything about the band, but he was told it was drawing big crowds.

Starting right after returning to the hotel from the game, they took a cab to a location where they could get the big red Pacific Electric street car that ran all the way to Santa Monica.

During grammar school Dave had learned to play the accordion. He played cowboy music and was very good. Every morning he listened to Dude Martin and his Happy Roving Cowboys on a San Francisco radio station. They had an accordion player and Dave wanted to see him in action. Dave's dad took him to a dance where the group was playing in San Jose. George Mason said, "He is a good accordion player, but his big attraction is his continuous smile." Dave always remembered that and it may have accounted for his reputation as a smiley person.

When Del and Dave arrived, the dance hall was packed. Dave had heard about the crowds and the popularity of the Play Boys, but he was surprised, seeing it in person. Del was immediately off to look over the ladies stag line, while Dave listened to the music at the band stand.

In 1941 Bob Wills had written an arrangement called the New San Antonio Rose. It had started out as a fiddle instrumental, but was later given lyrics that conjured up romantic images of the Southwest. The recording was solidly in the big-band style, the swinging arrangement revealing the formidable group of musicians that Wills had at the time. Bing Crosby made his own version of the song, and later sang it with Wills and the Playboys at a Tulsa war-bond rally.

The band tonight included fiddlers, a steel guitar player, bass and reed sections. Dave learned that Wills and his band had dominated the southern dance halls from 1935 with their unique blend of Texas fiddle music, pop songs, jazz and blues. It was later to be known as Western swing. Some time after the war Wills had moved the band to the the Santa Monica pier and become a legend.

It was too late when they left the music of Bob Wills to find the Aragon Ballroom and learn about the band that played there. Dave would learn about the band years later, when the band had a weekly TV show.

San Francisco International Airport South San Francisco, California 10:00 PM August 21, 1949

In a phone call with Jill earlier in the week, Dave learned she would be returning to San Francisco on a flight tonight at 10:30 PM. Dave said he would meet her if the team returned in time from L.A.

The team had split the Sunday double header, so the Lions had won the series 5-2. Dave thought they should have won another game. It was one they lost because of two errors. Dave went out to the gate where Jill's flight was to park and waited. The flight was on time and Jill was soon coming through the gate. Dave took Jill's suitcase and they walked to the parking lot. After some welcoming kisses, Dave said, "I'll go with you to your apartment. Later I'll call a cab and go to Palo Alto. I'll bet you are tired Jill." "No, it was an easy fight, even though it was full."

At Jill's apartment, only Jane was there and about to turn in. She and Woody had gone to dinner. Jill and Dave talked for a while, but he soon called a cab. After some good night kisses, Dave was off to Palo Alto.

The Mason Residence 10:30 PM August 21, 1949

Ann was still up when Dave arrived. He gave her a report on the games in Los Angeles as well as his trip to Santa Monica. Ann said Pam would be home on the 31st. "I think you will still be in town, wont your?" "Yes, what time does she arrive?" "I think its 10:30 in the morning. If that's the time I can go with you and dad. Will you be able to attend the game on Sunday?" "Your dad will talk to you about it." "Good. Now I will turn in. It's been a long day."

The next morning Dave and his dad were having breakfast in Motley's Restaurant. George Mason reported on his discussions with Bill Fox regarding Dave's appearance in the ads for Lavell Chevrolet. They had agreed on $25.00 per advertisement publication with a seven insertion minimum. Fox indicated it would likely run for two weeks, and might run longer if the response is good.

We had some preliminary discussions about radio commercials. Fox indicated they were covered for the baseball season, so any commercials would be for after the season. "I said I would need to do some research before I could talk about the radio work. How do you feel about doing the commercials?" "I'd like to do them. I spent a half hour on the sales floor last week, talking to potential car buyers. I turned two over to salesmen and I think they bought cars." "That's great Dave. That experience will help you in what ever you do in the future."

"Will you be able to go with us to meet your sister?" "Yes, I talked to mother about it last night. I think Jill will be home that day and I will ask her to come with me." "That's fine Dave."

"Mother said to talk to you about attending the game Sunday. "We will be there for the second game Dave. That's the one you will pitch in isn't it?" "Yes, your seats will be in Mr. Dent's box. I don't know if he will be there or not." "Jill has a meeting to attend so she won't be able to attend." Now dad, please take me to the S.P. depot."

Approaching San Francisco Aboard a Southern Pacific Train 9:30 AM August 22, 1949

Arriving at the Third Street station, Dave took a taxi to his apartment. He called Jill to ask her if she could go with him to meet Pam. She said, "Sure, I'll be in town." Jill had met Pam when she visited Dave at Christmas in1948.

Dave reported he had tickets for A Streetcar Named Desire at the Curran Theater on Saturday night. It stars Anthony Quinn and Judith Evelyn. "That sounds interesting, Dave." "How do you want to do it?" "I'll come to the game and let a handsome baseball pitcher take me to dinner." "Oh, do you know a handsome baseball pitcher?" "I sure do." His name begins with D and ends with e." "Oh, Dickie." There's no Dickie on your team." Dave couldn't hold his laughter any longer, so he laughed and Jill joined in. "Your ticket in the Lavell box will be in will call" "Thank you Dave."

Chapter Sixteen

Lavell Chevrolet

4:00 PM August 22, 1949

DAVE HAD COME to the dealership to have pictures taken for the advertisements he would appear in. Bill Fox said, "I have worked out a contract with your Dad. Has he told you about it?" "Yes, just this morning." "He also said you had a preliminary discussion about radio commercials."

After his last showroom appearance, Dave had asked Bill Fox if he could spend some of the time during the next appearance talking to potential customers on the show room floor. Bill readily agreed. He thought show room lookers would be eager to talk to Dave. He would do it for 30 minutes following his talks with the kids and signing balls.

With no pre-announcement, Dave ended his meeting with the kids and walked to the show room floor where a special Fleetline two door sedan just like Dave's was on the display. Almost immediately he had a young man walk up to him and started asking questions about the car. Dave's answers must have been good ones because the fellow wanted to talk about buying one. "Great," Dave said. Let me get a salesman over here to work out the details." Dave called a salesman, and introduced him to the customer. Dave said, "Sam will take care of you, and thank you." Dave talked to at least five showroom lookers during his 30 minutes and two were interested enough for Dave to call a salesman.

Later, Dave asked Bill Fox for some suggestions in talking to lookers about cars. Bill said, "The best approach is to be friendly and ask what the person wants the car to do for him or her. Are they just buying transportation or do they want the car to be a status cymbal. This will indicate what model they may be interested in." "Thanks Bill, I'll remember that." Dave had spent two and a half hours at the dealership and felt he had achieved much and had learned some good pointers about sales.

Kiwanis Club Meeting
12:05 PM August 23, 1949

Members of the club including President Kenneth greeted Dave with hand shakes and backslap. Many members were reading the sports page. Dave contributed a happy dollar for his win on Saturday.

Club members were encouraged to start requesting items for the club auction in October.

Children, who had been able to attend summer camp because the club had paid their registration fee, attended the meeting with their mothers.

The program was presented by a representative of the San Francisco Chamber of Commerce. The subject was the promotion of tourism and conventions. San Francisco has a high rating among cities people would like to visit. The chamber was promoting the city to attract more visitors and conventions.

Sea Lions Stadium
Oakland at San Francisco
9:30 PM August 24, 1949

Dave was pitching the second game of the series tonight. The Sea Lions had won the first on Tuesday 5 to 1. C.C. Chuker was the winning pitcher.

It was the start of the eighth inning and the Lions held a 3 to 2 lead. Dave was having the rare experience of not placing his sinker pitches where he wanted them. Oakland had gotten nine hits, all singles. The inning didn't start well. The Oaks lead off batter drew a walk on a 3 and 2 count. Then Dave threw three fast balls that the next batter fouled off twice trying to·bunt the runner to second. With the count 0-2, the batter tried to bunt again and missed for a strike out. The next batter hit the first pitch to Billy May who started a twin killing.

In the Sea Lions half of the inning the Lions wanted to produce an insurance run. They were batting at the bottom of the order, but Del Hoffman singled. Ray Chess sacrificed Hoffman to second. Les Short struck out. Catcher Jim Jarvis hit a ball down the first base line where the Oaks first baseman's only play was to first, Hoffman going to third. With Dave coming up, would he get an intentional walk? He did. Runners were now on first and third and there were two outs. Billy May was coming to bat. Billy fouled off a a pitch and took a ball. On the next pitch he hit a low line drive into the left field power ally, a ball that went all the way to the fence. It was his first hit in nine at bats. Hoffman scored and Dave got the go sign at third and slid in under the catcher's tag. The Sea Lions now led 5-2. Bill Vaughn popped out to third and the inning was over

Dave threw eight pitches in the ninth for a perfect inning. The game was over and the Sea Lions had a 5-2 win. It was Dave's 17th win.

Dave made his usual rounds to thank the players for their good play. He told them, "I threw more pitches than I like to tonight, but we won the game."

Oakland at San Francisco
9:20 PM August 26, 1949

The Lions had won the first three games of the series, but were losing 4-2 tonight in the bottom half of the eighth inning. The Sea Lions had started a rally, scoring a run with one out, and Ray Chess was on first base. Less Short was due up, but Dave was sent to the on-deck circle to pinch hit. He had devastated the Oaks during their series in Oakland earlier in the month.

Dave, batting left against the Oakland right handed pitcher, took the first pitch for a ball. He fouled off the next pitch, a high fast ball. You could tell he wanted to hit that pitch, but didn't get the bat on it in squarely. The next pitch, a slider, slid out of the strike zone for a ball, making the count 2-1. Would the pitcher chance another fast ball or give Dave something else. Dave thought he would get a change. He did, and he was ready. He met the pitch on the fat of the bat, but the pitch being slow, Dave had to supply all the power. The ball skied into right field. The right fielder went back to the warning track, almost to the fence and waited. He jumped just as the ball was about to go over his head and the ball landed in the web of the right fielder's glove, for a long out. Two outs and catcher Bill Parks was coming to bat. Parks hit the first pitch into center filed for a single and Ray Chess moved to second. Catcher Jim Jarvis came to bat as a pinch hitter for pitcher Al Armor. The Oaks pitcher, now frustrated, walked Jarvis. Bases loaded and Billy May coming to bat. Billy was still experiencing a hitting slump and was two for his last 12 at bats.

The Oaks manager, "Kid" Youngman came to the mound, removed his pitcher and called for a right hander from the bull pen. In this era of baseball you wouldn't call such a pitcher a relief pitcher because there were few of them. A "replacement" pitcher was usually a starter or at least a part-time starter. Youngman called Les Smiley, a part time starter who matched his name with a big smile when he pitched.

Billy watched a ball, low for the first pitch. He had a good rip at the next pitch, but only hit air. The count was now 1-1. Expecting a breaking pitch next, Billy was not prepared for a fast ball, but he recovered and hit the ball down the third base line just fair. The hit cleaned the bases scoring three runs and Billy was standing on second base. Lions led 6-4 and hopefully Billy's slump was over. Bill Vaughn popped out to the catcher and the inning was over.

C.C. Chuker came on to pitch the ninth inning. He got a one, two, three inning and the Lions won the game 6-4. It was the fourth win in a row for the Sea Lions, their longest winning streak of the season. The Lions led 4 to 0 in the series.

Oakland at San Francisco
3:30 PM August 27, 1949

In this Saturday afternoon game the Sea Lions were going after their fifth win. It would be another season high winning streak. Pitching for the Sea Lions was Ray Littlejohn. Ray was recently called up from the Yakima Bears of the Western International League where he had won 18 games. Littlejohn, of American Indian heritage, was born in White Swan, Washington on the Yakima Indian Reservation. When it was apparent that Ray had baseball talent, his father sent him to Toppenish, Washington to live with Ray's uncle so he could play baseball on the high school and American Legion team. The Sea Lions signed him after high school graduation. He was sent to San Jose, in the California State league. In two years he progressed to Yakima and this had been his second year with the Bears.

Ray had pitched well through seven innings. He had a live fast ball and above average slider and a good change up. His curve ball was not the best so he seldom used it. Today, the Oaks were hitting lots of fly balls into the big outfield of Sea Lions Stadium. In the last half of the seventh inning the Lions were leading 3-1. After lead off batter Dino Roselli singled, he was left stranded at first base.

In the top of the eighth Oakland rallied for two runs and tied the score 3-3. The Lions got nothing in their half of the eighth. In the top of the ninth, Oakland got their lead off man aboard, but he went no further as Littlejohn got the next three batters to fly out to center field.

With the Lions coming to bat, shortstop Les Short would be leading off. Les was a quick out, on a ground ball to second. Bill Parks was up next. Bill hit a Texas League single just back of first base. With the pitcher due up, would Tub call on Dave to pinch hit again? Littlejohn, who was in the on-deck circle, was called back and Dave emerged from the dugout. The first two pitches were balls. It was obvious the Oaks were not going to give Dave a good pitch to hit. The third pitch bounced in front of the plate, high enough for Dave to swung and hit the ball between second base and the shortstop. The ball was going to roll all the way to the wall. Parks, not a fast runner, took off from first and slid into third ahead of the throw. Dave was on second.

Billy May was up with a chance to win the game. Billy took the first pitch for a strike. The second was a ball. He fouled off the next, a fast ball. 1-2. was the count. Two pitches later it was a full count 3-2. "Kid" Youngman visited the mound to give the pitcher some advise. Youngman departed when the umpire came to end the conference. The Oaks pitcher threw Billy a slider that didn't slide very far and Billy hit it into center field just past the second baseman, driving in the winning run. Billy slump was over and he was becoming a clutch hitter. He received a big welcome from his teammates including Dave, who ran to first base as soon as Bill Parks had scored, for a 4 to 3 win. Five straight wins for the Sea Lions and a first win for Ray Littlejohn in his first start in the PCL.

Jill and Lisa May had watched the game sitting in Larry Lavell's box. Bill Fox had told Dave they could sit in the box whenever seats were available.

St. Francis Hotel Coffee Shop
7:00 PM August 27, 1949

Dave and Jill had met after the game and gone to his apartment where they changed clothes. They decided to have dinner in the St. Francis coffee shop so they could walk to the Curran Theater to see Streetcar Named Desire.

First Presbyterian Church
9:30 AM August 28, 1949

Dave was welcomed by Dr. Milligan and members of the class. The class had progressed to the 24th Chapter in their study of Acts. In this chapter, Paul was on trial before Governor Felix of Caesarea, accused by Ananias, High Priest of the Jews.

When the class was over Dr. Milligan asked Dave how the outline of the life of Jesus was working out. "I made a good start before we went to Los Angeles but I didn't get much done last week. I'll be in town for two weeks now before we go to Seattle so I should make more progress."

Sea Lions Stadium
Oakland at San Francisco, Doubleheader
3:30 PM August 28, 1949

Dave's mother and dad had arrived and were sitting in Walter Dent's box. Walter was there too. Luke Devore, the West Coast scout of the New York Dukes was also in attendance today. Devore had followed Dave's baseball career since he was a skinny 14 year old high school sophomore.

The Sea Lions had lost the first game of the double header 5-1 to end the unbeaten streak at five games. With Dave pitching the second game the Lions were confident they could start a new win streak. It was important with the league leading Hollywood Stars coming to town next week.

Baseball has great terms for its games. "A laughter" is a game that is over in the first one or two innings. However such a game can not be branded as such until it's over. That's because the game is not over until the last out is made. It would be described by a future Hall of Fame catcher in this manner. "It ain't over until it's over."

In the first inning of this game, Dave threw eight pitches and got three ground ball outs. Billy May led off the Lions' first inning with a single, Vaughn and Roselli also singled, scoring two runs. Mike Roc hit the right field fence and the ball bounce off the wall back towards the infield, and Roc kept running for a triple, Roselli scoring. That made the score 3-0. Del Hoffman hit a deep fly ball to center field and Roc scored after the catch. The Lions were now leading 4 to 0 with one out. Ray Chess doubled to right field and that was enough for "Kid" Youngman. He called for a left hander from the bull pen.

With a new pitcher on the mound, Lions' manager Warren wanted to make him throw strikes, so he had Les Short taking the first two pitches that were balls. To get a strike, the pitcher served up a fast ball and Les hit it out of the park. It was his first home run of the season. He was hitting just .221. The Lions dugout emptied to greet Les at home plate. The Sea Lions now led 6-0. Dave was up next. He fouled off two pitches and ran the count to 2-2. He hit the next pitch high over the right filed fence 320 feet away. It made the score 7-0. The next two batters went out to end the Lions' batting practice.

It was now a game to end as soon as possible. Working with his usual speed, Dave threw a total of 80 pitches, allowed four hits and the game was over in one hour and twenty minutes. It gave the Sea Lions a record of 77 wins and 78 losses, only one game under .500. They were now in fifth place in the PCL, a half game ahead of Seattle. Would the team continue to win?

Sitting behind home plate so he could watch the pitches, Luke Devore had a decision to make. The PCL season had only a month to go. What would he recommend to his baseball club about Dave Mason?

Emerging from the clubhouse, Dave was greeted by his mother and dad. Dad said, "Your mother almost jumped out of the box when you hit the home run." "Thanks mom."

They went to dinner where they talked about the game within the game that only the ball players know. Ann found it fascinating.

"Jill and I will meet you at the Ferry Building Wednesday morning. What time should we be there?" Dave's mother, the travel expert of the family, said, "Nine o'clock. Pam's train is scheduled to arrive at ten." "We'll be there to meet you."

Dave's Apartment
8:00 AM August 29, 1949

Dave had called Jill when he returned to his apartment last night. He advised her that he had an appearance at Lavell at noon, but they could do something in the evening. "How about having dinner with three girls?" "Boy, do you think I can handle that?" "I don't think you will have any trouble at all." They laughed together.

Dave had finished his bible study and breakfast and was off to do some shopping and pick up dry cleaning. He was due at Lavell

Chevrolet at 11:00 AM, a half hour earlier than usual. Bill Fox wanted to have Dave meet with the kids early, so Dave could spend more time talking to potential customers on the show room floor. Bill thought Dave had great potential as a sales person.

Dave spent the noon hour on the show room floor, talking to lookers. He referred three to salesmen. At one o'clock, Dave went to the office of Bill Fox to report his activity. Bill was not surprised at what Dave reported. Bill told Dave that the newspaper ads that Dave appears in would start running on Wednesday in three San Francisco papers. They would be run for a week and then evaluated. Dave said, "It will be interesting to learn what the response is."

Jill's Apartment
6:30 PM August 29, 1949

Jill had put Jane and Sally up to giving Dave a hard time about his popularity and notoriety. Jane started off by parroting a radio announcer saying, "And now we introduce that sensational baseball pitcher and king of the automobile showroom, San Francisco's hero Dave Mason. What do you have to say for yourself Mr. Mason?" "It's a "put up job, and I know who put you up to it." They all had a big laugh. This went on for some time from both Jane and Sally. They both said, "Jill didn't want you to get the 'big head.' "I'm sure Jill won't let me get the 'big head' or anything else."

Later it was Sally's turn. "This is the well known news correspondent Claire Booth Luce. I've heard so much about you Dave, I wanted to interview you.

Q Are you surprised at the reaction of people in San Francisco to your success on the baseball diamond?"

A "Yes I am. No one has ever paid any attention to me in the past."

Q "In all the reports I have heard, you are described as a nice guy"

A "That depends on what your definition is of a nice guy. My roll model for behavior is Eric Liddell, who won the gold medal at the 1924 Olympics in the 400 meter race. He later became a missionary in China and he died in a Japanese internment camp during the war."

Q "It's reported that you plan to attend Stanford University following the baseball season to work on a master's degree in mechanical engineering. Is this true?"

A "Yes I will start classes the last week of September."

Q "Does this mean you will limit your baseball career in the future?"

A "No, I won't limit my baseball career until I don't have a good future in baseball."

Q "Are you interested in pitching in the major leagues?"

A "Every young baseball player dreams of playing in the major leagues and I do too." "Thank you very much Mr. Mason." "You are welcome." They all had another big laugh. Dave said, "You ought to become a reporter Sally."

Sports Center
10:30 AM August 30, 1949

Dave bowled a quick three games, working on covering splits. Dave wanted to become a member of a good team at the Indian Bowl when the baseball season was over.

Kiwanis Club Meeting
12:00 noon August 30, 1949

This was Dave's second meeting without a miss. He reported he would be gone two of the next three meetings and then the season would be over. As soon as the Key club starts meeting, he hoped they will schedule a Saturday morning meeting that he could attend.

Dave contributed two happy dollars for his two wins during the Oakland series. "Now we face the league leading Hollywood Stars starting tonight in a nine game series."

Sea Lion Stadium
Hollywood at San Francisco
9:45 PM August 30, 1949

The Sea Lion were losing this game. It was batting practice for the Stars. They had teed off on three Lions pitchers for a 12-3 win. I took the steam out of the Lions who had done so well in the Oakland series last week. Gordon Enson the rookie bonus player hit a three run home run in the third inning that put the game out of reach. Luke Devore who signed Enson for the Dukes will be happy read the report of this game.

Oakland Mole
San Francisco Bay
Southern Pacific Terminal
10:25 AM August 31, 1949

Dave, his parents and Jill waited under the big train shed that covered the eight tracks of the Mole. Trains were lined up ready for departure and trains were arriving from the north, south and east.

Pam's train arrived right on time and she was greeted with hugs and kisses. Pam was happy to see Jill again. On the ferry ride to San Francisco, Ann asked Pam if Jim Smith had a job yet. "He thinks he has one in Chicago, but it will be a week before he knows."

Arriving at the Ferry Building, Dave and Jill departed for lunch at Fisherman's Warf. Pam and her parents were off to Palo Alto.

Chapter Seventeen

Sea Lion Stadium

Hollywood at San Francisco

9:35 PM September 1, 1949

THE STARS HAD won the Wednesday night game 5 to 1. The Sea Lions were not getting timely hits.

The game tonight had been a pitching duel between Dave and Frank Lester, the Stars top pitcher. There was no score through seven innings. In the top of the eighth Hollywood scored a run on a single, sacrifice, an infield single and a sacrifice fly ball fly that scored the run. The Lions matched it in their half of the inning on a home run by Dino Roselli. Both pitchers were fast workers, so the game was only an hour and fifteen minutes old. The score was tied, 1-1.

Dave retired the first two batters in the top of the ninth on six pitches. The next batter was Gordon Enson. In a battle of pitcher verses batter, the count progressed to 3-2. Dave thought he had thrown the correct pitches to Enson. Sinkers and change ups but no fast balls. He decided to throw a change on the 3-2 count. It was a good pitch, but Enson, looking for a walk, not a home run, timed it perfectly and hit a 325 foot home run that just cleared the fence in left field. It gave Hollywood a 2 to 1 lead. In the Lions last chance in the bottom of the ninth inning they went out one two three. Dave had lost his second game 2 to 1. He had allowed seven hits struck out two and walked one. Dave's record was now 18-2, an outstanding record for an unknown rookie just two months ago.

In the club house Dave gave a big thanks to Billy May and shortstop Les Short for two double plays at critical times in the game. Even though it was a loss, the team had played well. The loss gave Hollywood a 3-0 lead in the series.

Dave's Apartment
10:45 AM September 2, 1949

Dave had been catching up on his reading while listening to the radio this morning. On the morning after he pitched, he had adopted the practice of not reading the sports page account of the game. He found the San Francisco writers were too enthusiastic about his pitching and he didn't want to get to the point where he believed everything they wrote. He would read the articles on all the games in which he didn't pitch. He did wonder what they would write about the loss. He thought they would probably sugar coat it.

Dave stopped his reading to listen to a new song, Riders in The Sky sung by the Sons of the Pioneers. Dave had always liked cowboy music. When he played the accordion in grammar and junior high school, that's the music he played. However the record by the Sons of the Pioneers didn't catch on. Band leader and vocalist Vaughn Monroe's more dramatic rendering of the song reached number one on the pop charts.

Dave was going to the ball park early today to study the pitching chart of last night's game.

He would face the same hard hitters in the second game of the Monday Labor Day double header. He particularly wanted to review the pitches he had thrown to Enson when he got no hits.

Benjamin Franklin Hotel
7:25 PM September 3, 1949

Jill and Dave were having dinner and then would attend the second show. How Green Was My Valley, staring Walter Pidgeon and

Maureen O'Hara. It had received good reviews and was a good movie. Jill enjoyed the feisty O'Hara.

Later Dave drove into the hills behind Burlingame where they looked at the moon and with Jill in her usual position on Dave's lap. Dave gave Jill some romantic moments. It was good medicine for Dave because Hollywood had defeated the Sea Lions again today for their third win in the series.

It was late when Dave took Jill home and he didn't return to his apartment until 2:00 AM. He set his loud alarm clock for 7:30 so he would be up in time to get to Sunday school.

First Presbyterian Church 9:30 AM September 4, 1949

Dave had been awakened out of a sound sleep at 7:30 and taken a cold shower to wake up. By the time he arrived at the church he was wide awake. The study in the 24th chapter of Acts was continuing. Governor Felix had sent for Paul. With his wife Drusilla, who was Jewish, he listened to Paul. Paul talked about his faith in Jesus Christ. As Paul went on discussing goodness, self control, and the coming Day of Judgment, Felix became afraid and dismissed Paul. Felix was hoping Paul would give him some money. He knew that Paul had charge of large sums of money collected from many churches.

After two years, Porcius Festus replaced Felix as Governor. Felix wanted to gain favor with the Jews, so he left Paul in Prison.

After class, Dr. Milligan asked Dave how much longer he would be in San Francisco. Dave replied, "The baseball season ends on September 25. We will be playing in Sacramento that week. I will move back to Palo Alto before the end of the month. I start classes at Stanford in October. So we will see you for a while longer." "Yes, I'll be gone next week, but return the following week." Dr. Milligan was not yet ready to tell Dave that he had a daughter attending Stanford who worshiped at Menlo Park Presbyterian Church.

Sea Lions Stadium
Hollywood at San Francisco, Doubleheader
5:30 PM September 5 1949, Labor Day

After losing both games of the Sunday doubleheader and the first game today, the Sea Lions had finally won a game from the Stars, winning the second game of the doubleheader. It broke Hollywood's eight game winning streak.

Dave had won the second game, pitching one of his better games. It was a 5-0 shut out. Dave allowed only two hits and threw only 68 pitches. He contributed one hit, a double, getting an RBI and scoring a run. The game took only an hour and fifteen minutes.

After the game, Dave said to all his team mates, "It was a big relief to get the win." He thanked his position players for their errorless play. The only negative was the realization that the Sea Lions would have to face the Stars again after the Lions' trip to Seattle.

Dave's Apartment
9:00 AM September 6, 1949

Dave had not talked with his mother or dad since he and Jill met Pam at the Oakland Mole. He wanted to call before he left on the trip to Seattle. "How is Pam doing," he asked. "Oh she's fine. She is glad to be done with school and she's in love." "Well, I assumed that. What does she plan to do?" "It now appears she will go live in Chicago. Jim got his job there. She thinks her friend Adell will be based there when she completes her United Airlines stewardess training. They would share an apartment." "How does she plan to support herself?" "That's the problem. She plans to take a typing course so she can at least type. Four years of college and she has to take a typing course to get a job!" "Well mother, don't you know the only reason girls go to college is to catch a good man?" "Oh Dave, that's not true." Dave laughed.

"I wanted to call before we leave on our trip to Seattle. Please tell dad I called and I'll try to call him at the office before I leave." "Thank you Dave."

Lavell Chevrolet
6:30 PM September 6, 1949

Dave was surprised at the long line of youngsters waiting for him to arrive and sign baseballs. He decided they had come because it was their last opportunity before school started tomorrow. Tonight, Dave spent all the time signing balls and talking to the kids. The newspaper ads with Dave standing by his Chevrolet had brought many potential customers to the showroom. The salesmen were all busy.

Dave and Bill Fox talked about Dave's schedule of appearances in the next two weeks as the season wound down. Bill had asked Dave if he could continue after the baseball season. Dave has said he could, but would have to wait for scheduling until he had his class schedule at Stanford.

Dave called Jill from Lavell to learn if she was home from her weekend flights. Sally reported Jill had been called to fill in on an afternoon flight to Denver and would return tomorrow afternoon. Then she would be at home for at least four days. Dave asked where the crews were staying during Denver layovers. Sally thought it was the Brown Palace. Dave thanked her and said, "I'll call her later tonight. " Dave didn't reach Jill until the next morning when they had a long conversation. She was so tired when she arrived in Denver she turned the telephone off and went to bed early. She would fly back to San Francisco this afternoon and would be home until Monday afternoon. Dave said, "I'll call again later in the week."

Dave decided to call his dad at home. Pam answered the phone and Dave asked her if she had started learning to type yet. He got a not-so-happy answer of no! Pam reported, "Dad is at a meeting." "Ok, I'll call in the morning. Good night."

Dave talked with his dad early Wednesday morning. He asked how Pam was really doing. His dad said, "It was hard to tell because she's in love. I just hope she does well in the typing course so she can get a job in Chicago." "I'm sure that's what she wants to do,"

Dave said. "I'll talk to you when I return dad."

Battleship Missouri
Bremerton Navel Shipyard
Bremerton, Washington
10:30 AM September 8, 1949

A group of the Sea Lions had signed up for a tour of the battleship, where the surrender of Japan had taken place in 1945. The group had taken a ferry from Seattle to Bremerton, then boarded a bus that took them to the ship. Dave was amazed at the size of the ship. As a young boy he had visited the Battleship Oklahoma during Fleet Week in Santa Barbara. Later he had been aboard the Arizona in Monterey. Both ships had been sunk in the Pearl Harbor attack. There was a large photo display of the surrender proceedings as well as others showing the ship in action during the war in the Pacific. It was an interesting tour.

Before going to the Stadium, Dave had called Jill and they talked briefly. Jill was about to go shopping with Jane. Dave said he would call Sunday night when the team returned home.

Sick's Seattle Stadium
San Francisco at Seattle
8:45 PM September 9, 1949

Dave was pitching tonight with a goal of reversing the downward slide of the team. The Lions had lost the first two games of the series and 10 of their last 11 games. Through two innings Dave had not allowed a hit and his sinker was working well. All the outs had been ground balls to infielders. The Sea Lions had not produced any offense, so there was no score in the game.

In the top of the third inning the Seattle pitcher got two quick outs and that brought Dave to the plate. Pitcher and batter dueled through six pitches, including two foul balls. With the count 2-2, the Seattle pitcher threw his best fast ball. It was a bit high and Dave hit a towering ball that cleared the left field fence by ten feet for a 1-0 lead.

Dave sailed through the bottom of the third, allowing no hits. Dave's home run energized the Lions and Billy May led off the fourth inning with a single. After failing to get the bunt down with a two strike count, Bill Vaughn singled to center field, May going to second. Dino Rocelli flied out to deep right field, May going to third after the catch. Now there was one out and runners on first and third. First baseman Mike Roc battled the Rainiers' pitcher to a 3-2 count. Would the next pitch be a fast ball? It was the Seattle pitcher's his best pitch. The next pitch was a slider, a good pitch on the outside of the plate, but Mike hit it into the right field gap for a double, scoring May and Vaughn. The Lions now led 3-0. Roc died on second base as the next two batters struck out.

Dave gave up a hit in the fifth inning, ending the no-hitter and one in the seventh. There was no more scoring and the game ended 3-0 for the Sea Lions. It was just their second win in the last 12 games. Dave's record was now 19 wins and 2 losses.

Dave was a happy man in the clubhouse. Stopping the losing was his goal and he had accomplished that. He made his usual rounds to all the players, thanking them for their play. He particularly thanked catcher Bill Parks for a good fast game in calling the sinker pitch locations.

Hong Kong Cafe
International District
507 Maynard Avenue
Seattle, Washington
7:15 PM September 10, 1049

Dave and Billy May had come to the Hong Kong to forget about the loss of today's afternoon game. Dave had remembered Sam Wong's invitation. Dave asked to see Sam Wong. "Tell him Dave Mason is here." Sam was soon in the dinning room giving Dave a big hello and hand shake. Dave introduced Billy May and then asked Sam to order for them. We are here to forget that we lost the game today."

"Oh, the Rainiers are beating you up?" "You could say that." Sam had the waiter place the order and said, "I'll be back to see how you like it." "Okay, Sam."

Approaching San Francisco International Airport 9:35 PM September 11, 1949

The Sea Lions were returning home after the Seattle series. They had won only the one game Dave had pitched, losing both games of the double header today and the series 5-1.

At 9:00 AM this morning Dave had walked up to the First Presbyterian Church to attend the adult Sunday school class. He had heard that the First Presbyterian Church of Seattle had at one time been the largest Presbyterian Church in the country with a membership of 10,000. The class was a large one of at least 35 adults. The study was in 2nd Corinthians, Chapter 8. Paul was reporting on the generosity of the churches of Macedonia in giving to the Saints, even though the members of the churches were poverty stricken.

The team's record for the week didn't make the players feel very good on the flight home. Their record was now 82-91 and they were back in seventh place, one game out of sixth. The thought of facing the Hollywood Stars again during the coming week didn't make them feel any better. The series would be at home, but that didn't help much last week when Hollywood won all but one game. Dave would pitch the first game on Tuesday night. Winning the first game and getting off to a good start in the series would help. Dave would be going after his 20th win, an amazing record for only three months of pitching.

Dave's Apartment 8:30 AM September 12, 1949

Dave had called Jill from the airport, even though it was late. They had a brief talk before Dave boarded the bus to the stadium. He was finally home at 11:30 PM. This morning he had slept in. The week in

Seattle had drained him because the team was losing. Could they turn it around this week? It would be a big challenge. The Stars were leading the league and would be pressing to win the pennant. Dave would call Jill later to learn her schedule for the week. She had been the first called lead stewardess when substitutes were needed during the past week. Hopefully there would be no calls this week.

When they talked, Jill said, "If you can get me a seat outside the wives box again I'll come to the game tomorrow night to watch you pitch." "That's great. I've talked to Sam Ducket the ticket man who said he would give you a ticket in another box. I didn't want to ask Bill Fox again for seats in the Lavell box. I'll ask Billy if Lisa would like to sit with you. If she does I'll ask her to call you. Pick up your ticket in will call." "Thank you Dave."

Will you join me for my after game meal?" "Sure." "Are you at Lavell tonight?" "Yes, from 6:30 to 8:00." "Are you still getting lots of kids?" "Oh yes, there were more than ever last week." "Good. I'll see you tomorrow night." "Great."

Chapter Eighteen

Lavell Chevrolet

8:35 PM September 12, 1949

IT HAD BEEN another busy evening at the dealership. The Lavell advertisement with Dave and his car was still running and bringing people to the show room. Dave had a few minutes to talk to those looking at the cars on display. Lavell was promoting its end of the year sale to clear out cars for the new 1950 Chevrolets.

About this time a young lady entered the show room and started looking at cars. As soon as one of the salesmen, Del, was finished talking with a "looker" he immediately went to talk to the attractive blonde. "Good evening," Del said. "My name is Del." She said, "Hello Del" and didn't give her name. She proceeded to tell him she had always driven Fords, but might consider changing.

She asked why all the kids were in the show room. He replied, "Because of the appearance of Dave Mason, the pitcher for the San Francisco Sea Lions, who has become a local hero." "What do the kids want, his autograph?" "Yes, on a baseball and the opportunity to talk to him. It makes each one a hero at their school." "That's interesting, maybe I should meet this Dave, you said." "Yes Dave Mason." To change the subject back to Chevrolets Del asked, "What model of Ford do you drive now?" "It's a two door coupe, the smallest Ford. It's a 1947 model." "We can provide you with a 1949 Chevrolet coupe at a year ending discount. Your Ford is a relatively new car. How many miles do you have on it?" "I think it's about 25,000 miles. It was a used car when I bought it" "We can give you a good trade in for your Ford."

About this time Dave spotted Jill from across the show room. He watched the conversation for a few minutes, then excused himself from the table and walked up to the salesman and asked if he could meet this customer. Del said, "Well she isn't a customer yet, but I think she does want to meet you." Dave said, "Hello, my name is Dave." "Hello, I'm Jill." "Del broke in and said, "How do you do Jill." Both Dave and Jill were trying to keep straight faces so not to embarrass Del.

Finally, Dave excused himself by saying, "Nice to have met you Jill. I must go pick up my autograph pens." "Oh, may I come and get your autograph?" By this time Del probably thought something was "fishy" about this conversation so he said, "Go right ahead." Jill followed Dave to the autograph table where Dave wrote his name on a piece of paper with a note that said, walk outside and I'll be right out. He gave it to Jill just in case Del was still watching. Jill left the showroom and Dave followed soon after.

When they got outside they started to laugh and couldn't stop. When Dave got control of himself, he said, "Shame on you Jill. You really confused Del." "I'm sorry, I didn't mean to. I hoped to just walk in and surprise you but you were talking to a kid, and before I knew it, Del came up to me." "You surprised me alright. I couldn't believe it was you talking to Del and I did a double take."

Jill said, "I came to take you to dinner." "Wow, what a surprise. Where are we going?" "Just follow me and you'll find out."

Dave followed Jill to Mc McCarthy's Big Serve on Van Ness Avenue. After they were seated, Jill said, "I have great news. Jane is engaged! Woody took her to the Portola House for dinner and proposed right there in the restaurant over coffee." "Well, the Portola House is romantic enough with the low lights and candle light. That's great," said Dave. "I'll have to call Woody and congratulate him." "Jane has been so concerned about her age and not being married. All her college friends have husbands, many they met in college. Also, she had a long time relationship with a friend who was a high school classmate that ended when the fellow found some one else. It took

Jane a long time to get over that." "I'm glad for Jane. Have they set a date?" "No, I think it will depend on how much longer Jane wants to work as a stewardess." "I'll call Woody in the morning."

Dave's Apartment
8:30 AM September 13, 1949

Dave was on the phone talking to Woody Block. He offered congratulations and invited Woody to have breakfast with him on Wednesday or Thursday morning. "Thursday would work best for me Dave." "Okay, I'll meet you at 7:00 on Thursday morning at the Trucker's Restaurant in San Bruno." "Do you know where that is?" "Yes I do. The food is good."

Kiwanis Club Meeting
12:00 noon September 13, 1949

Dave was now being accepted as just a member of the club and not a celebrity. During happy dollar time, Dave had one for his 19th win in Seattle last Friday.

The Sponsored Youth chairman advised there would be a Saturday morning meeting of the Key Club at Washington High School on October first at 10:00 AM. Dave was asked if he would give a talk to the club members. He said, "I'll be glad to."

Ward, the Chairman of the Day introduced the speaker James Thompson from the Port of San Francisco. He talked about the changes likely to come as the result of the way products are shipped. It was just a hint at the big changes that would come as the result of containerization.

Sea Lions Stadium
Hollywood at San Francisco
9:05 PM September 13, 1949

The game had started ugly for Dave. The first two batters singled through the infield. The next batter sacrificed the runners to second and third. With one out and two on base Gordon Enson was coming to bat. Dave threw nothing but sinkers for a count of 2-2. The next pitch, a change, had Enson out in front of the pitch, but he got just enough for a foul tip.

The count was still 2-2. Next, Dave fed Enson another sinker that he hit on a line to Dave who had his glove in the right place. Dave threw to third, but the play had happened so fast the runner had not started to run and dove back to the bag, so no double play. Now there were two outs. The next batter for the Stars was Frank Hamilton. He was an aggressive hitter with big power, but had lots of strike outs. Dave started with a change that Hamilton lunged to hit but only got air. Strike one. The next pitch, a sinker was hit into center field that scored the runner from third. The runner from second tried to score, but a great thrown by Dino Roselli to catcher Jim Jarvis nailed the runner at home.

Dave staved off another bad start in the second inning. A double and a walk put two on with no outs. The next batter popped out to catcher Jim Jarvis. An infield hit loaded the bases. With the infield in, a pop single just beyond shortstop Les Short scored the runner from third. The bases were still loaded with one out. The Sea Lions needed a double play. Dave threw sinkers to get the ground ball double play they needed. The batter hit a line drive to a diving Billy May who made the throw to first while seated to double up the runner. The double play kept the score 2-0 for Hollywood.

Through the next four innings there was no scoring. Dave had improved his pitch location and had retired 12 batters in a row, but Hollywood still held the 2-0 lead. In the bottom of the sixth inning, the Lions started a rally but it was snuffed out by a double play. In the bottom of the eighth, with the score still 2-0 singles by Vaughn, Roselli and Roc produced a run. But the Lions left two runners on base. The score was now 2-1, with one more chance for the Lions. Dave pitched a no hit ninth inning on only nine pitches.

With the bottom of the order coming up, it didn't look promising for the Lions. However, Del Hoffman led off with a single. Ray Chess was not bunting and drew a walk. The Stars manager came to the mound and had a talk with his pitcher, and decided to leave him in the game. George Holly, the Stars pitcher responded by striking out Les Short. This brought Dave to the plate. Could he win another game with his bat?

The Hollywood pitcher threw nothing but sliders and breaking pitches, no fast balls to Dave. The count went to 1-2. Dave fouled off two pitches. Dave hit the next pitch down the third base line just inside the bag, past a diving third baseman. It scored two runs and the Sea Lions won the game 3-2. It was Dave's 20th win. This win could be credited to Dave's hitting.

The clubhouse was a loud place celebrating the come back win over the league leaders. Dave was exhausted. He had not felt good on the mound tonight and the results reflected his feelings. The San Francisco baseball writers all said again that if Dave didn't make the big leagues as a pitcher he could as a hitter.

Dave thanked all his teammates for their play. He led a big cheer for Dino Roselli. His great throw from center field to nail the Hollywood runner at home was critical.

Jill and Lisa had been given tickets in Walter Dent's box. They had been sitting among Walter's guests although he was not in attendance. When Dave came to the box Jill could tell he was drained. Lisa said, "Jill almost jumped out of the box when you hit the double Dave." He gave Jill a big hug. Jill suggested they pick up something to eat and take it Dave's apartment.

Unknown to the girls Fern had seen them entering Walter Dent's box and she was furious. She would have words with Sam Ducket tomorrow!

While they ate, Jill and Dave talked about the soon to end baseball season and what Dave's schedule would be. Dave said he wouldn't know until he registered at Stanford and received his class schedule. I will move back to Palo Alto as soon as the season is over. I must be out of my apartment by the 30th. Jill departed soon after they had eaten and Dave went to bed.

Trucker's Restaurant El Camino Real San Bruno, California 7:00 AM September 14, 1949

In this day and age the best restaurants, particularly for breakfast were at truck stops. Truck drivers were particular about food and if they stopped, that was the place to eat. Dave and Woody looked out of place dressed in coats and ties among the truck drivers, but the food was good and the servings were large.

Dave again gave Woody congratulations. "You and Jane make a great couple." "Thank you Dave. It's a good feeling, especially when you start getting close to 30." "I asked Jill if you had set a date, but she said Jane hasn't decided when she wants to cease being a stewardess." "That's true. I think she hesitates to go back to public relations work and hasn't come up with something else she'd like to do."

"What is your relationship with the future in-laws?" "Mrs. Graham is my friend. She is so happy that Jane is finally getting married, I can do no wrong. Foster Graham is a typical attorney, so we are not really on the same wave length. But he does fly United and I think he must have a 100,000 mile card, although he's never shown it to me. He does talk about meeting or knowing W.A. Patterson, the President of United Airlines. I'm sure they will plan a big wedding. My guess is in late spring." "That sounds good, Woody."

Dave's Apartment 9:30 AM September 14, 1949

Dave had returned from breakfast with Woody. He called Jill saying' "I have interesting news." "What's that," said Jill. "Orval Overwall has been released so Fern is gone! When you and Lisa sat in Walter Dent's box Fern was furious. The next morning she called Sam Ducket and unloaded on him for giving you and Lisa those seats. Sam had taken much abuse from Fern and this was the last straw. He complained to business manager I.T. Botumline and my source told me it went all the way up to Walter Dent. Walter met with Orval and told him he was being released now because of Fern. Otherwise the team would have kept him on the roster until the season was over. He did tell Orval that he would not be offered a contract for next year. I understand the wives are ecstatic! None of them liked being bossed around by Fern. I have no report on Fern."

They agreed on a lunch date for Friday in Burlingame. Jill would be on a flight over the weekend. Dave planned to attend the Sunday evening worship service at Temple Baptist Church.

After the win Tuesday night, The Sea Lions were confident they could continue to defeat the Stars. But it wasn't to be. Hollywood pounded three Lions pitchers for 15 hits and 10 runs, winning the game 10-2. Dave was hoping for a better effort tonight.

Sea Lions Stadium
Hollywood at San Francisco
9:30 PM September 15, 1949

Tonight, unlike last night, the Lions were getting good pitching from rookie Ray Littlejohn. After winning his first game against Oakland he had pitched well in Seattle. However, he left the game with a tie score and no decision. This was his third start since being called up from Yakima.

It was the first of the eighth inning with Hollywood leading 3-1. Hollywood had put two men on base via a single and a walk with no outs. It would be a test for Ray to get out of this situation. He struck out the next batter, the Stars passing up the sacrifice to move the runners. The next batter ran the count to 2-2 and then fouled off six pitches. On the next pitch he fouled out to catcher Jarvis.

Now there were two outs and runners on first and second. The next batter would be the real test. Ray fed the batter an assortment of pitches, starting with a slider, then a fast ball and then a change. This brought the count to 2-1. The batter fouled off the next pitch a good slider. What should Ray's next pitch be? With veteran catcher Jim Jarvis calling the pitches, all Ray had to do was pitch, not decide.

Jim signaled for a fast ball. Ray, thinking about what he had been told about overthrowing a fast ball in a tight situation, relaxed and threw an aspirin tablet fast ball by the batter who had a mighty swing and only hit air. The threat was killed and Ray had taken another big step in becoming a good pitcher.

In the bottom of the eighth inning the Sea Lions came to life with singles by Mike Roc and Del Hoffman, after a first out by Roselli. Ray Chess was the next batter. After running the count to 3-1, he singled to center, scoring Roc from second. With the score now 3-2, two men on base and one out, what would Tub Warren do? Shortstop Les Short, the team's weakest hitter was due up. Les was called back and Dave came to the on-deck circle. Hollywood changed pitchers, bringing in a right hander. The wisdom was that Dave was a weaker hitter batting left handed, since he was a natural right handed batter.

After his warm up the Stars pitcher had trouble getting the ball over the plate and threw three balls. On a 3 and 0 count, would Dave be given the green light to swing at the usual strike? He was, and he hit a line drive down the first base line that hit the turf just foul by an inch. 3-1 was now the count. After fouling off the next pitch, for a 3 and 2 count, Dave hit a drive into right field. The right fielder raced back and caught the ball just before he would run into the fence for a long out. Billy May struck out and while "It's not over until it's over," the game was a win for Hollywood 3-2 because the Lions went out 1-2-3 in the ninth inning. The "Twinks" now led 2-1in the series.

Jill's Apartment
1:15 PM September 16, 1949

Dave had taken Jill out for an early lunch. They were back in Jill's apartment, talking about what changes would occur after the baseball season was over in a little more than a week. Dave said, "I will continue to make appearances at Lavell Chevrolet and attend Kiwanis in San Francisco, when my Stanford class schedule allows. I look forward to attending worship services at Menlo Park Presbyterian Church and I want you to come with me when you can. I want to bowl on a team and I want to spend time with that beautiful lady with blonde hair named Jill." "Oh Dave, sometimes I wonder if we will ever satisfy ourselves that we should spend the rest of our lives together, and then you tell me something like that and I know I love you so much." "That's why I say them Jill. It's because I love you. Now, come and sit on my lap so I can give you some tender loving care"

Sea Lions Stadium
Hollywood at San Francisco
3:00 PM September 17, 1949

C.C. Chucker had pitched well the night before and the Sea Lions had defeated Hollywood 5-3. The Lions were gaining confidence by winning against the league leader. The win for the Lions had tied the series at 2 -2.

As they say in baseball, Dave was in a groove today. His sinker pitch was being hit into the ground for infield outs, and he had not allowed a hit through five innings. The Sea Lions had scratched out one run in the third inning for a 1-0 lead. In a tension filled game, Dave's no-hitter was ended in the seventh and that was the only hit he allowed. A number of fly balls were hit deep into the outfield, but were hauled down by Vaughn, Roselli, and Chess. When the last Hollywood batter grounded out to Billy May, all the Sea Lions and their fans heaved a sigh of relief. They had won another tight game 1 to 0 and Dave had won his 21st game, a one hitter. The Sea Lions now led in the series 3 games to 2.

First Presbyterian Church
9:30 AM September 18, 1949

After missing one week Dave was eager to pick up the study in Acts, now in the 25th chapter. Paul was still in prison in Caesarea. The Jewish leaders had come and made many charges against Paul. He appealed to the Emperor. A new Governor, Festus had replaced Felix. After conferring with his advisors, Festus said, "You have appealed to the Emperor, so to the Emperor you will go."

In the meantime, King Agrippa and his queen Bernice came to visit Festus. Festus asked Agrippa to hear Paul because he, Festus had no charges to send to the Emperor with Paul. He told Agrippa, "It seems unreasonable to me to send a prisoner without clearly indicating the charges against him." In the 26th chapter Paul will defend himself.

Sea Lions Stadium
Hollywood at San Francisco, Doubleheader
6:16 PM September 18, 1949

With a chance to win the series from the Stars, manager Warren had planned to have three pitchers ready to pitch. He might let each pitch three innings. Ed Dean started and pitched three shut out innings. With the Sea Lions leading 1-0, Al Armer came on in the fourth inning to pitch a 1-2-3 inning. The Lions added a run in the bottom of the fourth. It gave the Sea Lions a 2-0 lead. It looked like Warren's strategy was working. However, in the fifth inning the Stars scored one run to make it a 2-1 game. It stayed that way until the seventh inning.

The third Lions pitcher, Ray Ball had come into the game and the stars tied up the score at 2-2. The Lions could not generate any offense, so the ninth started with the game still tied. Ball walked the lead off batter. He was sacrificed to second. With one out, Ball got the next batter to pop out to second baseman Billy May. Now there were two outs and a man on second. With the count 0-2 on Gordon Enson, Ball made a mistake, leaving a curve hanging and Enson hit into centerfield for a single, scoring the run. The Stars now led 3-2. Ball struck out the next batter, but it was too late since the Lions mounted no rally in the bottom of the ninth. Hollywood won the game 3-2, tying the series 3-3.

C.C Chucker, the Sea Lions number two starting pitcher started the second game to go after the win and the series. He pitched well, but not good enough. Hollywood scored four runs in the third inning and it stood up for a 4-1 win and the series 4-3. The Sea Lions lost an opportunity to rally in the seventh inning because of poor base running.

The Sea Lions did gain in the standings, moving up to sixth place, one game ahead of Portland. Could they hold on to sixth place?

Dave's Apartment
9:15 AM September 19, 1949

Dave was on the phone talking to Jill. Dave had offered to take her to dinner at the famous Cliff House restaurant after his appearance at Lavell's tonight. "Well, I'll have to find out what my other boy friend is offering tonight." Jill said it while finding it difficult to not laugh. "Well," Dave said, playing along "You'll just have to call him up and ask him." Then Dave went silent. "Dave, Dave," Jill said, "Are you still there?" "Oh I'm here, waiting for you to make your call" About that time Jill could not hold out any longer and started to laugh about the same time as Dave did. They both went into hysterics. When they finally stopped laughing, Jill sheepishly said, "I would love to go to the Cliff House with you for dinner." "Oh, I'm so glad." That started more laughter.

Finally, Dave said, "I think we should end this conversation before we come down with laughing sickness." "I agree. I should meet you where?' Meet me at my apartment at 8:15 so we won't confuse Del again." "Ok, I'll be there."

Dave always got a lift by talking to Jill. He had been down this morning because the team had lost the double header yesterday.

Dave was thinking about starting his packing to vacate the apartment next week. He planned to take a load to Palo Alto next Monday or Tuesday. His mother had called with information about his Stanford registration schedule. He had to be there on Wednesday, September 28.

Lavell Chevrolet
8:00 PM September 19, 1949

Dave had just ended a conversation with a potential customer and turned him over to Del. He hoped Del made a sale after the trick he and Jill played on him last week. He hadn't said anything to Dave about it, so Dave decided Del didn't have a clue about them.

He was now off to his apartment to meet Jill.

The Cliff House
1090 Point Lobos Avenue
San Francisco, California
9:00 PM September 19, 1949

San Franciscans dined late. Any dinner date before 8:00 PM was not in style. So Jill and Dave were right in style having arrived just before 9:00. Dave had a college classmate who had gone to work for Douglas Aircraft in Santa Monica. He came to San Francisco to take a stewardess friend to dinner at a very fancy restaurant. The friend was not a San Franciscan, so she didn't object when Justin made a reservation for 6:30 PM on a Saturday evening. They arrived to a scene of the waitresses sitting around relaxing and waiting for the evening work to began. They had a dinner with no one else in the restaurant, and deathly silence. Justin was from Nebraska.

Jill and Dave had a delicious dinner with a great view of the Pacific Ocean. Jill said, "I read an article on the sports page about baseball players being sold to a major league team for money and sometimes players. Are baseball players sold just like cattle?" "Yes Jill, they are sold. Maybe not exactly like cattle. Ball players are not sold by the pound, but based on performance. Except for Los Angeles, teams in the Pacific Coast League, sell players to major league teams for money and players. Los Angeles is owned by the Chicago Cubs, so their players would just be promoted to the Cubs."

"Dave, will you be sold to a major league team?" "I have no idea Jill, but I doubt it. Most baseball teams and their scouts look for fast ball or strike out pitchers. I am not a popular style of pitcher in most baseball expert's view. Some teams don't have a good defense, something I need to be successful. Some have small .baseball parks with small outfields so they don't want batters hitting the ball. They want strike out pitchers. Even pitchers who walk lots of batters are preferred to control pitchers whose best pitch is a sinker. Also, I've only had a short four month season. That's not much professional experience."

Sacramento Solons Baseball Park
Sacramento, California
San Francisco at Sacramento
9:30 PM September 21, 1949

Dave was having another good game of sinker ball. The Solons got just two hits through seven innings and the Sea Lions had a 4-0 lead. The Solons played in what is called a "band box" stadium. It had short fences, 300 feet to right and 290 to left field. Lots of home runs are hit here that would be fly ball outs in Sea Lions Stadium. Dave had hit one over the center field fence in his first at bat. It was a solo home run with no one on that made the score 4-0.

In the ninth inning the Lions added two more runs and the final score was 6-0. It was the team's 89th win and Dave's 22nd.

In thanking his team mates Dave commented, "It was just like pitching in a basketball court the field was so small." It was the second win of the series, the Sea Lions having won the opener last night 8-2. Dave expected the team to end the season winning games.

The California State Capital Building
Capital Park on L Street
Sacramento, California
10:00 AM September 22, 1949

Dave, Billy May, and two other young players were on a tour of the capital building. It was a first for Dave. He had visited Sacramento in 1937 when his dad was President of the California Newspapers Publishers Association. The family had spent a day at the State Fair. In the afternoon they had sat in the Governor's box to watch the horse races. Dave and Pam wanted to go on the rides for which they had been given free tickets. They finally did that after the races. Dave had never been in any capital or legislative building, so it was a new experience. The tour was interesting and gave Dave a little knowledge of the legislature.

Room 950
Saint Francis Hotel
San Francisco, California
2:00 PM September 22, 1949

In this large suite of the hotel, four men with big baseball responsibility were meeting. The players were Walter Dent, President and major owner of the San Francisco Sea Lions. James Whitlock, Esq., the attorney for the Sea Lions, Donald Newton, General Manager of the New York Dukes of the American League and Lester W. Locke, the attorney for the Dukes. The subject at hand was negotiations for the purchase of Dave Mason by the New York Dukes.

The purchase had been recommended by Luke Devore, the Dukes West Coast scout who had such a good record in finding and evaluating baseball talent that his recommendations were rarely challenged. He felt so strongly about his recommendation that the Dukes buy Dave Mason that he traveled to New York so he could make his recommendation in person to Donald Newton and Fred Duke. Newton had questioned this recommendation more than usual because Dave Mason was not the power pitcher most teams desired, and he had less than a year of professional baseball. However, Luke Devore had followed Dave's pitching progress since he was a skinny 14 year old and was convinced he was a future pitching superstar.

The big issue today, was not over money. That had been settled after much give and take. Now it was over the players the Dukes would send to the Sea Lions. As an independent baseball team with no working agreement with a major league team, players were critical to supplement the Sea Lions' small farm system.

Donald Newton had a list of players divided into three categories. Players they would send to the Sea Lions, players they might send to the Lions and players they didn't want to send to the Sea Lions. Walter Dent wanted one or more of the last group. Dent's priority was pitchers.

Finally, at almost 5:00 PM a compromise was reached and the Sea Lions got one pitcher from the highly rated list, one other pitcher plus two position players. Dent and Newton shook hands on the deal and the attorneys went to work on the contract and bill of sale.

No announcement would be made until Monday, September 26 at a news conference. Dave Mason would be advised Sunday evening when the team returned from Sacramento. Luke Devore would represent the New York Dukes at the press conference.

Donald Newton and Locke had registered in the hotel under assumed names representing a non-baseball company owned by Reggie Duke. Dent and Whitlock entered the hotel separately from a side entrance. The Sea Lions wanted to have a good public relations story about this, and did not want a newspaper to break it first.

Sacramento Solons Baseball Park
San Francisco at Sacramento
6:15 PM September 25, 1949

After winning the first two games of the series, the Sea Lions had lost on Thursday and Friday nights. The Lions had won the Saturday afternoon game, so it came down to the Sunday double header that would determine the series winner. The Solons won today's first game. That made the 7 inning second game the series decider. Dave was the starting pitcher.

Dave pitched probably his best game of the season. He threw only 62 pitches, for an efficiently rating of 2.93. In the first inning the Sea Lions scored three runs. Dave had hit a double and drove in a run. That was all the scoring, the Sea Lions winning 3-0. Dave had allowed only two hits and the game took only one hour and 14 minutes. It was Dave's 23rd win.

The Sea Lion players were all happy to end the season on a winning note, even though they didn't have a winning record. Dave went to every player and thanked each for their effort and support. He even led a cheer for the Sea Lions. The season record of 89 wins and 98 losses earned the team sixth place in the PCL, four games ahead of Portland.

Dave's pitching was mainly responsible for the season's record. He had won 23 and lost only 2 games. His ERA was .881, less than 1 run per 9 inning game. His batting average was .318. In 66 at bats he had seven doubles and six home runs. His slugging average was .590. It had been quite a season for a rookie from a small unknown college baseball program.

San Francisco International Airport
8:55 PM September 25, 1949

The Sea Lions' plane had landed and the team was on the bus ready to travel to the stadium. Tub Warren came down the aisle and told Dave that as soon as arrived at the stadium he was to go to the clubhouse and then to Walter Dent's office. Dave wondered what it was all about but didn't ask.

Entering the club's executive offices, Dave was met by Walter Dent and James Whitlock, the team's attorney. Dent wasted no time in telling Dave that he had been sold to the New York Dukes for $125,000 and four players." "Unbelievable," Dave said. "Oh it's believable, Tub Warren said as he entered the office. No pitcher I have known or even heard of has made the impact you've made as a rookie. I'm just so glad you've done it for the Sea Lions. It has been a privilege to coach and know you Dave. You are a young man mature beyond your age." "Thank you very much Tub."

"Some time after the World Series when Vic Marko comes back to town, I will set up a lunch so you can meet him and he can give you some pointers about living in New York. Have you ever been there?" "Yes, but I was only nine years old. That would be great Tub. Thank you."

Walter Dent advised Dave there will be a press conference tomorrow morning at 11:00 AM. It will be in the Sir Francis Drake Hotel. I don't have the room, but it will be posted. So come early in your Sunday suit. "I'll be there with bells on." They all laughed. "We want this to be a good public relations event for the team, so we don't want any leaks to the newspapers. That's the reason Tub had you go into the club house before we came here to make sure the writers weren't hanging around."

"It's okay to tell your dad and Jill, but mums the word." "I understand." "Is your car here Dave?" "No, I came in a cab." Tub said, "I'll take him home, it's on my way."

Dave's Apartment
10:35 PM September 25, 1949

Jill had asked Dave to call her when he returned from Sacramento. It was later than he expected, but he called anyway. Jill was waiting for his call. She said, "Great game, Dave." "You listened?" "Yes, I got here when the game was in the second inning. I couldn't believe how fast the game was played." "That's the way I like to play them. No standing around waiting for the pitcher to pitch." "How are you Jill?" "I'm fine we had a good flight today. It was full but right on time."

I have something to tell you that you can't repeat until after a press conference tomorrow morning that starts at 11:00. I have been sold to the New York Dukes of the American League." "Oh that's amazing Dave. Were you surprised?" "I could hardly believe it. That's all I can tell you now. If you want to, you could attend the press conference. It's being held in the Sir Frances Drake Hotel. I don't have a room name but it will be posted." "I wouldn't be a distraction would I?" "No, but you may be the only lady in the room." "I think I'll skip it Dave. You can tell me all about it when it's over" "Yes I can do that." "Okay, please call me as soon as you get to your apartment." "I certainly will Jill." "I love you Dave" "I love you too Jill. Good night."

In the morning Dave had called home and talked to his mother. Ann was excited about the news and told Dave to call his dad as soon as he hung up. He did and gave him the news "That's surprising Dave." "Yes it is. I'll be down to see you in the next day or two. I'll let you know when I'm coming. I have to register at Stanford on Wednesday." "Yes, I remember."

Franciscan Room
Francis Drake Hotel
11:00 AM September 26, 1949

The room was crowded with baseball writers, radio sportscasters, a few people from the news media, television, and just interested members of the sports media. As soon as the press conference was announced, rumors flew about the subject. The Sea Lions seldom called a press conference so this must be something big! The last one was when Walter Dent bought the team. Was he selling the team? The team had done well after a fourth place finish in 1945, the year Dent purchased the club. A pennant in 1946 and two second place finishes in 1947 and 48 had turned the club around. This year's sixth place was the lowest since Dent took over the ownership. As soon as the press started to assemble and saw Dave Mason sitting in the first row, they expected it had something to do with him.

Walter Dent came to the podium. "Thank you for coming on such short notice. As you know, major events in baseball do not stay secret for long and I wanted this announcement to be the original. I am pleased and proud to announce that the New York Dukes of the American League have purchased Dave Mason for cash and four players. Two of the players are pitchers.. The announcement produced lots of mummers in the audience. Dave will join the Dukes in spring training next year. Now, let me introduce Mr. Luke Devore, the West Coast scout for the Dukes. Before Devore could start speaking some members of the media ran from the room to telephone the news to their papers, radio stations or news service.

"Thank you Walter. Gentlemen, I first saw Dave Mason play in a baseball game when he was 14 years old. When I saw him pitch, I was amazed at his control at such an early age. When batters began hitting the sinker pitch into the ground for infield outs, I was convinced that this fellow was a once in a lifetime gem. This would be true particularly if he continued to work hard on his pitching. I was even more convinced when I talked with Dave and asked him how he developed such good control at his young age. He said he had been pitching to a unique target for four years, throwing 100 balls five days a week, except when he was pitching. A fellow who worked that hard at developing control could be a great pitcher."

"I tried to sign him out of high school and again when he finished college, but failed. Finally, after an unprecedented first season in professional baseball, I got a hit, and batting .333 is not bad. Dave, please come forward so I can put this New York Dukes shirt on you. Now Dave, it's your turn." "Thank you Mr. Devore."

"My thoughts go back to that Sunday school picnic many years ago when an elderly gentleman watched me throw the baseball and said I had a natural sinker ball. But he told me I must develop control if I wanted to be a sinker ball pitcher because batters would lay off the sinker if they could. To this day I don't know who he was, although there has been much speculation. Whoever he was I want to thank him. The advice he gave me on how to develop control and its importance was golden. I want to thank my high school coach, the late Bert Briley, my college coaches Captain B.B. Bell and Bob Trotter, and all my teammates through all the years of baseball."

"I want to thank you Walter and Sea Lions for signing me to my first pro contract. For me a sinker ball pitcher to be successful I must have good infielders, because I keep them busy. The infielders of the Sea Lions made my season. If they had not been so good, I wouldn't be here today. I thank you fellows and all my teammates. I just wish we could have won more games for Tub Warren, a very good manager. Thank you Tub for having the confidence in me to allow me to pitch on three days rest and to be a hitter. Finally, to you the members of the press and radio, you have treated me swell and I do like newspapers." This brought a laugh, since most were aware that Dave's dad was a newspaper publisher and owner.

Walter Dent thanked Dave and then asked Manager Drew Warren to say a few words. "Thank you Walter. It has been a once in a lifetime opportunity to have a player of Dave Mason's ability, work ethic and character on our team. I have never observed or even heard about a player who has had the impact that Dave has had in his first, not even full year of professional baseball. Dave is the ultimate team player and you haven't seen all the small things he has done to lift the spirit of this team. Dave is not a holler guy, but he has a quiet impact on his teammates"

"Some players on other teams in the PCL have been critical of Dave talking to and encouraging young players before games. I can assure you when the game starts Dave is a bulldog in his effort to win a baseball game. Some of you may remember what Dave's response was following the loss of his first game. 'It was bad, I lost the game.' I wish you all the success in the world next year in the American League. Please come back and see us Dave."

Walter Dent again thanked the members of the press and radio.

Immediately, the members of the press crowded around Dave where he was seated and started asking questions.

Q "Did you see this coming, Dave?"

A "No, I had recently talked about my future in baseball and I thought I would be here next year."

Q "Why did you think that?"

A "Because I've had only four months of experience in professional baseball. I thought I would need more."

Q "Why do you think the New York Dukes had such an interest in you?"

A "Mr. Devore told me a few years ago that the Dukes' manager liked sinker ball pitchers because the team always had a good defense and their stadium had a big outfield"

Q "The New York Dukes are in the World Series again. Will you be rooting for them?

A "Sure I will."

Q "The Dukes have at least four good starting pitchers plus others. Do you think you can break into the starting rotation?"

A "Baseball experts have said, "A team can't have too much pitching. I'll do my best."

Q "I understand you will be attending Stanford graduate school this fall. Will that interfere with the baseball season?"

A "No, I will complete a quarter in my study for a master's degree. Then I'll go to spring training. I plan to continue my study next year after the season is over."

The writers and reporters thanked Dave.

Chapter Nineteen

Jill's Apartment

5:00 PM September 26, 1949

DAVE HAD CALLED Jill as soon as he returned to his apartment from the press conference. He said, "It was good you didn't attend. There may have been a couple of female radio assistants there, but that's all. You might have had to answer some questions asked by reporters. I'll tell you all about it when I see you."

"My Lavell Chevrolet appearance has been changed to Tuesday this week. Now that the season is over they want to try out other days to see if more show room lookers come. I need to load up the car and run some errands, so if I come to your apartment about 5:00 we can go have dinner later." "That's fine Dave."

Dave arrived to a streamer and confetti welcome by the three girls in celebration of his sale to the Dukes. Jill had put them up to it. They had even made up a sign, "Dave Mason Major Leaguer." Dave said, "I'm floored, let me sit down." Jane said, "Jill told us that your sale was a big surprise." "Yes it was. I talked to Jill about it just last week, saying it wasn't going to happen."

Dave took Jill to the Benjamin Franklin Hotel where she had a glass of wine and Dave ordered ginger ale. First, Dave gave Jill a report on the press conference. "There were lots of reporters there and Walter Dent was happy that it was a big surprise to them. There was no scoop." "The more I thought about it after your phone call last night the more excited I got," said Jill. I thought this could result in our getting married because you wouldn't want to go off and leave me here while you are in New York."

"For just that reason I must tell you about the life of a major league baseball player Jill. You need to know so you can decide if you might want to be the wife of one." "Is that a sneaky proposal?" Jill said with a grin. "No, it's information you should know. I don't know everything, but I know the basics. First the schedule is different than what the PLC plays. The series are only two to four games long so there is more traveling. Road trips can last two weeks. The season lasts from early March when spring training starts in Florida, until the end of September. If your team is in the World Series it could last another two weeks."

"So you live in New York for seven months and then come home for five months. The big problem comes when you start a family and kids become school age."

"There are some other considerations too. The weather in the summer is hot and humid, not like California. Dad took me to New York and Connecticut when I was nine years old and I remember how hot it was. Also, I will have to make the team in spring training and could be optioned to a Dukes farm team. However the potential is unlimited. Bob Ball, the pitcher makes between 80,000 and 100,000 dollars." "That much," Jill said. "Yes."

"When will you have to go to spring training?" "It will be some time in February. I'll know better when I meet with Vic Marko, a member of the Dukes." "Dave, I want to be where you are, so when it's the right time I'll put in for a change of base to New York." "That will likely be some time in the spring. In the meantime I will be here for the next four and a half months with no traveling and no baseball games so we can enjoy our time together. I do want you to attend worship services with me at Menlo Park Presbyterian Church. Our biggest need now is to be together on faith. It's not only important in our relationship, but is vital for children."

Jill said, "This week I fly Wednesday and Thursday, home Friday and Saturday and out again on Sunday. Maybe I can trade with Rene and go to church with you. Her boy friend has to work some weekends so she doesn't mind flying on Sunday. I'll check and let you know." "Good, we could celebrate Saturday night and hopefully attend church together on Sunday. I'll think of something different to do Saturday evening".

Following dinner, Dave drove into the hills above Burlingame. He found a good location to park and invited Jill to sit on his lap. "Jill, right now I want to spend the rest of my life with you. But I want our future to be good, without problems because we didn't solve them before marriage. My family has had a history of divorce that I won't go into now and I have heard about the pain it causes. I don't want either of us to be hurt so potential problems must be dealt with before we make a commitment to each other. What are your thoughts about what I have said?"

"You know that I agree, it's just that I love you so much that some times I don't think about real life problems. We haven't had any real disagreements that I can think of." "That's true, but it could be because I have not pushed the things I'm concerned about. But let's not push them under the rug and then wish we hadn't." "I agree Dave, and as I have said before, you are so mature for a young man." "Thank you Jill and now how about letting me romance you." "Romance me Dave."

Jill took her usual position on Dave's lap. They had been doing this almost from the start of their relationship. Because of their relative height, they were face to face when Jill sat on Dave's lap. Jill was experiencing very high excitement tonight. "Dave, you have me so excited tonight." "Oh my Jill should I stop kissing you?" "No, don't stop Dave. I love your kissing and romancing. "I get excited too. What should we do Jill? I like to romance you so much by hugging and kissing you," Dave said. "Our solution Dave is to agree on our remaining concerns, and get married." "I'm all for that."

Dave thought he should search the Bible for some direction regarding his romancing of Jill.

The Mason Residence 9:00 AM September 27, 1949

Dave had arrived home after midnight and had gone right to bed. He had been up at 7:00 in the morning to greet his dad and go out for breakfast with him. Dave gave his dad the story on his sale to the Dukes, and the press conference. George Mason said, "The sports editor of the Times attended the press conference and had a brief article on the sale in yesterday's paper. He will do a more complete article today. However, he has standing instructions not to over do it." "I understand Dad."

George Mason said, "I'm still talking to Bill Fox about the radio commercials. I have put off any agreement until the end of the season because your mother was sure you would be sold to the Dukes. Your sale raises your value in regards to these commercials. I'll call Fox, and I think we can wrap it up." "That sounds good dad. Since there will be no more baseball pay checks, I can use the money."

"It's been a long time since we've talked about world news. I learned so much during those family diners while I was in high school. What do you think about Russia exploding an atomic bomb?" "I suppose it was inevitable but not so soon. I don't think it will improve our relations with the Soviet Union." Dave said, I read that a congressman has charged the Atomic Energy Commission with a lack of security." "Yes, I read that too," said George "I don't know how true it is. We live in a continuously changing world Dave .The communists have taken over in China. What country will be next?"

Dave had returned home and was now talking with his mother, giving her the story. "I'm so proud of you Dave. You have accomplished something few have done." "Thank you very much mother."

"How is Pam doing on her typing?" "So far so good. Her class starts at 9:00 each morning. It's an accelerated course. She wants to get to Chicago as soon as possible."

"Now I must get back to the City to attend Kiwanis and do an appearance at Lavell tonight. I'll be back tonight so I can get out to Stanford for registration tomorrow. "Good Dave, it will be nice to have you here. The house will not seem so empty with both you and Pam here. We will go to Rickey's for dinner tomorrow night." "That sounds good." On his way out of town, Dave stopped at Mac's Smoke Shop to pick up all the San Francisco papers so he could read what had been written about his sale to the Dukes. Mac's is a Palo Alto institution that is still in business today.

Kiwanis Club Meeting 12:00 noon September 27, 1949

Dave received many congratulations from the members for becoming a major leaguer. Dave thanked everyone. He said, "I will order a directory so I can make up as much as possible when I'm in New York and on the road. I'll try to get to all the meetings while I'm still in California. For my season and the sale to the Dukes, I have a happy $20.00." This resulted in a big cheer from the members.

President Kenneth reminded the members about the Key Club meeting on Saturday morning at Washington High School. Dave will talk for about 15 minutes.

The program speaker, James Donovan, Vice President of Bank of America was introduced by Steve, the chairman of the day. Donavan's topic was, "Will the Economy Improve in 1950?" Donovan thought so.

Following the meeting Dave went to his apartment to clean out more stuff he had accumulated in just four months and load into his car. Jill called, and Dave said he would take her to dinner after his appearance at Lavell Chevrolet. But Jill said, "How about a candle light dinner here? Both the girls will be on flights" "You've sold me." It will likely be 9:00 before I get there." "That's okay. Just call me when you are about to leave." "I will and I'll see you soon."

Dave got out his bible and the Phillips translation to learn what he could to help him in the romancing of Jill. His Bible referred him to I Thessalonians Chapter 4, verses 3 and 4. They said that you should avoid sexual immorality. And you should learn to control your body in a way that is holy and honorable. Not in passionate lust.

The Christian faith is incompatible with sexual promiscuity. Christians should please God. Dave was glad to know he had made the correct decision four years ago, not to have sex with Jill. At the time he was not a Christian, and had made the decision for practical reasons, and how it would affect his relationship with Jill. The scripture confirmed he had made the right decision. He would have to cool his romancing of Jill, so they wouldn't get so excited.

Lavell Chevrolet
7:30 PM September 27, 1949

The crowd tonight was larger than ever with more adults in the show room. After giving out the supply of baseballs, Dave talked to show room lookers. He passed three of them on to salesmen.

Bill Fox was pleased with the Tuesday turnout and asked Dave if they could change the regular day to Tuesday. "I'll let you know as soon as I register for Stanford classes tomorrow. I would prefer Tuesday because that's my Kiwanis meeting day. I'll call you tomorrow."

Jill's Apartment
10:15 PM September 27, 1949

Dave had arrived a little after 9:00. Jill was dressed in new house dress for cooking and she had an apron bedecked with flowers. She looked like a young lady in a magazine advertisement. The dinner by candle light featured meat loaf in tomato sauce, mashed potatoes and carrots, Dave's favorite foods. This was preceded by a different fruit salad. They were about to have desert, an ice cream pie. Dave was overwhelmed. He had been to the apartment for dinner in the past, but the food had never been so good. "My complements to the chef," Dave said. "When you retire from flying, you could be a chef."

"The only chef I want to be is your permanent chef Dave, hint, hint."

Dave helped Jill clear the table and dried the dishes. Then, they had coffee in the living room. Jill asked Dave just what he would be doing now in addition to attending classes at Stanford University." Dave said, "I will spend all the time I can with a certain young lady when she's not flying off some place" "Oh Dave, you flatter me so much. What will you do when that young lady is flying off somewhere?" "I will make a weekly appearance at Lavell hopefully on Tuesday and attend the Kiwanis meeting the same day. I would like to bowl on a team so I can get my exercise. I hope to spend some time at the ranch riding the horses." "I think that certain young lady will have to fly more if you're going to do all that." "Never fear, the lady is first priority!" "Oh thank you Dave, I was getting worried." Again they both broke out in laughter. "You know Jill we could form a comedy team and go on the radio, maybe even that new fangled thing they call TV." That produced more laughter. Jill did wonder If Dave was going to be a workaholic, something she had heard talked about on flights.

Later with the lights down low they had danced to records. Dave had decided to cool their necking after the other night. Dave departed after midnight.

Room 35
Stanford Quad
Stanford University
9:00 AM September 28, 1949

Dave was meeting with his advisor professor, James English a member of the College of Engineering faculty. Professor English welcomed Dave, and he had done his homework because he knew much about Dave. They talked about what Dave wanted to achieve in his master's program. Dave related his experience in discovering consulting engineering during the SAE meeting. "I want to broaden my education so I may have the opportunity to enter the field of consulting as a young engineer." "Good Dave. I'm sure we can design a program for you to meet that goal. We have relationships with local consulting engineering firms that can give you on-the-job experience." "That would be great." "For your first quarter, I suggest the following courses that I have marked. Since your mechanical study has been specialized in the aviation field, you need to have that area broadened. The classes and schedule are listed." Dave reviewed the list that included the following:

Strength of Materials Review: MWF 9:00 AM.

Advanced Mechanical Engineering: MWThF 10:00 AM.

Introduction to Heating & Ventilating Engineering: MWThF 1:00 PM.

A Study of Mechanical Engineering Occupations & Requirements: Th 9:00-11:00 AM.

Dave said, "The schedule is just fine with me." "Good, you can go sign up for these classes. Please feel free to contact me at any time to discuss anything regarding your study." "Thank you."

As soon as Dave returned home he called Bill Fox at Lavell Chevrolet to tell him the change to Tuesday for his appearances was fine. "Great, Dave. I'll see you next Tuesday."

Jill called about 5:00 PM and was happy to report she had been able to trade her flight so she could go to church with Dave on Sunday. "I'll have to work extra flights next week, but that's okay." "That's great Jill."

Rickey's
6:30 PM September 28, 1949

Mr. and Mrs. Mason, Pam, and Dave were seated at their table. Ann and Pam ordered a drink, Dave and his dad ordered ginger ale. Dave wanted to get to the food, so they soon lined up at the smorgasbord table. As usual the food was super and Dave had to restrain himself from making a second trip around the table. He could not eat all he wanted anymore without putting on weight.

George Mason asked Dave how his finances were. "My finances are in good shape. Please tell me what you want me to pay for room and board or just room and I'll pay for my meals." George said, "I think room and board of $45.00 per month will be adequate and we won't keep track of meals. You won't be here for all the meals anyway." "That's true." "So far I have earned $575.00 for my appearances at Lavell. Added to that is the $25.00 per publication for the advertisement I was in. It ran for 14 days in two papers. I have picked up about $60.00 from bowling competition. That's a total of $1,335.00. It has paid for all my entertaining during the baseball season. I haven't had to spend any of my salary on that. So I've saved about half of my salary or about $2,000.00."

Dave had taken the figures from a small notebook he had carried since he started winning money from bowling at the age of 14. This was his third book. Dave's dad congratulated him on his financial management. "As I have told you in the past, it's a lot easier to make money than it is to hold on to it. You are doing a good job Dave. Keep it up."

Pam said, "You were in newspaper advertisements?" "Yes and next will be radio advertisements. Your dumb brother isn't so dumb any more" "Now Dave," his mother said." "I apologize. I just couldn't pass up that dig."

Dave's Apartment
10:15 AM September 30, 1949

Dave had employed a cleaning lady to clean the apartment. He was ready to leave for Palo Alto with the last of his clothes and belongings loaded in his car. Dave had made a suggestion to his mother that he set up his TV in the big bedroom at the end of the hall. Even with a bed in the room, there was plenty of room for the TV and chairs. Ann had agreed. Now he was off to Palo Alto.

Broadway Theater
Burlingame, California
9:30 PM September 30, 1949

The movie, A Connecticut Yankee staring Bing Crosby and Rhonda Fleming had just ended. Crosby was always good and Rhonda was a beautiful girl.

Over a cup of coffee, Dave said, "I have tomorrow evening planned." "Oh what new and exciting things are we going to do?"

"It's a secret and I'll never tell." "Okay for you," as Jill mustered a pout, trying to keep a straight face, while Dave just grinned at her. Finally, she couldn't suppress it any longer and broke out in laughter which Dave joined. "You always defeat my stories with that grin of yours." "The grin is why we are together isn't it?' "Yes, Yes!" It was Dave's big grin and smile that first attracted Jill to him in the Snow White Creamery in San Luis Obispo four years ago. "I'll pick you up at 5:30 tomorrow afternoon and we will go celebrate our fourth anniversary together a little early. Also, we will celebrate Dave Mason's sale to the New York Dukes." When Dave took her home, Jill was still trying to get clues about what they would do tomorrow night, just to give Dave a bad time. She didn't want him to get the "big head" over this major league baseball business. Dave closed off her questions by kissing her repeatedly. Then he was off to Palo Alto.

Washington High School
600 32nd Avenue
San Francisco, California
10:20 AM October 1, 1949

The meeting started just like a Kiwanis meeting with the Flag salute, a song, God Bless America and a prayer. The Kiwanis members attending were introduced by the Chairman of Sponsored Youth.

Later, Dave was introduced and said "Good morning. This morning I want to talk to you about encouragement. But first I want to take your picture so I can remember this occasion.

You may need some encouragement in your life or you may know a friend who may be a fellow student who could use some. When I was in high school I was a poor student. I wasn't interested in school work because I had no interest in the subjects of most of the classes I was required to take. My interests were sports, particularly baseball, learning about the Navy so I could volunteer when I finished high school. The war was still on."

"My dad always gave me encouragement no matter how poor my report card was. He had me tutored so I could pass geometry. Since

I didn't read any books, only the newspaper and mainly the sports page, my reading speed was slow. To increase my reading speed I was sent to a summer reading school at Stanford University."

Dave then told the story of his attending Samuel Gompers Trade School; and Cal Poly. "The odds of my earning a degree in engineering were not good when I started. But the interest I had developed in the classes I was taking allowed me to overcome the odds. I encourage you, and ask you to encourage others in school work and in all aspects of life. What you are learning by helping others, particularly children, as a member of your Key Club will help you throughout your life. Thank you for the opportunity to talk to you this morning." Dave received a big round of applauds. The Key Club President thanked Dave and gave him a Key Club pen.

Stanford Stadium
Stanford University
2:30 PM October 1, 1949

Stanford was playing Michigan in the football game today. George Mason had to attend an afternoon meeting, so Dave took his mother to the game and they were sitting in the press box.

Michigan, still running the single wing offense, ran all over the Indians. Reverses to the right halfback were devastating. Every time Michigan needed 10 yards they got it with the reverse. The final score was 27 to 7 for Michigan.

Merry-go-round bar
Fairmont Hotel
7:30 PM October 1, 1949

Dave had brought Jill to the Fairmont Hotel for her surprise. Driving into the garage, Jill said, "I didn't know we were staying over night. I didn't bring my suitcase." She wanted to tease Dave, knowing what his response would be." Dave, going along with her tease said, "How should we register, Mr. and Mrs. Garber?" "Oh Dave, you always foil my teasing." "You pull my leg Jill Garber and I'll pull yours." Jill laughed first before Dave could muster one.

Jill had not been in the hotel previously and when they walked out of the elevator she was amazed at the bright lobby carpet. Dave led Jill to the merry-go-round bar. It was a real merry-go-round that moved very slowly. You didn't have to ride a horse to drink, but they were there. Jill said, "This is a first for me. I've never seen anything like it."

Tonga Room
Fairmont Hotel
8:15 PM October 1, 1949

The Tonga room was created from the former hotel swimming pool. In the 1940s the hotel sponsored a girls swimming team that was a leader in national competition. The star of the team was Ann Curtis.

The Tonga room is located around the pool. There was a float in the pool that held the band that played south sea island music. The real show was when there was thunder and lighting and it rained into the pool to reproduce a tropical storm. Dave had requested a poll-side table so they would be close to the storm and the music. Also, he thought it would restrict the view that people would have of them. They had a nice dinner and the only request for an autograph was from the bus boy, who said he wasn't supposed to ask, but could accept one if offered. Dave signed a menu for him, and was thanked by a grinning boy.

"Now, Miss. Garber, would my queen like to go up to the Venetian Room and Dance the light fantastic." "If I am your Queen Mr. Mason, yes I'll dance, but only with you, not that light fantastic!" Almost on queue, they both laughed. "You must be prepared to be recognized and pointed at, my picture having been in those Chevrolet ads for two weeks in two papers." "They will be looking at you, not me." "Ha ha, you are much better looking than I am." "You jest, Prince Charming. In any case, lead the way."

Dave was right; he was immediately recognized as they entered the Venetian Room, as the host said, "Good evening Mr. Mason."

"Good evening, we came to dance to Mr. Garber's music." "I would like a table near the wall please." They were seated at a table near the north wall of the room, where they would not be surrounded by people. The Mr. Garber Dave mentioned was Jan Garber, the band leader of the band that played very danceable music and appeared in hotels most of the time. When Jill heard him say it, she thought he was making "funny."

After dancing a few numbers they returned to their table and Dave soon spied Hattie Arnold, who was San Francisco's number one gossip columnist. He had never met Hattie, but had seen her picture on her column and true to her name she wore wild hats. Hattie was headed Dave's way. In a low voice, Dave said, "Be prepared for Hattie the gossip, she's heading this way."

"Dave Mason, I've wanted to meet you, and this must be Jill." "How do you do Hattie? Yes this is the beautiful Jill Garber, no relation to our band leader." "How do you do Jill? Are you out celebrating your ascending to the major leagues of baseball Dave?" "Yes, you could say that." "Jill, I understand that you and Dave have been a couple since college days." "Yes, that's true." "And you are a United Airline Stewardess based in San Francisco." That's also true." "Dave, what do you plan to do until you report for spring training." "I'm going back to college at Stanford." "Oh my you are a scholar baseball player." "You said it Hattie." "Well thanks, Dave and Jill. Read about yourself in my column Hattie's Hat."

"How did she know all about us Dave?" "She talks to hundreds of people each day, mostly by telephone and I'm sure she has talked with Stanton S. First the senior baseball writer in San Francisco, and for her paper, the San Francisco Tribune. First is the guy who had a tantrum when I gave my first interview to Dan White, that young writer for the Times. His motto is, First will be first." "You've never told me about that." "I didn't?" "No, I don't remember it" "Well, I'll tell you about it sometime, but now, let's dance."

They danced until midnight and then were on their way to Palo Alto. Jill was staying at the Mason home tonight so she could go to church with Dave in the morning. They arrived a little after 1:00 AM, and after a few good night kisses they went to their rooms.

Menlo Park Presbyterian Church
11:00 AM October 2, 1949

After breakfast, Dave had driven with Jill to the church, arriving early for a good parking place. Jill looked like she had just stepped out of I. Magnin in a new dress. Jill really knows how to dress, Dave thought. The music by the choir was great. It had been a long time since Dave had been in a morning worship service.

The sermon, preached by The Rev. Don Emerson Hall, was about the story of Nicodemus from John, Chapter 3. In verse 2 Nicodemus said… "We know that thou art a teacher come from God: for no man can do these miracles that thou doest, except God be with him." In verse 3 Jesus answered him. "Verily, verily, I say unto thee, except a man be born again, he cannot see the Kingdom of God." Dave smiled to himself. There is nothing like getting right to the heart of the matter for Jill. He glanced at her out of the corner of his eyes. She was riveted on the speaker and continued to be.

The service concluded, and they made their way out into the bright sunshine. Jill said, "That sermon was so different Dave. I'll have to get my thoughts together and tell you what they are." "Good. Now, let's go have some lunch."

Peninsula Creamery, "The Pen"
Emerson Street. & Hamilton Avenue
Palo Alto, California
12:35 PM October 2, 1949

Dave told Jill, "This was and likely still is, the after school "hang out" for the high school students. It's called "The Pen." Their milk shakes have always been the best in town." After ordering, Jill said "The church service was so different from the few I've attended. I didn't understand all of it. You'll have to explain it to me." "I will Jill. We'll set some time aside to talk about it." "Thank you Dave, I'll look forward to that." Now, Dave said, "Let's go home."

The Mason Residence
1:45 PM October 2, 1949

Jill and Dave had arrived in front of the Mason home. Mr. Mercier, the across the street neighbor, was watering the sidewalk, his method of removing the leaves. He was a big baseball fan, particularly of Stanford baseball. He was a Stanford alumnus. He called to Dave and he took Jill's hand and they walked across the street. Dave introduced Jill. Mr. Mercier said, "I always knew you would make it to the big leagues Dave, but I was amazed you did it so fast. Congratulations Dave." "Thank you Mr. Mercier." As they walked back across the street, Dave told Jill that Mr. Mercier is President of the Southern Pacific Railroad.

Jill's Apartment
8:00 PM October 5, 1949

Dave had suggested he come to Jill's apartment this evening to explain the Sunday sermon, so Jill invited him to dinner. They had finished another tasty dinner prepared by Jill, and Dave was ready to be a teacher.

"First, I want to set the scene for you as described in the Bible in John Chapter 3. If you have any questions Jill, please ask immediately." "I will." "It was early in the first year of the ministry of Jesus. He was about 30 years of age. This was his first trip to Jerusalem since he started his ministry. He had come from Capernaum, a walk of about 80 miles. He had been in town only a few days."

"It was evening when there was a knock on the door of the house where he was staying. When the door was opened, Jesus found Nicodemus, one of the Jewish leaders of the city standing there. He was a member of the Pharisees Party. They were masters of the oral traditions which had come down over the past four centuries. They believed that one earns merit with God by scrupulously observing every technicality of the law and traditions. In spite of this, the Pharisees had broad support among the common people, particularly because they held to a belief in life after death, which some other sects denied. Many Pharisees had been chosen for high government positions, including the Sanhedrin which was the highest tribunal of the Jews. Nicodemus was a member of the Sanhedrin."

"Now Jill, consider the situation; a meeting between Jesus, a young, not well known teacher and a great man who was curious about the ministry of Jesus. Since the Pharisees opposed Jesus, Nicodemus had come in the night so fellow Pharisees would not be aware."

"Jesus had to decide what he would tell Nicodemus. Should Jesus show respect by thanking him for coming to see him? Nicodemus is a successful older man. Jesus was just starting his ministry. He could have asked Nicodemus for suggestions on how to proceed in his ministry. But Jesus asked no questions of Nicodemus. Jesus was very direct in answering. In verse 2 of Chapter 3, Nicodemus said, ". ... we know that thou art a teacher come from God: for no man can do these miracles that thou doest, except God be with him.' At this point Jill asked, "What was he after Dave?" Dave said, "He was seeking something beyond what the Pharisees believed, that would make them right with God. You may have noticed that Nicodemus said we and not I, at the beginning of the passage"

"Jesus did not take it easy on Nicodemus. " ... Verily, verily I say unto thee, Except a man be born again, he cannot see the kingdom of God.' In verse 4, Nicodemus answers Jesus by saying, 'How can a man be born when he is old? Can he enter the second time into his mother's womb and be born?' In verse 5, Jesus answered, 'Verily, Verily, I say to thee, Except a man be born of water and the Spirit, he cannot enter into the Kingdom of God.' The water refers to water baptism and the Spirit is the Holy Spirit." Jill asked, "What is the Holy Spirit?"

"That is a good question Jill. Better said is who is the Holy Spirit? The Bible makes it clear, that the Holy Spirit is a person who lives within every Christian. It also teaches that the person is God, the third person in the Trinity that includes, the Father, Son and Holy Spirit."

"The scriptures give us five clear evidences that the Holy Spirit is a person, not just a mystic force or strange power. So being born again results in a person being filled with the Holy Spirit which is God. You could say the person is filled with God. In layman's language, the Holy Spirit is God who lives within every Christian."

"In verse 9, Nicodemus says, '...How can these things be?' Jesus answered him with many reasons that I won't go into tonight. After verse 9, we hear no more from Nicodemus. He fades from the scene." Jill asks, "Is this the basis of Presbyterian religion?" "Yes. To be a member of a Presbyterian Church you must believe in Jesus Christ and have accepted him as Lord and have been born again." "Thank you Dave. This is very interesting. I'll have to think about all of this." "You're very welcome Jill. Now, how about that desert you promised." "There you go again, always thinking about your stomach." "Guilty."

After Dave gave Jill some romancing, he departed for home.

The Mason Residence
4:00 PM October 26, 1949

Dave had returned home from Stanford classes. Greeting his mother in the living room, she said, "There is a phone message for you with the mail in the hallway. Dave picked up the message that said to call Drew Warren in San Francisco.

Dave placed the call and was soon talking to Tub. He said, "I have great news for you Dave. You have won the Sam Gibson Award as the best pitcher in the Pacific Coast League. The league makes this award each year and it is a coveted award. You are the first rookie to win the award." "I'm amazed Tub. I had heard something about the award, but I hadn't given it a second thought." "That's not all Dave. You were also selected as Rookie of the Year." "Well, that's a little more believable," said Dave. Tub said, "You will receive a letter from the league office about the awards and a place and time for their presentation. I would expect it to be made in San Francisco."

"There is one more award that is being voted on by all the minor leagues as I speak. The award is that of Minor League Player of the Year." "I'm wondering why you're telling me about that award" "I'm telling you because from what I hear there is a good possibility that you will be selected." "That is more amazing than the PCL awards, Dave said." "I don't think so Dave. Just think about your performance in only four months of your first year in professional baseball. If you are selected you may hear about it in the newspaper or on the radio. The voting is not too secret." "Ok Tub, but I won't be expecting."

"In about a month I will be in touch with you about lunch with Vic Marko. He and his wife Marie are going to Hawaii for a three week vacation next week. Vic has promised to call me about a date for the lunch when he returns." "That's fine Tub. Thank you for the call." "You're welcome Dave."

Returning to the living room, Dave reported to his mother what Drew Warren had told him. Ann was excited and gave Dave a big hug. "Your dad should be home soon so you can tell him the good news."

The Mason Residence
4:00 PM November 3, 1949

Dave had just returned from Palo Alto High School where he went to do some running. He had run on the large expanse of turf that surrounds the baseball field. He wanted to stay in shape in the off season so he would be ready for spring training. Running also let him relax from his heavy class load on Thursdays.

He stopped in the hallway to see if he had any mail. There was no mail but there was a phone message for him to call the Pacific Coast League office in Los Angeles. He picked up the message slip and went into the living room to greet his mother. Dave said, "I better return this call now."

The purpose of the call was to set up a time for a press conference to present the Sam Gibson and Rookie of the year awards to Dave. The press conference would be held in San Francisco and Dave could select the day during the week of November 14-18. The press conference would be held at 10:30 in the morning so the newspaper writers would have plenty of time to write their stories for both afternoon and morning papers. Dave selected Tuesday, November

15. It was his Kiwanis meeting day and evening at Lavell Chevrolet. Dave had been talking to the league's Director of Public Relations. He said, "Please hold the line for Mr. Sagimore, he would like to talk to you." Sam "Shag" Sagimore was president of the PCL.

"Hello Dave, how are you?" "I'm doing just fine Mr. Sagimore." "Just an hour ago I learned that you have been voted the Minor League Player of the Year. Congratulations to you Dave." "That is really unbelievable Mr. Sagimore." "From my information I think it was your accomplishments in just four months that won the award for you. I will try to work out the presentation of that award at the same time as our PCL awards." "That would be fine," said Dave. "In a few days we will send you a letter with the location and details of the press conference." "Thank you, I'll look forward to receiving your letter." "Good by Dave." "Good by."

By the time Dave was finished with the phone call his dad had come home and was in the living room with Ann. Dave came into the living room, sat down and said, "I can't believe it. I won the Minor League Player of the Year award!" His parents said in unison, "Congratulations Dave." George Mason said, "Remember what I have told you in the past. Do not get carried away with these awards Dave. Remember the Mason philosophy about not promoting yourself." "I will keep it in mind dad. The presentation of the awards will take place in San Francisco on November 15 at a 10:30 press conference. I would like you both to be there." Ann said, "We'll be happy to be there Dave."

Franciscan Room
Sir Francis Drake Hotel
10:30 AM November 15, 1949

The press conference to present the PCL awards to Dave was being held in the same room where his sale to the New York Dukes was announced. George and Ann Mason were seated in the front row with Dave. Because she was not flying on Sundays, Jill was on a flight so she could not attend. There was a large turn out of the sports press. Dave thought it was even larger than when his sale was announced.

Mr. Ron "Rip" Rowan, Director of Public Relations of the PCL, was the master of ceremonies. He thanked everyone for attending. "We are here today to honor a baseball player who has brought great credit to the Pacific Coast League. Now let me introduce Mr. Sam Sagimore, President of the Pacific Coast League who will present the awards." "Thank you Ron. The three awards we are making today are, PCL Rookie of the Year, the Sam Gibson award for the best pitcher of the league and to top it off the Minor League Player of the Year. Now Dave Mason will you please come forward."

Mr. Sagimore described each award prior to making the presentation of plaques for the first two awards. The Minor League Player of the Year award was a first for the PCL. It is an award voted on by a select committee of baseball men who have no affiliation with any baseball team or organization. They review the performance of outstanding players from all the minor leagues, not just triple A leagues. I think I can safely say that Dave Mason won this award because he established such an outstanding record of pitching and hitting in less than four months in his first year in professional baseball. "Now Dave I present to you this trophy that includes sculptures of a pitcher and a baseball batter with an appropriate inscription that reads as follows: 'Presented to Dave Mason the 1949 Outstanding Minor League Baseball Player of the Year.' (Applause).

"Thank you Mr. Sagimore. All of these awards have been overwhelming to me, particularly the last one. When I learned that there was such a award I thought surely there would be a player in some other baseball league who had played the entire season who would be selected. I again thank all of my teammates who helped me be a good baseball player during the season. Also, I thank Drew Warren who is an outstanding baseball manager. Mr. Sagimore I thank you and the Pacific Coast League for these awards."

Ron Rowan thanked the members of the media again for attending and, "we will see you next season."

The baseball writers had questions for Dave, so he did not leave the Hotel until 11:30. He had invited his mother and dad to be his lunch guest at the Kiwanis meeting. After Dave took his awards to his car he returned to the hotel. Then they rode the cable car up Powell Street to the Fairmont Hotel for the Kiwanis meeting.

Kiwanis Club of San Francisco 12:00 noon November 15, 1949

Dave, his mother and father entered the meeting room and Dave obtained guest badges for them and paid for their lunch. They seated themselves at a table and members came by and congratulated Dave for his baseball awards. Newspaper articles had announced the press conference of this morning.

Visiting Kiwanis members were introduced followed by guests. Dave said, "I am honored to introduce my mother Ann and my father George."

During happy dollar time Dave had nine happy dollars, three for each of the awards he had received this morning. Dave said, "I had my Kiwanis pin on so any photographs that were taken should show my pin." That brought a big cheer from the members. George Mason had a happy dollar because Dave followed his suggestion to join a service club. Dave said, "I won't tell you what service club my dad is a member of, but it begins with "R." That brought a "Bronx" cheer from the members.

Lester, the chairman of the day introduced the speaker William Donavan, manager of the San Francisco International Airport. He presented the plans for the new greatly expanded airport and terminal. Compared the small terminal of today the new one would be gigantic.

Following the meeting Dave, his mother and dad rode the cable car down to the garage where their cars were parked. George and Ann were going back to Palo Alto. Dave was meeting Jill's flight at four o'clock. They would have dinner then Dave would go to his Lavell appearance. Dave said, "I'll be home about ten o'clock."

The Mason Residence
8:00 AM November 16, 1949

Dave was up having his breakfast while he read the morning San Francisco Chronicle. The article about the press conference was just a description of what had transpired and photos of Dave and the awards. Dave planned to pick up a San Francisco Times at Mac's Smoke Shop on his way to class. He wanted to read Dan White's article about the press conference.

The Union
Stanford University
Stanford, California
12:00 noon November 16, 1949

Dave was having his lunch while reading the article by Dan White in the San Francisco Times. Dan had learned that Dave's competition for the Minor League Player of the Year was a young hard hitting switch hitter like Dave who played shortstop, but not very well. He made lots of errors. Dan did not give the name of the player, probably a condition for obtaining the story. He had played in a double A league of the New York Giants organization. There were rumors that the Giants planned to convert him to an outfielder. At least one baseball man who had seen him play said he was a potential home run king. Dave thought he would be interested in knowing the player's name so he could follow his career in the minors. It was obvious that Dan White had gone the extra mile to get his story. Dave thought Dan had a big future as a sports reporter.

Following lunch Dave had gone to his one o' clock class on heating and ventilation. Soon Alex walked into the classroom. Dave could tell that Alex was upset because his face was red and his body language transmitted stress. Alex was considered the top student in the class. He was a Stanford graduate in mechanical engineering. Someone had told Dave that Alex had straight A grades through high school and Stanford.

Dave got out of his chair and walked to the chair Alex was sitting in. He asked Alex "Is something wrong?" Alex said, "I lost my class notebook with all my notes. I can't remember what I did with the notebook." "Relax Alex. After class I'll loan you my notebook and you can take it home and copy it. I'm sure my notes aren't as good as yours, but they should give you the basics of the lectures." "Oh thank you Dave. I'll return your notebook tomorrow." "That's fine Alex."

On his drive home Dave felt good. He had helped a fellow student who was in need.

Chapter Twenty

Bayshore Highway

Approaching San Francisco

10:30 AM November 22, 1949

DAVE WAS DRIVING to San Francisco to have lunch with Sea Lions Manager Tub Warren and Vic Marko the All Star center fielder of the New York Dukes.

Vic Marko's history starts with Giuseppe Markotinelli who was born in Rome, Italy in 1855. His father was a chef in the best restaurants of Rome. Giuseppe was taught to cook as soon as he could reach the stove, standing on a box. He was a member of the boys choir, an alter boy, and later an all around helper for the Priests. He started cooking in the small restaurants of Rome. However, he volunteered to cook for church dinners and other events when he wasn't working. At the age of 30, he became the youngest chef in the kitchen of the Vatican. By 1900 at the age of 45, he was a chief chef.

Priests who visited the Vatican from America told Giuseppe about the opportunities to cook and own restaurants in the U.S. Giuseppe decided he would encourage Napoleon, "Nap," his eldest son, 25, to immigrate to America to seek those opportunities. The Priests suggested he have his son go to San Francisco because there was more growth and opportunities there. Also there was a large Italian population in the city and it was becoming one that enjoyed good food.

So Nap traveled by ship to New York and by train across the U.S.

to Oakland, California and a ferry boat to San Francisco. He was amazed at all the open unpopulated land in this country. He wondered what kind of a city he would find in San Francisco.

Nap had no trouble finding a cooking job. His parish church had English classes so he could learn the language. In 1906 at the age of 31, he was a chef in the kitchen of the Palace Hotel, the best hotel in town. He had just been married and he and his wife had been sent on a honeymoon to Hawaii by his wife's parents. So he missed the 1906 San Francisco earthquake.

Back in town, Nap cooked for the children in relief camps while the city cleaned up and rebuilt. Later, he went back to cooking in the rebuilt Palace Hotel.

In 1920, at the age of 45, Nap decided it was time to open his own restaurant. Located in North Beach, it was to be named Markotinelli's. When the sign painter advised what the sign would cost Nap thought it was too much. He asked the sign painter, "How can I reduce the cost?" The sign painter said, "Shorten your name. It's too long." Nap thought for a few seconds and said, "How much for Marko?" The sign painter replied, "It would cut the price in half." "Do it.," said "Nap." "I'll go see a judge in the morning and change my name." So the family name was shortened to save money on a sign.

That same year marked the birth of Nap and Marie's youngest son, Victor. Victor was a surprise. Nap and his wife thought they had a finished family of three girls and two boys. He decided the Lord wanted to even up the boys and girls.

Victor was a different boy right from the cradle. He immediately tried to climb out of it. He was not interested in the kitchen. Vic wanted to be outside, and was soon playing all the games. His favorite sports were baseball and football. He was a good athlete. In high school he excelled in baseball as a power hitting outfielder. He was so talented he was signed to a professional baseball contract by the San Francisco Sea Lions upon high school graduation at the age of 17. He played part of the 1937 Pacific Coast League season, finishing second in batting. In 1938 he led the league in hitting and hit 35 home runs. The Sea Lions turned down a $50,000 offer by the

Boston Red Sox for him at the end of the 1938 season. After another record setting year in 1939, he was sold to the New York Dukes for $80,000 and three players.

Luke Devore had tried to get the Dukes to buy Marko following the 1937 season. He had recommended they let him play the 1938 season for the Sea Lions and bring him to the Dukes in 1939. The Dukes general manager had vetoed Devore's recommendation and no offer was made.

Then in 1938 the Dukes offer for Marko was $10,000 less than Boston's. Following the 1939 season the Dukes won the contest for his purchase from the Sea Lions.

In 1940 and 41 Vic Marko led the Dukes to American League pennants and World Series wins. In January of 1942 after the Pearl Harbor attack, Vic Marko joined the Navy. He turned down the opportunity to be assigned to Great Lakes Naval Training Station as a physical training instructor and requested cook's school. He served on cruisers, battleships and aircraft carriers in the Pacific. He was discharged in late August, 1945, too late for the baseball season. In November he married his long time girlfriend, Marie. It was one of the biggest weddings in the history of North Beach.

Vic returned to the Dukes in 1946. However he was rusty after four years away from baseball and didn't have a good year. The Dukes finished a poor second in the American League. With a new manager, Vic and the team recovered in 1947, winning the pennant and the World Series. They did it again in 1948 and 49. Vic Marko led the team, winning two American League batting titles. He had patrolled the big center field of Dukes Stadium, called the "big pasture," catching every fly ball in sight.

Dave was thinking about the last month and a half since he was sold to the New York Dukes. He thought about his explanation of the Nicodemus sermon to Jill. It had been the first time he had done any teaching of a Bible message.

The following weeks flashed by, the time consumed by dates with Jill, attending classes, studying and bowling. He had found an opening on the Peninsula Creamery bowling team and was their leading bowler. He had traveled to the "City" (San Francisco) each week for his Lavell appearance and the Kiwanis meeting. Early in October he had recorded the radio ads for Lavell on electrical transcriptions, the high tech of the day. They had been running on two radio stations since, and according to Bill Fox, the response was the best they had ever had from a radio ad. They offered a gift if a listener came to the show room and said they came because of Dave's commercial So many had come the first week, Lavell had run out of gifts and had to scramble to find a new supply.

Pam had gone to Chicago at the end of October, soon after completing her typing course. She and her college friend, Adell were living in a small apartment in the south side of town. Adell was a United Airlines stewardess flying out of Chicago, so she was on flights much of the time. Pam had obtained a job as a file clerk at an insurance company. She, of course was spending most of her time with Jim Smith. His home was in Evanston, just north of Chicago.

Jill's flight schedule had changed in October and she was home most Sundays. This had allowed her to attend church with Dave and she even started to accompany him to Sunday school. He had been doing more teaching.

Dave had received many requests to speak at meetings of groups and organizations. Because of his schedule, he accepted only an invitation to speak to the Kiwanis Club of Palo Alto. He did so on the condition that the leaders of their Key Club were invited to attend. While attending the Palo Alto club meeting he learned that J. Hugh Jackson, a member of the club is the 1949-50 International President of Kiwanis.

Jill planned to take a week's vacation during the week of Thanksgiving so she could go home and visit her family. She invited Dave to come with her and he accepted. They would leave tomorrow morning to drive to Hopeton for Thanksgiving and the weekend. Jill would stay through the end of the month.

Marko's Ristaurante
Taylor & O'Farrell Streets
San Francisco, California
11:45 AM November 22, 1949

Dave was early for the lunch. He was recognized immediately by the hostess and led to a small private room. He was asked what he would like to drink. "Coffee would be fine." Soon Tub Warren and Vic Marko entered and Tub introduced Vic to Dave. Dave said, "Congratulations on another World Series win." The Dukes had defeated Brooklyn 4 games to 1."Thanks" said Vic. After ordering Vic asked Dave if he had ever been to New York. "Yes, when I was 9 years old, I'm sure it's changed since then." "Yes, it has, but I don't know if it's better. When I arrived as a rookie in 1940 I found it so different from San Francisco or any other big city on the West Coast. The only part of town that I felt good in was along the river or at least somewhere near water. The hot humid summer weather really gets you." "Yes," Dave said. "On that trip in 1937 we stayed in Connecticut for three weeks and I learned about the heat and humidity. What part of the city do you live in?" "When I arrived in 1940, I was told to live close to the stadium, then in the Bronx so I wouldn't need a car. So I rented an apartment six blocks from the stadium. When the new stadium was built in Queens after the war we moved to Flushing. I needed a car then. When children started coming we rented a house in Flushing. A year ago we bought one, also in Flushing. I suggest you look for an apartment in Flushing. There are plenty of them."

"Tell me about contracts and salaries, something I've heard lots about." "Contracts are the standard baseball contract that all teams use. They are mailed out each year in late November with a salary. The general manager expects you to sign the contract and return it with no questions. Your options are to reject it, saying you want more money and naming a figure or signing and returning it. The owner has control. Until you have a few years of good performance you have no negotiating power. If you hold out, you may get a small increase, or you may be traded. Based on my experience, if your first contract salary is below what you expect, I would challenge it, if for no other reason to let the general manager know that you won't be a push over." "Thanks, that's good advice."

"One more bit of advice. Rookies are treated coldly by veteran baseball players. So don't expect them to be friendly or even say hello to you, and I won't either. It's not the best system, but it's the culture. If you perform well, it will soften some as the season progresses. However, some players will not be friendly until you have been on the team for at least two or three years. It's because that's the way they were treated.

Dave asked if Vic still saw Ty Cobb in the off season. "Yes, I see him at least once when I'm at home." "I would like to meet him some time." "I'll keep that in mind." "Thank you Vic for taking the time to meet with me." "Well, I look forward to you being a teammate. The Dukes can never have enough pitching, and I hear you hit the ball too." "I try." "He's too modest," said Tub he hits the ball."

G Bar R Ranch
Hopeton, California
1:35 PM November 23, 1949

Dave had picked Jill up at 10:00 AM. They had driven south on highway 101 to Gilroy where they took the cutoff to state highway 152, heading east. At Highway 59 they turned north, driving into Merced. They stopped there for lunch. From Merced they continued north on 59 to county highway 117, where Dave turned left. A short trip down that road brought them to the entrance of the G Bar R Ranch. A gate guarded the entrance that Jill opened. A half a mile down the road they came to a tree lined oasis where the ranch house, barn and other buildings were located. The house was a one story rambling structure with a red tile roof and white stucco exterior.

Jill and Dave were greeted by Jill's mother and father and her younger brother, Ted, now 19 and a student at Cal Poly. Jill's older brother Willie, wife Stella and their boy Leslie 3 years old had gone to Fresno on ranch business. Willie managed the ranch with his Dad, but lived in Snelling, a couple of miles east. Willie, who had been interested in rodeo competition when he was in his teens, had gone to Texas A & M. He was a member of the college rodeo team, but had to give it up when he broke an ankle that required surgery. He met his wife in Texas and worked on a ranch near her family ranch for a year before they married. Two years ago Willie's Dad offered him a future managing the family ranch, and he came home.

Ted was a sports fan and he immediately wanted to talk to Dave about baseball. That was fine with Dave as it let Jill visit with her parents.

Highway 101
Approaching San Jose
4:35 PM November 27, 1949

Dave was almost home. Throughout the drive from Hopeton Dave had thought about the visit with Jill's family. He had been given a good reception. Jill's brothers, both sports fans had lots of questions for Dave. Jill's dad was interested in the Mason ranch and the cattle raising of Dave's dad in the Merced area years ago. He had a few questions about playing baseball in the east. Dave told him he would play no more than ten years and then only if successful. He said his goal was to be a consulting engineer. Mrs. Gerber was a reserved country lady. Dave thought it was because she had no experience with "city boys."

The Thanksgiving dinner had been huge and delicious. Dave was stuffed when it concluded and got Jill to go for a walk with him.

Jill had given Dave a tour of the home country, including parking spots for young lovers. On Friday night Jill had picked out one, and asked Dave to park. Jill was sitting on Dave's lap as they hugged and kissed. Dave was doing his best to restrain himself in his romancing.

On Saturday, they had gone to Merced to see Top o' The Morning with Bing Crosby, Anne Blythe and Barry Fitzgerald. Dave was a Crosby fan, so he liked the movie.

Dave and Jill had attended the worship service at Central

Presbyterian Church in Merced this morning. Jill's interest in the service did not appear too overwhelming. Dave was committed to encouraging her interest.

Soon Dave drove through the gate of the Mason driveway and was home.

The Mason Residence
2:36 PM November 30, 1949

Dave had come home from class at Stanford to find his Dukes contract in the day's mail. The Dukes wanted him to pitch for only $4,000.00 for the season. Dave had made that much pitching only four months for the Sea Lions. Remembering what Vic Marko said, he would send it back with a letter. But first he would show the contract to his dad and tell him what Vic Marko had told him.

When Dave showed the contract to George Mason and told him what Vic Marko had suggested. George said, "I have a listing of information sources on the baseball contract and the reserve clause. It was provided by an attorney in San Francisco who has done much research on the clause. I talked to him when I was looking into a player's share of a sale to a major league team. He is a big baseball fan and has done the research just because he is interested. Attorney Christopher "Chris" Monroe would be in the forefront of the legal challenges that broke the reserve clause 26 years later. George Mason suggested to Dave that he compose the letter and he would review it, "But you will have to handle this matter yourself from now on. It will be good experience." "Thank you dad for your good advice."

Dave learned from his research that baseball had no reserve clause in the year 1871. That was the year the first professional baseball league was formed. It was the National Association of Professional Base Ball Players. The league was dominated by the Boston Red Stockings who won the championship in four of the first five years. The Red Stockings owner, Harry Wright would sign star players as soon as other teams developed them.

Because of an economic depression, the league was in trouble by 1876. William Hulbert, owner of the Chicago team, decided he could take advantage of the situation. A rich coal baron, he lured Adrian "Cap" Anson, the great star of the Philadelphia Athletics to his team along with four top players of the Boston team.

He was sure that the league would object, so Hulbert formed a new league, the National League of Professional Base Ball Clubs. Once formed, the club owners wanted to have the power, not the players who could move from team to team for more money. The league soon added a reserve clause to the player's contracts of the five best players on each team. A player's services were "reserved" in perpetuity. Players who objected were fired and then "blackballed." Soon the reserve clause was extended to all the players on each team. Each player was the property of his team until he was traded or released. The National League owners would control baseball for the next 25 years. The players would be just like slaves.

By 1919 there were two major leagues, the National League and the American League. The later was formed by owners in big cities who had been left out of the National League. There was a World Series played between the season winners of each league.

In 1919 the Chicago White Sox, winners of the American League were preparing to play the Cincinnati Reds, the National League winner in the World Series. Chicago was the big favorite. However, the Chicago players were very unhappy. Charles Comiskey, the owner was one of the "cheapest" owners. He was so cheap he wouldn't have the player's uniforms washed. The players renamed the team the Black Sox in 1918 after many weeks in dirty uniforms. Eddie Cicotte, the Sox star pitcher had a grudge against Comiskey. He had promised Cicotte a $10,000 bonus if he ever won 30 games in a season. When he had won 29 in 1919, Comiskey ordered him benched so he wouldn't have to pay up.

The player's discontent was a big motivation for a number of them to agree with gamblers to "throw" the World Series. It resulted in the Black Sox scandal. This resulted in the hiring of Judge Kenesaw Mountain Landis as baseball Commissioner to clean up the game.

In 1949 baseball owners were not quite as cheap as Charles

Comiskey but, they were in firm control, and all but dictated what the players were paid. The forgoing was in Dave's mind as he composed his letter to Donald Newton.

This is the letter Dave sent to Donald Newton, General Manager of the New York Dukes.

December 5, 1949

Mr. Donald Newton, General Manager
New York Dukes Baseball Club
Junction & Northern Boulevard
Queens, New York

Dear Mr. Newton:

Thank you for the contract to play baseball for the New York Dukes in 1950. I am looking forward to being a member of the team.

The salary to be paid to me for my services shown on the contract is $4,000.00 for the season of 1950. This salary is not acceptable. In 1949 I was paid $4,000.00 for my services by the San Francisco Sea Lions Baseball Club for only four months of the Pacific Coast League season. That salary was at the rate of $1,000.00 per month. For the six months American League season, I request a salary of $6,000.00.

While I like to play baseball, I am not required to do so to support myself. I have a degree in aeronautical engineering. 1948 graduates from my college entered the work place with starting salaries of $3,900.00. I'm sure they are making more this year. I am aware that this is for a period of twelve months, but they do not have to endure the heat and humidity of the east or the travel involved in playing baseball.

I am also a very good bowler, Mr. Newton. I have been told I could make a very good living on the Professional Bowlers Tour.

I am now enrolled in a master's degree program at Stanford University. I plan to complete one quarter's study in pursuit of this degree before traveling to Florida for spring training. If not playing baseball, I could continue this study that will lead to a very good position in a consulting engineering firm right here in my home town of Palo Alto.

I really do want to play baseball for the New York Dukes, but for a reasonable salary. For the reasons stated above, I am returning this contract to you for revision. I look forward to receiving a revised contract.

Very truly yours,
David D. Mason
David D. Mason

P.S. When I signed with the San Francisco Sea lions, I requested a letter from the manager insuring that I could take daily batting practice with the position players. I request the same letter from the manager of the New York Dukes.

DDM

Office of the General Manager
New York Dukes Baseball Club
Queens, New York
10:00 AM December 12, 1949

Donald Newton was reading the letter from Dave Mason, and he was not happy. Newton had opposed the purchase of Dave Mason on the basis of Dave having had only a partial season in pro baseball. Because of pressure from Luke Devore to sign Mason, Newton had suggested they buy Dave for delivery after the 1950 PCL season. The price could be based on what his record is in 1950. Newton had lost that battle so was undecided what to do about Dave's salary.

He would think about it for a few days. It appeared to him that Luke Devore had the support of Fred Duke, president of the club.

Spartan Bowling Lanes
East Santa Clara Street
San Jose, California
10:35 AM December 12, 1949

Dave had entered the California State Amateur Bowling Tournament. Even if he won a regional he would not be able to compete for the championship because it would be held in the spring of 1950. He decided to enter for the experience of competing in a tournament.

He was bowling in his first match, and bowling at a big disadvantage. Dave had always kept his bowling ball in the trunk of his car. Earlier in the week he had taken it out to clean it up and left it in his room. He had been busy during the last week of November and had forgotten he had not returned the ball to the car. Arriving at the Spartan Lanes he discovered he had no ball. So he was bowling with an unfamiliar ball.

After the first three frames Dave game had improved and was able to win the first match. He won his second match, doing even better. In the third match this evening, he met a very good bowler from here in San Jose. He was bowling on his home lanes. The match went down to the last frame in which Dave was bested by one pin and he lost the match. Would he have won with his ball? It will never be known. So Dave was ready to drive home and get back to studying for Stanford final exams.

The Mason Residence
9:00 PM December 2, 1949

Dave entered the house from the backyard, and greeted his parents in the living room. Ann asked, "How did your do?" "Not so good. I really goofed. I forget I had taken my ball out of the car to clean it up, and I went off leaving it in my room. So I had to use a ball of the lanes, and that may have cost me the third match. I lost it by one pin. I just allowed myself to get too busy and not think about what I was doing. It was a very good lesson."

George Mason said, "I'm glad you understand it as a good lesson, Dave. It will help in the future." "Thanks dad."

4:15 PM December 15, 1949

Dave had just returned home after completing his last final examination. Because of his studying and Jill's flight schedule, he had not seen her in a week. He had made a date with her for tomorrow evening to celebrate the end of finals. Dave planned to take Jill back to the Portola House Restaurant for a candle light dinner. He wanted to invite Jill to spend Christmas with him in Palo Alto.

Portola house Restaurant
Portola Valley
9:10 PM December 16, 1949

Francis Frank, the chef and owner had come to the table as he always did when the entrée was served. He waited while it was tasted. As usual the food was delicious. Jill and Dave talked about Christmas. Jill would not have to fly on Christmas Eve or day, so she could come and stay with Dave at the Mason home. They planned to attend the Christmas Eve service at the Menlo Park Church. As the evening progressed, Jill thought she might be coming down with a cold, so Dave took her home.

The Mason Residence
12:00 noon December 17, 1949

Jill had just called to tell Dave she was down with a bad cold. She had called in sick and would just stay in the apartment until she recovered. Dave advised, as his dad always did when he had a cold, "Drink lots of liquids." "I will, Dave."

3:10 PM December 21, 1949

Returning home from a trip to the cleaners, Dave picked up his mail in the entryway of the Mason home. Included was an envelope with the New York Dukes return address. Dave told his mother as he sat down in the living room, "The contract has returned." "What does it say?" "I'll tell you in a minute." Dave tore open the envelope and read the contract. There was no letter included. It's $5,500.00." "Well," Dave said. "They came up more than I thought they would. I was thinking they would raise it to $5,000.00, so it's better. I'll sign it." "You should tell your dad what you plan to do." "Yes, I'll talk to him tonight."

Later, Dave told his dad what the salary had been raised to and that he planned to sign the contract, but only after he received the letter about batting practice. George Mason said, "It's your decision. I think you did a good job on the letter and that resulted in the increase." "Thanks Dad."

Dave thought it would have been interesting to be a fly on the wall when Don Newton received Dave's letter. According to Vic Marko Donald Newton was not tolerant of the salary demands of players. He knew he had the reserve clause club over them, and most baseball players had no alternate job in which they could make near what they earned playing baseball. Dave Mason would be an exception that would cause Donald Newton much grief. Dave received the batting practice letter a week later. He then returned the signed contract.

7:30 PM December 21, 1949

Jill called to report she was recovering, but had decided to stay on sick leave until December 28. "Is it okay if I come to your house on Friday?" "Sure, that would be fine.

I cleaned up the room for you. No one has occupied the cook's room for a while so I thought I should do that." "Thank you Dave." He had not only cleaned up the room but hung a banner in the room that read "Merry Christmas Jill."

Homer Market
Homer Avenue
Palo Alto, California
1:45 PM December 22, 1949

Dave had come to the store to pick up some items for his mother. Ann didn't do much shopping any more because they eat all their dinners out, and George was never home for lunch. When she was grocery shopping in the past, she had abandoned Safeway, ordering by telephone from the Homer Market. Then the market delivered her order.

Dave was ready to pay for his purchase and was waiting in line to check out. A little old man was in front of him and he was having trouble counting out his money. It appeared he may not have enough. Dave stepped up and said to the cashier, please take it out of this, handing him a twenty dollar bill. The man protested, "I can't have you do that." Dave said, "I can afford it, and I cannot afford not to do it. Merry Christmas," Dave said.

The Mason Residence
4:00 PM December 23, 1949

Dave had just returned home from his last Christmas shopping trip. Jill was due some time before 5:00.

About 45 minutes later Jill drove up and parked her car in front of the house. Mr. Mercier was in front of his house watering the sidewalk, and when he saw Jill he called to her. Jill walked across the street to where he was watering. She was surprised he remembered her name since he had met her just the one time. Mr. Mercier asked if she was visiting during Christmas. "Yes," Jill said, "I'm staying for a week. I'm on sick leave because I'm just recovering from a bad cold." Mr. Mercier said, "I wanted you to know that I think Dave is a fine fellow. I've watched him grow up and if I had a daughter his age I'd be pleased if he was her friend."

About that time Dave emerged from the house and joined Jill

and Mr. Mercier. Mr. Mercier said, "I've been talking to your girl friend Dave." "He remembered my name," said Jill. Dave said, "Mr. Mercier is a very good neighbor." "Thank you Dave and a merry Christmas to both of you." Almost together Jill and Dave said, "Thank you."

Jill and Dave walked to Jill's car to get her suitcase. Jill warned Dave not to kiss her because of lingering germs. "Just give me a hug Dave." "I don't know how long I can be under that restriction." "You'll just have to suffer Dave." Dave responded with a laugh.

Entering the house, Jill was greeted by Ann. "How are you feeling Jill?" "Better Mrs. Mason." Jill followed Dave to her room behind the kitchen. When he opened the door and she saw the Merry Christmas sign, she gave Dave a big hug.

"When dad gets home we will go to dinner. Now I'll let you unpack. When you are done, come to the living room." "Thank you Dave."

Menlo Park Presbyterian Church
8:15 PM December 24, 1949

Dave and Jill were leaving the church following the Christmas Eve service. The music had been outstanding. It included hymns by the children's choir. Dave liked to see and hear children sing. He was always watching for those children who wave to their parents. The message of the birth of Jesus was told in an interesting way by Rev Hall. Dave thought that Jill's interest in attending the service was more enthusiastic than in the past.

The Mason Residence
9:00 AM December 25, 1949

It was time for gift giving. Dave gave Jill a designer dress she had seen at I. Magnin and told Dave she would love to have it but it was too expensive. Jill was thrilled. Jill gave Dave a book, The Big Four. It was the account of the men who built the Central Pacific Railroad over the Sierra Nevada Mountains.

Jill was overwhelmed with gifts from Dave parents. She said, "You have been overly generous." George and Ann Mason said, "It's our pleasure."

The foursome went to Ricky's for Christmas dinner. While having their desert, Ann said to Jill and Dave, "I do hope you can survive another separation. How many have you had?" Jill answered, "If you count the short ones in 1946 and 47, it must be seven or eight. I just hope this will be our last."

In the evening Jill and Dave watched TV in the big bedroom upstairs. Then they talked until midnight.

4:30 PM January 2, 1950

Dave and his mother were listening to the Rose Bowl football game between California and Ohio State. Even though California was the big rival of Stanford, they were rooting for Cal. In a close game Ohio State won on a field goal 17 to 14.

Jill had gone home on Friday to return to work. She was on a flight New Years Eve so Dave had a quiet evening. He had gone to Sunday school and church on New Years day. Tomorrow it would be back to classes at Stanford. The quarter would be over in just a month.

Black Mountain Ranch
10:00 AM February 11, 1950

Dave was on Capt., his favorite horse on a ride around the ranch. He had completed his first quarter in the master's program and felt good about how he had done. His grades would be mailed to the Mason home in about two weeks. He would be on his way to Florida and spring practice by then.

In the first week of January Dave had asked the Stanford baseball coach if he could pitch batting practice for the team. His offer was immediately accepted. This had given Dave a month pitching to batters to get his arm ready for spring practice.

Tuesday was Valentines Day and Dave planned to take Jill to the Portola House for dinner. Dave would leave for New York the next morning, so it would be their last night together for some months.

Enjoying his ride in the cool mountain air, Dave hoped his dad would be able to keep the ranch so he and his family of the future could enjoy it.

Portola House Restaurant
9:15 PM February 14, 1950

When Dave went to Jill's apartment he had a giant Valentine card for her and a dozen red roses. Jill was overwhelmed. She was wearing the dress Dave had given her for Christmas and she looked fantastic to Dave. Both Jane and Sally were in the apartment and he said, "Isn't she beautiful?" The both agreed. "Dave, you flatter me so much, I'm getting spoiled." "That's my intention."

Dave had requested Jill's favorite desert that had just been served. It was a chocolate cake cable car. The lettering, Powell & Hyde Sts., was done in white frosting. Vanilla ice cream was served on the side. The desert was an original creation of Frances Frank the chef and owner of Portola House.

Over coffee, Dave turned serious. He said, "I want you to feel free to date others while we are separated. If Jane or Sally would like you to double date, please do so. Our separation will be at least four months. Jill was silent for a while… .then she said, "Dave, I'll consider doing so if you agree to do the same. I know you are going to a new city where you won't know anyone, but maybe one of your new teammates has a sister or will fix you up. Will you agree to that?" "Yes I will, primarily so you will feel free to date." "All right," Jill said. "We have agreed and let's not talk about it any more."

On the drive to Jill's apartment Dave stopped at a location where Jill could sit on his lap for the last time for a while. Dave romanced Jill for a long time and they said their goodbyes. Dave then took Jill home and they were separated again.

PART FOUR

NEW YORK CITY, NEW YORK

FEBRUARY 20, 1950

Chapter Twenty-One

25 Miles East of San Francisco

Highway 50

February 15, 1950

DAVE WAS ON his way to New York and the next adventure in his young life. He had departed Palo Alto at 5:00 AM so he would be out of the morning city traffic crossing San Francisco Bay on the San Mateo Bridge. He drove through Oakland and then to Sacramento where he entered highway U.S. 50. He had planned a six day trip across the country to New York City. He wanted to find an apartment before going to Florida for spring training. He would take the train since the team would return to New York by train after playing teams on the trip north. Dave planned to stay overnight in YMCAs wherever he could to save money. His schedule was to start at 5:00 AM and arrive at the next overnight city at 4:00 PM so his chances of finding a room in the Y were good.

Dave's primary thoughts were whether he had helped Jill progress in her interest in church. Dave had given Jill a copy of The Man Nobody Knows. He had found two copies in a San Francisco used book store. They were the 22nd printing of December, 1927. Dave hoped the book would spark Jill's Interest in Jesus as it had his. Dave had reinforced his feeling that their relationship could not proceed to a proposal until Jill made a commitment to the Lord.

In late January, Jill and Dave talked about Jill's future home base.

They decided she should not make a change request until Dave made the team and was reasonably sure he would stay and not be farmed out. Dave suggested this would be about June first. So it would be another four month separation. It would be another test of their relationship.

One of Dave's two radio commercials had started airing on the first of December. The second commercial started on the first of January. He was receiving ATRA scale plus a fee paid over three months. If the spots ran for a total of three months each, Dave would earn more than $800. He had continued his weekly appearances at Lavell Chevrolet right up to yesterday.

The Peninsula Creamery bowling team had won their fall league championship at the Indian Bowl. Dave led the team with a 260 average that was tops in the league. He bowled a 300 game.

George Mason had suggested that Dave find an advertising agency to represent him if he was successful with the Dukes. He cautioned Dave, saying that business men in the east were much more formal and tough to deal with compared with those in the west. George advised Dave to be sure to take his safe with him so he would have a safe place for cash. Dave had obtained the name of a Flushing, New York bank from his Palo Alto bank, the American Trust Company.

Dave had given Jill another pack of penny post cards, their method of communication whenever they had been apart. Dave would write his first card in Denver.

Dave drove into New York City on Monday morning, February 20th.

Flushing Hotel
Flushing, New York
12:00 noon February 20, 1950

When he was sure he would arrive in New York on February 20th, he called his mother and had her make a hotel reservation for him. Before checking in, he bought a New York Times so he could look through the apartment advertisements. He found some possibilities in Flushing, not far from the Dukes stadium. After lunch he found a travel agent who made a reservation on the West Coast Champion, an overnight train to St. Petersburg. Then he was off to look at apartments.

Dave didn't find what he wanted in the afternoon, so he checked into the hotel. The next day he found an apartment at the Hunter Gardens Apartments located at 149th Street and Northern Boulevard. It was a one bedroom apartment with a small kitchen that rented for $98.00 per month. A garage for parking his car was included. It was located within walking distance of a Long Island Railroad station on Main Street. The train would provide transportation into Manhattan's Penn Station. Also, it was close to the Dukes Stadium at Junction and Northern Boulevards. Dave paid the first and last month rent, a cleaning deposit and had his apartment.

Ann had shopped for bedding and a few basic kitchen items so he wouldn't have to shop for those items. Dave bought a few items of furniture that would be delivered the next day, and he was ready to travel to Florida.

Pennsylvania Station
3100 Seventh Avenue
New York City, New York
3:15 PM February 26, 1950

Dave was waiting for his train to arrive from Boston. Departure was scheduled for 3:50 PM. The train would arrive in St. Petersburg at 5:00 PM tomorrow afternoon. Penn station was the biggest train station he had been in since he came to New York in 1937. He and his dad had walked on the red carpet in Grand Central Station to board the Twentieth Century Limited.

Dave attended church this morning at the North Presbyterian Church in Queens. Upon his return to New York with the Dukes, he would locate and visit the 5th Avenue Presbyterian Church in Manhattan. It was a church suggested to Dave by an elder of Menlo Park Presbyterian Church who was from New York.

As soon as Dave was on the train he wrote one of the post cards to Jill. He gave her his apartment address so she could send cards to him. He had suggested she write even though he would not return for a month. He gave Jill his first impression of New York City. He said it was just a big place.

Dave settled down in his seat and started to read the Sunday New York Times sports section. He found a feature article on the New York Dukes. It was entitled "The Dukes." "The Dukes Baseball Club, named after owner, Reginald "Reggie" Duke has become a dynasty. Duke bought a struggling baseball team called the New Yorkers in 1920. He has built them into what the team is today."

"Reggie Duke made his money importing. He imported many items from all over the world. One of his specialties was French wines. He realized a bonanza in the 1930s, anticipating the repeal of probation he had his warehouses full of wines. However Duke is a tea totaled."

"In the 1920s Duke started investing his money in real estate not the stock market. His capital was not depleted as a result of the stock market melt down."

"Reggie Duke is a staunch Presbyterian, the faith of his family for generations. He is a long-time member of the 5th Avenue Presbyterian Church in Manhattan. Reggie has a large family of five children and he is considered a good family man."

"During World War I, Reggie joined the Navy and became an aviator. After discharge, he became an aviation booster. He was convinced that in the future, people would fly on trips of long distance and drive their car on short trips. For these forward thinking reasons he sold the old Dukes stadium located in the Bronx, and built a new one near La Guardia Airport. He wanted more parking spaces for cars and to be near the airport when the team would start flying to road games."

"The stadium was built on land owned by the Duke family and there is even more land for expansion of parking. The stadium capacity was reduced from the 90,000 of the former ball park to a more realistic 60,000. Crowds of over 50,000 were the exception and seldom reached during the season. Being an astute real estate investor, Reggie felt more people would live in the suburbs following World War II. He wanted the stadium to be closer to where people lived. Reggie managed the construction of the stadium himself. He battled through the shortages of steel and other items to complete the stadium in 1948 in time for the opening of the season."

"When World War II ended in 1945, Reggie Duke was 65. He turned the Presidency of the baseball team over to his eldest son, Fred. Fred was just 25 years old, however he had been around and worked for the team since the age of five. Fred is a Princeton graduate who majored in business. He had learned to fly as a teenager and had earned his private pilots license at the age of 18. Reggie had built an air strip on the Duke estate located on Long Island so he could use his plane to save time on short trips. It is also a great way to look at land when deciding on a purchase."

"Fred Duke spent two years in the Army Air Force flying transport planes. It included a year stationed in England. He was discharged early because of a problem with his eyes. Baseball observers have watched Fred concentrate on increasing the income and profit of the club. Since the club is privately held, no financial information is available, however most observers think the club is making more money each year."

"Donald Newton has been the general manager of the team for five years. Prior to assuming the position he had built the Dukes farm system into one of the best in baseball. However, he is willing to purchase promising players from minor league teams and make trades when needed."

Harvard University
College of Business
Cambridge, Massachusetts
9:00 AM February 17, 1950

Fred Duke along with 19 other top executives and business owners were attending a new 90 day case study program developed by Harvard.

The program featured simulated business problems in which the participants were challenged to provide solutions. Then the solutions were critiqued. These and informal "bull" sessions outside of the study sessions caused Fred to come to the following conclusions about the future of the economy and the entertainment business.

1 Americans would have more money to spend on entertainment and vacations.

2 Americans would work harder and longer hours to earn that money.

3 All weekday entertainment would move to the evening.

4 While movies were currently a strong contender for the entertainment dollar, the biggest threat was stay-at-home television.

5 TV could be both a great promoter of baseball or it could be a negative force by reducing attendance.

6 Saturday fall entertainment and leisure would be dominated by college football and weekend golf.

7 Sunday afternoons would continue to be dominated by baseball. The one threat to this was if professional football survived the league verses league competition for college players without going bankrupted, it could become a competitor for the Sunday dollar.

8 While Fred could not get a consensus, there was a strong feeling that a professional baseball team needed one or more superstars to produce a good profit.

9 With the dominance of a few teams in each major baseball league, it would be necessary to offer more than baseball to the fans when the weak teams came to town.

10 Fred confirmed his opinion that baseball was a business with a bottom line and not just a sport called America's national past time. Most baseball owners and general managers would not admit this. To them it was a game to be revered, and its traditions were to be continued at all cost.

11 Future transportation of the team to out-of-town games would be by air travel for long road trips and by bus for short ones. Train

travel and service will decrease.

12 More baseball fans would come to the stadium in their car, so more parking spaces would be required.

During his time at Harvard, Fred was developing a plan to meet the changes and challenges of the future. He developed the following plan.

1 He would create a position of Vice President of Entertainment & Promotion. The person who would fill this position would be one with broad experience in the entertainment business. He would create non-baseball entertainment on a more conservative basis than that of the Cleveland Indians. He would develop new methods to promote the star players of the team. He would find ways to bring off-season entertainment to Dukes Stadium.

2 Good lights would be installed in Dukes Stadium by June 1, 1950.

3 The advertising budget would be increased.

4 A program of education would be developed directed to the players regarding the advantages of air travel (some players refused to fly). The savings in time that would allow more time at home with player's families would be emphasized

5 Initiate a study of the make up of the fans who attend the games. The many empty box seats in the Bronx stadium was something Fred noticed as a teenager. His father said they were boxes purchased by firms. For many games they couldn't give all their tickets to customers or employees. In the Queens location fewer boxes were bought by business firms, but more by individuals. Should the current policy of not charging for parking be continued? Charging for parking would add income.

6 Initiate a study of ticket prices in comparison with other entertainment. Consideration must be given the fact that baseball operates for only seven months of the year.

Petersburg Hotel
Petersburg, Florida
5:00 PM March 1, 1950

Dave was talking to his mother about spring baseball training that would start tomorrow. He had called to learn what his Stanford grades were for the fall quarter. Ann said, "I'll let your father tell you about your grades." "Hello dad, how are you?" "I'm fine Dave. I'm happy to tell you that you received three A grades and one B in your first quarter of your master's study. Congratulations Dave, you really excelled." "Thank you dad, it proves that Cal Poly is not an easy college that some people have claimed."

George asked how the weather was in Florida. "It has been fine so far. They say this is the best time of the year. How are Pam and Jim doing?" "They are doing fine. She and your mother are starting to plan the wedding." "I hope to see them when the team travels to Chicago for games with the White Sox." "I hope you do well in your spring training. Keep us advised on how you're doing." "I will dad. Good night."

Knickerbockers' Field
St. Petersburg, Florida
10:00 AM March 2, 1950

The New York Knickerbockers Base Ball Club was the first organized club in America. Some time in the spring or summer of 1842, a group of young gentlemen began getting together in Manhattan each week to play one or another version of baseball, depending on how many showed up at game time. On September 23, 1845, at the instigation of Alexander Cartwright, twenty-eight young men formed the New York Knickerbockers Base Ball Club. It was named after a volunteer fire company to which Cartwright and others belonged. The group was made up of merchants, Wall Street stock brokers, salesmen, a U. S. Marshal, a portrait photographer, a doctor and a dealer of cigars. These were men who were not at work after three o' clock in the afternoon. They played for recreation and exercise only. They also showed a great interest in improving the game. In honor of the Knickerbockers, Reggie Duke named the team's spring training facility Knickerbockers' Field.

On this March morning spring training of the New York Dukes commenced. The first event was calisthenics. Dave was one of nine rookies that included Gordon Enson, the bonus player who played for the Hollywood Stars of the PCL last season. There were 37 veteran baseball players in camp.

Dave's big surprise was to see his former American Legion catcher B.B. Katcher at breakfast on Monday morning. B.B had signed with the Dukes following the 1947 baseball season. Following high school he had played two years at San Mateo Junior College. Dave knew he had signed with the Dukes, but had not followed his progress through the minors. B.B. had progressed through two minors the first year, and played for the Dukes triple A farm team in Buffalo last year. He told Dave he was surprised to be invited to the major league camp. He thought sure he would return directly to Buffalo. B.B.'s hitting was his big asset, but he was still progressing in throwing to second base and other defensive techniques. He would be tutored during spring training by the retired Dukes Hall of Fame catcher Ray Woodall.

Dave and B.B. were glad to be able to walk into the Dukes Club House together so they would not be so intimidated by the veteran players. Vic Marko had to act like he had never met Dave because the veteran players did not make it easy for rookies.

Since the Dukes had a big investment in Dave, he was wondering how he would be handled during spring training. Would he be challenged early to show his talent or would the Dukes manager ease Dave into the major leagues.

Manager Ozzie Felton (he had legally changed it from Oswald) was a former catcher who played eight years in the major leagues. While he was an average hitter for a catcher, his strength was handling pitchers and defense. Upon becoming the Dukes manager two years ago he did not hire a pitching coach. He would handle that task with a bull pen catcher. So Ozzie knew what rookie pitchers faced in spring training. Some would be nervous and couldn't throw strikes. Others would throw too hard too soon to impress and end up with a sore arm. Ozzie planned to ease Dave into action to reduce the pressure on a "high priced" rookie. Having worked out with the Stanford baseball team during January and February, Dave thought he was well prepared to face the challenge of spring training.

Ozzie Felton had adopted the game philosophy of Hall of Fame Catcher, Mickey Cochran. When he became manager of the Detroit Tigers in the 1930s, Cochran's formula for winning a pennant was to win 80 to 90 percent of the games against the lower division teams, and play .500 baseball against the top teams. He would not use second line pitchers against the poor teams. Also, he avoided pitching his ace against an opposing team's ace.

In this era of baseball, few players worked out in the off season to keep in physical shape to play baseball. Most players had to work in the off season to make ends meet. No pitchers appeared prepared to throw batting practice and Dave did not volunteer. For the first time the Dukes employed a pitching machine. Machines had been used for some years by other teams. The players gave the machine a name: Rapid Robert Robot.

An article on the local newspaper's sports page of March 3, 1950 reported that major league players are quietly but effectively launching a campaign to kill all payments of bonuses to unproven players. Marty Marion, National League representative to the players' committee, revealed he planned to present to the executive council at the next meeting a proposal to eliminate the payment of any kind of bonus to unproven players. Marion stated, "Something must be done. When the Pittsburg Pirates gave Paul Pettit, an 18 year old pitcher from Southern California $100,000 to sign, each member of the Pirates lost about $4,000. That is not good for the club."

To complete the story, Pettit hurt his arm in 1953, his second year in the league. His major league record was 1 win and 2 losses. He later tried to make it back to the major leagues as a first baseman/outfielder. He played eight years in the Pacific Coat League for Hollywood, Salt Lake City and Seattle. He didn't make it back to the majors.

Dave's first outing was in the second inter-squad game among rookies and non-regular players. B.B. was his catcher, another choice of Ozzie to encourage Dave. Dave thought they were making things easy for him now, but wait until the veterans start playing. He pitched three innings and threw only sinkers and change ups. No fast balls. Dave threw 27 pitches, allowed one infield hit, and no walks. He was satisfied. He looked forward to pitching in the next inter-squad game against the veterans.

Two days later Dave pitched in the last inter squad game. All the pitchers in these games were rookies and second line pitchers. No likely starters had pitched. So far, Dave was the only rookie pitcher who had been impressive. In this game Dave pitched the first three innings. He allowed two hits, one each in the first and second inning. He issued no walks and got two fly ball outs on his rising fast ball. It was an impressive outing.

Games with other teams would start the next day, but it would be a few days before Dave would pitch in a game. The Dukes had four returning veteran starting pitchers. Three other veterans were competing for a spot in the pitching rotation. The ace relief pitcher, Ed Edgar was a sure member of the pitching staff. The team would carry 9 or 10 pitchers and Dave wanted to be one of them. He didn't want to be farmed out to Buffalo, the Dukes Class AAA farm team.

Dave mailed one of his post card to Jill. He told her what spring training was like. He also told her about his performance. He wrote, "I miss you." Love, Dave.

March 12, 1950

Dave was scheduled to be the second pitcher in the game today against the St. Luis Cardinals .The National League team had some good hitters, if they played, who would challenge Dave. The Dukes regular catcher, Joshua Ben Felton, know as J. B., would be today's catcher (He was a distant cousin of the Dukes' manager). Ozzie Felton instructed J. B. to call for more fast balls and change ups in today's outing. Felton wanted to learn what the velocity was on

Dave's fastball and find out if good hitters could drive it instead of hitting fly balls. Dave entered the game in the fourth inning with the score tied 1 to 1. In the fourth he threw 12 pitches, three sinkers, three change ups and six fast balls. The batters hit two fly ball outs to the outfield and one ground ball to second base for the third out. Dave had pitched a shutout inning.

In the bottom of the fourth the Dukes scored three runs to go ahead 5 to 1. Dave got his first chance to bat in any spring training game. He hit a double, batting in two runs for the Dukes.

Like his agreement with the San Francisco Sea Lions Dave had been taking batting practice with the position players. His motivation had always been to be a good hitter so he would not be lifted for pinch hitters in the late innings of games. As with Pacific Coast League pitchers, major league pitchers were going to throw fast balls to a pitcher. That was the advice of Hall of Fame catcher Mickey Cochran of the Detroit Tigers. He said, "Pitchers are notorious late swingers," so give them three fast ball strikes and they should be out. Manager Felton knew about Dave's hitting, but it had to be proven against major league pitching.

Dave allowed one hit in each of the next two innings, but no runs. In his three innings of work he threw 36 pitches, got five fly ball outs, three from ground balls and one strike out. He issued no walks. Manager Felton was satisfied with the velocity on Dave's fast ball. But it was the rise that made it such a good pitch. His change up, thrown with the same motion as all his pitches, looked very good. The Dukes won the game 7 to 1. Dave was encouraged by his outing.

Dave wanted to use the evenings during spring training to sharpen his bowling. He had not bowled for more than two weeks. He invited B.B. Katcher to bowl with him. Dave told B.B. about the amateur tournament he entered in December, and his mistake of leaving his ball at home. Dave and B.B. bowled at least three nights each week at various bowling lanes in St. Petersburg. Dave wanted to get experience on different lanes, something a bowler had to contend with in tournaments. Lanes varied in their surface. Some were fast and some slow.

Dave would not pitch for four days while the regular pitchers and other rookies took their turns on the mound. During batting practice, Dave was turning some heads as the result of the balls he was hitting out of the park. Old timers were shaking their heads. A rookie pitcher is not supposed to hit like this.

Dave continued his morning bible reading and in his study of the life of Jesus. His references continued to be The Man Nobody Knows and the J. B. Phillips translation of the Bible.

Stevens Hotel
120 South Michigan Avenue
Chicago, Illinois
7:00 PM March 18, 1950

Jill had met Kent Ross, a new co-pilot on the flight to Chicago. He had a big smile like Dave's. He asked Jill and Beth the other stewardess on the flight to have dinner with him. Beth declined, saying she had friends in Chicago to visit. Jill decided to accept.

During dinner Jill learned that Kent was 26 and recently left the Navy after eight years. He resigned because he could not get into combat aircraft. He few only transports during his tour of duty. That made him a good candidate for a United Airlines position.

Since tomorrow is Sunday, Kent wanted to know where the closest Catholic Church is located "Do you know Jill?" "No, I don't know." "Are you Catholic?" "No. I suggest you ask at the front desk." After that exchange, Jill didn't talk much.

March 18, 1950

Dave was the starting pitcher in a game with Brooklyn. Dave pitched four innings and left the game with the Dukes up 2 to 1. Dave had allowed his first run of spring training in the second inning when Brooklyn batters hit two singles aided by an infield sacrifice put runners on second and third. A sacrifice fly ball scored the run. In the four innings he pitched Dave allowed three hits, struck out one and did not walk a batter. In his only time at bat, he singled to right field, batting left handed. Dave's left handed hitting had shown big improvement.

All through spring training, Dave had made an effort to be a good clubhouse player for a rookie. He congratulated players for their play and encouraged all players. He had his ever present smile that helped get through to some of the "crusty" veterans. His practice of giving thumbs up with his back to home plate after a good fielding plays was winning over infielders. Even when an infield error was made he gave the player a thumb's up. He had approached some of the veteran pitchers, asking them how they pitched to certain good hitters. He was trying to learn all he could.

Dave sent off another post card to Jill. He looked forward to Jill's cards when he returned to his apartment.

Jill's Apartment
Burlingame, California
7:30 PM March 27, 1950

Jill had thought about Kent since their dinner in Chicago. He had been on another flight with her, but she turned down his dinner invitation in Chicago. She thought maybe she should have accepted so she could make a comparison between Dave and another man. While Jill and Dave had agreed to date others during their separation, she had dated only two other fellows since she met Dave. She hadn't found them interesting. If Kent called, she might accept a date. Was she wondering if she and Dave would get married? She was still having difficulty becoming interested in church and religion. She would have to make a decision at some time about transferring to New York. She wished life was not so complicated.

Kent did call back and Jill accepted an invitation to attend a play at the San Mateo Playhouse. The play was interesting and she learned more about Kent over coffee and hamburgers following the play. Kent said his only ambition was to become a United Airlines Captain. It was the time off between flights that interested him the most. When he had a family, he would be able to spend lots of time at home with them. Jill immediately recognized the difference between Kent and Dave. Dave was so much more ambitious.

Knickerbockers' Field
March 28, 1950

As spring training wound down, seven players were sent to the Buffalo farm team and three to the class double A team at Binghamton, New York. The Dukes lost their game with Boston today 5 to 4. Catcher J. B. Felton committed an error when he dropped the ball on a throw to home plate, allowing the winning run to score. A home run was hit off rookie pitcher Ed Card.

Office of the President
New York Dukes Baseball Club
Junction & Northern Boulevards
Queens, New York
9:00 AM March 30, 1950

President Fred Duke was progressing in his plan for the Club. The design of lights for the stadium had been completed and the project was out for bid. Fred wanted to have them installed by June first or sooner if possible.

He was about to start interviewing candidates for the position of Vice President of Entertainment & Promotion. He had received a flood of applicants for the position. He was encouraged that he could select an outstanding man for the position.

He had been working on the outline of an increased advertising budget. It would be given to the V.P. of Entertainment when he was hired.

He had requested programs from United and American Airlines that would encourage team members to be willing to use air travel to road games.

The other items including the market studies would be the responsibility of the V.P. of Entertainment.

Pelican Restaurant St. Petersburg. Florida 7:30 PM April 8, 1950

B.B. Katcher was treating Dave to dinner on his 22nd birthday. They were each doing a self evaluation of their spring training performance to date. B.B. said, "My big problem is the mechanics of catching and the throw to second base. I think it's just something you have to do over an over again by playing games. It's called experience." "I agree B.B. there is no substitute for experience. I would have liked to pitch against some of the better hitters, but I didn't face many. The teams played lots of rookies when I pitched."

In another week the team would depart for games on the way home to New York.

April 14, 1950

The Dukes completed their trip home with games in Cincinnati and Pittsburg. On April 15 three more players including Dave's friend B.B. Katcher and pitcher Ed Card were sent to Buffalo. This reduced the roster to within one player of that required. Randle White the third baseman dental student who always reported late because of his off season dental school had reported

Dave's record during spring training was outstanding. He pitched 21 innings, allowed seven hits, two runs, he struck out six and walked one batter. Only one of the hits was for extra bases and no home runs were hit off Dave. While he didn't face many opposing team's regular players, on any other team Dave would be an immediate starting pitcher. But the Dukes had many hurlers proven by experience. Dave would have to wait for his opportunity. He also showed he could hit major league pitching. In limited opportunities he hit .400 including two doubles and a home run.

Dave's Apartment
10:30 AM April 15, 1950

The team had returned to New York the morning following a game in Pittsburgh. In his mail box, Dave found five post cards and a letter from Jill. Most contained private words but all contained the words, "I love you." However, only one post card mentioned Jill had attended church. The letter reported Jane and Woody had set a date for their wedding. It will be on Saturday, June 10, in Grace Cathedral, the big one on Nob hill. A big crowd is expected. Jane plans to resign from United on April 30. She will move back home to San Francisco soon after. "Jane has asked me to be a bride's maid and I want to do it. If necessary I will take vacation time."

"I'm thinking I should wait to put in for a transfer until you're sure you will stay with the team. The San Francisco Times is keeping us supplied with all the news about you Dave, but I don't know if you've made the team. What do you think about that? I want to be where you are Dave. I miss you so much." The letter included Jill's flight schedule for April. She is home today, so Dave planned to call her this evening.

"Operator." "Operator, this is Dave Mason, I want to place a person to person call to Miss Jill Garber in Burlingame, California. The number is Diamond 6-5232." "One moment please." "Hello." "I have a person to person call for Miss Jill Garber." "Just a minute please." "Hello." "Is this Miss. Jill Garber?" "Yes." "Go ahead sir." "Good evening, this is Mr. Dave Mason calling from New York City. I am now a member of the world champion New York Dukes Baseball Team." "Dave, it's so good to hear your voice and that's great news. Did you receive my letter?" "Yes, I did, and that's why I called, to tell you that I agree with you're putting off requesting the transfer for now. I suggest you wait until June. I should know by then if I'm going to be with the team for the whole season. I do miss you Jill." "Oh Dave, I have missed you so much after our eight months together. You've been gone for a month an a half but it seems like years."

I have learned that my Denver friend and apartment mate,

Dorothy, is based in New York." "Oh, I thought she got married." "She was going to, but just a month before the wedding, with invitations out and all plans made, she learned her pilot future husband was a womanizer who tried to take every stew he flew with to bed. He was very sly about it and threatened the girls if they talked about it, so he got away with it for some time. One of the girls of his past learned about his impending marriage and passed the word through her supervisor. Dorothy confronted him and he didn't deny it. He said he was sowing his wild oats while he could." Dorothy told him, "Men like you don't change," and gave his ring back."

She was so devastated that she took a leave of absence. She went back to her home in Montana to get over it. When she returned, she wanted to be as far away from Denver as possible so she would not likely fly with him. I told her I might be transferring to New York. She said, "Call me if you do." "She lives in Flushing." Dave said, "Dorothy is fortunate she learned about him before they got married. I don't think a womanizer can change easily. Pilots have too many opportunities. Please keep the post cards coming Jill, I look for them each day." "I will Dave." "I love you Jill." "I love you, so much Dave." "Good night." "Good night."

April 15, 1950

The scheduled game with Brooklyn was snowed out. It was a first for Dave. He had only seen snow in Yosemite National Park in California. This gave Dave some time to buy food and additional items for the apartment. His plan was to eat a big breakfast in the apartment, take a snack with him to the ball park and eat dinner in a restaurant following home games. Games started at 2:30 or 3:30 in the afternoon. It would be nice to have evenings free.

Dave had located the Kiwanis Club of Flushing, organized in 1927. The club met on Tuesdays at 12:30. He would need to find another club that met in the morning or evening to make up.

Jill's Apartment
7:30 PM April 15, 1950

After calling for Jill at least twice, and missing her because she was on flights, Kent Ross was successful tonight. He asked her for a dinner date next Friday and Jill accepted.

Dukes Stadium
Brooklyn at New York
5:35 PM April 16, 1950

Brooklyn had won the pre-season game today. The Dukes pitcher, Louis Leon, was his usual wild self. The score was 6 to 4.

On Tuesday the Dukes would open the season in Boston. Before today's game, manager Felton, announced his starting lineup and pitching rotation for the Boston series. Felton favored a set lineup as opposed to the platoon system. To play regularly for Felton, position players had to be more than specialists who just hit right or left handed pitchers. They also had to be good defensive players.

The Dukes batting order for the season opener in Boston:
Billy "Long Arms' Duke, Shortstop
Larry Mann, Second base
Tommie Hoff, Left field
Vic Marko, Center field
J. B. Felton, Catcher
Mike Hudson, Right field
Glen Close, First base
Jim Essick, Third base
Doug Abbott, Pitcher

The pitchers for the three game Boston series will be Doug Abbott, Lindsey Barrett and Vic Carlisle.

The Dukes' compete roster was handed out to the reporters.

Infielders:
Billy Duke, ss
Larry Mann, 2b
Glen Close, 1b
Len Ogle, 1b
Jim Essick, 3b
Randle White, 3b
Rick Loud, 2b
Roger Lamb, ss
Larry Small, ss, 2b

Outfielders:
Tommie Hoff
Vic Marko
Mike Hudson
Gordon Enson
Cliff Nelson
Jim Fielding
Hank Wilkes

Catchers:
J. B. Felton
Ray Silva
Ralph Hoffman

Pitchers
Doug Abbott
Lindsay Barrett
Vic Carlisle
Louis Leon
Ed Edgar
Jake Filner
Bob Pennell
Tom Harris
Ray James

Two rookies had made the team, Dave and outfielder Gordon Enson.

The first question from one of the writers was, "What are your plans for the expensive rookie and Minor League Player of the Year, Dave Mason?" Felton replied that he would have Mason watch his first major league baseball game from the dugout and then he would probably be in the bullpen. "Do you have a plan on when he might start a game? " "No," said Felton. "I will probably have him get his feet wet by pitching in relief first."

The next question was how Felton planned to use pitcher Jake Filner? Filner had come to the Dukes in an off season trade with last place St. Louis. Both Felton and General Manager Donald Newton thought Filner was a much better pitcher than his record for the lowly St Louis team. In the trade, the Dukes sent a promising young catcher, Howard Trent, two players and cash for Filner. Both Felton and Newton said you can't have too much pitching. "Initially, Filner would be a spot starter, Felton said. "We will see how he pitches." The next question was, "Are you trying to change the focus of the team from a power hitting big inning team to one that features pitching?" Newton replied, "We are trying to make the team better so we will keep winning. Keep in mind, our power hitters are aging and we must develop replacements in the next few years. If we don't, we will have to rely on improved pitching."

Monday afternoon the Dukes left Grand Central Station on the Yankee Clipper train for the four hour trip to Boston.

Chapter Twenty Two

Fenway Park

Landsdowne Street & Yawkey Way

Boston, Massachusetts

New York at Boston

5:30 PM April 18, 1950

DAVE WAS WALKING to the visitor's clubhouse following the end of the opening game of the season in Boston. He had witnessed his first major league baseball game. And what a game! At the start of the sixth inning the Dukes were trailing by a score of 10 to 0. Starting pitcher Doug Abbott had been racked for six runs in the first two innings. The Dukes had managed only one hit off southpaw Mel Powell. But in that sixth inning the Dukes came alive and scored four runs.

Then two innings later, they exploded for 10 runs. Fireman Ed Edgar came on to shut out the bean towner's and preserve the 14 to 10 victory. It was a great demonstration for Dave of how a game can change, no matter what the score.

Dave had been assigned to watch his first game in the Dukes dugout because manager Felton had no plans to use him in the game. Dave watched ace pitcher Doug Abbott get knocked out of the game in the second inning. Halfway through the sixth inning

Dave thought the game was over.

Dave had brought his pitching chart to record how Boston batter faired against the Dukes pitchers. This would be the start of his catalog of the good hitters in the American League. It would help him if and when he got the opportunity to face them.

At dinner this evening with Randle "Randy" White, Dave reflected on the advantages of playing baseball in the day time compared with the night games he played in the Pacific Coast League. White said, "I like day baseball for the playing conditions because you can see much better. Also, I like to have evenings free. But I think it's only a matter of time before most games will be played at night."

Dave asked Randy what manager Felton's practice was in brining relief pitchers into a game. "Since we have veteran pitchers, he usually gives them time to work out of trouble. However, he will bring Edgar into a game at any point because he can pitch extended innings. Also the team's ability to score runs allows Felton to be more patient with starters."

Dave had been matched with White as a road roommate because White had requested him. It put two college graduates together.

The Gallery
1 West 3rd Avenue
San Mateo, California
7:30 PM April 18, 1950

Three thousand miles away, Jill was having dinner with Kent Ross. They were dining in a new restaurant in San Mateo. They had ordered their dinner and when the waiter served the food there was an error in Kent's order. He had ordered a baked potato, but received mashed potatoes. He was very rude to the waiter and demanded the plate be returned to the kitchen and the order corrected. He did this in a loud voice that attracted the attention of other dinners. Jill was embarrassed. She thought about the times when a mistake had been made in hers or Dave's orders and how kind Dave was in dealing with the waiter or waitress. He would say something like, "We all make mistakes. I encourage you and your kitchen staff to learn from your mistake." He never raised his voice. Jill became silent, while Kent acted like the incident had not happened. Jill decided this would be her last date with Ken Ross.

New York at Boston, Doubleheader
6:00 PM April 19, 1950

Baseball scheduling didn't make sense sometimes and this was one of them. Scheduling a doubleheader on the second day of the season could not be explained.

The starting pitcher in the first game for the Dukes was Lindsey Barrett. He did not pitch well and lost the game 6 to 3. The Dukes won their second game of the season in the nightcap when Vic Carlisle was supported by lots of hits and runs, winning the game by the score of 17 to 8.

The final game with Boston was rained out, so the Dukes returned to New York with two wins and a loss.

Dukes Stadium
Junction & Northern Boulevards
Queens, New York
Washington at New York
2:30 PM April 21, 1950

It was opening day in New York. The opponent was the Washington Senators, "First in the country, last in the American League." The Governor would participate in the opening ceremonies.

Today, Dave was sent to the bullpen, indicating he might pitch, but only if the Dukes were losing big. Louis Leon, the starting pitcher was hit hard, but survived until the seventh inning when Ed Edgar took over to quiet the Senator's bats. Vic Marko, Tommie Hoff and J. B. Felton hit home runs that helped produce 15 runs. The game ended with the score 15 to 7 for the Dukes. The Dukes' pitchers were not doing well and Dave thought he would have an opportunity to pitch soon. Only time would tell.

Washington at New York
5:35 PM April 23, 1950

Dave was in the bullpen again today. He couldn't see the pitches from the pen, so he could only talk to the relievers about hitters, which he did. Jake Filner, the starting pitcher today was hit hard and reliever Edgar had to be called on again. He entered the game in the ninth inning with the score 6 to 6. Edgar allowed a single to the first batter he faced, Gil Coates, that scored Eddie Voss from second and a 7 to 6 lead for Washington. The Dukes could not rally in the bottom of the ninth and Hunky Ferris, the Washington manager finally got some revenge for his firing as the Dukes' manager in 1947. Dave did warm up, but did not see action.

In this young season, relief pitcher Ed Edgar had pitched in three of the five games played by the Dukes. Edgar was the first relief pitcher in recent years, but not the first. The first real relief pitcher, one who expected to enter games in the late innings to save it for a starter, was a pitcher with the unusual name of Firpo Marberry. Firpo was a pitcher for the Washington Senators in the 1920s. Marberry became the relief pitcher for Hall of Fame pitcher Walter Johnson as his career came to a close. In 1926 Marberry became the first pitcher to save twenty games. Then it wasn't until Ed Edgar's rise after World War II that relief pitching started to become a practice.

Independence Hall
Independence Park
Philadelphia, Pennsylvania
1:30 PM April 24, 1950

The final game of the Washington series was rained out. From Penn Station the team took the Pennsylvania Limited night train at 10:25 from Penn Station, arriving in Philadelphia at midnight. The team was here for a two game series. The first game on Monday, April 24 was an early rain out. This gave Dave time to look around Philadelphia. He went to Independence Hall and spent the afternoon there. It was his interest in history that sent him there.

Shibe Park
21st & Somerset Streets
Philadelphia, Pennsylvania
New York at Philadelphia
5:30 PM April 25, 1950

After starting pitchers had failed to go the route in the first five games of the season, Doug Abbott did it, defeating the Athletics 6 to 3. Dave was back in the dugout charting the hitters. Two double plays at critical times helped Abbott. Abbott's pitching style was quite different than Dave's. Abbott walked seven and allowed ten hits, but still won the game.

Dukes Stadium
Boston at New York
5:45 PM April 26, 1950

Back in New York, Boston was in town for a two game series. Dave was back in the bullpen today. He watched Vic Carlisle limit Boston to two runs and pitch a complete game. The Dukes had produced four runs in the first inning on home runs by J.B. Felton and Randy White. The Dukes won the game 11 to 2.

Since the season started, all Dave had time for was baseball, eating and sleeping. He confirmed that eating a big breakfast, having a snack before the game and eating dinner after the game was a good schedule.

Boston at New York
4:00 PM April 27, 1950

Louis Leon was the starting pitcher today. He had pitched well for the first four innings. The score was 1 to 1 on solo home runs by each team. Now in the top of the fifth inning, Leon's typical wildness took over. He had just walked the leadoff batter. He couldn't find the plate and walked the next three batters, forcing in a run. Then two hits and the Red Sox had a 5 to 1 lead.

That was enough for manager Ozzie Felton. He summoned Dave from the bullpen. When he entered the game there was one out and a man on second base. Dave threw a sinker for a strike. On the second pitch, the batter hit a hard ground ball down the first base line that first baseman Glen Close fielded and stepped on the bag at first for one out. The runner at second took off for third, but Close threw a bullet to third to nail the runner. A double play and the Dukes had escaped further damage.

In the last half of the fifth inning, second baseman Les Mann hit a double to left field. Most thought Dave would be called back from the on-deck circle for a pinch hitter. But Felton wanted to see Dave hit against a good pitcher. Switch hitting, Dave batting left handed, hit the second pitch into center field for a single scoring Mann. That brought a big cheer from the Dukes dugout. The Dukes did not extend the rally, and the inning ended with the score 5 to 2.

Over the next four innings, Dave allowed one hit, struck out two, walked no batter and shut out the Red Sox for the rest of the game. He got six ground outs and four fly balls to the outfield. It was a great start for Dave even though the Dukes mounted no rally and lost the game 5 to 2.

Manager Felton had many questions to answer from the writers following the game. The most asked was, "Will you put Mason in the starting rotation?" Ozzie was non-committal. He said, "We'll see. Jake Filner will pitch the opening game of the Washington series in the Capital tomorrow night."

The team was bused to Penn Station where they took the Mount Vernon to Washington, arriving at 11:00 PM.

Griffith Stadium
Washington, D. C.
New York at Washington, Night
10:15 PM April 28, 1950

In the first night game of the season, Washington defeated the Dukes 5 to 4. Jake Filner took the loss. Dave was in the bullpen, but did not warm up.

New York at Washington
4:00 PM April 30, 1950

Saturday's game had been rained out and the team was sitting out another rain delay of today's game. Yesterday the Dukes had traded former bonus player, Jim Fielding to the Chicago White Sox for outfielder Hank Wilkes and cash. Fielding came to the Dukes in a trade with Cleveland for outfielder Jim Hart during the winter. Fielding, a member of the Ohio State baseball team, had been signed in 1940 for a bonus of $60,000. He had an indifferent career in Cleveland and took a big pay cut in salary to see if the Dukes uniform would make a difference. Following the trade announcement, Fielding said he would insist on restitution of the twenty five percent cut in salary he took to join the Dukes. He may not report to Chicago.

The rain did not let up and today's game was called. The team took the afternoon Congressional Limited, arriving in Penn Station at 7:15 PM.

Dave's Apartment
10:40 PM April 30, 1950

Dave has arrived at his apartment house and picked up his mail. There were two post cards from Jill. In the most recent she reported talking to two stewardesses who had just transferred from New York. "They didn't like New York. I'll write a letter about it later." That didn't sound too good to Dave. If he didn't get the letter soon, he would call Jill.

10:00 AM May 1, 1950

There was no game today, so for the first time since the season started, Dave had time to get some things done. He went shopping for a television set. The newspapers were full of advertisements for TVs. Dave visited a TV store in Flushing where he selected a 20 inch RCA table model he could take to his apartment in the car.

In the afternoon, Dave drove to the Fifth Avenue Presbyterian Church to locate it and find out about a Sunday school class. He learned there was a young adult class at 9:30. Dave would attend the class on Sunday to see if he liked it. The class schedule would give him time to get to the stadium for Sunday afternoon games.

In the evening Dave watched The Lights Out Drama Playhouse on his new TV. The play was The Devil to Play, starring Grace Kelly.

Dukes Stadium
Chicago at New York
5:35 PM May 2, 1950

There was more rain today, so after sitting out the delay, Dave located the bowling lanes in Flushing. After bowling three games, he was approached by a young man about 18 or 19. He asked if Dave would like to bowl three games for $20.000. Since he was willing to risk $20.00, Dave thought he must be a confident bowler. His name was Don. Dave learned that Don was a passenger agent for United Airlines at La Guardia Airport. He was older than he looked. He had worked at United for two years after two years in the Air Force. Don won the $20.00 that afternoon, and it started a long time friendship. When Don asked Dave what he did for a living, Dave said he was a baseball player. This sparked Don's interest because he had played in high school and now pitched for a Flushing semi-pro team. Don liked to play the game, but said he was not much of a follower of major league teams. He didn't know Dave was a member of the Dukes. Don worked the graveyard and some swing shift. This gave him free daytime for bowling and baseball.

Following a discussion about pitching, Dave thought he might have found a person who could count and chart his pitches during home games. Dave and Don Frank exchanged phone numbers and planned to bowl again. Dave wanted to recover his $20.00.

Chicago at New York
5:30 PM May 4, 1950

The Dukes had won yesterday 4 to 3. Lindsey Barrett pitched well. Rookie Gordon Enson had started in left field, but went hitless.

Today it had been veteran pitcher Vic Carlisle against Chicago rookie Bill Coates in his first start. Carlisle was routed, allowing eight runs in two and a third innings. Before being relieved he had made 59 pitches. He was followed by Tom Harris who gave up four more runs. In the eighth inning with the score 12 to 0, Dave was sent into the game. Dave made nineteen pitches in two innings, got five ground balls and one fly out. He allowed no hits or runs. The game ended with the score 12 to 0 for Chicago.

After the game the first question by a writer was, "When will Mason start a game?" Felton's reply was, "Louis Leon will start tomorrow's game against Cleveland. I'll announce the pitchers for the next two games tomorrow."

Dave had not attended a Kiwanis meeting since he left California. He had found a club that met on Thursday evening at 7:00 PM. It was the Kiwanis Club of Five Towns located in Valley Stream on Long Island. Dave was introduced as a visiting Kiwanian from the Kiwanis Club of San Francisco.

Dave said he lived in Flushing and worked in Queens. He didn't say, nor was he asked what his occupation was. Dave contributed a happy dollar because he had found this club where he could make up. He said he couldn't attend lunch meetings.

Chicago at New York
4:15 PM May 5, 1950

The game was rained out early today. The writers had plenty of time to question manager Felton. When a doubleheader was announced for the next day, Felton said, "Doug Abbott will pitch the first game and Dave Mason the second."

Dukes Stadium
Cleveland at New York
6:15 PM May 6, 1950

In today's doubleheader, Cleveland, powered by Luke Jackson and Ben Rose home runs won the first game 5 to 4. In 1949 Jackson hit 25 home runs and batted in 92 runs in Just 80 games for the San Diego Padres of the Pacific Coast League. He was one of two Black players on the Cleveland team. This would prompt Dave to ask Randy White when the Dukes would have such players.

In the second game, Dave's first major league start, the Cleveland lead off batter singled through the infield. The next batter hit a pop up behind first base that fell in for a single. This put runners on first and second with no outs. To the next batter, Dave threw two sinkers for a strike and a ball. A change up was hit back to the mound. Dave fired to second base and the relay to first completed the double play.

Now there were two outs and a Cleveland runner on third. Dave decided he needed a strike out. With cleanup batter Luke Jackson coming to the plate that was a tall order. However Dave had faced Jackson in the PCL with reasonable success. Dave thought Jackson would be over aggressive, so he fed him a change on the first pitch. Jackson was way out in front of the pitch for strike one. A sinker on the inside tied up Luke and he watched it catch the inside corner of the plate for strike two. Next, Dave threw his rising fast ball on the outside to try to get Jackson to fish for it. He didn't. With the count now one ball and two strikes, Dave thought Luke would be looking for a fast ball, so Dave threw him another sinker on the inside that Jackson watched for a called strike and Dave had his strike out. He had met the first big challenge of his young major league career.

There was no score starting the last half of the third inning and Dave was coming to bat. On a two ball, two strike count, he stroked a double down the first base line. He scored on a single by Billy Duke. Cliff Nelson doubled to left, Duke going to third. Tommie Hoff cleaned the bases with a three run home run. The Dukes now led 4 to 0. Dave breezed through the next four innings, allowing just two hits. No runner reached second base. In the top of the sixth inning it was getting dark. While the game was official, having gone five innings, Dave hoped to pitch one more inning. He threw six pitches, got three ground outs, and the game was called because of darkness.

Dave had won his first major league game, a shut out. He allowed four hits, had one strike out and issued no walks. He had given lots of thumbs up to his infielders who played good defense without any errors. It was a good start for Dave.

Both Dave and manager Felton had many questions from the baseball writers following the game. The main question put to Felton was, "Would Dave Mason join the regular pitching rotation?" Felton didn't hesitate, he said, "Yes."

Fifth Avenue Presbyterian Church
7 West 55th Street
New York City, New York
9:30 AM May 7, 1950

This was Dave's first Sunday attending the young adult class at the Fifth Avenue Presbyterian Church. As Dave entered the classroom, he saw a beautiful brunette girl sitting in the first row of chairs. While young people entered the room, Dave couldn't take his eyes off of this girl. He thought; why am I looking at this girl? Have I subconsciously given up on my being able to marry Jill? Was it her lack of reports on church attendance?

The class study was on Paul's first missionary journey. The lesson today covered the preparation for the journey. Paul was in Antioch, Syria, where it was becoming the center of the church's activity. Many of the believers in Antioch had come from Gentile families. They thought of their relatives located throughout the Roman Empire. The church leaders decided a missionary party should be formed and sent out to nearby countries to spread the message of salvation. Paul and Barnabas were selected to make the journey.

The class teacher, Steve Early, was a young man in his early thirties who Dave would learn was an assistant professor of history and political science at Columbia University. There were about twenty five young people attending the class most of whom appeared to be college students.

When the class was over Dave couldn't resist asking the fellow sitting next to him who the brunette was. Barry Wold had introduced himself when Dave sat down. Dave gave only his first name, a habit he had gotten into in San Francisco. "Oh that's Sharon Knox. She is a pre-law student at Columbia. She wants to be a Wall Street Lawyer. Her father is a Wall Street broker. If you're thinking about asking her for a date, beware! She is very particular, and turns down four out of five. Believe me, I speak from experience." "Thank you Barry. Are you a Columbia student?" "No, New York University." Dave felt it would be a challenge to get a date with Sharon.

Following class, Dave drove to the stadium, arriving just after 11:00, more than the required time prior to the 2:00 PM game time.

Dukes Stadium
Detroit at New York
5:25 PM May 8, 1950

Yesterday the Dukes won 6-3 before 54,000 fans. Louis Leon was the winning pitcher. Today, Detroit won 7-1 defeating the Dukes number two starting pitcher Lindsey Barrett.

Dave's Apartment
9:30 AM May 9, 1950

There was no game today so Dave called Don Frank to set up a bowling date. They agreed on Saturday morning at 9:00.

It had been a week since Dave had received Jill's post card about the girls who didn't like New York. There had been no letter but Dave decided to wait instead of calling Jill.

Dukes Stadium
St. Louis at New York
4:00 PM May 10, 1950

It was another afternoon of waiting out the rain until the game was called. Dave decided he would start bringing a book to the games so he could read while waiting on the rain.

The Dukes management had been concerned about the health of their veteran players. Donald Newton decided a good hitter was needed. So far their bonus rookie, Gordon Enson had not hit major league pitching.

Bill Wood had won the Pacific Coast League batting title in 1946. He had been purchased by Cleveland for the 1947 season. However he didn't get continuous playing time and did not hit well. Cleveland decided he was a minor league hitter, but could not hit major league pitching. They traded him to Pittsburgh of the National League. Again, he did not hit well, so he was optioned to San Diego of the Pacific Coast League. Wood tore up the PCL again, hitting .380 in 1948. Pittsburgh brought him up for the 1949 season; He had a fair season, batting .264. In the off season the Dukes tried to work a trade for Wood, but the teams could not agree on a player to complete the trade. Wood started the 1950 season playing left field and leading off for Pittsburgh.

With the Dukes injury problems mounting, a trade was worked out for Wood. He was installed in left field and was hitting over .300. Was it the Dukes uniform magic? No one was sure.

Dave's Apartment
6:30 PM May 10, 1950

When Dave arrived at his apartment house he ran into Wes Jones. He was just coming in the door in his Pan American uniform carrying his bags. Dave asked Wes if he had stopped for dinner. Wes said, "No, I didn't stop." Dave invited him to join him. Wes accepted saying, "Give me twenty minutes to get out of his uniform, and I'll meet you here in the lobby."

Dave had met Wes early in April when Dave saw him in uniform and asked if he was a pilot. When he learned Wes was a flight engineer, Dave knew they had something in common. Wes was a baseball fan, but his team was the New York Giants.

Over a steak dinner in the Golden Pheasant Restaurant in Westbury, Wes had some great stories about Buenos Aries and the beautiful girls he saw during his layover. Since he was there for just twenty four hours, he could only observe. The trip took many hours and he had used up half of his flying time for the month. He would not fly again until May 26th, then on a trip to the Caribbean. Dave asked if he was still flying Constellations. Wes said, "Yes and we have all but eliminated the past engine problems." Dave had told Wes previously about his experience with the Constellation engine problems during the summer he worked at Pan American in San Francisco.

Wes said he planned to spend some extra time at the Air National Guard outfit he belonged to. Dave asked if the guard service helped his Pan American career. Wes said, "No, seniority is the only thing that counts at Pan Am. The extra money I make is going into flying lesions. I think the flight engineer will be eliminated in the future when the airlines are flying jets. I want to be prepared." "That's interesting, because I've heard that before. A friend of mine who is the director of flight engineer training for United Airlines has told me the same thing. What aircraft do you fly at the guard?" "It's a B-29 outfit. We have limited funds, so we fly the simulator most of the time. We get little air time."

Dave had no interest in military reserve service. Little did he know how that would change in the future?

Dukes Stadium
St. Louis at New York, Doubleheader
6:00 PM May 11, 1950

Doug Abbott pitched a 5 to 1 win for the Dukes in the first game.

In his second start in the nightcap, Dave allowed nine hits, but only two St. Louis base runners reached second base. Three double plays were significant. In this game, Dave walked his first batter of the season and struck out two. Still, he threw only four pitches per out. Again, Dave was a productive hitter. In the second inning he led off with a single and later scored. In the seventh, batting right handed, Dave hit a line drive solo home run into the left field seats about 363 feet away. Wanting the shut out, Dave retired the last six batters in the eighth and ninth innings, all on ground balls. It was a 5 to 0 win for the Dukes.

The writers and the radio reporter had many questions for Dave following the game. He responded with good answers and didn't leave the stadium until six o' clock. Dave drove directly to the Kiwanis meeting of the Five Towns club for a make up.

Dave's Apartment
9:00 AM May 12, 1950

Dave had gone out for breakfast. He picked up a New York Tribune. Dave liked the baseball writer for the paper. He was a young fellow, but was very knowledgeable about the game. Dave had learned that Dane Sullivan had played baseball at Columbia. On the sports page Dave found a column by Sullivan with the headline, "Dave Mason, a different kind of pitcher."

"Yesterday at Dukes Stadium, rookie pitcher Dave Mason demonstrated what a different kind of pitcher he is. Dave throws strikes, but doesn't strike out many batters. He throws pitches that have so much 'stuff' on them that batters hit the ball into the ground to infielders and fly balls for outs. Mason's best pitch is a sinker that sinks into the strike zone from his over arm delivery."

"In yesterday's game, Mason had no strike outs and issued no walks. The fans like his game because there is constant action. Yesterday, Mason allowed nine hits, mostly ground balls through the infield, but no St. Louis runner advanced past second base. Mason's ability to get ground ball outs in critical situations resulted in three double plays. I'm told the Dukes infielders like his fast work on the mound because it keeps them alert with little standing around. Mason takes little time between pitches."

"Another difference in this pitcher is he is a hitter. A lead off single in the second inning started the scoring for the Dukes. In the seventh inning he hit a 360 foot home run into the left field seats. Although a natural right hander, Mason taught himself to be a switch hitter. He started in his senior year in high school. Mason says his motivation for hitting and switch hitting is to avoid being lifted for a pinch hitter in the late innings of games. Mason takes hitting practice with the position players, something pitchers don't usually do. He has demonstrated his ability to hit major league pitching and has gained the respect of the position players. Initially they questioned his taking their time in the batting cage."

"Yesterday's performance by Dave Mason is another feather in the cap of Luke Devore, the Dukes west coast scout who signed Vic Marko almost ten yeas ago. Devore discovered Mason in 1942 when he was a tall skinny high school sophomore and was immediately interested because Mason had the making of a good sinker ball pitcher. With their good defense and large outfield, sinker ball pitchers have done well for the Dukes."

"However, Devore had to wait until Mason had graduated from college and played part of a season in the Pacific Coast League where he was a big winner. The Dukes bought" Mason from the San Francisco Sea Lions at the end of last season for a reported $125,000 and players. Dave Mason made a good start yesterday in paying back the Dukes for their investment."

Before departing for the ball park Dave picked up his mail. There was a letter from Jill. She described her talk with the stewardesses who transferred from New York. She had put it off until the end of the letter. Dave wondered about that. Jill said the girls did not like the big city. Both had grown up in small mid west towns. They had been based in Seattle and wanted a change in climate. They did say the made a mistake in renting an apartment in Brooklyn to be close to plays and other entertainment in Manhattan.

"I must tell you that my supervisor told me about these girls because she doesn't want me to transfer." Jill was planning to write a letter to Dorothy to learn her opinion about living in Flushing and flying out of La Guardia airport.

Chapter Twenty Three

The Home of Larry Lavell

Divisadero Street

San Francisco, California

7:30 AM May 12, 1950

LARRY LAVELL, OWNER of Lavell Chevrolet, was sitting down to breakfast alone because his wife was not a morning person and his two children were away at college. The sporting green of the San Francisco Chronicle was the first section of the paper he read. Turning to the major league baseball results, he read about Dave Mason's pitching and hitting in the game yesterday. Larry had an immediate idea. When he arrived at his dealership he would call his good friend Bill Turner, owner of Turner Chevrolet in New York City. Larry and Bill had been good friends for many years and had shared many sales and promotion ideas to sell Chevy's. Bill Turner was a baseball fan like Larry and Bill was a New York Dukes fan. At a Chevrolet dealers meeting in New Orleans last fall, Larry told Bill about Dave Mason and the personal appearances he had made in his show room. Also the advertisements his dealership had put him in, and the radio commercials that featured Dave.

Over the years Bill Turner had heard many reports from other dealers about minor league players in the Dukes organization who can't miss. While the Dukes had a reasonable rate of success by rookies, many did not make it, so Bill was not ready to jump on the band wagon for Dave Mason.

Lavell Chevrolet
San Francisco, California
8:30 AM May 12, 1950

Larry was on the phone talking to Bill Turner. His first question to Bill was, "Have you read yesterday's baseball results?" Bill replied that he had attended an early breakfast meeting of the Mayor's committee on traffic problems, so he had no time to look at the morning paper. Larry proceeded to remind Bill of their conversation in New Orleans about the Dukes rookie pitcher Dave Mason. "He pitched his second win yesterday and got two hits including a home run. What I suggest is that you line him up for personal appearances before some other dealer does. Go after the kids and they will bring their parents. Offer the kids a baseballs autographed by Mason. He is very good with kids. So when Dave sells many cars for you Bill, just remember where you got the tip." Turner said, "I'll think about it Larry." "Okay Bill, just remember that I called about Mason." Bill Turner thought it couldn't be that good, but I'll follow Mason's progress and if he continues to do well, maybe I'll try him.

Flushing Lanes
Flushing, New York
9:00 AM May 13, 1950

The Dukes had won yesterday's game 3-2. Louis Leon was the winning pitcher. This morning, Dave and Don Frank were bowling for $5.00 per game and $10.00 for the three game series. Dave won the first game 230 to 206. Don took the second, 235 to 230. Dave won the rubber game 245 to 205 and the series, winning $15.00.

Over a cup of coffee, Dave asked Don if he would be interested in seeing all the Dukes games he could attend free, sitting in a box seat behind home plate. "Sure, what's the catch?" "In return for the good seat, I would like you to chart my pitches and those of the other Dukes' pitchers so I can learn what pitches get batters out." Dave showed Don his chart. "I need someone who knows the difference between pitches. Also, I would like you to count my pitches when I pitch, using this mechanical counter. "Sure Dave I'll give it a try. I may not be able to attend all the home games." "That's okay. The most important are the games in which I'm pitching." "Okay, give me a schedule and I'll start." "Good, I'll leave your ticket in will call." "For now, please keep what you're doing quiet. This worked for me in college and in the PCL, but I want to see how it works here before I talk to my manager about it. If anyone asks you what you're doing, just say it's a hobby."

"Try it for a couple of weeks and then we can review and go from there." "I'll start with tomorrow's game against Philly." "Good. Here are envelopes to put the chart in. Bring it to the clubhouse and give it to the guard. My name is on it."

In the game the next day with Philadelphia, the Dukes won 9-3 powered by Vic Marko's three hits, including a home run. Lindsey Barrett was the winning pitcher. The envelope with the pitching chart arrived soon after the game. It looked to Dave that Don had done a good job.

Fifth Avenue Presbyterian Church
9:30 AM May 14, 1950

Anticipating the Sunday school class this morning, Dave had to decide if he would try to get an introduction to Sharon Knox or just introduce himself. Jill's letter about New York had not been encouraging. He was wondering if Jill would come to New York. Dave decided he would talk to Sharon one way or another.

In the lesson today, Paul, Barnabas and a traveling companion, young Mark had departed for their first destination, the island of Cyprus. It was the home of Barnabas. The travelers landed at Salamis the chief city of the island.

Paul and Barnabas told about Jesus wherever they could. In the synagogues, orchards, mines or wherever people gathered.

When the class was over before Dave could approach Sharon, Steve Early came up to Dave and asked, "Have you met Sharon Knox." "No I haven't had that pleasure." Steve then called Sharon over to where he and Dave were standing and said, "Sharon, I would like you to meet Dave Mason." "Hello Dave, you pitched a good game Thursday." "Well, thank you. Are you a baseball fan?' "Yes. All the members of our family are fans and rooters for the Dukes." "That's interesting, can I have your phone number so I can call and we can talk about baseball." "Sure, it's MU 3-2855," "Thank you Sharon. Now I want to talk to Steve and then I must head for the ball park. Goodbye Sharon." "Goodbye Dave."

Dave asked Steve Early for a suggested book on the travels of Paul. Steve suggested The Life and Journeys of Paul by Charles Ferguson Ball, published by Moody Press.

As Dave drove to the ball park, it did not enter his mind that the introduction to Sharon had been a set up initiated by Sharon. Dave still didn't have an ego when it came to girls.

Later that morning Sharon told her mother she had met Dave Mason. "Oh, just as you planned?" "Yes, and he is very polite and asked me for my phone number." "You didn't give it to him did you?" "Yes I did mother." "You're not playing hard to get with Dave?" "No mother, I want to know him, the sooner the better." "My, My. My daughter is so out of character." By now they had entered the sanctuary for the morning worship service. Sharon's father and younger brother soon joined them.

Dukes Stadium
Philadelphia at New York
5:47 PM May 14, 1950

Philadelphia won the game 9-8. Dave pinch hit in the seventh inning. He doubled and drove in two runs, but it wasn't enough.

The Dukes took the Penn Texas from Penn Station at 7:50 that evening for the overnight trip to St Louis. This was the first overnight trip of the season and Dave's first since he was a nine year old boy. Many of the players played Poker. Not being a poker player, Dave tried to get a game of hearts started, but could not get a foursome interested. He watched one of the poker games for a while. Soon he went to his seat and read until bedtime. Being a rookie, he had a top bunk with his roommate Randy White in the lower.

In the morning after breakfast Dave wrote letters to his parents and to Jill. The train arrived in St. Louis at 3:40 PM on Monday afternoon and the team was bused to their hotel.

Dave saw the movie Asphalt Jungle starring Sterling Hayden and James Whitmore, advertised in the St. Louis paper and asked Randy White if he would like to see it. He did, and they took a cab to the theatre.

May 16, 1950

On this day the Dukes had to reduce their roster by four players to get down to 25 players. Three players were sent down to Buffalo. The baseball Commissioner had ruled that the Dukes must either trade or release Jim Fielding, the bonus player who was traded to Chicago but refused to report. The Dukes released Fielding. He was not signed by another major league club so he played 87 games for Oakland of the Pacific Coast League. In 1951he played only five games for Oakland and was released. He was signed by St. Louis of the American League in 1952, but appeared in only three games and was released. That brought his baseball career to an end.

Sportsman's Park
Dozier & Spring Streets
St. Louis, Missouri
New York at St. Louis
5:16 PM May 16, 1950

Dave had pitched a shutout in his first game against the lowly Browns. Using sinkers, his improving change up and a few rising fast balls,

Dave threw less than 90 pitches.

There was added excitement in the fourth inning when the Browns pitcher threw at Vic Marko's head. Vic had hit a home run in the first inning for a 1-0 Dukes' lead. When the St. Louis pitcher came to bat, Dave drilled him in his hip with a fast ball. The Brown's pitcher limped to first and had to be taken out of the game.

Dave continued his hitting with a single and a double. The double drove in two runs in the fifth inning, increasing the Dukes lead to 3-0. Dave had hit in every game he had played and was batting .600.

The Duke added two more runs in the eighth inning for a 5-0 win. It was Dave's third shutout.

After the game, Dave and Gordon Enson went bowling. Enson wasn't playing much because he had not hit when he did play. Dave wanted to cheer him up, by getting his mind off baseball.

Dave and Gordon bowled for $5.00 per game and $20.00 for a three game series. Enson was good competition, but Dave won two games and the series to win $30.00.

In the evening, Dave placed a call to Sharon. "I have a person to person call for Miss. Sharon Knox." Sharon's mother had answered the phone, and called Sharon. "You have a person to person call." "Ask who is calling" "Operator, who is calling?" "Mr. Dave Mason." "It's Dave Mason." Sharon was at the phone in a flash. "This is Sharon Knox." "Go ahead sir." "Good evening Sharon how are you?" "I'm fine Dave. Where are you calling from?" "I'm in St. Louis where we defeated the Browns today. The purpose of my call Sharon is to invite you to have dinner with me on Monday evening, May 29 when I return to New York." "Oh sure I accept." "May I pick you up at 6:30?" "That will be fine Dave." Thank you Sharon." "What was the score of the game today?" "It was 5-0." "Oh another shutout." "My, are you keeping tract?" "I always keep tract of the Dukes." "That's great Sharon. I'll see you on the 29th. Good night." "Good night Dave."

Dave had not planned to date any girl even when he agreed to do so in order to encourage Jill to date others while they were separated. He didn't know why this was happening.

Sharon's mother, Alexis, said, "Is this my hard to get a date with daughter?" "Yes mother, I think I have found a potential dreamboat." "Oh, My."

New York at St. Louis
6:05 PM May 17, 1950

Dave watched the game from the dugout, while charting. He couldn't see where the pitches were except high or low, but he could tell what kind of a pitch was thrown. He could also ask the pitcher what opposing players were hitting. New York won the game 6-5. Vic Marko and Randy White hit home runs. Jake Filner pitched the win.

That evening the team boarded the Chicago Special of the Gulf, Mobile & Ohio Railroad. Following dinner, manager Felton asked to talk to Dave in his compartment. Felton said, "Louis Leon has a sore arm and I don't know how long he will be out. It will take time to call up another pitcher from Buffalo, so we need to do something in the meantime. I know you pitched on three days rest in the PCL. Would you be willing to try it here?" "Sure, I liked to pitch every four days. It helped me stay sharp." "Ok, I'll start you Saturday in Chicago. We will watch how it goes and make sure your velocity holds up."

The train arrived at Chicago's La Salle Street Station at 9:00 AM Thursday morning, and the team boarded a bus for the Stevens Hotel.

Dave had written to his sister Pam, who was working in Chicago, offering tickets for one of the Dukes games against the White Sox. Pam was living with her college friend Adell, a United Air Line stewardess. Pam was there because that's where Jim Smith was working. Pam and Jim were now engaged to be married.

Dave had called Pam Thursday evening to learn what day she and Jim would attend a game. Pam said Saturday would be the best day for them. "Great, you will be able to watch me pitch." He told Pam he would leave their tickets in will call. He also invited them to have dinner with him Saturday evening following the game. He said they would go to the Palm Court in the Palmer House Hotel.

Comiskey Park
35th Street & 34th Place
Chicago, Illinois
New York at Chicago
3:35 PM May 20, 1950

The Dukes had won the first game of the series Friday night 2-0. Vic Carlisle pitched a shutout giving up only two hits.

Dave was pitching his first game in the majors on three days rest. The game was in the fifth inning and there was no score. In the top of the sixth, Glen Close singled. Dave laid a perfect bunt down the third base line and both runners were safe. Duke struck out and Larry Mann singled to center field, scoring Close. After fouling off two pitches, with the count 2-2, Tommy Hoff doubled, scoring Dave and Mann. New York now led 3-0.

In the seventh inning Dave allowed his first earned run in 33 innings. The lead off batter singled through the infield. He was sacrificed to second. The next batter fouled out to catcher Felton. On the next pitch the runner on second stole third. A ground ball hit by the next batter down the first base line was fielded by Close, but his throw home was late and the runner on third, off with the pitch scored. Dave retired the next seven batters and the Dukes won the game 3-1. It was Dave's fourth win.

Dave had agreed to an interview with Leon Jones, the senior baseball writer and columnist for the Chicago Register. Jones' son Larry was a friend of Jim Smith. Dave had declined all the interview requests by the New York writers because he didn't want to call attention to himself. He was a rookie and he was concerned about the reaction of the team's veterans. Also he didn't want a repeat of the controversy he created in San Francisco when he granted an exclusive interview to Dan White.

The interview was being done before today's game.

Q "What makes your sinker ball pitch so effective?"

A "The most important factor is control. A veteran baseball player once told me I must have good control, because if your sinker is effective, batters will lay of that pitch. Also, a good sinker must have lots of spin on the ball."

Q "You only throw two other pitches, a fast ball that rises and a change. Why don't you throw a breaking pitch?"

A "One of my American Legion coaches suggested I not work on a curve ball or other breaking pitch because it puts more stress on your arm. With the sinker pitch I didn't need a breaking pitch."

Q "All your pitches are thrown from an over arm motion. How do you get your fast ball to rise from that delivery?"

A "I'll never tell."

Q "I understand you practiced control by pitching to a target"

A "That's true. The target was not the usual out line of the strike zone, however. The target had slots on the inside and outside of the strike zone that extended beyond the strike zone because umpires are not perfect. The idea was to practice pitching to the slots so I could master pitching to the inside and outside edges of the strike zone. I wanted to be able to throw strikes but not over the heart of the plate. Also, I wanted to get the first pitch over for a strike."

Q "What is your pitching philosophy?"

A "It is called pitching efficiency. I want to throw as few pitches as possible to get an out. The perfect game for me would be one where I threw 27 pitches and got 27 outs in a nine inning game. It will never happen because the human baseball player is far from perfect."

Q "Because of your engineering degree, I'm told you have a very technical approach to the game of baseball. Is this true?"

A "I use whatever I've learned in technical knowledge to improve my pitching and the ability to get batters out. In college I started counting my own pitches which wasn't too accurate, so I recruited a fellow engineering student to count for me. As a result, I could learn how many pitches it was taking to get an out."

Q "Most pitchers aren't good hitters and don't work on it. Why are you a good hitter and why have you worked on it so much?"

A "I have always been a good hitter. My hitting even improved when I mastered switch hitting starting in high school. Most pitchers were good hitters in high school, but stopped working on hitting when they became professional players. I wanted to continue to be a good hitter so I would not be taken out of games for a pinch hitter. To be a good hitter you must get at-bats and you must take batting practice. Most pitchers don't. When I started in professional baseball I insisted that I be able to take the same batting practice as position players. The big key to hitting is the ability to recognize the type of pitch coming at you."

Q "Many baseball people have said that college graduates, intelligent people, are not dedicated baseball players because it isn't their whole life. Is this true?"

A "I disagree. Randle White and I are very competitive baseball players. We may have other interests, but when the game starts it's only baseball."

Q "Do you think you can continue to pitch every fourth day throughout the season?"

A "In the years since high school, I have pitched at least 200 innings. Last year in the Pacific Coast League I pitched more than 200 innings. And that was after I had pitched almost 100 innings in the college season. It's mainly because I throw fewer pitches in a game. Also, I think my pitching to the target when I was young, built up my arm strength."

Q "Are you surprised at your success in the American League?"

A "I'm always surprised about my baseball success because I didn't have great success in winning games in high school. To be successful with my kind of pitching, I need a good team like the Dukes supporting me."

"Thank you for your time Dave" "You are very welcome."

The Palm Court
Palmer House Hotel
17 East Monroe Street
Chicago, Illinois
8:45 PM May 20, 1950

Pam, Jim Smith and Dave were enjoying an excellent dinner in what was likely the best restaurant in Chicago. Pam and Bill had been telling Dave their wedding plans. Pam would be going home at the end of June to prepare for the big day on September 2, 1950. The wedding would be held in the Stanford Memorial Church on the Stanford campus. The Rev. Arthur Cassiday, Pastor of the Palo Alto Congregational Church would perform the marriage ceremony.

Pam would have long time Palo Alto friend, Jane French Thompson, Adell and Nancy Smith. Jim's sister as bride's maids. Larry and Wayne, friends of Jim would complete the wedding party. Jim said to Dave, "If you were available, you would have been included." "Thank you Jim. I'm sorry I can't be in two places at once. I would love to be there!"

New York at Chicago, Doubleheader
6:00 PM May 21, 1950

At the beginning of the day, the Dukes and Detroit were tied for the league lead. Each team had a record of 16 wins and 8 losses. Dave watched the double header while he charted the pitches from the dugout. The Dukes won the first game 4-1 behind the pitching of

Lindsey Barrett. Doug Abbott was the losing pitcher in the second game 6-4. Detroit had split their doubleheader so the teams were still tied for the league lead starting the series in Detroit tomorrow.

The team was on the bus traveling to La Salle Street Station to board New York Central's Lake Shore Limited for Detroit.

Chevrolet Assembly Plant
2:15 PM May 22, 1950

The game with Detroit today was an early rain out. Larry Lavell had given Dave a phone number to call if he had an opportunity to tour a Chevrolet assembly plant when he was in Detroit. Dave called and took a cab to the plant. Dave found the plant tour interesting, watching how the assembly line worked.

Briggs Stadium
Michigan & National Avenues
Detroit, Michigan
New York at Detroit, Doubleheader
1:55 PM May 23, 1950

New York won the first game 6-4, gaining one game on Detroit in the race for the pennant. Carlisle was the winning pitcher. J.B. Felton hit a home. In the second game, Jake Filner lost a close game 3-2. As the result the teams were tied again in the pennant race.

Following the game, the Dukes took the Interstate express to Cleveland, arriving at midnight.

Cleveland Municipal Stadium
West 33rd & Boudreau Boulevard
Cleveland, Ohio
New York at Cleveland, Night
8:15 PM May 24, 1950

A pitching match up between Dave, the winning rookie and

Cleveland's number two ace, Bob Orange brought more than 50,000 fans to the game on a Wednesday night. The Dukes scored two runs in the first, produced by a Vic Marko double, driving in both runs.

The first batter to face Dave swung at the first pitch and hit a single between second and third. The second batter also swung at the first pitch and hit a ground ball single up the middle. The third batter swung at the first pitch and missed. On the second pitch, a change up, the batter hit a double play ball to second and the lead runner went to third. The next batter continued first pitch swinging, but grounded to first, and the inning was over. The Indians manager had evidently decided to have his batters swinging at the first pitch because Dave usually threw a strike.

In the second inning the Dukes put two men on base but Dave hit a hard line drive right at the third baseman to end the threat. The bottom half of the inning was almost a mirror of the first. Cleveland batters continued to swing at the first pitch and another single was hit through the infield. The runner moved to second on a slow roller to third that Randy White's throw just nipped the runner at first. Dave struck out the next batter on four pitches. With two down the next batter fouled off two pitches and then struck out. It was an unusual two strike out inning for Dave. Two a game is high for Dave.

The Dukes scored two more runs in the fifth inning to go up 4 to 0. Over the next five innings Dave allowed one base runner to get to third, but shut out Cleveland. The Dukes won the game 4-0 and Dave registered his fifth win and fourth shutout.

New York at Cleveland
5:35 PM May 25, 1950

Bob Pennell pitched a good game, allowing only 4 hits and won 3-1. Randy White hit a home run.

After the game, the team was on their way to Union Station. It was on to Philadelphia on the Clevelander departing at 8:05 PM. They would arrive at Philadelphia's North Station just before 7:00 AM the next morning.

Shibe Park
21st & Somerset Streets
Philadelphia, Pennsylvania
New York at Philadelphia
3:36 PM May 28, 1950

The Dukes had split the first two games of the series. Doug Abbott won 4-2 on Friday, but Lindsey Barrett lost 6-1 on Saturday.

Dave was pitching today. He had been almost perfect through the first six innings, allowing only one hit. His sinker was working to perfection. The Dukes had scored single runs in the second, third and fourth innings. In the fifth the Dukes broke the game open scoring five runs that included a base clearing double by Dave. He allowed two more hits, but no runs and ended with an 8-0 shut out win for the Dukes. He allowed three hits, struck out one and issued no walks. He had one hit in three appearances.

Following the game the Dukes took The Embassy to New York, arriving in Penn Station at 8:55 PM. During the trip some of the players talked about changing the travel from train to plane. A number of the American League teams were flying, reducing the travel time between games. The players with families could see the switch giving them more time at home. The problem was that a few players still refused to fly, and among them were veteran starters. Some thought it would take at least a year or two until the veterans retired.

It had been a good road trip for the Dukes with 10 wins and 3 losses. Their record was now 22-11 and they were in first place by a half game.

Dave's Apartment
11:00 AM May 28, 1950

Dave had picked up his mail and found a post card from Jill. It was the second one in a month. She reported nothing about transferring. Her card said nothing about attending church.

The Knox Residence
Park Avenue
New York City, New York
6:30 PM May 29, 1950

Dave had arrived at the Knox Town House to be greeted by Alexis Knox. He was introduced to Sharon's father, Tom. Thomas A. Knox III was President and sole owner of Thomas A. Knox & Company, a third generation Wall Street stock broker. On the street, the firm was known as TAK. It was a relatively small firm but had many long term clients with old money. The firm handled all of Reggie Duke's investments. Dave had learned this information from an article on the financial page of the New York Times.

Dave had made a reservation at Hoots Rohr's for dinner. He had heard about the restaurant for many years. It was reported to be a favorite of baseball players. When Dave and Sharon entered the restaurant, they were greeted by the maitre d' who said, "Good evening Dave, and Miss Sharon. Dave was surprised his name was known, but, Sharon said, "I've been here many times." So she was well known. They were given a table up front and soon Hoots Rohr himself was at the table to welcome Dave and Sharon. "It's nice to see you again Sharon. Please give my best to your father." "I will."

On the way to the restaurant Dave was asking questions of Sharon. He was learning all about her and her family. She had older and younger brothers. Thomas A the IV was 29 and worked in the family firm. William was 17 and a senior in high school. Sharon had wanted to be a Wall Street Lawyer ever since she observed her father's lawyers at work. She realized she would be working in a man's world, but had the advantage of the family firm. Sharon said, "I could start as an in-house counsel if no firm would hire me. I won't work as a paralegal or legal secretary like some trained women lawyers have." Dave kept up the questions so he did not have to talk about himself. About all he had to relate was his home town and family members.

They had an excellent dinner and enjoyed watching the well known people enter the restaurant. Sharon was well versed on the well known customers of the restaurant. They did talk about baseball and the past teams of the Dukes. Sharon had attended two World Series games in 1949.

Sharon and Dave seemed to have good chemistry for a first date. Dave thanked her for a very nice evening at her door and was gone.

Sharon's mother was waiting up for her. She was egger to learn if the date was what Sharon expected. "Well, how was it," her mother asked. "It was wonderful mother. He asked me so many questions I did most of the talking. He's not like most ball players who talk about themselves all the time. I hardly learned anything about him. Only that his home town is in Palo Alto, where Stanford is located and he has a sister who is engaged to be married and is working in Chicago. His father is in the newspaper business. He is so polite and just a nice fellow." "Just be careful Sharon, don't get carried away." "I won't mother."

Dukes Stadium
Boston at New York, Doubleheader
6:06 PM May 30, 1950

Today was Memorial Day, so the teams would play a doubleheader. Manager Felton applied his pitching philosophy by starting Jake Filner and Bob Pennell in the games. Both were second line pitchers, but the Dukes were short of pitchers and Felton had used his best against Philadelphia, a lower division team. The two pitchers came through in fine style, Filner winning the first game 7-3 and Pennell the second 4-1. It increased the Dukes lead over Detroit to 1-1/2 games

Following the double header, the writers had questions for Manager Felton.

Q "What are you doing about your shortage of pitchers?"

A "We have called up right handed pitcher Ed Card from Buffalo. He will join the team on Thursday."

Q "When will Mike Hudson play again?"

A "It's not known because knee injuries heal slowly."

Q "What about Tommie Hoff?"

A "He will start pinch hitting, but no field play. As mentioned before the season, when we traded for Jake Filner, our veteran players are aging and more subject to injury. We traded for Bill Wood who has been hitting well. So far, Gordon Enson has not shown he can hit major league pitching."

Q "You have been starting Dave Mason with only three days rest. Won't this catch up with him late in the season?"

A "I'm sure you are aware that Dave throws fewer pitches than our other pitchers.

He did this last season in the PCL, a hitter's league, after pitching almost 100 innings in the college baseball season. We are watching closely to see if he's getting tired or his pitch velocity is dropping, but we see no signs of this."

Flushing Lanes
Flushing, New York
4:30 PM May 31, 1950

After catching up with laundry and shopping for groceries, Dave went to the lanes to bowl. He bowled four games alone and thought he was wearing off some of the rust of not bowling enough.

He then went to dinner and to his apartment to watch TV. He didn't find much on, so he read a book.

A team meeting at 10:30 tomorrow morning prior to the game had been announced. No reason was given.

Chapter Twenty Four

Dukes Stadium

Chicago at New York, Night

5:00 PM June 1, 1950

A TEAM MEETING was being held. The subject was travel by airline. President Fred Duke made the presentation to emphasize the importance of the issue. First he showed a movie of airline travel provided by the Airline Transport Association. Then he talked about the time savings that would mean more time at home with members of the player's families. Fred said, "At some time during the season we will schedule a trip by airline when those who do not wish to fly can travel by train. The other reasons for switching to air travel are, it's becoming less expensive than train travel and we should start before the league decides to make up a season's schedule based on air travel.

The game tonight was a first in Dukes Stadium. The newly installed lights were state of the art, and provided great light on the playing field. Dave would be the first Dukes pitcher to pitch under the home lights. Having pitched many games in the Pacific Coast League at night, he was an experienced night game pitcher

New Yorkers had read and heard about Dave Mason and they came this night to see this pitcher who makes batters hit the ball to fielders and when he bats he isn't an automatic out. Almost 60,000 came and Dave did not disappoint them. For 10 innings he threw pitches that Chicago batters hit on the ground or in the air for outs.

Chicago got seven hits through 10 innings, but no runner reached third base. Three double plays helped. The Chicago pitcher, Mel Brough, matched Dave for eight innings.

A Chicago relief pitcher came on in the last half of the ninth inning. Third baseman Jim Essick led off with a single. He was sacrificed to second by Larry Mann. Glen Close struck out. The next batter would be Dave. Would manager Felton send in a pinch hitter maybe, Randle White? Dave was not called back to the dugout. He waged a battle of batter verses pitcher, a battle he knew well. Thinking what he would do as a pitcher, he did not expect any fast balls. He was right. The first three pitches were curves and a slider. With the count two balls and one strike, Dave timed a change up just right and hit a single to center field. The run scored, and the crowed roared. The Dukes had won the game 1-0.

The next morning, Bill Turner of Turner Chevrolet was trying to contact Dave Mason about a personal appearance at his dealership. However, he couldn't obtain Dave's phone number because Dave had an unlisted number. Turner called the Dukes office but they would not give out his phone number. They would take a message for a player and give it to him when he came to the stadium. Since Dave didn't know who Turner was, he didn't leave a message.

Bill Turner called Larry Lavell to see if he could find a phone number for Dave Mason. Larry said, "I'll have to call Dave's dad to get it. I'll let you know. When Larry called George Mason he was advised that Mr. Mason was out-of-town until Monday. Larry called Bill Turner and relayed the message. It would be a while before he could get a number. Turner didn't want to wait, so he had to contact Dave some other way. I can attend a Dukes game and try to talk to Mason. Yes, that's what I'll do. I'll take Bill, Jr. and see if I can talk to Mason after the game.

Dave's Apartment
9:00 AM June 2, 1950

Because of the many questions from the writers and radio reporters, Dave had not left the stadium until 11:00 PM Thursday night. He stopped to eat something on his way home. He fell into bed and slept until 8:30 this morning.

Dave decided to call his mother and tell her about the game last night. He would have to wait until at least noon because of the time difference. He would call before he departed for the stadium.

Now, he was off to have a big breakfast. During breakfast he decided he should do something about an advertising agency to represent him as his dad had suggested. He thought he would call Sharon, and invite her to a movie Saturday night. When he picked her up he could ask her father if he could suggest some advertising agencies. He might invite Sharon to the doubleheader Saturday afternoon. I'll see if she would like to sit in the wives box? I'll do it tonight.

At noon Dave called his mother and described last night's game to her. She hadn't read the paper yet so she was learning about the game for the first time. Ann said, "All those scoreless innings must have had everyone on the edge of their seats." Dave said, "It was one of those games. How is dad, Sarge and Pudge?" "They are all fine Dave." Say hello to dad for me." "I will Dave, and thanks for calling."

Dave made his call to Sharon early Friday evening. He invited her to the game Saturday and she thought sitting in the wives box would be interesting. Dave asked her to go to a late movie of her choice Saturday night. She accepted that too. "I'll leave your ticket to the game in will call." "Thank you Dave."

Chicago at New York
4:00 PM June 2, 1950

Chicago had defeated the Dukes 6-5. Ed Edgar who had relieved Doug Abbott allowed the winning run and took the loss.

Chicago at New York, Doubleheader
5:40 PM June 3, 1950

The Dukes split the games, the Dukes winning the first game with Lindsey Barrett getting the win, 4 to 2. In the nightcap Vic Carlisle started, but was relieved in the fourth inning by Tom Harris. Carlisle was the loser 6 to 3.

Dave visited Sharon in the wives box following the games. Showing her lawyer like ability, she was having a ball fending off the wives questions and teasing about Dave. Her defense was, "I just met him a month ago and we have had one date." Dave had asked Sharon to wait in the box with the wives so he could walk her to her car.

Bill Turner and his son were waiting at the clubhouse gate, hoping to see Dave leaving the stadium. Turner thought he knew what Dave looked like from his picture in the paper. He watched the players leave without seeing anyone who looked like Dave Mason. Finally Turner asked one of the last players leaving if Dave Mason was still in the club house. The player thought he had gone to the wives box where a girl friend had been watching the games.

When he was dressed, Dave had gone to the wives box and walked Sharon to her car. . Bill Turner had missed him.

Paramount Theatre
Times Square
New York City, New York
9:00 PM June 3, 1950

When Dave arrived at the Knox residence, Tom Knox and his wife were entertaining guests. When the guests learned who was coming to pick up Sharon, they wanted to meet him. So Sharon brought him to the living room and he was introduced. Before Dave and Sharon departed, Dave asked Mr. Knox if he could talk to him for a couple of minutes. He made his request for suggested advertising agencies that could represent him for personal appearances. Tom Knox said, "I'll talk to our agency on Monday and get back to you Dave." Thank you Mr. Knox."

Sharon's movie choice was Father of the Bride with Spencer Tracy, Joan Bennett, Elizabeth Taylor and Billie Burke. They had arrived for the second show. They enjoyed the story that would be repeated with different casts in future years. Dave was happy to learn that

Sharon had a good laugh. Dave said, "Taylor is beautiful but I think you are just as beautiful Sharon." "Oh Dave, "You are so complementary. I like it and I like you so much." "I like you too Sharon and I say them because they are all true." A stop for hamburgers and coffee completed the date.

During this date, Sharon asked most of the questions, so she learned more about Dave. She was interested in his plan to continue his education at Stanford in the baseball off-season. She told Dave that one of her high school friends is at Stanford. Her family came from California and she wanted to attend the best college possible to major in political science. She was our school Vice President and wants to enter politics.

Sharon was interested in Dave's education at Cal Poly. His description of the upside down system and learn-by-doing was new to her." She had not heard of Cal Poly. She said she would be spending the summer working as an intern in a Boston law firm, headed by a college friend of her father. She would be learning by doing. It was the only firm that would give her such an opportunity. None of the New York firms even her father's lawyers would accept her. "Law is still a man's world Dave." "That's true. I think it will change, but it will take a while"

Dave said goodnight to Sharon at her door, saying he would see her in Sunday school the next morning. There was no good night kiss. He wasn't sure Sharon was anticipating or not, but he was not ready to make their relationship more serious.

Fifth Avenue Presbyterian Church
9:30 AM June 4, 1950

When Dave entered the classroom he saw Sharon sitting in her usual place in the first row. He found a chair a couple of rows back.

The study of Paul's first missionary journey found Paul and Barnabas in Antioch of Pisidia, once a Greek city. A Roman army garrison was now stationed there.

Paul preaches his great sermon in the Antioch Synagogue. After recounting Jewish history, he introduced Jesus Christ, his crucifixion and his rising from the dead. When the sermon was over, the people sat spellbound. His message was new. "Could it be true?"

Dave stopped to say good morning to Sharon and was off for the ball park.

Dukes Stadium
Chicago at New York
5:00 PM June 4, 1950

The Dukes won the game 6-2. Jake Filner pitched another good game going nine innings for the win.

Flushing Baptist Church
Flushing, New York
7:00 PM June 4, 1950

This was the first Sunday evening since Dave arrived in New York that he could attend church and hear a sermon.

The title of the Sermon was, Are You Worry Free? The scripture was Luke 12: 22-31. The key verses were 22 and 23. "And he said to his disciples, therefore I say unto ye, take no thought for your life, what ye shall eat; neither for the body, what ye shall put on. The life is more than meat, and the body is more than raiment." Dave took notes and later wrote out his summary of the sermon.

Most of us do not worry about food and clothes as they did in Jesus' time. We worry about other things. The mother worries about her children. Will they grow up to be good people? The father worries about being successful in his work. Will he get that promotion? Will he make a critical sale? And if he does, will the product be shipped on time? The daughter worries about her looks. Is she attractive and will the boy she likes, be attracted to her? The son worries about how he will play in the big game? Does the girl he likes, like him?"

Why do we worry? We worry because we want certain good things to happen, and bad thing not to happen. What happens?

We suffer from eating disorders, ulcers and depression. Nothing very good happens to us. God sent his only son to earth in a human body. This allowed him to experience some of the same problems and challenges that you and I face. He understands. So how can he help? Jesus can help by taking all your worries off your hands. Give your worries to Jesus and you will be worry free. If you believe in the power of our Lord Jesus Christ, you will willingly give your worries to him and be worry free.

Dave's Apartment
1:30 PM June 5, 1950

Dave was on the phone calling the advertising agencies provided by Tom Knox. His secretary had called with suggestions just before noon. The first one, J. P. Morgan, was obviously not a follower of baseball. Mr. Morgan appeared to be using the name of the famous financier to feather his nest.

The second was just the opposite. Henry "Hank" James had played baseball at Yale. He said one of his teammates was a fellow by the name of George Bush, who was the youngest Navy pilot in World War II at the age of 19. Hank knew who Dave was and after Dave told him what he had done in San Francisco, he wanted to meet him as soon as possible.

Hank James had grown up on Long Island, son of Lester and Marge. Lester was a Vice President of J. Walter Thompson, the big international advertising agency. The members of the family were all sailors. So when the war started Hank, a freshman at Yale, volunteered for the Navy and ended up as a P.T. boat captain in the Pacific. Discharged early in 1945, following combat injuries, he returned to Yale, graduated in 1948, and took a job with J. Walter Thompson in Chicago. He endured the big organization in the Chicago office for a year, and then asked his dad if he would help him start his own agency in New York. Les thought Hank needed more experience, but agreed to give Hank a loan and advice. Hank opened Henry James & Associates in the summer of 1949 in a low budget office with one girl Friday. Hank had made steady progress towards turning a profit in the eight months he had been in business. He had concentrated on small businesses of all kinds to build his clientele and reputation. Talking with Dave and learning more about what he had done in San Francisco, had him excited. He thought Dave might be an individual who could help put the agency over the top.

Dave had suggested to Hank that he call Larry Lavell, the Chevrolet dealer in San Francisco who had started Dave in personal appearances. Tentatively, they agreed to meet later in the week after Hank had talked to Lavell.

Dukes Stadium
Cleveland at New York, Night
8:00 PM June 5, 1950

Another big crowd was on hand for a night game to see if Dave could win his first eight games. The attendance would be 60,000, the stadium capacity. His opposing pitcher would be the great Bob Ball. It would be a contrasting style of pitching. Ball, the strike out pitcher verses Dave, the ground ball pitcher.

At the end of seven innings the game was tied 1-1. Vic Marko's home run had given the Dukes the lead in the fourth inning. Cleveland matched it in the sixth. A single, sacrifice, and an RBI single had produced the run. It was the second earned run allowed by Dave in 73 innings. In the bottom of the eighth, the Cleveland leadoff man beat out a ball hit to third sacker Randy White for an infield hit. He was sacrificed to second. The next batter stuck out on a great change up. Dave's change was getting better and better. Now there were two outs and a runner on second. The next batter ran the count to 2-2. Dave threw a good sinker and the batter hit it hard to short. Billy Duke didn't have to move to field the ball, but somehow the ball skipped by him into left field for an error. The Cleveland runner raced home with the go ahead run. The next batter popped out to second. In the middle of the 8th inning, Cleveland led 2-1.

In the bottom of the inning, the Dukes tied it up on Vic Marko's second home run. Vic always hit Ball well and had hit lots of home runs off of him. As the game entered the ninth inning it was all tied up at 2-2. The first two Cleveland batters went out on infield grounders. Luke Jackson was the next batter. With the count 1-2, Jackson hit Dave's good rising fast ball for a 370 foot home run. It was the first home run hit off Dave in the majors. It gave Cleveland a 3 to 2 lead.

The Dukes did not mount a rally in the bottom of the ninth. Ball struck out two and got a fly ball to center field for the final out. It had been a classic baseball game with excellent pitching and home run hitting. Even though the home town team lost, they had seen a good game and watched Dave pitch well. After the game, Bob Ball came to the Dukes clubhouse and congratulated Dave for his pitching. In the loss, Dave had allowed eight hits, had no strike outs and no walks.

Dave's Apartment
8:00 AM June 6, 1950

Unbeknown to Dave, the wheels were turning to start his appearances at Turner Chevrolet in Manhattan. George Mason had returned Larry Lavell's call and agreed to call Dave. He would have him call Bill Turner. That was fine with Larry. He called Turner and reported Dave Mason would call him at the dealership. George Mason was not able to reach Dave on Monday, so he called Tuesday morning, and told him about Bill Turner. George asked Dave if he had someone to represent him, and Dave told him about Hank James. Dave said, "I will call Turner and have him talk to Hank." "That's the way to do it Dave." "How's mother?" "She's fine. Pam will be home at the end of the month to get ready for her wedding." "Yes, I learned about the wedding plans when I took Pam and Jim to dinner in Chicago." "Good luck with Turner Dave." "Thanks for calling dad."

Dave called Turner Chevrolet and asked for Mr. Bill Turner. "May I ask who is calling," said the receptionist. "My name is Dave Mason." Bill Turner was soon on the line. "Good morning Mr. Mason, I've been trying to contact you about appearances in our showroom. Larry Lavell has told me about what you did for his dealership in San

Francisco. Are you interested?" "Yes I am. I have a small advertising agency representing me, Henry James & Company. You can call Hank James at Plaza 7-1950 and tell him I asked you to call." "Thank you Mr. Mason." "Call me Dave, I'm a Californian and we're informal." "Okay Dave, thank you."

Later in the morning Bill Turner talked to Hank James about appearances by Dave in the Turner show room. Hank James quoted the fee Dave had suggested of $100.00 per hour. Turner had learned what Larry Lavell paid and tried to negotiate with James. Hank James pointed out that Dave was now in the major leagues, not the minor leagues. What he was paid in San Francisco was a minor league rate. "Are you aware of how many fans came to the game last night to see Dave pitch?" "Yes, I saw the headline, 60,000 come to see Mason." "Ok, I agree on $100.00 per hour. When can Dave start?" "How about this Friday evening?" Dave had given Hank a possible schedule. "That would be great. I suggest 7:30 to 8:30." "That's fine. Give me your address and I'll have a contract sent over to you by messenger." "The address is 1700 Broadway." "Good, I'll have Dave call you as soon as the contact is signed and returned." The contract listed four dates for Dave's appearances; June 9 and 28 and July 13 and 19.

Kiwanis Club of Flushing
Flushing, New York
12:30 PM June 6, 1950

Since the Dukes were playing a night game this evening Dave was able to make up at the Flushing club for the first time. He was recognized soon after he put on his visitor's badge. Many of the members were surprised when Dave was introduced as member of the Kiwanis Club of San Francisco. Not many professional athletes were Kiwanians. Following his introduction, Dave told the members that his father George Mason graduated from Flushing High School in 1904.

The president of the Flushing High School Key club, sponsored by the Kiwanis club was attending the meeting. He reported on the club's last program of the school year. It was a Saturday children's play day at the high school that included games and a free lunch.

The speaker of the day talked about the relationship of Kiwanis and the Freedoms Foundation of Valley Forge. The Freedoms organization encouraged members to "speak up for freedom."

Dukes Stadium
Cleveland at New York, Night
5:00 PM June 6, 1950

In another night game, Cleveland clubbed Bob Pennell and Ed Edgar for 15 runs. The bright spot in the game was the debut of Ed Card, the recently called up rookie. Card was a New Yorker and a brash one. On arrival from Buffalo, he immediately talked to manager Felton about his pitching and that he wanted to start a game. Felton replied the he would have Card start in the bull pen and likely pitch in relief once or twice before he would get a start. Card was disappointed but didn't let on to his teammates. However, he kept after Felton.

Card entered the game in the seventh inning with the score 15-2. He pitched three good innings, allowing no runs just two hits, striking out two and walking two. Felton was encouraged. Maybe his pitching problems were on the way to being solved. At the end of the game Dave was the first player out of the dugout to congratulate Ed Card when he came off the mound.

Following the game, Dave had a steak dinner at Bob's Restaurant where you ordered your steak by the ounce. If you could eat a 72 ounce steak, it was free. Dave selected an 8 ounce rib steak to drown his sorrows for the Dukes' two game losing streak and the battering they had taken today.

Dave's Apartment
7:30 PM June 6, 1950

Hank James had called to tell Dave of his deal with Bill Turner. Hank related his fending off Turner's attempt to negotiate the fee down. He gave Dave the schedule and said, "I'll let you know as soon as I have the contract back. Then you can call Turner and work out details." "That sounds good, Hank. You did a good job." "Thank you Dave."

Soon after Dave hung up the phone, Sharon called. "How are you tonight Dave?" "Not so good, we got bombed today 15-2." "Oh, I'm sorry about that. I called to ask you if you would take me to a party Saturday night. My good friend Angela is have a graduation party for some Columbia students who are about to graduate." "Sure I'll take you. What time?" "Pick me up at 8:15." "I'll be there with bells on." "Oh Dave, you are so refreshing." "Now that's a new description." They both laughed.

Dukes Stadium
Detroit at New York
4:55 PM June 7, 1950

Detroit was in town for a three game series. The Tigers were tied with the Dukes for the league lead.

The Dukes won the game today 5-4, halting their two game losing streak. Abbott was the winning pitcher with relief by Ed Edgar. Vic Marko hit a two run home run in the sixth inning. The win gave the Dukes a one game lead over Detroit in the pennant race.

Dave's Apartment
7:00 PM June 7, 1950

Hank James was calling to advise Dave that he had the signed contract back from Turner Chevrolet. "Okay, I'll call Turner in the morning. What's his phone number?"

"UN 4-4000. Hank said, "I think we should meet as soon as possible Dave. So far we've done all our business over the phone. If I attend the game Saturday can we have dinner afterwards?" "We can if we eat right after the game. I have an engagement at 8:15 in Manhattan." Hank said, "That's fine." "Okay, I'll leave your game ticket in will call. Meet me at the player's gate about thirty minutes after the game." "Fine Dave, I'll see you then."

8:30 AM June 8, 1950

Dave was talking to Bill Turner on the phone. He had asked Turner how many baseballs he wanted to give away?" "Our ad in today's and tomorrow's paper said the first 30 children under 18 could receive a baseball. Can you supply the balls? Yes I can supply them this time." "Good, we can work out our purchase of the balls in the future." "I plan to arrive a half hour early at 7:00." "That's fine. When you arrive see Dick Chevrolet, our Sales Floor Manager. That's his real name, so he couldn't sell any other cars." "I'll be there."

Dukes Stadium
Detroit at New York, Night
10:00 PM June 8, 1950

In a night game the Dukes started fast scoring four runs in the first inning, highlighted by Randy White's two run home run. They kept producing runs and won the game 12-4, giving the Dukes a two game lead. Barrett was the winning pitcher.

Detroit at New York
4:05 PM June 9, 1950

The game after a loss is always a challenge for a pitcher. This is particularly if he had been winning before the loss.

New York was leading 4-1 in the seventh inning. Dave had allowed seven hits, but two double plays had cut down base runners. He had singled and driven in a run. It was now time for Dave's late inning performance. In the top of the seventh inning he threw eight pitches and got three ground outs. In the top of the eighth Dave recorded three outs on seven pitches. In the ninth inning, it was seven more pitches, three ground ball outs and the game was over. The Dukes had won the game 4-1 completing a sweep of the three game series producing a three game lead in the race for the American League pennant. The win was number eight for Dave.

Turner Chevrolet
1700 Broadway
New York City, New York
8:30 PM June 9, 1950

Dave's appearance was just over. When he arrived at 7:00, there must have been at least 50 kids and parents lined up to get an autographed baseball. Dave had met with Dick Chevrolet who was surprised at the turn out. "I don't know what it is, but it was the same in San Francisco Dick. As time went on, more came out." "That means the word was passed by those who came, and they obviously enjoyed themselves." "I will always encourage the parents to look at the cars on the showroom floor." "That sounds great Dave."

It had taken Dave the hour to sign the 30 balls and talk to the kids and their parents. He watched as many looked at the Chevy's, after they left the table where Dave was signing baseballs.

Dave was now talking with Dick Chevrolet in his office. "Do you have any suggestions to make it better Dick?" "I wouldn't change a thing. We will have more time to advertise your next appearance, so we may get more people." "During one of the appearances I would like to have some time to talk to parents on the floor who are looking at cars. In San Francisco, if I got someone interested in buying, I turned them over to a salesman. I've learned that some people want to avoid talking to a salesman initially, and I've been an ice breaker." "I'll sure consider that Dave."

Dukes Stadium
St. Louis at New York
5:30 PM June 10, 1950

In this Saturday game the lowly Browns beat the Dukes 6-2. Vic

Carlisle started and was relieved by Ed Edgar. Carlisle took the loss. It was becoming obvious that the Dukes were not getting the power hitting they had in past seasons. Except for Vic Marko, no one was getting extra base hits. The team was not getting any power from either first baseman, Glen Close or Len Ogle. Veteran outfielders Tommie Hoff and Mike Hudson were not hitting with power. They were getting old and were frequently injured.

Fairmont Hotel
San Francisco, California
7:00 PM June 10, 1950

Three thousand miles from New York, Jill was enjoying the reception following Jane and Woody's wedding in Grace Cathedral, two blocks away. Jill had been matched with Woody's Navy buddy, Rex Ryan. Rex was a Navy pilot officer stationed at Alameda Naval Air Station. He had flown with Woody during the war. He had the looks of a dashing aviator and appeared to be Woody's age or a bit older. Jill was immediately attracted to him. They were dancing and had good chemistry. Rex soon asked Jill to a party at the Officers Club on the following Friday. Jill said, "I accept if I'm not flying." She later confirmed she would be home. Rex planned to get a room at the Benjamin Franklin Hotel in San Mateo so he could pick Jill up and drive her home without making another round trip. He would have to figure out how he was going to break his date with Shelly for the same party. He would think of something.

The Home of Angela
Park Avenue
New York City, New York
8:30 PM June 10, 1950

Arriving at the home of Sharon's friend Angela, the party was in full swing. The fellows appeared to be veterans, 24 to 25, who were about to graduate from College. The girls were a bit younger.

Dave was soon introduced to Angela and her husband to be, Ray Daley. Sharon said he and Angela were both graduating from Columbia next week and would become Mr. and Mrs. Ray Daley in another week. "That's doing it all at once," Dave said. "Yes, we didn't have a choice because I have a job in Chicago that starts in July." "What's your field?" Dave asked. "I'm a business major, starting in sales with General Electric in their home appliance division, selling refrigerators, etc." "That sounds like a good field. Everybody with a house needs appliances." Ray said, "I'm happy to meet Sharon. I've heard lots about her from Angela." "Dave said, "Isn't she beautiful?" Sharon seemed stunned, but recovered to say, "Complements will get you everywhere Dave." They all laughed. Dave and Sharon spent most of the evening dancing. Sharon was a good follower.

They departed the party about midnight. On the door step of Sharon's home, she turned, threw her arms around Dave's neck, said, "You are such a sweet fellow, and kissed him full on the lips. Surprised at first, Dave recovered and kissed her back. Sharon turned, and without a word entered the house. Dave stood on the door step for a minute, recovering from the surprise kiss, and then went home.

Fifth Avenue Presbyterian Church
9:30 AM June 11, 1950

As Dave entered the classroom he received a big smile from Sharon who was sitting in her favorite seat in the front row. Boy, she is a beautiful girl with a wonderful smile! Dave took a seat a few rows back.

The class teacher Steve Early announced that the Senior Pastor had requested all classes study a lesson on kindness. The study will tie in with his sermon this morning. Our scripture is one verse from Ephesians Chapter 4, verse 32. "And be ye kind one to another, tenderhearted, forgiving one another, even as God for Christ's sake hath forgiven you.

"What I'd like to do is ask you to give examples of kindness and even some examples when someone did not show kindness."

"I think we are not kind many times because we let our tongue get out of control and we say things that are not kind to another person."

"Kindness is helping an elderly person across the street."

"Helping a person who appears to be lost in the big city is an act of kindness."

Sharon said, "I have a real life act of kindness to describe. Leaving a hotel a lady was trying to help her husband to their car but he was very drunk and she just couldn't hold him up. A couple came out of the elevator in the parking garage and saw her problem. The fellow immediately said, 'I'll hold him up. Where is your car?' The wife said, 'Just outside the door to the garage.' 'Okay, lead the way and I'll carry him to your car.' He did and put him in the car. He told the wife not to give him any coffee or try to get him out of the car when you get home. 'Leave your garage door open for air and let him sleep it off. He will have a headache in the morning but he should be okay.' The lady thanked him and tried to give him some money but he refused. I don't think many men would do what he did."

Steve challenged the members of the class to do at least one act of kindness each day. You will be blessed by what you do.

When the class ended Dave went to talk to Sharon. "Good morning." "Good morning yourself," Sharon said with a sly smile. "I'll be gone until the 26th, so I wanted to know what day you would be leaving for Boston?" "Mother and I will go up on Wednesday or Thursday to move me into wherever I'm going to live, probably an apartment hotel. We will return in time for Angela's wedding on Saturday. I'm one of her bridesmaids. I'll go back Sunday." "Okay, I invite you have dinner with me on Monday evening, the 26th." "I'll have to let you know Dave. The folks may have something planned." "In that case I'll give you a call around the 22nd or 23rd." "That's fine Dave. Good luck today." "Thank you."

Dukes Stadium
St. Louis at New York, Doubleheader
6:00 PM June 11, 1950

It had been a long afternoon because of two slowly played games. The scores didn't indicate it, but the pitchers had thrown lots of pitches running long counts. However it was a good day for the Dukes winning both games. Jake Filner pitched another good game winning the first 1-0. He was proving the opinions of General Manager Don Newton and Manager Felton that he was a good pitcher and that's why they traded for him in the off season. He allowed just four hits, although walking five. Double plays got him out of jams.

In the second game manager Felton decided to go against his practice of starting his best pitchers against lower division clubs, and started rookie Ed Card. He pitched well through seven innings and then was relieved by Ed Edgar, but he got the win. Dave gave him the first greeting when Card came to the dugout after being lifted. It was a good way to end the home stand and start a road trip.

Grand Central Station
Park Avenue & E. 42nd Street
9:30 PM June 11, 1950

The team had been bused to the station to take the New York Central's Chicagoan, departing at 10:05 PM. They would arrive in Chicago at 3:05 PM tomorrow afternoon. This is a schedule the flying advocates said would have given them a night at home if the team had not been riding the train. Dave went right to his upper bunk and was soon sleeping. He was up early the next morning, taking his bible into the men's lounge and then having an early breakfast. He spent the day writing letters to Jill and his parents. Then he read a book.

Comiskey Park
New York at Chicago
5:00 PM June 13, 1950

It was the end of the eighth inning with the Dukes leading 6-0. Dave had allowed just two hits and had contributed two hits to the New York 10 hit attack. He sailed through the ninth inning on eight pitches and a 6-0 Dukes' win. The shutout was his seventh. He had thrown only 84 pitches and had gotten 18 ground ball outs. The game had taken just an hour and 45 minutes. Dave record was now 9-1. His ERA was a microscopic .150.

In the clubhouse, Dave gave his infielders a big thank you for their errorless play. All thanked Dave for his quick work that meant less standing around and a fast game.

New York at Chicago
5:30 PM June 14, 1950

Chicago had won the game 6-2. Lack of power was again haunting the Dukes. They banged out nine hits, but all but two were singles. Doug Abbott pitched well enough to win, leaving in the seventh inning with the score tied at 2-2, but with the bases loaded. Tom Harris came on to get the side out, but he allowed two runs in the eighth and Bob Pennell gave the other two in the ninth. Up to this time, Manager Felton had not used Dave often as a pinch hitter. He wanted Dave to be able to continue pitching on three days rest and didn't want to tire him out.

Stevens Hotel Dinning Room
Stevens Hotel
120 South Michigan Avenue
Chicago, Illinois
8:45 PM June 14, 1950

Pam had invited Dave to dinner during this trip to Chicago. He had

selected this evening and suggested she and Jim Smith come to the team hotel. Pam was updating Dave on her wedding plans he had learned about during his last trip. Pam was going to fly home on June 30, her first cross country flight. Dave said his next trip would be July 28 through the 30th. "I hope we can get together then Jim"
"I'm sure we can."

Kiwanis Club of Chicago
Morrison Hotel
12:15 PM June 15, 1950

Dave was able to attend the meeting and get a make up because the Dukes were playing a night game. According to Dave's Kiwanis Club directory, Chicago was club number 23. After Dave signed in as a visiting Kiwanian and put his badge on he was recognized. When he was introduced as a visiting member of the Kiwanis Club of San Francisco, many members were surprised that Dave, a major league baseball player was a Kiwanian.

During happy dollar time Dave contributed a happy dollar for his ninth win on Tuesday. That brought a few boos from the Chicago White Sox fans.

The program was one of the club's sports days. They were honoring the Chicago Cubs and had some current and former players attending the meeting.

Dave learned the Club sponsored a Key Club at the Cooley Vocational High School. The club had about 200 members.

When Dave mailed his make up card to the Secretary of his San Francisco club he included a note to the members so they wouldn't forget him.

New York at Chicago, Night
5:55 PM June 15, 1950

The Dukes were still chasing Detroit for the league lead. Detroit's lead was now 1-1/2 games. Today's game was another of good pitching, but little power hitting. Lindsey Barrett was in a 2-2 tie as late as the eighth inning. Then an error allowed an unearned run that opened up a four run rally by Chicago. The Dukes had only one inning of offense. Bill Wood singled with no outs in the seventh inning. Dave has called to pinch hit. On a 2-1 count, Dave doubled to left center field. With two on and no outs, a rally looked good. But a strike out and two infield pop ups ended the threat with no runs scored. Chicago won the game 6 to 2.

Between the end of the game and the trip to the La Salle Station, manager Felton made a phone call to Donald Newton. They talked about what they could do to get some power hitting. Felton again suggested bringing up B.B. Katcher to play first base. Although a catcher, he had played first base in high school. Newton had opposed the suggestion when Felton first mentioned it because of defensive liabilities. But now he said they might have to do it. Newton said, "I'll talk with Buffalo manager Ike Lofton and get his opinion. I'll call you when you get to St. Louis."

The team traveled on the St. Louis Moonlighter of the Gulf, Mobile and Ohio to St. Louis, arriving at 9:30 the next morning.

Sportsman's Park
New York at St. Louis, Night
10:10 PM June 16, 1950

In this night game the Dukes did some hitting for a change. Vic Marko and Mike Hudson hit home runs and the Dukes scored seven runs. Vic Carlisle scattered nine hits and won a complete game 7-3. It was a big help since the bullpen did not have to be called on.

Before the game, Don Newton had called and after talking to Ike Lofton, he had decided they would call up B.B.Katcher. Newton advised Felton he would have Katcher report on June 26th when the team returned from the road trip. Manager Felton was happy with the decision.

Officers Club
Alameda Naval Air Station
Alameda, California
10:30 PM June 16, 1950

It was a gala party that Rex had brought Jill to. It was a send off party for the officers of an aircraft carrier departing for Japan on Monday. Rex was a training officer and was not departing. He and Jill had enjoyed the dinner and they had danced together most of the evening. Rex was a joker with funny stories and didn't appear to be too serious. Jill was making a comparison with Dave. Jill felt an attraction to Rex unlike she had felt for any man. What was it? The party broke up at midnight. Jill thought the evening had gone fast because she was enjoying herself.

While they traveled to Jill's apartment, Rex kept her entertained with his humor. The attraction Jill had not experienced made her do something she had never done before. When she said good night to Rex, she wrapped her arms around his neck and kissed him on the lips. It was such a surprise to him, he didn't kiss her back and he departed. Jill immediately realized she had never kissed a fellow on the first date. She continued to wonder about this relationship.

Sportsman's Lanes
Spring Street
St. Louis Missouri
10:00 AM June 17, 1950

Dave invited Gordon Enson to go bowling with him. Enson was still not playing much and was down. Dave hoped to raise his spirits with some bowling competition. They bowled for fun and Dave thought Gordon felt better when they were finished. Dave did not have his ball, but was satisfied with his games

New York at St. Louis
4:00 PM June 17, 1950

The Dukes had started fast scoring three runs in the first inning giving Dave a lead before he faced a batter. Dave hit a double to drive in two runs. He did not allow a run until the seventh inning. A single, sacrifice and an infield single put a runner on third. The run scored on a fly ball to center field. The next batter struck out.

The Dukes scored five runs in the eighth highlighted by a three run home run by Vic Marko. That gave the Dukes an 8 to 1 lead. St. Louis scored another run in the bottom of the eighth on a single, sacrifice, error and another fly ball to center field. That was the end of the scorning and the Dukes won the game 8 to 2.

Dave and Randy White went to see the movie Two Corridors East with Paul Douglas and Montgomery Clift. It was the story of the Berlin Airlift, necessitated by the Russian blockade of Berlin. It was a great example of human kindness. The airlift prevented the people of Berlin from starving and freezing to death.

New York at St. Louis, Doubleheader
6:00 PM June 18, 1950

The New York players had been reading about their lack of power hitting and today they reacted. In the first game, Marko, Hoff, Hudson and Jim Essick hit home runs for a 16-4 win for the Dukes and Doug Abbott. The team kept it up in the second game, staking Lindsey Barrett to a three run first inning lead. Barrett responded by pitching a shut out, allowing just 4 hits. The Dukes didn't stop after the first inning scoring 6 more runs for a 9-0 win.

At 10:30 PM, the team took the Cleveland Special of the New York Central, arriving in Cleveland at 10:55 on Monday morning. There was no game, so Dave spent most of the afternoon bowling. He really needed practice.

In the evening Dave took a ride on the interurban electric car service to the Cleveland suburbs, an area that had been developed by brothers O.P and M.J Van Swerigen, Cleveland real estate developers. The brothers had promoted the building of the Cleveland Union Train Station. A17 mile electric rail line kept steam engines out of downtown Cleveland. The station completed in 1930, included a 52 story office tower that was the tallest building outside of New York City when it was built.

In Jill's apartment in Burlingame, she had just accepted another date with Rex Ryan for dinner on Friday night.

Cleveland Municipal Stadium
New York at Cleveland
3:30 PM June 20, 1950

Starting the day the Dukes record was 38-18, one game out of first place. For the first three innings of the game today, Vic Carlisle was in a pitcher's duel with Bob Orange. The score was 2-2. Then in the fourth inning, the Dukes generated power again and scored five runs for a 7-2 lead. Vic Marko continued his hot hitting parking a home run over the right field fence at 332 feet. Later Randy White hit one to left field. The Dukes added two more in the sixth inning and Carlisle pitched a shut out from the fourth inning on. The final score was 9-2 for the Dukes.

Before the game, Dave talked to Cleveland rookies. Some of the players were weary of Dave's encouragement as this was new to them. No opposing player had encouraged them during their baseball career. However, Dave was so sincere, most began to accept Dave's encouragement. Some of Dave's teammates had questioned his practice, saying he was "soft." Gordon Enson had told the players." "Don't kid yourself. When the game starts, Mason is a bulldog."

New York at Cleveland
2:45 PM June 21, 1950

Dave pitched two perfect innings allowing no hits on just 12 pitches. In the third inning the bottom of the Dukes order produced two runs.

Singles by Glen Close and Jim Essick with no outs brought Dave to the plate. After running the count to 3-2, Dave hit a hanging curve for a double down the left field line. Both runners scored. At the end of the sixth, the score was still 2-0. Dave was getting ground outs and had allowed only four hits.

Then, scoring erupted. Cleveland produced two runs in the top of the seventh to tie the game, 2-2. Both runs were unearned. The Dukes responded in their half of the inning scoring four runs on three singles, a double and a home run by J. B. Felton. The Dukes now led 6-2. Dave pitched his typical late innings, retiring six batters on ground balls in the eighth and ninth innings. The Dukes won the game 6-2. Dave allowed 6 hits, had no strike outs or walks. His record was now 11-1.

Kiwanis Club of Cleveland City Club 12:00 noon June 22, 1950

Dave had asked manager Felton if he could be a little late for the game warm up so he could attend Kiwanis and get a make up. Dave said he would leave the meeting early and would be at the stadium by 1:30 for the 2:30 game. Felton gave his approval but said, "Don't make it a practice Dave." "I understand," Dave said.

The Cleveland Club, the number two Kiwanis club, had a good turn out of members. When Dave was introduced, he got cheers and a few boos reflecting his pitching win against the home team yesterday. As at other clubs most members were surprised to learn Dave was a Kiwanis member. At happy dollar time Dave gave his dollar for his win yesterday, saying, "I'm sure it won't be a popular dollar."

A report was made on the children who were attending summer camp paid for by the club. The club sponsored a Key Club, but Dave did not learn the name of the high school.

Dave had advised the Secretary he would have to leave the meeting at 1:00 to get to the ball park and he departed at that time.

New York at Cleveland
2:30 PM June 22, 1950

Bob Ball was the scheduled Cleveland pitcher today so manager Felton applied his practice of not pitching his top starter against an opposing team's ace. He gave the ball to the rookie, Ed Card. It was a surprise to Card, but Felton wanted to see what he could do against a top team and pitcher. Card had continued his requests to pitch following his first start and win. Ball started the game by striking out the side in the first inning. He continued shut out pitching through seven innings. Card matched Ball for three innings, but gave up two runs in fourth inning on two singles and a double.

In the sixth inning, Cleveland loaded the bases and the next batter cleaned the sacks with a double to left field for a 5-0 lead. Ed Edgar then came on in relief. The Dukes scored two runs in the eighth inning on Vic Marko's fifth homer of the year off Ball, a two run shot to right center field. That ended the scoring and Cleveland won the game 5-2. It ended the Dukes seven game winning streak.

Following the game the team returned to their hotel and had dinner. Before dinner Dave had called Sharon to learn about his dinner date offer on Monday. Sharon said, "The family is having a going away dinner for me on Tuesday night and I am inviting you." "That's very nice of you Sharon, but are you sure I will not be intruding in a family affair?" "No you won't be intruding at all Dave. All the members of the family were very agreeable to my request to have you attend." "All right, what time." "Come about 7:00." "I'll be there and thank you Sharon." "You're welcome Dave. Good night." "Good night."

The team's New York Central train did not depart until 11:55 PM. It was a short overnight trip, arriving in Detroit at 6:50 AM. After checking in at their hotel, Dave had breakfast and took a nap. After that it was time to go to the stadium.

Briggs Stadium
New York at Detroit
2:30 PM June 23, 1950

This would be an important series. The Dukes were in first place, a half game ahead of Detroit. By starting Ed Card in Cleveland, Manager Felton had his best pitchers starting in this series. Doug Abbott was pitching this first game. Unfortunately it was not one of his better days. He was wild high in the strike zone that resulted in three home runs in the first four innings. The Dukes matched the Detroit slugging, Marko, Hoff and J.B. Felton hitting round trippers. At the end of the fourth inning the score was tied at 5-5.

Ed Edgar had relieved Abbott and held Detroit scoreless through the sixth inning. In the top of the seventh the Dukes scored three runs on Marko's second home run and one by Randy White. The Dukes led 8-5 in the middle of the seventh. The Dukes lead didn't last as Detroit came back with two more home runs that produced four runs to make the score 9-8 for Detroit. Tom Harris had replaced Edgar during the Detroit outburst.

In the eighth inning, the Dukes regained the lead on Mike Hudson's two run shot to left field. The Dukes now led 10-9. Detroit got two runners on base in their half of the inning, but a double play ended the inning. The Dukes did not add to their lead in the ninth inning, so the game was on the line in the bottom of the ninth.

Tom Harris was still on the mound for the Dukes. The Detroit lead off batter singled to right field. The next batter popped out to catcher J.B. Felton. Then it was a strike out for Harris. Now it was just one out away from a win for the Dukes but the Detroit clean up batter was coming to the plate. Harris got two strikes on the batter. Then trying to work the corners of the plate, he missed for a 2-2 count. Harris threw a slider on the next pitch that didn't slide far enough and it was belted for a 325 foot home run that gave the Tigers an 11 to 10 win. The Detroit players celebrated at home plate while the Dukes walked off the field in disappointment. 12 home runs had been hit, a new American League record. The Dukes were now a half game behind Detroit.

In trying to cheer up the players following the game, Dave said, "There was no lack of power out there today." Dave talked to all the pitchers who had pitched in the game. Tomorrow there is another game.

Dave and Randy White went to a movie to forget the game. They saw The Gunfighter starring Gregory Peck. It was a movie that made your forget about anything except what was on the screen.

The Gallery
1 West 3rd Avenue
San Mateo, California
10:00 PM June 23, 1950

Rex and Jill had enjoyed their dinner in this newly opened restaurant. The food and the service had been outstanding. Jill could not depress her good feelings for Rex. He was being his funny best tonight. They were just departing the restaurant. On the drive to Jill's apartment, Rex said, "I will be in San Diego next week for a training meeting. When will you be home after the weekend?" Jill checked her schedule and said, "I'm flying Saturday and Sunday and home on Monday." "Okay, I'll call you then. At her door, Jill did not invite Rex in. She was not sure she could control her emotions about him and might get carried away. She gave him a good night kiss and she went to bed.

New York at Detroit
3:45 PM June 24, 1950

Lindsey Barrett was in a pitcher's duel through five innings. The Dukes scored a run on Vic Marko's third home run in two days. It continued 1-0 until the last half of the seventh inning. Then Detroit scored three runs on three singles and a double. Detroit now led 3-1. In the top of the eighth inning, Larry Mann singled with two outs. Dave was called to pinch hit for Billy Duke who was in a slump. Dave hit the first pitch for a single to right field. With Tommie Hoff coming to bat the Dukes were confident of a rally. With the count run to 3-2, Hoff struck out, ending the threat. Detroit added a run in their half of the inning and the game ended 4-1 for Detroit. The win increased Detroit's lead to 1-1/2 games.

Following dinner Dave spent an hour on his chronological study of Jesus. He was learning more and more as he studied.

The next morning Dave went to breakfast at 7:00 AM. Picking up a Detroit Free Press on the way, he read a front page headline NORTH KOREA INVADES THE SOUTH. In the short article that followed, it was reported that the army of North Korea equipped with Russian tanks had pushed across the 38th parallel, the dividing line between the North and South. Since the war, countries dominated by Russia had been invaded or taken over, but the U.S. hadn't done anything about it. Dave thought it would be the same in this situation.

New York at Detroit, Doubleheader
3:15 PM June 25, 1950

Dave was pitching the first game with a goal of stopping the losses. It was the first of the seventh inning. The Dukes had started the game with a vengeance scoring three runs in the first, two in the second and three runs in the sixth inning for an 8-0 lead. The three runs in the sixth resulted from Dave's three run, 350 foot home run. Dave had not allowed a hit, so had a no hitter through six innings.

In the top of the seventh Detroit's lead off batter singled. He went to second when a double play ball was booted by Billy Duke for an error. After Dave retired the next two batters, it appeared Dave would get out of the inning unscathed. However, the next batter singled to left and the runner from second just beat the throw from Tommie Hoff to score the run. Another single scored Detroit's second run. Dave had just gotten the final out of the inning. The score was now 8-2 with the Dukes leading.

In the Dukes half of the seventh they put two men on base with one out, but a double play ended the threat. In the eighth Dave needed only seven pitches to retire the side. The Dukes scored no more runs, and Dave needed only five pitches in the ninth to end the game and give the Dukes their first win of the series 8 to 2. Dave had allowed just two hits. He contributed two hits and three RBIs to the offense. The win reduced Detroit's league lead to a half game.

Vic Carlisle started the second game of the doubleheader and pitched well for five innings. The game was tied at 2-2. In the sixth Detroit scored two runs, all on singles. The Dukes got one run back on Vic Marko's home run to left center field, a 390 foot clout. This made the score 4-3 for Detroit. The Dukes could not mount a rally and Detroit added two runs in the eighth inning for a 6-3 win. Detroit had won the series three games to one. Detroit now had a game and a half lead in the pennant race.

It was not a very happy team that was on the way to the train station following dinner. After the series loss they faced the longest train trip of the season to get home to New York. They would depart Detroit at 11:35 PM on a New York Central train, arriving in Cleveland at 5:37 AM, where they would change trains. The team would depart Cleveland at 6:15 AM, arriving at Grand Central Station at 7:05 PM.

After breakfast, Dave was asked to visit manager Felton in his compartment. Ozzie Felton wanted to tell Dave that they had called up B.B. Katcher to play first base. "We need some power hitting and Katcher has been power hitting at Buffalo. I'm sure he will contact you as soon as he hits town today. He was advised to get a room at the Flushing Hotel for the immediate future." "That's good news. B.B. played first base back in high school, so it won't be completely new to him. His manager in Buffalo thought he could do a reasonably good job at first for a right hander. We can always sub Glenn Close in the late innings. What we need immediately is power." "When I get home, I'll call the hotel and talk to B.B. I know my apartment house has vacancies." "Thanks Dave. How are you feeling after 10 games on three days rest?" "I feel fine. As I said when you proposed it, my pitching style fits pitching every four days."

It was ironic that newspapers picked up in Cleveland reported the major league baseball owners had decided during their meeting that the 1951 schedule would be based on all teams flying on long road trips. Players who had a fear of flying would have to conquer their fear or retire. The owners were aware that most of those who did not want to fly were older veteran players.

Chapter Twenty Five

Dave's Apartment

9:00 PM June 26, 1950

AS SOON AS Dave arrived in his apartment he called the Flushing Hotel and asked for B.B. Katcher. "Hello B.B., this is your old sinker ball pitcher calling." "Dave. I was hoping to hear from you. I'm a small town boy almost lost in the big city." They both laughed. "In the morning I'll come and get you and we will have breakfast. Later I'll take you to the ball park. What time do you want to eat in the morning?" B.B. said, "How about 8:00 Dave?" "That's fine, wait for me in the lobby." "I'll see you then Dave."

Dave found a post card and a letter from Jill in the mail. The letter described the wedding of Jane and Woody. She said, "The wedding was fantastic. Grace Cathedral was full. Jane was her stunning self and Woody was very handsome in his morning coat. Jane had two other bride's maids, both Stanford sorority sisters. Woody had his brother, and two friends who had been in the Navy with him. His brother is much younger than Woody and is now a college student. One of the fellows is a Navy pilot stationed in Alameda and the other was from Southern California. I think he works for Douglas."

"We haven't invited any one else to live in the apartment yet. Sally wants to wait until I leave. I'm finding it hard to make a decision on transferring to New York. I have talked to Dorothy about New York. She said living in Flushing is not living in a big city. Also, it's close to the airport and you can travel to Manhattan on the Long Island

Railroad and subway. She admitted the summer weather was hot and humid, but a stewardess is flying about half the time. She also said her apartment mate was close to getting married, so I might have a place to live." Jill wrote nothing about attending church.

Dave had picked up a New York Times on his way to his apartment. The headline read: NORTH KOREAN ARMY THREATENS SEOUL. The North Korean army supported by Russian tanks and equipment had swept across the 38th Parallel, the dividing line established to separate the country between Russian and American influence following the end of the War

The North Korean Army had pushed the poorly equipped ROK (Republic of Korea Army) back across the 38th parallel with little trouble, and was moving towards the capital city of Seoul. The Korean Military Advisor Group (KMAG) was made up of American Army officers and men, who did just that, advise the South Koreans. The commanding general of KMAG had departed for home the day before and there was no replacement on board. The Chief of Staff of KMAG, an artillery colonel, was acting commander.

Dave didn't think this was a serious situation. Just another take over by a Russian supported communist country. So far the U.S. hadn't take any action except to criticize.

Ruby's Restaurant
Flushing, New York
8:15 AM June 27, 1950

Dave was giving B.B. the run down on the team and its problems. "We are getting good pitching in many games, but no extra base hits. Our veteran outfielders are not producing power. Bill Wood, who the team traded for, is a good singles hitter, but doesn't supply power. The biggest problem is no power from first base. So that's why they brought you up. What do you think about playing first base?" "I'll play anywhere to stay in the majors Dave." "Yes, most of us would. After breakfast let's go over to my apartment house and you can check out apartments. It's good place and the rent is reasonable."

"Sounds good, Dave."

B.B .looked over the apartments available, and chose a one room bachelor unit. He wanted to be close to Dave because he had wheels. Dave took B.B. back to the hotel so he could check out and move what he had brought with him into the apartment. Later they went to the stadium for the game.

Dave had been too busy to read the morning newspaper. The front page was full of news about the invasion of South Korea by the North. President Harry Truman had requested the United Nations demand the North Koreans stop their invasion and return above the 38th parallel. The North Korean government did not respond to the request so the U.N. approved military action to defend South Korea. On June 27th President Truman ordered General MacArthur to send troops to South Korea.

Dukes Stadium
Washington at New York
11:00 AM June 27, 1950

Dave and B.B. Katcher had arrived in the clubhouse and Dave was introducing him to his teammates. Some had remembered B.B. from spring training. Manager Felton had made the announcement about the call up of B.B to the team on the train returning to New York. Before the announcement he had talked to Glen Close and told him he would be replaced as a regular as soon a Katcher arrives and gets acclimated. He said, "You and Ogle were just not supplying any power hitting." Ogle was being sent to Buffalo, although he may retire.

Jake Filner was the starting pitcher today. Filner had been pitching well lately and had won his last three starts. He started off with a good fast ball and good control, and did not allow a hit for three innings. The Dukes scored one run in the third on Vic Marko's home run to dead right field. It was Marko's sixth home run in eight games.

In the fourth inning Washington scored two runs on two singles and a double. At the end of the fourth Washington was leading 2-1.

The Dukes tied it on two doubles hit by J. B. Felton and Mike Hudson. The tie held up until the ninth inning. The Dukes scored a run on a single, sacrifice, and a second single. So, at the end of nine, it was a 2-2 tie and the game went into extra innings.

In the 10th, Washington took the lead on a two run home run. The Senators now led 4-2. In the Dukes' 10th they scored a run on two singles and a wild pitch. The Dukes had a runner on first and one out with Vic Marko coming to bat. It looked like the Dukes would come back to win. It didn't happen. Marko hit a nasty slider to the second baseman who started a double play to end the game. The final score was Washington 4, New York 3.

Dave had told B.B. that he had a dinner to attend tonight, so he would be one his own. "That's fine Dave. I want to get my apartment organized and pick up some food." Dave told B.B, "There is a neighborhood grocery store around the corner that has the basics. The A & P Super Market is a few blocks away. We can shop there tomorrow. I need to do some shopping since I've been away for two weeks." Arriving back at Hunter Gardens Apartments, Dave said, "I'll see you tomorrow."

The Knox Residence
7:00 PM June 27, 1950

Dave was met at the door by Sharon with a hug. Up the stairs to the living room where Dave said, "Good evening." to Mr. and Mrs. Knox. Sharon introduced Dave to Tom IV, called Tommy and his wife Grace. Dave said, "How are you Bill, Sharon's younger brother who Dave had met on his first date with Sharon. Tom said, "You had a tough road trip." "Yes we did. We lost games we could have won with better hitting. Except for Vic Marko, our veteran players have not been getting extra base hits. The team has called up from Buffalo my American Legion team catcher, B.B. Katcher, yes, that's his real name spelled with a K, to play first base. He has been burning up the International League, hitting 30 home runs and driving in 50. He will start at first base in a few days. He played first base in high school before moving to catcher. He was with the team in spring training." "That sounds promising," said Tom.

"Dave asked, "How is the world of finance?" "It's about the same Dave. However, the economy is beginning to pick up. How did you do with those advertising agencies we suggested?" "I have retained Henry James & Associates, and I have a contract with Turner Chevrolet for personal appearances. I did the first on June 13th." Tom asked, "What do you do?" "I sit at a table and talk to the kids while I autograph a baseball for them. I ask their name and if they play baseball and if so, what position. I gave away 30 balls that night and I could have given away many more." "Have you done this before?" "Yes, it started when I bought my first new car, a Chevrolet in June of last year in San Francisco. The dealer sponsored the radio broadcasts of the San Francisco Sea Lions, the team I was a member of. When I went to pick up the car the owner of the dealership wanted to have a picture taken of him handing me the keys to the new car. He wanted to place it in a newspaper advertisement. It developed from there."

"Sharon tells me you are working on a master's degree in engineering at Stanford." "Yes, my goal is to enter the field of consulting engineering when my baseball career is over, so I'm broadening my engineering education." "Do you have any idea how long you will play baseball? "No, not now, but after earning the master's degree and getting some work experience, I would be ready to retire after being licensed as a professional engineer." "You have an interesting plan, Dave. Randle White is the only other baseball player I've heard of who is planning a professional career after baseball." "That's true, and Randy is my roommate on the road." "Oh they put you together." "Yes, Randy requested me. He could request a rookie and thought we would be compatible. We have been a good combination."

Mrs. Knox, Alexis, announced, "Dinner is ready." They all went to the dinning room and when seated, they all held hands while Tom said grace.

Dave asked Tommy, "How long have you worked in the firm?" "Almost two years now." "Where did you go to college?" "I passed up the family tradition and didn't attend Yale. But being a staunch Presbyterian, I attended Princeton." This brought a smile to Tom's face. Then, I attended the Wharton School of Finance." "That sounds like a good preparation for the business." "It teaches you the basics Dave, but you have to work in it to learn the real world." "I think that's true. Sharon is very fortunate to have the opportunity to experience just what being a lawyer is all about."

The dinner, served by the Knox cook, was delicious. Following dinner, Sharon took Dave's hand and led him to her father's den. She said, "I want to keep in touch with you this summer Dave." "You're reading my mind. I've used this method of communication with my parents and friends." Dave takes out a pack of penny post cards he has addressed and gives them to Sharon. "I've found writing a short message on the post card is less likely to be put off than writing a letter. However, if you don't want the mailman to read your message, you have to write a letter." They both laughed. Also, here's our schedule, so you will know when I'm out of town. "Thank you Dave. I'll be back at least a couple of times during the summer. Mother and I will drive back from Boston for Angela's wedding on Saturday, so I won't be able to talk to you in Boston"

Dave thanked Mrs. Knox for the dinner. "It was delicious." "You're welcome Dave." "Good night to all of you and thank you for including me. "I'll walk you to the door," Sharon said. At the front door, Dave embraced Sharon, and said thank you for a wonderful evening." Then he kissed her and she kissed back. "Good night." "Good night."

Sharon returned to the living room beaming, something all could tell. Tommy needled her by asking, "Did you get a good night kiss?" Sharon's face blushed and they all they all laughed. Sharon said, "I'll never tell!" "They all laughed again."

Tom said, "I congratulate you honey. That is an outstanding young man you have started a relationship with, and we all agree" "Thank you so much. You know how particular I've been about boys and dates. I think my wait has paid off." "We all hope so," said Alexis.

On the drive home Dave was thinking such a nice family of people and they are believers and Presbyterians. I don't know Sharon well enough yet to know what my true feelings are, but I like her. I must remember I have had only one long term relationship with a girl since high school.

Turner Chevrolet
7:30 PM June 28, 1950

Dave had listened to the radio news while he drove to Turner Chevrolet for his appearance. The reports on the Korean situation were not good. President Truman was planning an appeal to the United Nations, asking for a cease fire. The North Korean Army continued to advance south.

Dave had arrived about 7:00 PM to find the show room mobbed with kids and parents. Turner had run newspaper advertisements for a week promoting Dave's appearance. Turner was offering balls to the first 30 kids under 18.

Dave was just starting to talk with the young baseball players and autograph the balls. He could tell it was going to take the whole hour again to give away the 30 balls. At 8:20, Dave had a surprise when Randy White and Gordon Enson walked into the show room, came to the table and asked for an autographed baseball. One of the kids recognized Randy, and yelled out, "That's Randy White."

Randy told Dave they were checking up on him to learn if the crowd reports were true. "Gordon and I plan to take you out for coffee after your performance. In the meantime, we will look at Chevy's. They did and got a number of requests to sign their baseballs. The Turner sales staff had plenty of parents to talk to about buying a new Chevrolet.

At 8:35, Dave entered Dick Chevrolet's office and asked, "Are you selling cars?" "Yes we are Dave. We have never had a promotion that has brought as many people to our show room as long as I've been here. Thank you for the bonus of your teammates dropping in." "That was not my doing. Thank Randy White, my road roommate. He and Gordon came to see if what I had told him about the appearance was true." Dick said, "I made a request to Bill Buck, our Sales Manager, to extend the time of your appearances to 1-1/2 hours. If that's okay with you we would move the starting time up to 7:00 PM" "That's fine. I'll call Hank James in the morning and have him send a contract amendment to you." "Great Dave, we'll se you in about two weeks." "Yes, July 13th.

Randy and Gordon took Dave to a nearby coffee shop. While they ate, Randy and Gordon took turns giving Dave a bad time about his notoriety. Randy said, "We don't want you to get the big head Dave." "I know, my friends have all made sure I didn't get a big head by doing all sorts of crazy things. One pretended to be a newspaper reporter who interviewed me, asking outrageous questions." Randy said, "You told me how your got started in these appearances in San Francisco, but how did they get started here?" "Larry Lavell, the San Francisco Chevrolet dealer, is a good friend of Bill Turner. Larry told Turner about my appearances. Both Lavell and Turner are big baseball fans. Lavell's dealership sponsored the radio broadcasts of the Sea Lions' games in San Francisco.

In Burlingame, Rex Ryan had just called for Jill, but was advised by Sally that she was on a flight. He said, "Please tell her because of the Korean situation, I won't be able to call next week. I'll write to her as soon as I can. That's all I can tell her." "Thank you Rex."

Dukes Stadium
Washington at New York
2:30 PM June 29, 1950

On a Thursday afternoon, with Dave scheduled to pitch, Damon Holliday, Vice President of Entertainment, had designated the game as Ladies Day. They could purchase a reserved seat for 75 cents or a bleacher seat for 25 cents, so they would bring their children to the game. Children 12 and under were admitted free. It was working, as a flood of mothers with their kids came to the game. The crowd would reach a record 50,000 for a weekday afternoon game.

Dave pitched an almost perfect first inning, making only four pitches. Washington batters hit three balls to infielders for the three outs. The extra pitch was a strike on the first pitch of the game. In the bottom of the third inning, with the score still 0-0, Dave, batting left handed, led off with a single to right field. Duke and Wood followed with singles that scored Dave with a good slide at home plate. With runners on first and second J.B. Felton struck out. Vic Marko singled to center field, scoring Billy Duke for a 2-0 lead. Now there were runners on first and second and B.B. Katcher was coming to bat for the first time in the big leagues. With the count 2-2, he hit a fast ball into the left center field gap that went all the way to the fence for a double, scoring both runners. Katcher had come through supplying the power he had been called up for. The Dukes now led 4-0. That was the end of the scoring in the third.

Dave continued to shut out the Senators through the fifth inning on just two hits. In the Dukes half, Dave was up with two out and Randy White on second. The count ran to 3-2, and on the next pitch Dave hit a screaming line drive just inside the bag at first for a double, scoring White, making the score 5-0.

The Senators scored their only run of the game in the sixth on a single, sacrifice and another single. Two fly ball outs ended the inning for Washington. The score was now. 5-1.

In the seventh, Dave came to bat with no outs and no one on base. He hit the first pitch on a line to deep right center field. The ball hit the fence so hard it bounced away from the Washington center fielder. Dave saw it, kept on running hard. Third base coach Tony Morelli gave Dave the slide sign, and he made a hard slide into third just ahead of the throw. Wood hit a towering pop up just in front of home plate. The Washington catcher and the third baseman were in position to catch it, but they let it fall between them and Wood was on first. J. B. Felton walked to load the bases with Vic Marko coming up. Vic hit a ball deep to the third baseman that he beat out, and Dave scored. The Dukes now led 6-1.

Dave sailed along in the eighth getting three outs on seven pitches. Dave came to bat in the eighth with two outs and the bases clear. This was his opportunity to hit for the cycle if he could hit a ball out of the park. Would the Washington pitcher walk him? No, the Washington pitcher got two quick strikes. Dave, now batting right handed, watched three balls sail wide of the plate. With the count 3-2 Dave swung at an outside pitch, the best since the first two strikes, and hit a towering fly ball into deep left center field. It was hit so high the Washington centerfielder had plenty of time to get under the ball. The question was, would it come down inside our outside the ball park. As the crowd roared, Dave ran the bases like it was a triple. He was just past second when the ball slapped into the center fielder's glove for a long out and no cycle. The crowd still gave Dave a big cheer as he ran to the dugout to get his glove. Now, how would his running the base paths affect his pitching? With seven more pitches he closed out the ninth to end the game with the score Dukes 6, Washington 1. It had been a big day for Dave going 3 for 4 at the plate and winning his 14th game. As he walked off the mound he received another big cheer from the kids.

In clubhouse, the press had many questions for Dave. The inevitable one was asked by a young writer, "Do you ever think about becoming an every day player and giving up pitching?" "No, that question has been asked of me many times during my baseball career. My answer has always been I am a pitcher who likes to hit, but not every day. Now gentlemen, I must get dressed for the trip to Boston."

The team was bused to Grand Central Station where they took the New Haven Railroad's The Gilt Edge train to Boston, arriving just before midnight.

When Jill returned home from her flight to Chicago, she found the message Rex had left in Sally's handwriting. Jill had done much thinking about her feelings for Rex. She had concluded they were lust. She was relieved, because she now couldn't do something she might regret. She didn't even know if she would answer any letters Rex might write to her.

In the morning, Dave read in the Boston Globe the North Korean army had driven ten miles south of the 38th Parallel. President Truman had said, "We are not at war. This is a police action against bandits."

Chapter Twenty Six

Fenway Park

New York at Boston, Doubleheader

6:05 PM June 30, 1950

DOUG ABBOTT AND Ed Edgar pitched the first game a 9-6 win for the Dukes. Lindsey Barrett was shelled early in the second, and was followed by Tom Harris and Ed Card. Card was the only effective pitcher, shutting out the Red Sox over the last three innings. However, the damage had been done and Boston won the game 9-2. Detroit now had a 2-1/2 game lead over the Dukes.

New York at Boston
3:35 PM July 1, 1950

Vic Carlisle was pitching a good game, escaping the Fenway curse on left handed pitchers. Starting the top of the Fourth inning the score was 1-1. Tommie Hoff led off the inning with a single. Vic Marko hit a monster home run over the center filed fence for a 3-2 Dukes lead. B.B. Katcher followed with a high fly ball home run over the green monster in left field, increasing the lead to 4-1.

Carlisle sailed through the balance of the game allowing just three hits and no runs for a 4-1 complete game win. Detroit lost, so their lead was reduced to 1-1/2 games.

Back at the hotel, Dave listened to the latest radio report on the

Korean "police action." The first American ground troops had arrived in Korea by air followed by those arriving in Pusan by Naval transport. The troops were moving by truck to the front lines.

New York at Boston
3:25 PM July 2, 1950

In a pitching rotation change, manager Felton started rookie Ed Card, saving Jake Filner for the weak Washington Senators coming up next. He wanted to see what Card would do against the good Boston hitters. Card had pitched well in three innings in relief on Friday but Boston had substituted for some of their best hitters when Card entered the game. Card did well until he ran out of gas in the sixth inning. From a 2-2 tie, Card allowed three runs before Ed Edgar relieved. Edgar was not sharp and Boston won the game 6-2.

The start of the game had been moved up to 1:30 so the Dukes could take the Merchants Limited, departing at 5:00 PM for New York. They would have a close connection to make the train for Washington departing Penn Station at 10:00 PM. The team would arrive in the Capital at 2:00 AM, but would have to get to the stadium by 11:30 AM. With just a four hour trip, the players sat up, played cards or slept in the tilt back seats of the chair car. Dave wrote a post card to Jill and a letter to his parents.

Griffith Stadium
New York at Washington
8:00 PM July 3, 1950

Dave was going after his 14th win today. Since Washington had just visited the Dukes last week, Dave had current charts on Washington batters. The tendencies of some of their hitters had changed since the early part of the season. This was another value of the charting that Dave was discovering. He still had not talked to manager Felton about charting. He wanted to wait until he had more information to make a good case for having the charting taken over by the team.

While it wasn't costing Dave too much, the tickets for Don Frank were free, Dave was covering his transportation to and from the games. Dave didn't have the slightest notion that he was pioneering something that would be common practice 35 years in the future.

Using the chart information, Dave was pitching inside or outside to the Washington batters. Those who seldom swung at a first pitch strike got a sinker or fast ball strike. It was working very well. It took just eight pitches for three outs in the first inning. Through the fifth inning, Dave had a no-hitter. The Dukes had scored three runs in the second inning and one in the third, and now led 4-0.

Washington broke up the no hitter in the seventh inning with a single to center field. That was followed by two sacrifices that scored one run. The hit and the run in this inning were the only ones Dave allowed. In the eighth inning the bottom of the Dukes batting order produced three more runs. J.B. Felton led off with a single. He was sacrificed to second by Mike Hudson. Jim Essick walked. Dave came to bat with no hits for the evening. With the count at 1-2, Dave hit a three run home run over the left field fence. It increased the Dukes lead to 7-1. That's the way the game ended.

When the team returned to the Capital Hilton Hotel, Dave bought a Washington Post to catch up on the news. The big story on the front page was the Korean War. The North Korean army was not being stopped and in the paper's opinion, the draft would have to be started to supply enough men for the army. If the draft started, Dave knew he would be one of the older non veterans available. Randy White was also interested in the draft situation. "I thought you were in the Navy during the war," Dave said. "Yes, but I was attending college the entire time I was in the Navy. If the draft is started again there will be a dentist and doctor draft."

In the evening Dave was attending the Kiwanis Club of Washington Eastern Branch. The club's evening meeting time allowed Dave to get a make up. As soon as Dave gave his name when signing in, he was recognized. He contributed a happy dollar for his 14th win today. That brought a few hoots from the members.

On this eve before the 4th of July, the program was Speak up for

Freedom, a Kiwanis wide program to encourage Americans to do just that.

Griffith Stadium
New York at Washington, Doubleheader
2:30 PM July 4, 1950

Dave was wondering what kind of a turn out the Independence Day doubleheader would bring to the ball park. The Washington Club had requested a Marine Color Guard and the Marines volunteered to bring the Band to the game. They would play and march before the game. The stadium was almost filled at game time. The fans response to the Marine Band and Color Guard was enthusiastic.

Jake Filner started the first game, but was just the first of three Dukes pitchers. Ed Edgar and Tom Harris pitched well enough to win a hitters game 17-9. Vic Marko and Randy White hit home runs. B.B. Katcher continued his hitting with two doubles.

Doug Abbott started the second game. He matched the Senator's pitcher through nine innings. With the score 3-3, in the ninth, Larry Mann hit an unlikely home run that Abbott protected for the win, 4-3.

The team took the Evening Keystone train at 7:30 arriving in Penn Station at 11:35 PM. Dave entered his apartment at 1:15 AM. Even though he was tired, he read a post card from Jill. She said she was ready to request her transfer, but wanted to talk to him before she did it. She was concerned about the Korean War. She said, "Some of the pilots who are in the reserves are concerned about being called up." She said she would call after you return to New York.

Jill's Apartment
12:00 noon July 5, 1950

Returning from shopping, Jill picked up her mail. There was a letter from Rex Reynolds.

July 1, 1950

Dear Jill,

I'm writing this letter to let you know why I couldn't call you as promised. I had just arrived in San Diego when I received the news about the Korean War. Within a few hours, we were all ordered back to our bases. When I returned to Alameda I was given orders for immediate overseas transfer. Within eight hours I was on a United Airlines charter flight to Japan. That's all I can tell you now. Oh, by the way, I was promoted to Lt. Commander. When I get to a permanent ship or base, I'll write again.

Sincerely,
Rex

Jill thought I'm sorry. Rex has probably gone to the war, but it's just as well. He affected me in a way I've never been by another man, not even Dave.

Dukes Stadium
Philadelphia at New York
5:45 PM July 5, 1950

On the day after the fourth, Lindsey Barrett pitched a three hitter and the Dukes won the game 11-2. The win gave the Dukes their fifth win without a loss.

There was more good news. Louis Leon had started to throw again. He hoped to be ready to pitch in less than a week.

Following the game Dave and B.B. Katcher had gone to dinner at Bob's Restaurant. B.B. asked Dave, "What about this war?" "I just don't know B.B. If the draft is started I'll be one of the first to be selected." "I think I'm 4F Dave. I have flat feet." "That's probably true." B.B. said, "I heard that some of the fellows in Buffalo have joined the National Guard so they won't be drafted." Dave hadn't heard about that.

Dave's Apartment 8:15 PM July 5, 1950

Dave and B.B. were watching an old western on TV staring Bill Boyd. The phone rang and it was Jill calling. B. B. excused himself and Dave asked how she was and where she was. "I'm fine and at home. I have decided to wait to put in for my transfer until you know how the war is going to affect you. The war has increased travel to the West Coast and United is putting on more flights, so we need all the girls we can get." "I understand," Dave said. Jill reported that lots of girls are moving up wedding plans because their fellows are in the reserve and may be called up or might be drafted.

"When I was in Washington the newspaper said the draft could be started soon, Dave reported. So, I'm waiting for that announcement." "Dave, I just don't want to come to New York and have you get drafted and go into the army." "I agree, Jill. As soon as I know what's going to happen I'll let you know." "I knew you would understand Dave. I love you Dave, I just wish life was not co complicated." "I love you too, Jill. We just have to trust the Lord." There was no response from Jill and Dave noticed. "Good night Jill." "Good night Dave."

The next morning Hank James called. He asked Dave if he was keeping track of the crowds on the days you pitch. "No, I haven't been doing that." "I think it would be a good idea Dave. It could help you at contract time." "You're right Hank I'll start doing that and add up the past games." "I have received the contract back from Turner for the balance of your appearances. Let me know if you have any questions." "I will Hank."

"I'd like to attend the game on Friday." "That's fine Hank. How many tickets do you want? "Four. I'll bring Susan, Della my girl Friday and her husband Frank. He's a baseball nut." "How are you doing with Susan?" "I'm doing okay. The problem is that she is so career oriented that I don't know if she will ever agree to be tied down in a marriage." "What is her position over at J. Walter" (J. Walter Thompson, the big ad agency). "Oh she heads a copywriting group, but wants to get into ad creation, a tough move for a woman." "I'll leave your tickets in will call." "Thanks Dave."

Just before he and B.B. departed for the stadium, Dave received his first post card from Sharon. She said she was dizzy learning about the real world of law. She said cases and court dates change daily and it is hard to keep up. She wanted to know how Dave would be affected by the war.

Philadelphia at New York, Night
6:00 PM July 6, 1950

Vic Carlisle was pitching tonight in the Dukes effort to win their seventh straight game. With a 4-0 lead, Carlisle gave up four runs in the seventh inning and had to be relieved by Ed Edgar. In a closely played game the Dukes won the game 5 to 4 on a ninth inning home run by Vic Marko. B.B. Katcher also hit one, his second since being called up from Buffalo.

After dinner Dave and B.B. went bowling. They bowled three games for recreation with no money at stake. Dave wanted to relax tonight before pitching tomorrow.

Boston at New York
2:55 PM July 7, 1950

In the first inning Dave's sinkers were hit through the infield for three singles and one run. Then, a change up was poorly located and hit for a double, driving in two more runs. All this happened with no outs. Then Dave bore down and retired the next three batters. So Dave had allowed more runs in one inning than he had allowed in any game but one, the game he lost 3-2.

The score stayed the same until the sixth inning. Vic Marko led off with a single. Katcher hit a single to deep right field and Marko ran to third. J. B. Felton doubled down the left field line, scoring Marko and advancing Katcher to third. The score was now, Boston 3, Dukes 1. Mike Hudson struck out for the first out. Randy White singled, driving in Katcher and Felton for a 3-3 tie. Dave came to bat with an opportunity to keep the rally going, but with the count 2-2, he hit into a double play, ending the inning.

The game stayed tied 3-3 through the eighth inning. Dave pitched a quick ninth, getting three ground balls hit to infielders on eight pitches. In the bottom of the ninth Billy Duke hit the first pitch over the left field fence for a home run and a 4-3 Dukes win. It was Dave's 15th win and 16th complete game.

The baseball writers had lots of questions for Dave and Manager Felton following the game. Was Dave getting tired pitching on three days rest? His answer was, no he didn't feel tired. In the first inning he didn't have good location on the sinker pitch. He and B.B did not leave the clubhouse until after 6:30 PM. They decided to have a Chinese dinner at the Golden Dragon in Flushing.

Dave's Apartment
10:00 AM July 8, 1950

Dave was reading with the radio playing music. Soon the music stopped and a news bulletin was announced. "In Washington this morning President Harry Truman ordered the draft to be resumed. He said the reserves would not be called up at this time." It was expected that the oldest non-veterans would be called up first in the draft. However, there are few qualified men over the age of 22 who have not served in the armed forces. Dave immediately called his dad. He asked his dad about joining the National Guard. His dad recommended he not do that. He said, "The Guard is not the best of military outfits. I will find out what the Army plans to do with draftees who are graduate engineers." "Thanks dad."

After his phone call, Dave realized he would have four days off next week during the All-Star Game break. I think I will take a sight seeing trip to Manhattan. I'll go see the Statue of Liberty, the Empire State Building and visit the stock market on Wall Street. I'll ask B.B. if he wants to go along.

Boston at New York
5:34 PM July 8, 1950

The Dukes did not support Jake Filner's reasonably good pitching, and lost to Boston 4-2.

At dinner, Dave asked B.B., "Did you go to Sunday School when you were a kid?" No I didn't Dave. My parents were not church people. The story I got was that my Great, Great Grandfather, who came from Hungary, had a dispute with the Catholic Church and they excommunicated him. After that he didn't want to have anything to do with any church. That was handed down to each family. I've attended church a few times with friends in Redwood, but that's all."

"I want to give you a book entitled The Man Nobody Knows. It's a book about Jesus, written by a layman, Bruce Barton, who was an advertising man in Chicago. It was written in 1925 and more than 500,000 copies have been sold in English alone. Read it at your leisure and if you have any questions, let me know. I first read it in 1946, soon after I joined the church. I liked it because it was layman to layman." "I'll read it Dave."

Dave told B.B. what he had planned for the All Star break next week. He asked if B.B. was interested in going with him. B.B. said, "I can't Dave. I must take a trip back to Buffalo and ship my trunk and a big suitcase back to my apartment. I hope to see a game in Buffalo and visit the fellows.

Fifth Avenue Presbyterian Church
9:30 AM July 9, 1950

The lesson today was from Acts 14:10, the Miracle in Lystra. A man, crippled from birth, heard Paul's sermon, received God's spirit, and stood up on his feet, healed.

Dave had sat in the back of the room next to a slight not-so-good looking young man in his twenties. Dave had become aware of him because he asked very good questions. Dave asked others in the class who this fellow was. The typical response was, "Oh he's Rodney

Mann, the youngest son of Clearance Mann, a former Columbia football great who played for Coach Lou Little. He is not a chip of the old block." When Dave asked why, he was told that Rodney was not a sports fan or athlete like his father or two older brothers. This peaked Dave's interest and he decided he would meet and talk to Rodney.

Rodney Mann was the youngest of the three sons of Clearance and Olivia Mann. Clearance Mann was President and sole owner of Mann Athletic Equipment Company. Mann manufactured the equipment used in sports other than football, basketball and baseball (hardball). Mann specialized in softball equipment including balls mitts and uniforms for softball players. In 1950 more people played softball in America than any other team sport. Mann also made equipment for volleyball, handball, racket ball, squash, ping pong and the big ball used in push ball.

The two older Mann sons were husky, good looking men who were very athletic. Bill, the oldest, had played football at Columbia. Lester, the number two son was tall for those days at 6' 4" and had played basketball at Long Island University. Both were now working for the family firm.

Rodney Mann, 21, was not athletic and was not interested in sports. As a young boy he was a "bookworm." He read any book that sounded like a good storey or dealt with how people acted. Fortunately, Clearance Mann understood the difference in his youngest son, and encouraged him in his reading and other interests. Rodney was an inquisitive boy who asked lots of question of everyone, particularly in any learning environment. Otherwise Rodney was quiet and would not initiate a conversation. He was majoring in psychology at Columbia.

When the lesson was over, Dave talked to Rodney. It was the first of many talks they would have, that led to a long friendship.

Boston at New York
4:05 PM July 9, 1950

In a game started early so players could get to the All Star game in

Chicago, Doug Abbott pitched a six hitter and the Dukes won the game 3-1. The Dukes now led Detroit by 1-1/2 games.

After the game, manager Felton talked to Dave. He said, "I didn't select you for the All Star Game pitching staff because you wouldn't pitch in the game. I'll give veteran pitchers that opportunity. I'm sure you will be an All Star in the future. Now, Fred Duke would like to talk to you about the draft. Can you meet with him tomorrow morning at nine o'clock?" "Sure," said Dave. "I'll be glad to do so. And thank you for talking to me about the All Star game. I can use the time off."

Flushing Baptist Church
7:00 PM July 9, 1950

It had been a month since Dave had heard a sermon. The sermon tonight was entitled The Rock of Christian Giving. The scripture was II Corinthians 8:1-9. The scripture tells how the churches of Macedonia, even though in deep poverty, responded liberally to the call for a gift to help the ministry of the saints. Verse 9 is compelling. "For ye know the grace of our Lord Jesus Christ, that, though he was rich, yet for your sake he became poor, that ye through his poverty might become rich."

The sermon subject was one Dave was very interested in. Again, Dave took notes and he wrote out the following summary of the sermon.

1 A Christian cannot be totally committed to Jesus Christ without being a good giver.

2 Generous giving to the Lord's work is evidence that God has been working in people's hearts.

3 If people would chose to be directed by the Holy Spirit to create among us God's grace of generosity, the church could eliminate all of the special appeals that are made today. Grace is critical to giving. The word grace appears seven times in this 8th chapter.

4 Out in California a Bible study for ladies was started by a former

missionary to China. Soon there were expenses for lesson material printing and other expenses. The leader, Miss Thompson said there would be no appeals for funds. A plate was placed in the entry way of the house where the study was held so contributions could be made. All the funds necessary were contributed and no appeals have ever been made.

5 Paul, the author of Corinthians, had used the Macedonians as an illustration of Christian love and grace displayed toward others. Now he turned to the greatest example of all. Our Lord Jesus Christ, the Rock of Christian Giving.

6 He was born of poor parents in a stable. He never owned any real estate, stocks or bonds. He said, "Fox's have holes and the birds of the air have nests, but the Son of God has no place to lay his head." He spent his last hours with his disciples in a room loaned by a friend for the occasion. Having no money to leave behind, he entrusted his mother into the hands of his friends. He was crucified on a cross someone else provided. His coat was raffled in a lottery by those who crucified him. His forgiveness he gave to his enemies. His peace he gave to his friends. His love he poured out upon the whole world. They wrapped him in borrowed clothes and placed him in a borrowed tomb. Thus lived and thus died one of the world's poorest men. But thanks be to God for his unspeakable gift, for though he was rich, yet for our sake he became poor that through his poverty, we may become rich.

Office of the President
New York Dukes Baseball Club
Dukes Stadium
Queens, New York
9:00 AM July 10, 1950

Dave arrived dressed in his best suit for this meeting with Fred Duke. Meeting Dave for the first time, Fred liked Dave immediately. He asked Dave about his engineering degree. and training. "My degree is a B.S. in Aeronautical Engineering. It was a course heavy in aircraft and engine theory and maintenance. I hold CAA licenses in Aircraft and Engines that authorizes me to work on civilian aircraft and engines. However, I have only the experience gained in college and working one summer at Pan American as a mechanics helper."

Fred said he had learned about a reserve squadron of the Military Air Transport Service from his brother-in-law, a United Airlines Pilot who is a member of the squadron. There may be an opportunity for you to enlist in that organization. Fred suggested Dave call the squadron and ask for Lt. Frank Funk. "Tell him I suggested you call." Fred gave Dave the phone number and advised him the squadron is based at Republic Airport out in Farmingdale." "Thank you, I'll call today."

As soon a the draft was announced, Fred Duke had asked General Manager Donald Newton to determine what players on the Dukes' and the Buffalo rosters were subject to the draft. Also, I want to know about any players in the reserves who might be called up. Newton had determined that Dave, B.B. Katcher and Ed Card were the draft eligible players on the Dukes roster although Katcher says he has flat feet and likely could not pass an army physical. Randle White may be subject to a dentist draft and Glen Close is a Marine pilot who could be called up. At Buffalo there are at least four players subject to the draft.

As soon as Dave returned to his apartment he called Lt. Funk. "If you have some time this afternoon, you can come and see me at 1530, that's 3:30." "I can do that." Lt. Funk said, "We are located in the first hanger on the access road. Enter the airport off Broad Hollow." "Thank you, I'll be there.

Dave spent the rest of the morning and early afternoon shopping. The radio news reported that the Army's 2nd Division had been alerted for movement to Korea.

1st Military Air Transport Service Reserve Squadron RS-1 Republic Airport Farmingdale, New York 3:30 PM July 10, 1950

Dave reported to reception manned by an enlisted airman in an Air Force uniform. Lt. Funk soon came to meet Dave.

Lt. Funk said, "I'm one of two regular Air Force officers assigned to this squadron to assist in getting it organized and functioning. I'm the engineering officer in charge of aircraft maintenance and engineering."

"I know you are a well known baseball player, but tell me about your education and experience." Dave related his education, the A & E licenses he held and his limited experience.

'This unit is the first reserve squadron of the Military Air Transport Service. MATS was created in 1947 by combining the Air Transport Command (ATC) of the Air Force and the Naval Air Transport Service (NATS). The squadron was created as the result of the effort of Colonel Bernie Flyer, a Pan American Captain who was an officer in the ATC during the war. He is the commanding officer. It was authorized to start recruiting personnel on 01 January of this year. Our maintenance personnel are from the airlines and Republic Aviation. We have pilots from Pan American, United and American Airlines."

"Through the end of June our budget was very limited, so we could not recruit more than the initial manpower. The funds were increased 01 July, just in time for the Korean War. We expect to receive more funds by September. To enlist requires passing a written psychological examination and a physical exam. The enlistment period is four years but can be reduced at the pleasure of the government. You would be enlisting in the Air Force. We have funds from the Air Force and the Navy and that determines what service you join. The duty requirement is one weekend per month, now the third week end, plus a two week training period during the summer."

"We will review your qualification and get back to you later this week to give you an answer regarding enlistment." Dave said, "Thank you. I have a question. What is the possibility that the unit would be called to active duty?" "That is unlikely. MATS is reasonably well staffed and has plenty of airplanes. The most likely active duty calls would be for individual personnel who have expertise in needed in specialties." Dave said, "I do need to move as quickly as possible because I understand I must volunteer for the reserve before I receive a draft notice." "Yes, I believe that's true."

Statue of Liberty
New York Harbor
11:00 AM July 11, 1950

Dave had arrived at the statue and had climbed part way up the stairs. He decided not to attempt the climb to the top. This afternoon he would visit the stock exchange and the Empire State Building. Tomorrow he might go to Coney Island.

Turner Chevrolet
8:30 PM July 13, 1950

The first game of the series with Cleveland had been rained out. Dave and B.B had gone to an early dinner because Dave had an appearance scheduled at Turner Chevrolet tonight. This would be his first 1-1/2 hour appearance. During dinner Dave had told B.B. about the MATS reserve unit." "Do you want to get tied up for four years Dave?" "That's the maximum time. I don't think this war will last that long, so it may be less. I would not lose two years of baseball and I would be doing something I've been trained for. My big problem is should I do this while my friends have to take time out of their careers to serve in the army?

At Turner a big crowd of kids and parents had waited for Dave. Dick Chevrolet had told Dave, "They started lining up at 5:30!" The extra time allowed Dave to talk to parents on the show room floor. He developed interest with two families in buying a car, so he turned them over to salesmen. He was getting a real sense of accomplishment with this activity. Dick Chevrolet asked Dave if he would like to sell Chevy's after the baseball season?" "I think I'd better stick to engineering education."

Dave's Apartment
9:00 AM July 14, 1950

Dave was writing post cards and listening to the radio. Playing was a new Teresa Brewer number Music! Music! Music! It would become a juke box favorite. The phone rang and it was Lt. Funk calling. He advised Dave he had reviewed his qualifications with the squadron's Chief Maintenance Sergeant and "You are offered the opportunity to enlist in the Air Force Reserve and be assigned to MATS RS-1. One of our Navy mechanics attended a Navy aviation course at California Polytechnic so he was familiar with their aero program. We will need an answer by Monday Dave." "Thank you. I need to talk to Fred Duke about the duty time during the season and the summer training. I'll call you Monday."

In anticipation of this opportunity Dave had made an appointment to talk to one of the interns at Fifth Avenue Presbyterian Church on Sunday evening.

Dave called his dad and asked if he had any information about the draft? George Mason said, he had learned from one of the California's U.S. Senators that the army was working on a program for drafted engineers and others with special college degrees. However there is nothing specific yet. "The army's big need now is how they can train men quickly and send them to Korea. Dave described the MATS reserve opportunity and said "I'm leaning that way even though it requires a four year enlistment." George Mason said, "I agree Dave and I don't think this war will last that long. I think you will be out in a couple of years." "Okay, I'm meeting with one of the interns at church to talk about my concern for not spending two years of my life in the army like my friends will have to do." That compared to four years in the Air Force Reserve but not full time. That's a good approach Dave." "Let me know what you decide." "I will."

Dukes Stadium
Cleveland at New York, Night
8:30 PM July 14, 1950

Another big crowd had come to see this game and to see Dave pitch. If he won tonight it would be his 16th win of the season and ninth in a row without loss.

The game started as a pitchers duel. Dave retired the first nine batters using only 20 pitches. The Cleveland pitcher almost matched it, allowing one hit, but making 36 pitches. Dave allowed a hit in the top of the fourth, but continued to shut out the Indians. In the bottom of the fourth, the Dukes scored two runs on shear power. Vic Marko and B.B. Katcher hit back to back home runs. That's all Dave needed. He allowed just three more hits, pitching a four hit shut out and a 2-0 win for the Dukes.

Dave and B.B. were the focus of the baseball writers following the game. They answered many questions and did not leave the stadium until almost midnight. They were too charged up to sleep, so they had hamburgers and coffee before heading for their apartments.

With about three months of the season gone, how was manager Ozzie Felton's practice of using his best pitchers against the weaker clubs working out? The Dukes had won 30 and lost 12 games against the weaker teams for a .714 winning percentage. Against the best clubs, the team was doing better than .500, winning 22 and losing 14 for a .611 percentage. The Dukes had won 51 and lost 26 games and they were one game ahead of Detroit in the league standings. So the approach was working.

Dukes Stadium
Cleveland at New York
2:00 PM, July 15, 1950

In a close game, Doug Abbott pitched the Dukes to a 4-3 win. The Dukes continued to hit with power. Vic Marko and B.B. Katcher hit doubles and Randy White hit a two run homer.

Fifth Avenue Presbyterian Church
9:30 AM July 16, 1950

In the continuing study of Paul's first missionary journey, the lesson today was about the Apostles being received as Gods. Paul had to explain that they were ordinary men, not gods.

Dave asked Rodney Mann what he was doing this summer. Rodney said, "I'm going to summer school so I can get the last of my required courses out of the way before my senior year. I like summer school because I take just two classes so I have plenty of free time."
"Yes. I did that in college while I was playing summer baseball. I got some of my best grades during summer school. Good luck Rodney."

Dukes Stadium
Chicago at New York, Doubleheader
5:45 PM July 16, 1950

Another big crowd was on hand for the Sunday doubleheader. In the first game Lindsey Barrett pitched a four hitter. B.B. Katcher hit a home run in the eighth inning to break a 1-1 tie. That was the winning run and the Dukes won the game 2-1.

In the second game, Vic Carlisle was bested 5-2. The game was tied 2-2 for six innings. Then Chicago scored three runs in the seventh and that's they way the game ended.

In the clubhouse, B.B. Katcher was the center of the writer's attention because of his winning homer in the first game. He had lots of questions to answer. Dave stood behind the writers and made faces at B.B. It was all he could do to keep from laughing. It was the most attention he had received in his young major league career.

The writers next went to see manager Felton. They had head that Louis Leon was ready to pitch again. Felton advised the writers that Louis would start tomorrow's game. "This will really help our pitching rotation." One of the writers asked, "Will you take Mason off of the three days rest schedule?" "No, he prefers to pitch on that schedule so we won't change."

When the writers had departed to make their deadlines, Dave said, "I'll buy your dinner B.B." "I accept. You almost had me laughing in the faces of those writers." "I just didn't want you to get the big head." At dinner, Dave told B.B. that he had decided to join the MATS reserve squadron. He planned to call Lt. Funk in the morning." "How many pitching starts will you miss?" "It's hard to say. I'll be on duty one weekend each month and on a two week summer training period during August. Having Leon back in the rotation will cover my absence."

Detroit split their doubleheader so the Dukes had a 1/2 game lead over Detroit.

Fifth Avenue Presbyterian Church
7:00 PM July 16, 1950

Dave had an appointment with Norman Small. He was a church intern, serving for one year before returning to Princeton Theological Seminary for his final year. Dave's appointment had been set up with Small because he had spent three years in the Amy Air Corps during the war. He had become an assistant to chaplains and when the war was over he felt a call to the ministry. He had been raised in the Presbyterian Church so he enrolled at Princeton. Having had one year at City College before the war, he had completed his B.A degree and two years of seminary in five years by attending school year around.

Dave introduced himself, saying he was a member of the Menlo Park Presbyterian Church in California and had been attending the young adult Sunday school class when in town. My dilemma is should I accept an enlistment offer in a MATS reserve squadron or wait to be drafted. The reserve enlistment requires a four year commitment. By accepting the reserve enlistment I will be using my education and experience. Being drafted into the army, I don't know what I would be doing. However I am concerned that my friends will have to give up two years of their career, while I continue to play baseball and go to college in the off season. Since I received the enlistment offer Friday, I have been praying about it."

Mr. Small said, "I think the situation is different now compared to that of World War II. At that time the army needed soldiers as soon as they could be trained to use a rifle. They didn't much consider what a person's occupation or training was. They put bodies where the need was greatest. Today with many college graduates who haven't served in the armed forces, there is the need to consider that training. However, there is no guarantee that you if drafted, you would be able to use your training. You just don't know. I think, if you are willing to make the four year reserve commitment that's a good trade off. Dave said, "I should add there is no guarantee that I won't be called to active duty from the reserve unit." "If you feel good about the choice of the reserve enlistment, I think you should go ahead. But it is your decision. Let's pray about." And they did.

"Thank you very much for your time and counsel." It's my pleasure. Before you leave, the high school youth group that meets Sunday evening has requested that I talk to you about the possibility of you speaking to the group. Would you be willing to do that?" "With adequate time for scheduling and preparation, yes I would." "Good. What I would like you to do Dave is write out your statement of faith and get it to me. Then I'll get back to you." "I'll do that." "Thank you."

On the drive back to his apartment Dave felt much better about accepting the reserve enlistment. He would call Lt. Funk in the morning.

Dave's Apartment
8:30 AM July 17, 1950

Dave was on the phone talking to Lt. Funk. He had agreed to enlist in the Air Force and joint the MATS squadron. "Very good," said Lt. Funk. Can you report here at 8:00 AM tomorrow for testing and a physical?" "Yes I can. We have a night game tomorrow." "Fine, we will see you in the morning."

The radio news about the war was not good. The North Korean Army had driven close to Taejon, the temporary capital of South Korea.

Dave was continuing his study of the life of Jesus. He was studying the Parable of the Wedding Feast in Luke Chapter 12, verses 36-38.

The scripture reflects the ancient Palestinian wedding customs. The groom has gone to the wedding feast to be married at the home of the bride's parents. The slaves are to be ready to open the doors when the bridegroom appears, but they do not know when he will appear, so they must always be ready. It was just as we must be ready for the return of Jesus.

Dave called the office of Fred Duke to let him know that he had enlisted in the Air Force Reserve and will be a member of MATS. Fred was not in, so Dave left a message for him to call.

When Dave arrived at the stadium for game warm up, he first went to Fred Duke's office. "Dave Mason is here to see you," Fred's secretary said to the intercom." "Send him in." Dave said, "I have agreed to enlist in the Air Force Reserve and be a member of the MATS squadron. I will have one weekend of duty per month and a two week training period in the summer. This year it's August 12 through 26tn. "That's good Dave. I'll let Ozzie know." "Thank you."

Dukes Stadium
Chicago at New York
5:30 PM July 17, 1950

Louis Leon's time off with a sore arm helped his control and he pitched a game with just one walk and won it 4-2. The victory made Dave feel even better about missing some starts while on duty at MATS. Dave was one of the first out of the dugout to congratulate Louis.

1st Military Air Transport Service Reserve RS-1
8:00 AM July 18, 1950

Dave was reporting to take his written and physical exams. It all went well, and after lunch Dave was given the oath of allegiance to his country, and he was sworn in as a member of the United States Air Force Reserve. Dave was issued uniforms and was advised he would receive his dog tag and identity card when he reported for duty on July 22nd. The supply airman suggested that Dave would probably like to have his uniform shirts and blouse tailored.

Returning to his apartment, Dave picked up his mail. There was a post card from Sharon. She advised Dave that she would be coming home over the weekend of August 12 and 13 to attend the wedding of Loretta, a high school friend. "I'm sorry I won't see you because of your summer training that you wrote about."

Dukes Stadium
St. Louis at New York
4:35 PM July 18, 1950

When Dave arrived in the clubhouse he asked manager Felton if Fred Duke had talked to him about my Air Force Reserve enlistment. "Yes he did. I'll slide your next start to Tuesday in Cleveland. With Leon's return we are in good shape."

I'm glad you were able to work it out so you can continue to pitch and still meet your service obligation. If you have any other duty calls, just let me know and we will work around them." "Thank you Ozzie."

Ozzie Felton announced during a 5:30 team meeting that Dave Mason had joined the Air Force Reserve and would be a member of the MATS reserve squadron at Republic Airport. So he can continue playing baseball. "This required Dave to sign up for a four year hitch and he will be on duty one weekend each month and on two weeks summer training each year. He will miss some starts, but with Louis pitching again, I think we will be okay." Following the meeting, Dave received lots of pats on the back and hand shakes.

On a Tuesday night in the middle of summer, a big crowd to watch a baseball game could not be anticipated. But the fans were coming. It looked like another big crowd of close to 50,000.

The Dukes were starting a series with the lowly St. Louis Browns. Following manager Felton's formula for winning a pennant, he would start his better pitchers, Dave, Filner and Abbott so the Dukes could sweep the Browns. The teams would play a doubleheader on Wednesday to make up for rain outs.

After retiring St. Louis in the first inning on nine pitches and no hits, Dave watched the Dukes bat around. Vic Marko, B.B. Katcher, and Randy White all hit doubles. Dave contributed a single and an RBI. At the end of the inning it was Dukes 7 and St. Louis 0. Dave had a no hitter through five innings. In the sixth Browns broke it up when they scored their only run.

In the meantime, the Dukes added three runs in the sixth and three more in the eighth inning and the slaughter ended 13-1. It was a great way to end the day for Dave.

Dave's Apartment
9:00 AM July 19, 1950

Dave had read the morning sports page, something he usually didn't do after he had pitched. However the game last night was so dominated by the hitting of the Dukes, he thought that would be the focus of the articles about the game. He was only partially right. Below the headline, "Dukes Bomb the Browns," was a sub headline, Mason joins MATS Reserve, then wins his 17th. Most of the article did concentrate on the Dukes hitting and the resurgence of power hitting.

According to Jill's schedule she should be home this morning, so Dave was calling her to follow up on his promise to let her know what he did about military service. "Good morning, is this my beautiful blonde girl, I think her name is Jill." "I'll see if I can find her," Jill said. After a pause, "Is this the baseball super star who won his 17th game last night?" "Guilty." They both laughed. "I'm calling to tell you that I am now a member of the Air Force Reserve and have joined the MATS squadron here on Long Island." "I read that too." "Nuts, I wanted to be the first to tell you."

"That's great news Dave. Now that you aren't going to be drafted into the army, I'll put in for my transfer." That's fine Jill, but remember, I plan to go home after the season to continue my master's program at Stanford." "I'm aware of that Dave, but I have decided I must come to New York, and find out what it's like so I'll know what to expect when we get married." "My, my, is that a subtle suggestion? What brings on this confidence?" "It's the most important reason for my coming to New York" "What is that?" "I want you to lead me through my acceptance of the Lord as my personal savior!" "Fantastic, Jill. In your post card's you mentioned you had been reading and studying The Man Nobody Knows, but I didn't realize you were close to accepting the Lord." "Oh Dave, I can't wait."

"What convinced me Dave was the chapter entitled His Method. It talks about the cost of carrying the Roman civilization across the then known world and then the church that Jesus created did it with a tiny group of uneducated men and little money." "Do you have any idea of how long the transfer will take?" "No, it will depend on what the needs are in New York. There won't be any flight bidding until the end of the year." "Okay, Jill, lets pray about it right now." And they did.

Dave then called his dad to tell him the news." I think you did the right thing Dave. I haven't heard anything more about what the army plans to do with graduate engineers." "Okay, I'll call you after my first duty weekend and give you a report." "Thank you Dave."

Dukes Stadium
St. Louis at New York, Doubleheader
5:45 PM July 19, 1950

The Dukes still had hot bats and they clubbed the Browns 16 to 1 in the first game. Jake Filner pitched a seven hit complete game. In the second game, Doug Abbott shut out the Browns over the last three innings and won the game 4-3. The Dukes had accomplished their sweep.

That evening Dave and B.B. went to the show. They wanted to see Betty Grable in Wabash Avenue. It also stared Phil Harris and Victor Mature. Since they would have a day off tomorrow, they stopped for hamburgers and coffee, and didn't return home until midnight.

Turner Chevrolet
7:00 PM July 19, 1950

Turner's advertisements for Dave's appearance had stated that the first 30 kids under the age of 18 would receive baseballs and only 50 could enter the showroom. "So, come early," the advertisement said. The crowds had become so large Turner had retained Pinkerton to send one of their security men to keep order. Tonight there seemed to be a large number of 16 and 17 year olds, all of whom were baseball players. Dave thought many had come to see if Dave was really like they read in the sports pages.

Dave was able to complete his baseball autographing in time to spend some time on the showroom floor talking to parents about Chevrolets. Dave was enjoying this type of contact and liked to talk about his car. He began to think he could be effective in sales.

When Dave talked to Dick Chevrolet at 8:30, he mentioned that this was his last scheduled appearance. "I'll talk to Sales Manager Bill Buck about it tomorrow Dave."

Dave's Apartment
8:00 AM July 20, 1950

There being no game today, Dave had time to complete his statement of faith for Mr. Small.

STATEMENT OF FAITH OF DAVID D. MASON

God has given me all the abilities I have. He has also given me
the opportunities to develop and improve these abilities.

I am thankful that the Lord selected me
to be a member of his Kingdom.

I believe in Jesus Christ, God's only son
who came to earth in a human body to minister and serve.
Also, to experience the problems of life that I face
so I can turn my problems over to him.

I believe in Jesus Christ who shed his blood

and died on the cross to pay for my sins.
That he rose from the death to be the living savior
of me and those who trust in him.

Dave had talked with one of the younger baseball writers, Sherman West, of the New York Gazette about baseball history. Sherm said, "You remind me of Hall of Fame pitcher Christy Mathewson." Dave decided he would go the New York Library and learn about Christy.

Hank James called and reported he had scheduled appearances at Turner for August 7 and 28, and September 5 and 25. "I think these dates are all good according to your game schedule, but you should check to make sure." "I'll do that Hank, and only call if there is a problem. And thank you for all your help and support." "It's been my pleasure Dave."

Kiwanis Club of Five Towns
Valley Stream
New York
7:00 PM July 20, 1950

This was Dave's third make up at Valley Stream. Dave had a happy dollar for his opportunity to enlist in the MATS reserve squadron at Republic airport. Dave said, I signed up for a four year hitch in the Air Force Reserve. It will allow me to use my education and training in the Korean War effort.

The club was starting to plan their fund raising program for fall. The funds raised would be for the benefit of children and young people.

Dukes Stadium
Detroit at New York
4:00 PM July 21, 1950

The Tigers were in town to duel with the Dukes for first place. The Dukes had a two game lead over Detroit.

Lindsey Barrett was the starter for the Dukes. The game started out to be "a laughter" for the Dukes. They scored four runs in the first inning and by the seventh, led 12-1. Detroit made a threat in the eighth, scoring three runs making the score12-4. The Dukes added two in their half of the eighth and raised the score to14-4.

When he came to bat in the ninth inning, Vic Marko had hit a single, double and a home run. Could he hit a triple and hit for the cycle? With the count now 2-2, Vic hit a ball high into right field. It looked like it might go out for another home run. The ball came down and hit just below the top of the fence and bounded back towards the infield. Vic was almost to second when the ball hit the fence. The Tiger's second sacker ran into right field and retrieved the ball and fired to third. Vic beat the throw by three steps and had hit for the cycle.

Dave left the stadium as soon as the game was over to drive to MATS.

1st MATS Reserve Squadron
Farmingdale, New York
1700 hours (5:00 PM) 21 July 1950

Dave had arrived early so he could learn where his bunk was located and eat dinner in the mess hall. The third floor of the administration building had been converted into sleeping quarters for enlisted men. Officers quarters were located on the second floor. Dave reported in and received his bunk assignment. He located his bunk, and put his uniforms and toilet kit in the foot locker at the foot of the bunk. He was ready to sample MATS chow.

Lining up with other enlisted men, he was immediately recognized by an older Airman with two chevrons. "Aren't you Dave Mason, the baseball player?" "Guilty." "Chub Flabby is my name. My real name is Ray Underhill Flabby. R.U., get it? I try to live up to my name. (He was chubby). I've followed the Dukes for years starting back when they were in the Bronx." Where do you work Chub?" "I'm an engine man at United Airlines." "That's interesting. Engines have been my big interest. I'll have to pick your brains." "Okay. You can pick my brains about engines if I can pick yours about baseball?" "It's a deal Chub. Now let's eat."

Enlisted men had been directed to an orientation in the mess hall at 1900 hours (7:00 PM). Captain Peter Jergens, Executive Officer of the unit welcomed all the enlisted men, particularly the new recruits. "With the country in another war, security will be increased and starting right this minute don't talk about what you do, see or hear when you are away from this base. The summer training schedule will be from August 12 through 25, but you should not expect to return home until the Sunday the 26th. The training will occur at another Air Force base that will not be pre announced."

"Now, our information officer, Lieutenant Parks will come and give the history of MATS RS-1 and how it came to be." "I think most of you know that MATS was formed by combining the Air Force Air Transport Command (ATC) and Navel Air Transport Service (NATS). Colonel Bernie Flyer a pioneer Pan American pilot who flew for the ATC during World War II had the idea that MATS should have a reserve. He battled the Pentagon and then sold congress on an initial appropriation to start this squadron in January of this year."

"He had no problem recruiting pilots from Pan American, United, and American Airlines. With plenty of time off between flights, most pilots would rather fly than do almost anything else and it adds time to their log book. Maintenance personnel from the airlines and Republic Aviation were glad to sign up so they could make some extra money. In late January and early February we received our airplanes. Included were two C-47s and ten C-54s for a total of 12 airplanes. That's four less than our Table of Organization and Equipment (TO & E) calls for."

Although all the planes have reconditioned engines, the airframes are old and tired. Most of the planes flew in the Berlin Airlift .The big challenge has been to keep the systems working."

"On 01 July we received more funds so we could recruit more personnel and requisition more tools and equipment. We now expect more funds because of the Korean situation, just when is unknown."

"Our immediate goal is to be able to supplement MATS by flying domestic cargo trips. To meet our goal we need more personnel and training time. That is an updated picture of the unit."

Lt. Frank Funk was the next speaker. He gave out the revised maintenance squad roster. Each squad was composed of five men and each squad was assigned to two airplanes. "At 1930 all maintenance airmen will muster in the hanger and get acquainted with your squad leader and fellow members. You are dismissed."

In the hanger, standing in squad ranks, squad reports were made. All but two men were present and they were accounted for Lt. Funk said. "Lights out is at 2300 and reveille at 0600. The first mess call is at 0630 in the morning. All squad members are to report to their squad leader in the hanger at 0730." Following the announcements, Lt. Funk said to First Sergeant Norman Foster, "Take the detachment." Sergeant Foster gave the order, "Dismissed to your squad leader.

Dave's squad leader is Sergeant Sam Slade called "Gummy" because his the name being the same as San Francisco radio detective Sam Slade. Corporal Chub Flabby, Airman First Class Dick "Cub" Piper, Airman Ray "Mossy" Rock, and Airman Dave made up squad of five. Dave at 22 was the youngest and would be called "the Kid." The members of the squad spent the rest of the evening getting acquainted and sharing their experience. Then they inspected the two airplanes they were to maintain, both C-54s. The tail numbers were 23225 and 24360.

Sergeant Slade gave a run down on the history of each aircraft. Both were produced in 1943, and each had thousands of hours on them. Both had served in the Berlin Airlift. Sgt. Slade said, "You can still find coal dust in floor board cracks. The planes were fitted with overhauled engines before we received them. However, the systems of both have not been maintained and need work, particularly the hydraulics. Now lets get to know them." Sgt. Slade led a tour of each aircraft, pointing out some of the obvious problems. Both planes were well worn. At 2000 hours, Sgt. Slade dismissed the squad.

Dave and Chub went to the mess hall where the big coffee earn was on, and Dave answered Chubb's questions about baseball. Dave had said, "I'll ask my engine questions during our next duty.

By then I should know what questions to ask." On Sunday morning Chapel services were offered for Catholic and Protestants by a visiting Priest and Minister. Dave was surprised that the services were offered, but learned later that Col. Flyer was a practicing Catholic.

The first hour of Sunday morning was spent on basic military drill, including close order marching. The members of the squad then went to work on the list of pilot complaints for each airplane. One requirement instituted by Col. Bernie Flyer was that all maintenance personnel who worked on an aircraft would be aboard the plane during its test flight. At 1600 a Captain and Lieutenant pilot and co-pilot appeared and the squad went on two short test flights.

During the weekend, Chub Flabby was the only one who had said he recognized Dave, although it was well known by all that Dave had joined the unit. The word had been sent out to all personnel by Col. Flyer to accept Dave as an Airman, not a baseball player.

At 1900 the duty weekend came to a close. On the drive to his apartment, he concluded it was a rewarding experience. He looked forward to learning more about the aircraft, particularly the engines.

Dave's Apartment
8:00 PM July 23, 1950

When Dave entered his apartment he looked at the clock which read 8:00 straight up. Dave thought that's 2000 in MATS time, I think! There had been no newspapers at MATS so Dave had learned the game scores by word of mouth from others. The Dukes had won the Saturday game 10-4 and Detroit took the single Sunday game 6-5. Dave now read that Louis Leon had won the Saturday game and Jake Filner lost the Sunday game. This put the Dukes 2 games up on Detroit.

With no game scheduled on Monday, July 24, and the Tuesday game a night game in Cleveland, Fred Duke had decided this would be the road trip to do the trial on airline travel. Those who did not want to fly would take the train to Cleveland on Monday evening while the rest of the team would fly to Cleveland on Tuesday morning. The Clevelander departed Penn Station at 8:15 PM with five players and

Coach Ray Woodall. The train had arrived in Cleveland at 8:35 AM on Tuesday. The rest of the team members including Dave departed La Guardia Airport at 10:00 AM Tuesday morning aboard United Airlines DC-6 flight 1240. The flight arrived in Cleveland just after noon.

When the members of the two groups met in the hotel, the train riders took much ribbing from the plane riders. Catcher J.B. Felton, one of the train riders said, "If God had wanted us to fly, he would have given us wings."

Cleveland Municipal Stadium
New York at Cleveland Night
9:35 PM July 25, 1950

Dave had not thrown a baseball since Thursday, four days ago. How would he do after such a layoff? Over the first three innings it didn't appear to be a problem. Dave allowed just one hit and threw only 30 pitches. Cleveland batters were hitting fly balls into the spacious outfield of Municipal Stadium. The Dukes had scored a run in the second inning on Vic Marko's 21st home run of the season, a 325 foot blast over the right field fence. It gave the Dukes a 1-0 lead.

In the last half of the inning, the Cleveland lead off batter bunted his way on first with a perfect bunt down the third base line that would not roll foul. He was sacrificed to second. Dave struck out the next batter on a change up that had the batter swinging when the ball was ten feet away. Dave's change was getting better and better. Now, with two outs and a runner on second, Dave worked carefully to Luke Jackson. Jackson and Dave had met a number of times in the PCL and earlier this season. So far it had been a draw. Dave fed Jackson two sinkers, a strike and a ball that Jackson looked at without any notion of swinging. With the count 1-1, Dave threw him a change and Jackson hit it weakly to first base for the out. Advantage, Dave!

The Dukes scratched out another run in the fifth inning. With one out, Larry Mann, second baseman, singled. Randy White fouled off two pitches trying to get the bunt down. Then he hit a single into left field. Dave was coming to bat with two runners on base and one out. Dave fouled off two pitches and watched a ball, well outside the strike zone sail by. With the count 1-2, Dave hit a fast ball on the fat of the bat into the left field power ally for an easy double, scoring two runs. It increased the Dukes lead to 3-0. Dave did not progress from second as the next two batters popped out and the Dukes inning was over.

Dave allowed five more hits, but no runs and the game ended 3-0. The Dukes lead over Detroit had increased to 4 games.

Cleveland Municipal Stadium
New York at Cleveland
5:45 PM July 26, 1950

Louis Leon started his second game since rejoining the rotation. He was better than ever, pitching a shutout and the Dukes won the game 9-0. Since coming off the disabled list, Leon had cut down his wildness and issued only three walks in two games. The Dukes attack was let by Vic Marko and B.B. Katcher who each hit a home run and a double. Detroit lost, so the Dukes increased their lead to 5 games.

Following the game 20 players plus the manager, coaches and traveling secretary Ray Arnold took the bus to the airport. There they boarded United Airlines Flight 708 for the 45 minute flight to Detroit. The train five plus coach Ray Woodall took New York Central's train number 89 at 11:55 PM. They would arrive in Detroit at 6:50 AM.

Briggs Stadium
New York at Detroit
1:30 PM July 27, 1950

This was a one game make up of a rained out game. Jake Filner is the starting pitcher today. With the hot pennant race between the two teams there was a big crowd of almost 40.000 on a Thursday afternoon.

The Dukes started the game off with a bang. The first three batters reached base on two singles and a walk, loading the bases for

Vic Marko. After fouling off two pitches and being 0-2 in the count he watched two balls low in the strike zone. The next pitch, a fast ball that didn't move was hit for a grand slam. It almost reached the roof of the grandstands in right field. It gave the Dukes a 4-0.lead with no outs. Another single looked like the start of more, but it didn't happen. A double play and a deep fly to left field ended the inning.

Starting with a 4-0 lead, Dave thought Jake could pitch his game and flourish. Detroit batters hit the ball for ground and fly outs over the next five innings. In the sixth inning Jake Filner lost his control and poise. The first three batters singled scoring a run. A double added two more and it was a 4-3 game. With no outs and a runner on second, manager Felton visited the mound to give Ed Edgar time to warm up. Filner got the next batter to fly out to short left field for the first out. Filner pitched to one batter too many serving up a home run fast ball to the Detroit clean up batter and Detroit took a 5-4 lead.

Ed Edgar relieved and retired the side. The Dukes' bats went silent and they mounted no threats. In the eighth inning Detroit added two more runs for a 7-4 lead and that's the way the game ended. So Detroit picked up a game and they were now 4 games behind the Dukes.

The flyers went to the airport after the game to take a one hour Northwest Airlines flight to Chicago's Midway Airport. The train riders had to stay overnight in Detroit and take a 6:00 AM coach train to the windy city. They would taxi directly to Comiskey Park for the afternoon game, arriving at 11:30 in the morning. They got a big cheer from the flyers when they arrived.

Comiskey Park
New York at Chicago
2:30 PM July 28, 1950

Manager Felton had held Vic Carlisle out of his last scheduled start to see if the rest would help his pitching. On July 16 he lost 5-2 to Chicago and on July 6 he had to be relieved, losing a 4-0 lead in a game with Philadelphia. Carlisle pitched well scattering seven hits and winning the game 4-1. Detroit lost, so the Dukes lead was back to 5 games.

Dave had written to Jim Smith, inviting him to attend a game and have dinner. Jim had written back that Saturday the 29th would be the best and he would like to bring his dad to the game and meet Dave. It was going to work out well because Dave would be pitching Saturday.

Friday evening, Dave B.B. and Randy White went to see the movie The Big Hangover. It had a great cast including Van Johnson, Elizabeth Taylor, Leon Ames and Gene Lockhart. They had pizza at a Chicago pizza parlor that made it deep dish style.

Comiskey Park
New York at Chicago
3:00 PM July 29, 1950

In Comiskey Park there is lots of outfield. The left and right field fences are 363 feet away from home plate and it is 420 feet to center field. Dave thought he would feature rising fast balls and change ups to get fly balls to the big outfield.

He had started off with fast balls on three out of four pitches. He threw few sinkers because his approach was working. The first six White Sox batters had hit fly balls to the outfield or infield. In the meantime the Dukes batters had teed off on the Chicago pitcher for four runs in two innings.

Dave would allow two runs on five hits. He got 15 fly ball outs. He struck out two and issued no base on balls. It was his 19th win, and the 12th in a row.

Dave met Jim Smith and his dad after the game. They decided to have dinner in the Stevens Hotel dinning room. Jim gave Dave a report on Pam's preparations for the wedding. It was little more than a month away, on September 2nd. Dave told about his joining the MATS reserve squadron and why he did. He said, "I'll be on summer training from August 12 through the 26th." Jim asked, "Do you plan to attend Stanford in the off season?" "Yes, even if we are in the World Series. I can be a bit late for fall quarter and get another quarter in." They had a good dinner and good conversation that broke up at 10:00 PM.

Comisky Park
New York at Chicago Doubleheader
6:00 PM July 30, 1950

Pitching today would be the Dukes veteran starting pitchers, Doug Abbott and Lindsey Barrett. The Dukes needed to keep pace with Detroit in the pennant race. In the first game the Dukes clubbed their way to a 14-6 win. Abbott was not sharp, but didn't have to be with the run support. Ed Card relieved in the eighth inning and pitched two shutout innings.

The second game was a nail biter. The game was tied 3-3 going into the ninth inning. Lindsey Barrett had pitched well. In the top of the ninth, Larry Mann led off with a single. Jim Essick could not get the bunt down and was facing a one ball two strike count. Then he hit into a double play. There were two outs and no one on base. Barrett was due up. The decision for manager Felton was, leave Barrett in the game to pitch the last of the ninth or pull him for a pinch hitter. Ozzie decided to go for the win now.

He sent Dave to the plate for his fourth pinch hitting role. Dave worked the count to 2-2. The big Comiskey outfield offered a pitcher some latitude other parks didn't. The Chicago pitcher served up his best fast ball, expecting a fly ball to the outfield. Dave hit the ball on the fat of the bat with his arms extended. A fast ball pitch arriving at the plate at a high speed, will travel further if the batter has enough bat speed and power behind the swing. The faster the pitch, the further the ball will travel. It's a matter of physics. This ball was launched by bat speed and power on a line drive that cleared the fence at 363 feet, by at least ten feet. That made it New York 4, Chicago 3. Billy Duke stuck out, but the Dukes had their run. Ed Edgar came on to pitch a 1-2-3 ninth inning and the Dukes had a sweep of the doubleheader. It extended their league lead to 5-1/2 games.

Dave had to answer most of the questions from the writers. He kept repeating the fact that Lindsey Barrett kept the Dukes in the game by his good pitching. Give him some credit. The inevitable question was asked by a Chicago writer, "Don't' you think you could help the Dukes more if you played every day?" Dave said, "That's an old question that I have answered many times. My answer is the same today. I am a pitcher who can hit and I plan to continue in that role. Next question please."

The next day, Monday, was an open day of travel and the game on Tuesday in St. Louis would be played at night. The train riders took the St. Louis Special of the Gulf, Mobile & Ohio Sunday evening, arriving St. Louis at 9:35 AM Monday morning. The flyers stayed in Chicago Sunday evening and took a TWA flight Monday, arriving in St. Louis at 1:30 in the afternoon.

Dave spent the afternoon writing post cards and reading. He had written a post card to Sharon. Tuesday morning he planned to visit the National Railroad Museum. He planned to ask B.B. if he would like to go with him and B.B agreed.

Museum of Transportation
3015 Barrett Station Road
St. Louis, Missouri
10:15 AM August 1, 1950

Dave had heard that this museum had a good display of train cars and locomotives. He and B.B. spent a couple of hours at the museum looking at trains and the other transportation displays. B.B said, "I've never seen some of these trains before. They must have run in the east."

Sportsman's Park
New York at St. Louis
10:00 PM August 1, 1950

Louis Leon started this game and reverted to his wildness, walking five through eight innings. However, St. Louis stranded ten base runners so it was a 3-3 tie starting the ninth inning. The Dukes did nothing in the top of the ninth. In the bottom of the inning, Leon walked the first batter and he was sacrificed to second. Louis got the next two batters on a strike out and infield pop up. The next batter, the Browns weak hitting catcher, hit the first pitch over the short right field wall for a home run to win the game 4-3. Detroit won their game, cutting the Dukes lead to 4-1/2 games.

New York at St. Louis
3:35 PM August 2, 1950

This would not be one of Dave's better games. But when you can win without your best pitching it's a plus. The St. Louis batters were hitting Dave's sinker pitch through infield for hits and two runs in the first two innings. Fortunately the Dukes had also scored two runs in the first two innings. So after two innings the score was 2-2. Dave switched to more fast balls and change ups for the balance of the game and the Browns produced just one more run.

The Dukes produced four runs in the seventh for a 6-3 lead. Dave pitched his usual late innings, getting six outs in the eighth and ninth on 16 pitches. Dave had allowed three runs on eight hits in winning the game for the Dukes 6-3. Detroit also won so there was no change in the Dukes lead.

New York at St. Louis
10:20 PM August 3, 1950

In another night game the Dukes lost to the lowly Browns. Jake Filner pitched well, but the Dukes bats fell silent and they lost 3-2. Detroit split a doubleheader so the Dukes lead dropped to 4 games.

Dave was not happy about losing two out of three games to St. Louis. The team was not defeating the bottom division clubs like they should. The team needed some home cooking and wins at home.

Chapter Twenty Seven

Dave's Apartment

9:15 AM August 4, 1950

DAVE AND THE flyers had returned home last night, arriving at 10:00 PM. Dave and B.B. went directly home. Dave learned he had to have his mail held during road trips. He returned from the first trip to find his mail box stuffed with mail and note from the mail man that he should have his mail held. He just hadn't thought he would receive so much. A lot of it was advertising. There was no game today, so Dave could catch up on shopping and cleaning his apartment.

First, he placed a call to his dad. He gave him a report on his first duty weekend. George Mason was glad Dave had enjoyed his first military experience. He advised Dave that Senator Kay had called him and reported the army had decided to establish a program for graduate engineers and others with specialties the army could use, but hadn't worked out the details. So I think you did the right thing in joining the MATS reserve. "Thanks dad."

The Army did create a program for graduate engineers and others with specialized degrees. The Army called it Scientific and Professional Personnel, commonly known as S & P. Initially, the Army identified draftees with degrees and assigned them to the short or non-combat basic training cycle. They were then sent to Fort Myer, Virginia for assignment to an Army research station or other facility. Later, S & P men took the long infantry basic training and were assigned directly to a station or facility.

An example of the Army's utilization of the education and training of these draftees was those assigned to the Transportation Research and Development Station (TRADS) located at Fort Eustis, Virginia. In 1950-53 more than 100 S & P personnel were stationed at TRADS. They worked in the various branches of this, the research arm of the Army's Transportation Corps. The branches included air, rail, vehicles, aerial tramway as well as special projects. These draftees worked along with Army officers and civil service engineers.

The TRADS S & P barracks brought together college graduates from all over the country. When discharge time approached the S and Ps organized a recruiting program for civilian employment that resulted in many firms coming to Williamsburg, Virginia to interview TRADS Men.

Following discharge, TRADS Men had a number of reunions. Two big reunions were held in Williamsburg in 1990 and 2000. TRADS Men are still in contact with each other, more than 54 years after discharge.

Dave was about to leave to go the post office to pick up his mail and the phone rang. Jill's voice said "Good morning Dave." "Good morning Jill, how are you and where are you?" "I'm at home. It's only 6:45 here, but I wanted to give you the good news." "What's the good news?' "My transfer has come through effective September first. "Fantastic!" "Yes, I was surprised too. It seems five girls in New York have given notice to marry within two weeks. It's the war causing the rush to get married before the men get drafted or recalled from the reserves." "So when do you stop flying?" "My last trip will be on the 13th and 14th. I will pack up my clothes, and stuff to take to air freight and then go home for at least a week and leave the car." "Where are you shipping your things to?" "Oh, I forgot to tell you that Dorothy has invited me to move in with her. Her apartment mate left a month ago to get married. She married a United Airlines pilot who is a Marine. He is sure he will be called up." "I think you told me, but where is her apartment?" It's the Coral Gardens Apartments in Flushing." "That's good Jill. I think it's just a couple of blocks away."

"I do need to remind you that I will be returning to Palo Alto in

October to continue at Stanford, so I'll be gone for more than four months." "I'm aware of that Dave, but I must come to New York and experience it if I'm going to live there part of the year in the future. When I arrive can we get married Dave?" "That will be our first subject to talk about. When will you arrive?" "Right now I'm thinking I will stand by on Monday morning, August 28." "That's fine Jill. I will return from my summer training on Sunday." "Okay, I'll keep you advised on any changes Dave. I love you." "I love you too Jill."

New York Public Library
42nd Street & 5th Avenue
New York City, New York
1:30 PM August 4, 1950

Dave had decided if he was going to get the story of Christy Mathewson, he should to it before summer training. He could read a book or books during that time. He had no trouble finding a number of books on Christy. Since he had pitched for the New York Giants of the National League he was a New York story. Dave checked out the one book that looked the best.

Dukes Stadium
Boston at New York
4:05 PM August 5, 1950

Vic Carlisle was the starter today. He started okay and the Dukes produced a 3-0 lead in the first three innings. In the fifth inning the game began to fall apart for the Dukes. Boston scored four runs on three hits and an error for a 4-3 lead. The Dukes did not answer in their seventh, so at the start of the eighth inning, the score had not changed.

Boston went to work in the top of the eighth and produced two more runs, driving Carlisle from the mound. He was replaced by Ed Card, who had become manager Felton's first choice for relief since Louis Leon returned to the rotation. Now it was Boston 6, Dukes 3. Ed Card shut down the Red Sox, but the Dukes produced no runs and that's the way the game ended. Detroit won a doubleheader, putting pressure on the Dukes. Their lead was down to 2-1/2 games.

Fifth Avenue Presbyterian Church
9:30 AM August 6, 1950

After a two week absence, it was good to be in class again. The class study of Paul's First missionary journey had progressed to their arrival in Derbe a town about 25 miles south of Lystra, where Paul had been stoned. Paul and Barnabas lived quietly in Derbe during the winter. Paul made and sold his tents and used his home and the homes of others as centers for teaching of the new faith. As a result, a strong church was formed.

Following class, Steve Early came up to Dave and said, "I heard you have joined the Air Force Reserve." "That's right; I'm a member of the MATS reserve squadron out at Republic Airport. I decided my education and training would be used there, while I could not be sure of that if I was drafted. However it was a difficult decision. Some of my friends will not have a choice, so I was concerned about that." "I understand, Dave."

Dukes Stadium
Boston at New York
4:30 PM August 6, 1950

There would be only a single game today, a make up for a rain out. Dave was pitching. It was just his second game against the Red Sox led by the textbook hitter Denton Wilson a left handed batter. In 1940 Wilson had hit over .400, the first in ten years and he would be the last to do it through 2006!

Dave fed the Red Sox batters mostly sinkers and he had thrown only 45 pitches through the first five innings. However the score was still 0-0. In the bottom of the fifth inning, Vic Marko hit a double with two outs. B.B. Katcher worked the count to 3-2, and then hit a home run high over the left field fence giving the Dukes a 2-0 lead.

That's all the runs Dave needed. He allowed no runs on five hits. He hit a single in three trips to the plate. He finished the game with a five pitch ninth inning and a total of 85 pitches for the game.

After the game before he would talk to the writers he thanked every position player on the team for their errorless play. Detroit lost, so the Dukes increased their lead to 3 games.

Fifth Avenue Presbyterian Church
6:30 PM August 6, 1950

Dave had arrived to talk to the high school youth group. Following some enthusiastic singing, Mr. Small introduced Dave. "In response to your request, our speaker tonight is Dave Mason. Most of you know him as a baseball player, but I can assure you, there is more to Dave than baseball. He is a graduate of California Polytechnic College where he earned a degree in aeronautical engineering. He is a candidate for a master's degree in mechanical engineering from Stanford University. Dave is an Airman in the Air Force Reserve, serving in MATS-RS-1, a reserve squadron of the Military Air Transport Service, located at Republic Airport on Long Island. He is a member of the Menlo Park Presbyterian Church in California, and while in New York he has been attending the young adult Sunday school class. Dave Mason.

"Thank you Mr. Small. And thank you for inviting me to share my faith with you. But before I do that, I want to take a picture of you, so I can always remember this occasion" Using his Brownie camera, Dave snaps a flash photo of the group.

"First, let me tell you how I came to accept the Lord as my personal savior. I was raised in Presbyterian Sunday school, attending through the ninth grade. Then I dropped out. Inspired by the message of the speaker at my high school baccalaureate service, I started attending worship services at Menlo Park Presbyterian Church. It was a small church located in the small town just north of Palo Alto, my home town."

"Soon, I was off to college where I attended Sunday school at the San Luis Obispo Presbyterian Church. Because of the Sunday college cafeteria schedule, and no car, I couldn't attend worship services."

"Back home after my freshman year, I was attending the Menlo Park Sunday school and worship services. But I still hadn't made a decision to accept Jesus. Then in a men's breakfast meeting it happened. The speaker said that many non-Christians have better behavior than Christian. However, they have not made a decision to accept Christ, so they have not entered God's Kingdom. Dave said, "I thought I was a good person with good behavior. I didn't smoke, drink or swear or go with girls that do." That brought a laugh from the group. "I decided then and there to accept Jesus Christ and join the church."

"Since then, two events have been very important in my life as a Christian. First the Lord led me to find a book entitled The Man Nobody Knows. Written by layman Bruce Barton in 1925, it opened my interest in studying the life of Jesus and made the Bible interesting."

"Second, I learned about a man named Eric Liddell. Born in China of missionary parents, he became an outstanding sprinter and rugby player while in college in Scotland. Before each race and game Eric shook hands with his competitors and encouraged them. Because he would not run on Sunday in the 1924 Olympics, he would not compete in the 100 meters, his best event. Instead, he would run the 400 meters, thought to be too long a race for him. However, he won the 400 meter race and the Gold Medal. He also won a bronze metal in the 200 meters."

"Eric returned to China as a missionary following ordination in the Scottish Congregational Church. He married and had two children with another on the way when war clouds appeared. Sending his family home to Canada, his wife's country, he stayed in China. Eric Liddell was called home to be with the Lord at the young age of 43 while in a Japanese internment camp."

"Since learning about Eric, I have followed his example of meeting and encouraging my competitors before the game, particularly young players like me. Being a Christian is a full time commitment, every day of the week, not just on Sunday. I ask all of you to be kind to your fellow students, and to encourage them. And to everyone for that matter, so you will be a good Christian."

"Now that's enough from me. I'm sure you have some burning questions you would like to ask, and I'll try to answer them the best I can." Many hands went up and the questions started.

Q "On TV I see baseball players always chewing and spiting. What are they chewing?"

A "Most players that you see chewing are chewing tobacco. In the hot summer it helps keep a player's mouth moist. I didn't chew anything during games in California. Since the weather has warmed I have started chewing bubble gum. That brought a laugh from the group. It keeps my mouth moist and when I'm sitting in the dugout I can blow bubbles." That brought another laugh.

Q "I didn't know any baseball players had gone to college. Are there others on the Dukes?"

A "Yes, Randle White, my roommate on road trips has attended Stanford, UCLA and Tulane. He is studying to be a dentist. Gordon Enson attended the University of California. B.B. Katcher attended Junior College earning an Associate of Arts degree. As time goes on, and college baseball programs improve, I think there will be more college graduates in professional baseball."

Q "How have your teammates reacted to your talking to players on the other teams before games?"

A "I'm surprised you've heard about that. I heard there were questions by some of the veteran players. However, Gordon Enson, who played for Hollywood in the Pacific Coast League last year, was one of the players I talked to during last season. He told the veterans that when the game started I was a "bulldog" in trying to win the game. Sports writers at the 1924 Olympics asked Eric Liddell if he was happy winning the bronze medal in the 200 meter race? He said, "No, I lost the race." You can be friendly and give encouragement before the game, but play like a bulldog during the game. That's my approach."

Q "How long do you expect to play baseball?"

A "I don't really know. Pitchers are more prone to injury than the other players. We are particularly susceptible to arm injuries. Baring injury, I have told people that I will not play more than ten years."

Q "I have heard you have joined the Air Force so you can still play baseball."

A "I have joined the Air Force Reserve, and I am a member of the 1st Military Air Transport Service Reserve squadron located at Republic Airport on Long Island. I chose to join this MATS squadron primarily because I can use my education and training. I hold government licenses that authorizes me to perform maintenance on aircraft and aircraft engines. These are in addition to my engineering degree. If I had waited to be drafted I have no idea what I would be doing in the army. To enlist in the Air Force Reserve I was required to sign up for four years compared to the army service time of 21 months. MATS requires one weekend of duty per month, and a two week summer training period. It does allow me to continue to play baseball, but with longer commitment to military service more beneficial to the country.

Mr. Small stood and said, "One more question."

Q "Baseball players have a reputation for spending time in bars and doing lots of drinking. Why do they do this?"

A "The reputation as likely because baseball players are in the limelight. Men in other occupations spend time in bars and cocktail lounges, but you don't hear about them because they are not public figures. Most people are just not interested in, say businessmen who conduct business in bars and lounges. Since I am a so called "tea totaled," and don't drink anything stronger than a Coke, I'm really no expert on the subject."

"Thank you Dave," said Mr. Small. I would like to add something to Dave's answer to the question about military service. Dave took his decision about this very seriously. He made an appointment with me and we talked and prayed about it."

"Thank you again for taking the time to talk to the group." Applause.

Dave's Apartment
8:30 AM August 7, 1950

Dave had completed his daily devotions and his continuing study of the life and ministry of Jesus. He had studied the Parable of the Hidden Treasure in Matthew 13:44. The Kingdom of Heaven is like a treasure hidden in a field. The plowman finds the treasure (The Kingdom). On the other hand, the treasure could find the plowman. Dave thought; the Kingdom found me through the high school baccalaureate sermon. It sparked my interest.

He and B.B. planned to bowl this afternoon. Today B.B. said he would bowl Dave for money. Dave said, "Fine, I need some competition."

Flushing Lanes
2:00 PM August 7, 1950

Dave and B.B. were bowling three games for $5.00 per game and $10.00 for the series. B.B. had won the first game 146 to 140. Dave said, "I'm rusty." "No Dave, "I'm just better!" Dave won the second game 155 to 151, the same pin difference as in the first game. The third game winner would get all the spoils. B.B started out with a small lead, but then got a 7-10 split he couldn't cover. Dave kept bowling strikes and won the game and series 225 to 185. Dave pocketed the $15.00 for the game plus series win. "Just to show you my heart's in the right place, I'll buy your dinner tomorrow night!" B.B.

said, "I accept." They both laughed.

Turner Chevrolet
7:00 PM August 7, 1950

There was another big crowd in the showroom with kids lined up for baseballs. Turner had advertised an additional give away this evening. A drawing for three baseball mitts, infielder/outfielder, first baseman and catcher would be held at 8:30 PM. The fifty kids allowed in the showroom would receive tickets to the drawing.

Dave had about 10 minutes to talk to parents on the showroom floor before the drawing for the mitts. Two of the mitts were won by young boys 8 and 10 years old.

Dave asked Dick Chevrolet if Bill Buck had talked to him about a one time appearance of B.B. Katcher. "Yes he did, and we are going to talk about it with Bill Turner when he returns from vacation." "Sounds good." Dick asked, "When will you return from your summer training? "I'll return on Sunday, the 27th. I'll rejoin the team on Monday." "Where are you training?" "It's a military secret. We haven't been told." "Okay Dave I'll see you again on the 28th." "I'll be here, the Lord willing."

Dukes Stadium
Philadelphia at New York
5:15 PM August 8, 1950

Doug Abbott was the starter today against Philadelphia, one of the lower division clubs that manager Ozzie Felton wanted to sweep. Doug, who had not been winning lately, lost another 5-3. He was wild and did not make the clutch pitches he usually does. The loss left the Dukes with a three game lead over Detroit.

Dave bought B.B.'s dinner at the Golden Pheasant, and they returned to Dave's apartment to watch the Arthur Godfrey TV show.

Dukes Stadium
5:30 PM August 9, 1950

The Dukes wasted no time in producing runs for pitcher Lindsey Barrett, teeing off on the Athletics' starting pitcher for four runs in the first inning. B.B. hit a 340 foot, three run home run over the left center field fence producing the big lead. Barrett cruised through the game allowing seven hits and just one run. The Dukes added two runs in the sixth and one in the eighth for a 7-1 win.

Bob's Restaurant
6:30 PM August 9, 1950

Earlier in the week Randy White had asked Dave and B.B. to have dinner with him and Gordon Enson. As soon as they sat down, Dave asked Randy, "What have you heard about the dentist draft?" "I've heard nothing specific Dave. My permanent address is the home of my parents in San Francisco, so any call up I would receive would be sent there. So far nothing has come in the mail. I have talked to two of my dental school classmates, but they haven't heard anything either. I think the army has sent all regulars to Korea and then called up reserves to replace them while they get the draft organized. I doubt if I will be playing baseball next year."

Dave thought even though I'm in a reserve outfit, some members could be called to active duty according to Lt. Funk. However they would likely be experienced airmen.

Dukes Stadium
2:30 PM August 10, 1950

Dave was starting his last game for more than two weeks and wanted to get another win. Today he was throwing mostly sinkers and change ups. He had excellent control and the ball was going where he wanted. He allowed no hits through the fourth inning and had made only 15 pitches. The Dukes scored a run in the third on Vic

Marko's 29th home run, a 450 foot blast over the centerfield fence.

The Dukes added three runs in the seventh inning for a 4-0 lead. Dave had allowed just four hits and no runner past second. He pitched his usual late innings, allowing no hits on 12 pitches in the eighth and ninth innings Dave had won his 21st game, the 13th in a row, 4-0. The Dukes still had a three game lead over Detroit.

In the clubhouse, Dave talked to every player who had played in the game, thanking them for their great play. It had been an errorless game. All the players wished him well during his summer training.

In the evening Dave attended the Kiwanis Club of Five Towns for a make up.

Dave's Apartment
9:15 AM August 11, 1950

Dave had completed his devotions and study of Jesus and was packing. Soon the phone rang and Dave's dad said, "Good morning Airman Mason." "Good morning dad. How are you?" "I'm fine. I am calling to wish you good luck during your training. Do you know where you're going?" "No I don't dad. I'll find out when I report tonight." Dave asked how Pam was progressing with the wedding. "She and her mother are doing fine." "I had a nice visit with Jim and his dad in Chicago." "Yes Jim reported that in a phone call to Pam." "Okay, I'll send you a post card from wherever I am next week and thanks for calling." "Goodbye Dave."

At 1700 Dave reported in and was assigned a bunk in the enlisted men's quarters.

He was given a schedule for the evening and Saturday morning.

Schedule – Friday, 11 August 1950.

1800 Enlisted Airmen's Formation in the hanger—First Sgt. Foster

1830 Mess hall is open for dinner

1930 Maintenance Airman report to squad leaders

2000 All Airmen report to mess hall for briefing on the summer training

2300 Lights Out

Schedule – Saturday, August 12, 1950

0600 Reveille

0630 First Mess call

0800 All airmen and officers report to assigned aircraft for flight to training base.

0900 Departure

8,000 Feet over Maryland
0945 12 August, 1950

Dave's squad had been divided up. He, Chub Flabby and Ray Rock had been assigned to C-54, tail number 23225 for the trip to McDill AFB in Tampa, Florida. The location of the training had been announced during the training schedule briefing last night. Col. Flyer had addressed the men of the unit at the conclusion of the briefing. He encouraged each member of the squadron to take advantage of this training to increase their knowledge and become competent. "This will make our MATS unit the best and confirm my belief that we can make a great contribution to our nation's defense and support of the action in Korea."

The flight crew of Dave's C-54 had been introduced by Captain Wilton Le Donnell Blue, who said, "He was known as "Wild Blue", because of his initials." He didn't say it was really because of his tendency to be wild in his younger years. He was a 38 year old co-pilot for Pan American. He introduced Lt. James Grace, 30, a co-pilot for United Airlines. Capt. Blue said, "Its James not Jim. Cpl. Flabby will be acting as flight engineer."

The flight plan to McDill indicated a flight of five hours and thirty five minutes. It would take them over New Jersey, Pennsylvania, Maryland, Virginia, the Carolinas, Georgia and Florida. Tampa being located on the west coast of the state, the flight would be over land all the way. Capt. Blue had said, "Any problems with the aircraft during the flight will be reported to all members of the crew so you can have the experience of providing your diagnoses of the problem and its cure."

Dave was standing behind Chub Flabby so he could observe the work of a flight engineer. On the C-54 the flight engineer sat between the pilot and co-pilot on a jump seat.

Touching down at 1737, just two minutes over the flight plan, Dave was looking forward to the experience of a large Air Force Base and its operation. Also, Florida, a state he had visited only during spring training. Dave still hadn't had the opportunity to ask Chub his engine questions. He thought there would be time during the training period. The only mechanical problem the crew had encountered was a bit of a slow landing gear retraction and extension. Most members of the crew had it diagnosed as a hydraulic pump problem.

The main cabin door was opened and a blast of hot humid air hit Dave. Welcome to Florida!

8,000 feet Over Jacksonville, Florida
0830 August 26, 1950

Dave was stretched out on one of the pull down jump seats in the cabin of the C-54. They were on their way home to New York. Dave started thinking about the past 14 days and all that had happened. Upon arrival he and the airmen were assigned to a barracks and a mess hall where they had dinner. At 1930 all airmen mustered in a room for a schedule of training. There would be classes in basic military information followed by drill. Then there was a series of classroom sessions on the C-54 airplane. The systems of the aircraft were covered and tests were given. Dave had high scores on all the tests. Later in the week, flights with cargo were scheduled. Dave's crew flew on a flight to Lackland AFB in San Antonio, Texas. While there the airmen were given a pass to go into San Antonio. Dave took Chub Flabby to a meeting of the Kiwanis Club of San Antonio. It was a first for Chub and Dave got a make up. He thought the members in San Francisco would be surprised to get a make up card from Texas. After the meeting they visited the Alamo.

Dave had been concerned about keeping his arm in shape during his pitching layoff. He found the catcher of the base softball team

Sgt. Blake. Blake had played a little semi pro baseball, so he could catch a hardball. Dave had brought a catchers mitt with him that he gave to Blake. Dave had worked out a schedule with Sgt. Blake so he was able to throw at least three or four time each week.

Dave had gained experience working on the systems of the C-54 and trouble shooting the engines. On one occasion, Dave, Chub and Ray had completed the work on their airplane and went to see the other members of their squad. There was an engine problem on that airplane. Chub talked to Sgt. Sam "gummy" Slade about the problem. Sgt. Slade said they had gone through the trouble shooting procedure, but couldn't isolate the problem. Chub asked Sgt. Slade to run up the engine. As the result of the run up Dave suggested they check the magneto. He had remembered a simulated magneto problem on the test stand in the engine shop at Cal Poly. It sounded similar. The Magneto was checked and a short was found. The rookie mechanic had solved the problem. All members of the crew had a new respect for Dave's ability.

The most challenging training was the survival exercise. First there was a classroom briefing. The purpose of the exercise was training for crew members to be able to survive in case of a forced landing in an uninhabited area. Squads of six men including a leader would be taken to an area of wilderness by helicopter. They would be required to survive for three days on the minimal rations they took with them and what they could kill and catch. The problem was to walk out of the wilderness using the map the leader, Cpl. Frankland had been given. On the first day Cpl. Frankland fell and sprained his ankle so bad he passed out briefly. He had to be carried until crude crutches could be made from tree limbs. That was Dave's immediate suggestion before Cpl. Frankland had come to. Although at 22, he was the youngest member of the six man team Dave took over leadership and led the team out of the wilderness area in spite of their slow progress because of the injury to Cpl.Frankland. They were the only team to make it. The other teams had to be picked up by helicopter.

On the second cargo flight, Dave was given some experience as acting flight engineer. This flight was to Brookley AFB, Mobile,

Alabama. It was a large Air Force supply facility. It had warehouses and all methods of shipping including air, rail and sea.

While they were at McDill they received daily briefings on the progress of the war in Korea. The last had the North Korean army renewing their attack on Taegu, the major city north of Pusan. The United Nations forces were still defending a small southeast corner of South Korea. The army had announced the first call-ups of reserve officers who were not members of a reserve unit. In New York State 896 officers were included in the call up for physicals on August 23rd and duty on September 21. The British announced they were sending troops to Korea. Eventually there would be troops of 22 countries including the U.S. in the United Nations forces in Korea. It was the first confirmation of what the U.N. could do to stop an armed invasion of a country. This was the test that Dave's dad had talked about when the U.N. was being formed.

Members of Dave's squad were given a one day pass to go into Tampa. Dave took the opportunity to visit his Aunt Zeena Mae Mason. She was the widow of his Dad's brother Bill. She had sent Christmas gifts to him and Pam for years when they were young. Dave found her a very nice lady and they had a nice visit.

Dave had been able to attend a chapel service just once. Also, he had not had any time to read the book on Christy Mathewson. He would have to read it when he returned home.

Dave had tried to keep up with the Dukes during the past two weeks, but he couldn't always find a newspaper. He got some news from others on the base. Through Friday, August 25th the Dukes had won 10 and lost 5 games. The Dukes record was 79 and 39, four games ahead of Detroit. Dave thought the team had done well without him. He was glad his absence had not been a problem.

Dave was sure of one thing. He would not want to live in Florida in the summer. It was too hot and humid.

Dave's reverie was ended by the change in propeller pitch and the plane started its decent. They were nearing the end of the summer training. When the C-54 touched down at Republic Airport is was 1420. Since they were one of the first aircraft to land, Dave was able to watch most of the other airplanes land safely. During the summer training the MATS reserve squadron had flown many miles with only one emergency landing. It was a good record. Now that they were back at home base, the task for Dave's squad would be to fix any mechanical problems and clean up the aircraft. He expected they would be dismissed some time before noon tomorrow.

Chapter Twenty Eight

Dave's Apartment

2:30 PM August 27, 1950

DAVE HAD ARRIVED in his apartment about one o' clock. His squad had finished cleaning up their airplanes at 11:00 AM, and they had been dismissed soon after. Dave stopped off for some lunch and read the Sunday paper. The Dukes had won their game with St. Louis yesterday 3-2. The Dukes had a 4 game lead over Detroit. They were playing a single game today against Chicago. Dave would go to the ball park later.

The Korean War news was not any better. The U.N. forces were still defending a small area in southeast corner of South Korea.

Dave made a trip to the A & P Market to re-stock his food supply. He would pick up his held mail in the morning. He wanted to learn when Jill would arrive. At 3:30, he departed for Dukes Stadium. Upon arrival, Dave went to the future ticket window where he asked, "Do you think I could get a ticket to the wives box?" The ticket men were surprised to see Dave. Moe, a veteran ticket man said, "I thought you were still off in the wild blue yonder." "I've come back to earth Moe." Dave could hear the radio broadcast in the background, so he asked, "What's the score" "1 to 1" was the reply. It hadn't changed since Dave left his car. Dave was given a ticket and he walked to the wives box.

Sitting down next to Marie Marko, Dave said, "You ladies aren't doing so well. We should be ahead in this game." Marie and all the wives nearby turned and exclaimed "Dave!" Marie said, "We need you to put on a uniform and pinch hit. No one is hitting." "I haven't had a bat in my hands since I left. I don't think I could help. It looks like Ed Card is pitching well."

The game went into extra innings. In the Dukes half of the 10th inning Vic Marko was the leadoff batter. After working the count to 2-2, the next pitch was a high fast ball that Vic hit out of the park for a home run. You could tell it was going out of the park by the sound of the bat on the ball. Marie was up yelling and waiving her arms. It gave the Dukes a 2-1 win.

Dave visited with the wives and girl friends for a while so he wouldn't interfere with the celebration of the win in the clubhouse and the attention that Vic Marko deserved. Marie said, "That's Vic's 37th home run."

Detroit lost, so the Dukes had a 5 game lead in the pennant race. When Dave left for summer training, the lead had been only 3 games.

Dave went to the clubhouse only after he saw the writers returning to the press box to write their stories. He got a big welcome and told all the players that the game was a big win, he said, "I've been watching in the wives box since the eighth inning." B.B. came up and gave Dave a big hug. "You survived your war games!" "Oh it wasn't like that B.B., but, yes I survived." "Can I get a ride home with you? I've missed my taxi cab." "Well, I noticed I haven't much gas, you may have to push." "I'll even buy you some gas." "That's a deal."

Dave talked briefly with Ozzie Felton. He told him about his being able to throw at least three or four days each week while he was gone. "It only cost me a catcher's mitt." Ozzie said, "Lets see how you look tomorrow and then I'll pencil you in for a start." "That sounds good. Let's go home B.B."

Dave's Apartment
8:30 AM August 28, 1950

Dave had been at the post office when it opened. He picked up two boxes of mail. He was now going through the pile of mail, looking for post cards and letters from Jill. He found a recent post card that said she had been advised not to try and stand by on Monday. That's when businessmen fly. So she would start early Tuesday morning. If she arrived Tuesday, Dorothy could meet her. Jill gave Dorothy's address: Coral Gardens Apartments, 144-07 Sanford Ave., corner of Parsons, Flushing. It wasn't far from Dave's apartment. "The phone number is INdependence 3-9630." Dave found a letter from his mother and one from his dad. Dave had written letters to both during his training.

He also received a letter from his college friend Wes Witten. Wes had read about Dave joining the MATS reserve squadron so he wrote, "Aren't you glad you got you're A & E licenses?" Wes reported he was working for Pacific Gas & Electric Company at their power plant in Bakersfield. He also said he was married. That was a surprise to Dave. Wes had not been a social fellow at Cal Poly.

The last post card he found was from Sharon. It was the only one she had written while he was gone. Dave thought, Sharon must be very busy or she is losing interest because of our separation. Maybe I'll find out next week when we play in Boston.

Dave started reading the book he had gotten at the library on Chrisy Mathewson. In the book Christy was called a Christian Gentleman. This surprised Dave. He wasn't aware of many Christian baseball players. Mathewson played for the great John McGraw, manager of the New York Giants in the early 1900s. Christy was different than his teammates. He had attended Bucknell University, married his college sweetheart, a Sunday school teacher and had a spotless record on and off the baseball diamond. His teammates had come from families who worked in the coal mines or on the farm.

John McGraw and his wife helped the Mathewsons adjust to the rough world of major league baseball. There were doubters that this "gentleman" could be successful in the tough game of baseball. It wasn't long before he convinced the doubters. He could throw a baseball into a small cup from the pitchers mound. Mathewson threw many pitches. They included a fastball with an inside outside or rising movement. Also, slow ball, a drop curve, a fade away and a spit ball.

In 11 of his 17 seasons, Mathewson pitched more than 300 innings. He had a league leading 1.14 ERA in 1909 and his career record was 2.13. Dave was interested in his control. He had low walks ratio for nine innings pitched in 1913 and 14 of .62 and .66. His career record was 1.59 walks per nine innings pitched.

Christy Mathewson enlisted in the army in World War I. He along with Ty Cob became a Captain and served in France under Major Branch Rickey. During a drill, Mathewson was exposed to poison gas, his lungs were seared, and he never recovered. He lived just seven more years, dieing on October 7, 1925 at the young age of 45. John McGraw helped carry the coffin to the cemetery. He said, "Why should God wish to take a thoroughbred like Matty so soon."

The phone rang, "This is Hank James Dave. You must have survived your two weeks in sunny Florida and thank you for you for the picture post card with the bathing beauty." "I thought that would get your attention." "Is the Turner schedule still good?" "Yes it is. Have you had an answer on an appearance for B.B. Katcher." "Yes, Bill Buck said they would wait until the 1951 models were to be shown. He was not sure when that would be." "Okay, I'll let B.B. know. Thanks Hank."

"Can you come into town and have dinner with me tomorrow night?" "Yes, our game with Cleveland is in the afternoon." "Good. I'm working on an effort to get the advertising account at Turner and you would be a big part of my proposal." "Okay, what time?" "Come to the office about 6:30. We can walk to the restaurant." "I'll be there."

Headquarters
MATS Reserve RS-1
08:30 28 August 1950

Colonel Bernie Flyer was leading a review of the two weeks of training. Attending, were Capt. Peter Jergens, Executive Officer, Lt. Frank Funk, Engineering & Maintenance Officer, and Lt. Bill Parks, Information Officer.

The first order of the meeting was to congratulate Frank Funk who had been promoted to Captain. However, along with his promotion, orders were waiting for him upon his return from summer training, to report to FECOM (Far East Command) in Japan on 01 October. Col. Flyer said, "Frank has really been our guiding light and we are going to miss you." "Thank you sir. I had hoped to stay through my one year assignment, but I didn't expect us to be in another war. I will likely have an all expenses paid trip to that ancient oriental land known as 'frozen chosen.' They all laughed.

"To take Frank's place, I have appointed Captain Richard don't call him Dick, Tracy, acting Engineering & Maintenance Officer. He served in that capacity during the War and agreed to do it for no more than three months as long as he can get his flight hours in. I have one prospect at Pan American who is in the engineering department. He flew B-17s during the war and served two years as an E & M Officer. He held the rank of Captain. He wants to go to night school to get his master's degree, so his decision will depend on whether he starts this fall. He is not a reserve officer so he doesn't have to be concerned about a call up. I'm having the Air Force and Navy Reserve Officer lists checked to learn if there are any E & M officers who live in the area that we could recruit. The call up of reserves officers should help. If we can locate one he might avoid active duty."

"That brings me to my next subject of potential leaders discovered during the summer training. I have received the reports on Airman Dave Mason and Cpl. Ted Frankland. Mason for his leadership during the survival exercise and Frank told me about his solving an engine problem that had everyone else scratching their heads. Since Mason is a college graduate, I would like to get him into Officer's Candidate School (OCS). I have reserved a slot in the October class. If he agrees, I would get him into the E & M training that follows. It would make him late for spring baseball practice, but I think the Dukes would cooperate.

Frank, will you contact Mason and make the offer before you depart?" "Yes sir." "If you need any help, let me know. He will have to extend his service time by six months following commissioning. My thought is that Mason could be our assistant E & M Officer. This would help if it's necessary to have a pilot be the officer in charge.

Also, I would like to get some publicity about Dave Mason's leadership during the survival exercise. Take care of that Bill."(Lt. Bill Parks, Information Officer). "Yes sir." "I think that story could make the first section news, not just the sports page."

"I'm going to recommend Cpl. Ted Frankland for a promotion to Sergeant. In spite of his injury, he showed good leadership during the survival exercise."

"On 01 September, we will receive an increase in money. I have requested C-54s to replace our C-47s and get us up to 16 airplanes. I understand C-47s are in demand in Korea because of short runways. However, we may be offered C-119 Boxcars that I will turn down so we don't have to stock other than Douglas parts"

"I'm working on cargo flights to Presque Isle in Maine and eventually to England. Using us would allow regular planes and men to be used elsewhere. If the war lasts long enough, I think we will be flying across the water. That's all I have. Are there any questions?" "You are dismissed,"

Dukes Stadium
Chicago at New York
11:00 AM August 28, 1950

Dave and B.B. arrived early for the game warm up. Dave wanted to get extra batting practice as well as do some extra running. He thought his arm was in better shape than his legs.

Today's game was the final of a two game series with Chicago. The Dukes needed to keep winning to put Detroit away and wrap up the American League pennant. Doug Abbott was the starting pitcher. In a game with lots of hit and runs, the score was tied 4-4 at the end of seven innings. In the top of the eighth, Chicago scored two runs. The Dukes did not answer and Chicago won the game 6-4. Detroit also lost, so the Dukes' 5 game lead held up.

Turner Chevrolet
7:00 PM August 28, 1950

Upon his arrival, Dick Chevrolet told Dave, "I'm glad you survived your two week's training. The salesmen really missed you and the crowds you bring to the showroom." "Thanks Dick. It was an interesting experience. I hope we can sell some Chevy's tonight." For his first appearance in more than two weeks, the response was still overwhelming. Turner had increased the number of baseballs to be given away to 35. Entry to the showroom was still limited to 50. It took the whole hour and a half for Dave to autograph and give the balls away. When he was finished, Dave asked Dick Chevrolet, do you have a date for the introduction of the 1951 Chevrolets? "No we still don't have a date Dave."

Dave's Apartment
8:30 AM August 29, 1950

Capt. Funk was on the phone talking with Dave. He had tried to call him yesterday with out success. Capt. Funk first advised Dave about the press release regarding his leadership actions during the survival exercise in Florida. He said it would be issued to the press and radio today. "We didn't want it to be a surprise to you." "Well, it is a surprise, but thank you for letting me know about it." "Also, I have something to talk to you about that will take some time. Can you have dinner with me tomorrow evening?" "I can if it's not too early. We play a doubleheader tomorrow." "Fine how about 7:00 PM at the Golden Pheasant?" "Okay, should I bring anything?" "No just yourself."

Since Dave had not heard anything from Jill, he was concerned if she was trying to stand- by today. He called the number for Dorothy that Jill had given him, but there was no answer. He decided to Call Jill's Burlingame apartment. It was the same there, no answer. He decided to call Dorothy again after he returned from the Kiwanis meeting.

In the evening Dave went to the Kiwanis Club of Five Towns for a make up. Dave had Five happy dollars for making it through the two week summer training in Florida. He said, "After two weeks in Florida,

I'll never complain about New York weather. It was so hot and humid!" Two Key Club members had attended and Dave talked to them after the meeting. He continued to be interested in young people.

As soon as Dave returned to his apartment, he called Dorothy and she answered. "This is Dave Mason. Do you know where Jill is?" "Yes Dave, she is still in Burlingame. She couldn't get a non-stop to Chicago and didn't want to be bumped off in route, so she went home. She plans to try again tomorrow morning. If she gets to Chicago she will call and let me know what New York flight she will try for." "Okay, I'll call you when I return from my game tomorrow afternoon. I have a dinner appointment tomorrow night. Would you be able to meet her? "Yes, if she makes it tomorrow I can. If I'm not here when you call I've probably gone to the airport." "Fine, I hope she makes it tomorrow."

Dukes Stadium
Cleveland at New York
5:35 PM August 29, 1950

In this first game of a four game series, the Dukes built a 6 to 0 lead in the early innings and hung on for a 6 to 5 win. Lindsey Barrett pitched a complete game, although he had to work out of jams in both the eighth and ninth inning. Detroit had split a doubleheader, so the Dukes lead was now 5-1/2 games.

The Corner Grill
New York City, New York
7:15 PM August 29, 1950

Dave and Hank James were having dinner so Hank could talk to Dave about his plan to get Turner Chevrolet's advertising contract. Hank had just started giving Dave the history of Turner.

Hank said, "The dealership was started by Bill's father Sam Turner, as a repair garage in 1922. Sam was a good mechanic with a flair for sales. He had been trained during army service during World War

I. In 1924, Sam obtained a Studebaker dealership. He did so well, that Chevrolet came calling and he switched just about the time Chevrolet was passing up Ford in sales. Sam maintained a good service and repair business, hiring mechanics that were familiar with other cars. His garage wasn't limited to Chevrolet service and repair. This helped him get through the depression."

"When the war started in Europe, Sam was sure we would be involved sooner or later. He hired mechanics that were at least 40 years of age, so they wouldn't be eligible for military service. He also bought up used cars, ran them through his shop and built his inventory. Sam knew if we got into the war new cars would be limited and maybe not available at all."

"During the war he got a contract from the army to service and repair staff cars and trucks used by the army at New York City installations. He came out of the war in better financial condition than any auto dealer in New York."

"Bill started working in the garage at a young age, but was a better salesman than mechanic. Sam sent him to New York University to study business. He graduated in 1938 and joined the firm in sales. After Pearl Harbor, Bill joined the Army, was sent to OCS, and served as an Air Corps engineering officer, spending three years in England."

"Bill returned to the firm in 1945 and was made president in January of 1946. Sam was 60, at the time but continues as Chairman of the Board. He had been collecting cars he thought were classics, over the years, storing them in a warehouse on Long Island. Now he has hired a couple of mechanics who will start restoring the cars. Just what he plans to do with them, no one knows."

"Since 1946, an agency that specializes in print advertising has had the Turner account. They have done some radio commercials and a few billboards, but that's all. Most of their budget has been spent on newspaper ads."

"My plan is to propose more of a diversified program that would include radio, TV, and billboards, as well as print. I would propose they be a sponsor of Dukes radio broadcasts next year and TV in the future. In all of this I will propose to use you as spokesman and have you appear in the ads and on the billboards."

"That's overwhelming Hank. My immediate question is will I have the ability and time to do all this?" "I think you have the ability, with some practice. The time can be handled by good scheduling. The people at Turner have been amazed at the crowds you have drawn to the showroom on your appearance nights." "You can add me to that too."

"If you approve of this proposal, I'll work out the details, the budget, and what you could expect in income, and get it to you. It may take more than a month, so I may have to mail it to you in Texas." "That's fine Hank. Go ahead but keep me posted on your progress."

Dukes Stadium
Cleveland at New York, Doubleheader
5:55 PM August 30, 1950

Playing two games today offered the Dukes an opportunity to increase their league lead. In the first game, Louis Leon kept his walks down to only four, pitched well and the Dukes won 4 to 3. In the second game Vic Carlisle pitched a gem, allowing only two hits and shutting out the Indians. The double win increased the Dukes lead over Detroit to 6-1/2 games. Were the Dukes closing in on an early clinch of the pennant?

Golden Pheasant Restaurant
7:00 PM August 30, 1950

On his drive to the restaurant Dave wondered what this meeting was about. He really didn't have a clue. He was happy because of the doubleheader win today. Tomorrow he would pitch for the first time in more than three weeks and he wasn't sure how he would do after the long layoff.

Captain Funk was waiting for Dave when he arrived five minutes early. Dave noticed immediately that Funk had railroad track on his shoulders. "Congratulations, I see you are a Captain now." "Yes, you are very observant." "Railroad tracks are hard to miss." "Thank you Dave. Let's get to our table so I can bring you up to date."

"First, along with the promotion, I have been transferred to the Far East Command, (FECOM). I report on 01 October in Tokyo, with a two week delay in route, I'll be departing the outfit this weekend. I'll likely end up in Korea. Col. Flyer has appointed Capt. Richard Tracy, Acting Engineering & maintenance Officer, until a permanent replacement can be found."

"The press release I told you about in our phone conversation has been delayed and will be issued tomorrow. It probably won't get into the papers until Friday."

After ordering, Capt. Funk said, "The main purpose of this meeting Dave is to interest you in becoming an officer. During the summer training you showed great leadership potential and your knowledge of engines has surprised the older mechanics. Col. Flyer thinks you would make an excellent Engineering & Maintenance Officer. He has reserved a slot in the Air Force Officer's Training Course that starts in October. It's a 90 day course. This would be followed by a 10 week course for Engineering & Maintenance Officers. It would mean time between the first week of October and 24 March, 1951."

"Now, why do I think you should do this? First it would give you experience in leadership, something you can use in what ever you do in life. Second, it would give you broad experience in aircraft maintenance. It would also give you flexibility in your reserve service. Col Flyer's plan would be to appoint you assistant E & M Officer upon your being commissioned and trained. There would be a bit more money, probably not a major factor to you. The term of service after receiving your commission is four years, an additional six months. That's the proposal. Do you have questions?"

"Right now I can't think of any, it's such a surprise!" "Well, take some time to think about it and develop some questions. Col. Flyer needs to have an answer by 09 September." "Okay, I'll think about it and talk to my dad and the Dukes management. I'm sure I'll have questions." "After Friday, please call Capt. Jergens." "I just have to tell you Captain Funk, I'm overwhelmed!" "You really shouldn't be Dave, you have great potential." "Thank you very much sir."

Dave called Dorothy from the restaurant as soon as Captain Funk departed. There was no answer, so Dave drove to his apartment. He called again and Dorothy answered. "Did she make it? "Yes she did. Would you like to talk to her? I know, that's a silly question. Here she is!" "Hello Dave, when can you come to see me?" "Would right now be okay Jill?" "Right now would be great." "I'll be there in ten minutes." "I can't wait."

Coral Gardens Apartments
9:10 PM August 30, 1950

Dave had to call on the apartment intercom to be admitted to the apartment house. A voice, not Jill's asked who was there? "Dave Mason." The door was opened.

Jill had decided she would give Dave a different kind of greeting after more than six months apart. Before her trip east, she had gone into San Francisco to shop for a new dress. She found what she wanted at I. Magnin. A low cut red dress that bared he shoulders and was a great contrast with her blonde hair. Jill had Dorothy unlock the apartment door and then go into her bedroom. Jill sat on the couch in front of a lamp turned on low, the only light in the room.

Arriving at the door of the apartment, Dave knocked. A voice inside asked who was there? "Dave Mason." "Come in." Dave entered a dark apartment. All he could see was a silhouette of Jill. She said in a low voice, come in Dave. Then she turned the lamp up so Dave could see her in the dress. He stopped and just starred. "It's me Dave I've been waiting for you." Dave walked to the couch, picked Jill up and kissed her. He said, "You make the dress!" "Oh Dave, you are such a doll." Dave sat down with Jill still in his arms and they got reacquainted.

Dave's Apartment
9:00 AM August 31, 1950

Dave had placed a call to his dad that would be 6:00 o'clock his time. However, he knew his dad would be up. Dave gave his dad the offer he had received for OCS and E & M training. "What are your thoughts about it dad?" "I think it is a great opportunity Dave. It will give you leadership and management experience at a young age you cannot get elsewhere. What are your feelings about it?" "I'm thinking I should accept, but haven't made a decision yet. The experience and the management opportunity is one I should not turn down. But I did want to get you thoughts." "I appreciate that Dave. I think it would be a positive move." "Thank you dad. I will talk to the Dukes management, but I don't think they can object with the war on." "That's true. Please keep me posted." "I will."

"Jill arrived last night and is living here in Flushing. She will start flying in a few days." "I hope it works out for her Dave. Just be sure she knows what's involved in your life on two coasts." "Yes I will dad."

"Is everything ready for the wedding and did my gift arrive?" "Yes and yes. All the members of the wedding party have arrived and the weather has been great!" "Thanks dad, I plan to send the newly weds a telegram on Saturday." "That's very thoughtful of you Dave."

The phone rang just before Dave left his apartment to go see Jill. Lt. Parks, the MATS information officer was calling. He said, "The press release has been delayed because we want it to appear in the Sunday papers. It will get more exposure on Sunday. We wanted you to be aware of that." "Thank you sir."

Headquarters
MATS Reserve RS-1
0930 31 August 1950

The press release regarding Dave's actions during the survival training had been delayed because Col. Flyer wanted to read it before it was released. He had been on a Pan Am flight the past two days. It was now ready to be released to the newspapers, press services and radio.

MILITARY AIR TRANSPORT SERVICE RESERVE RS-1

Republic Airport

Farmingdale, New York

Press Release
31 August, 1950

Contact
Lt. Bill Parks
IN 4-7777

DUKES PITCHER DEMONSTRATES LEADERSHIP ABILITY

31 August 1950. Dave Mason, the sensational rookie pitcher of the New York Dukes baseball team demonstrated outstanding leadership ability during summer training of MATS Reserve RS-1, a reserve squadron of the Military Air Transport Service.

During a survival exercise, Airman Mason assumed leadership of his six person team when the leader, Cpl. Ted Frankland sprained his ankle so badly he passed out. Mason had crutches fashioned from a tree limb and using the map provided, led the team out of the wilderness to the destination location within the three day limit of the exercise.

Airman Mason, who joined the MATS squadron in July was participating in just his second duty since enlisting. During the three day survival exercise, Mason, the youngest member of the team at 22, kept the spirits of the team members positive by his encouragement and focusing on helping Cpl. Frankland with his injury. Mason challenged each member of the team to do their part, and more, to help the team succeed in reaching the destination point. Airman Mason's team was the only one of eight teams to reach the destination. .

Colonel Bernie Flyer, Commander of the MATS squadron said, "Airman Dave Mason demonstrated excellent leadership ability during the survival exercise. It is a quality the military service is always looking for in its men."

Coral Gardens Apartments
10:00 AM August 31, 1950

Dave had come for a short visit with Jill before he had to be at the ball park. Dorothy greeted Dave and said, "Jill is still getting the sleep out of her eyes and will be out in a few minutes.

It rook Jill longer than a few minutes and Dorothy served Dave a cup of coffee while he waited. When Jill did appear, she looked like she had just stepped out of a house beautiful advertisement. Dave greeted her with a big hug and a kiss and said, "You look beautiful Jill!" "I slept so hard I didn't know what I would look like when I got up. I was so tired after yesterday's trip." "I suggest you rest today and I will take you to dinner after today's game." "Are you pitching today?" "Yes I am against the Cleveland Indians." "Can I listen to it?" "Yes, the broadcast is on station WINS. I will call you when I leave the stadium after the game."

Dukes Stadium
Cleveland at New York
2:30 PM August 31, 1950

Dave had started the game with a lack of control. He thought it was being rusty. While he had thrown regularly during the layoff, he hadn't thrown to batters. It makes a difference. Cleveland scored two runs on three hits in the first inning. They added a single run in the third. In the fourth the Dukes tied it up with three runs. Dave walked and scored a run.

Dave's control improved as the game went on, and while he had allowed seven hits the tie held until the eighth inning when the Dukes scored two runs on back to back home run by Vic Marko and B.B. Katcher. It was number 38 for Marko and the fourth for B.B. since being called up from Buffalo in late June. Dave pitched a perfect ninth inning and the Dukes had a 5-3 win.

The win put the Dukes 7-1/2 games ahead of Detroit. It was looking like the Dukes would win another pennant and be in another World Series. However, "It ain't over till it's over."

Dave had to answer lots of questions from the writers, mainly concerning his layoff. He and B.B. finally departed at 6:00 PM.

Coral Gardens Apartments
7:00 PM August 31, 1950

Dave was knocking on the door of Jill's and Dorothy's apartment. Jill, remembering Dorothy's warning to check all visitors through the peep hole in the door, looked first to see Dave's smiling face. She saw he was carrying flowers. She opened the door and Dave gave her a dozen red roses and a big kiss." "What beautiful roses," Jill said.

Jill said, "We have the apartment to ourselves. Dorothy left this morning for a flight to Chicago. But before she departed she fixed a casserole for our dinner so we can stay here in the apartment. You can cancel our dinner reservation." "That was nice of her," Dave said.

While they ate dinner Jill gave Dave all the news from California. She covered everyone, starting with Jane and Woody. They have an apartment in San Francisco because Jane has gone back to work for a public relations firm in the city. Sally has a new boy friend and he may be Mr. Right."

Following dinner Dave said, "Now Jill, tell me about your decision to accept the Lord." "It was the book, The Man Nobody Knows that convinced me Dave. The part about how Jesus trained his band of uneducated disciples who had received the Holy Spirit to spread the gospel throughout the known world at a fraction of the cost of carrying out the Roman civilization. Now I want you to lead me through accepting the Lord." "I can do that Jill, but first you should decide on membership in a church so you will have the support of a community of believers, and can be baptized. On Sunday, I suggest we attend North Presbyterian Church Sunday school and you can inquire about membership. Is that acceptable?" "Yes Dave." "That's good Jill.'

"Jill, do you understand Romans 3:23 'For all have sinned, and come short of the glory of God?' "Yes I do." "Do you understand, 'For by grace are ye saved through faith; and that not of yourselves: it is the gift of God: Not of works, lest any man should boast?' "Yes I do." "Now, repeat after me, Dear God ... Dear God...I know I'm a sinner, I'm trusting in Christ alone for my salvation ... Dear God, I know I'm a sinner, I'm trusting in God alone for my salvation ... Lord Jesus, come into my heart and save me from my sins... Lord Jesus, come into my heart and save me from my sins... In Jesus name, Amen... In Jesus name, Amen."

"Jill, you've just made the greatest decision of your life" "I'm sure of it Dave."

Jill and Dave talked until midnight. Dave said, "The team has an unusual day off tomorrow and then games with Washington on Saturday and Sunday. In the morning what time would you like to go to the airport to learn what your flight schedule will be?" "Let's do it at 10:00." "That's fine. I'll be here at 10 o'clock."

La Guardia Airport
10:30 AM September 1, 1950

Dave had driven with Jill to the airport so she could check in with stewardess scheduling. Her supervisor was not in the office, but she learned her first flight would be Monday morning at 10:00 AM on flight 1834 to Cleveland.

Later they stopped for lunch and Dave took Jill to his apartment. He brought her up to date regarding his joining MATS and the summer training. He didn't talk about officer training because he had not come to a decision yet. Also, he wanted to talk to Fred Duke about it before he made the decision.

He thought Jill had not been happy with his military decision to join MATS. He thought she wanted him to wait for the draft which would give her the opportunity to push for them to get married. She had seen many stewardesses leave to marry because their men were called up from the reserve or drafted. If he decided to accept the OCS offer, it may cause more of a problem between them. However, I planned to return home in October to resume my master's degree study. I wouldn't be here for another five months anyway. I think Jill sees all the stewardesses getting married and is getting impatient.

Dave took Jill to dinner at the Golden Pheasant. Then they went back to his apartment. As soon as he was in his apartment, Dave called Western Union and sent his telegram to Pam and Bill so it would arrive tomorrow on their wedding day. Then Jill and Dave watched TV. When it was time to take Jill home, Dave said, "I'll take you dinning and dancing at Great Neck tomorrow night." "That name sounds interesting. It will be nice to dance with you again after so many months." "I'll look forward to it, Jill."

Dave's Apartment
9:00 AM September 2, 1950

This morning Dave had called Capt. Jergens and was asking him questions about OCS.

Q "Do you think the enlisted men will accept me an as officer? I'm very young."

A "I don't think that will be a problem and neither does Col. Flyer."

Q "Is there a possibility that I would be called to active duty?"

A "Very unlikely. The need in Korea is for experienced E & M Officers."

Q "In future years I will go home to California when the baseball season is over. Will my being an officer help me get on a MATS flight to New York for duty weekends?

A "Yes. Lacking a priority, boarding is strictly by rank". Thank you Captain Jergens sir.

Dukes Stadium
Washington at New York
4:45 PM September 2, 1950

Dave had watched Jake Filner pitch a good game backed by good hitting for an 8-2 win. As he always did, he made notes on the hitters and pitchers even though Don Frank was charting the game. He had decided to let Don finish the season as his private charter. Ozzie Felton may have known he was having it done, but he hadn't said anything. Dave would talk to Ozzie about it following the season. The win gave the Dukes a 7-1/2 game lead over Detroit.

Elizabeth Flynn's Restaurant
122 Middle Neck Road
Great Neck, New York
7:00 PM September 2, 1950

Dave had selected this restaurant because he had heard good things about it and it was away from Flushing and Queens. He was being recognized more lately and he was less likely to be recognized in Great Neck. However, the person who took his reservation must have been a baseball fan because he was greeted by the hostess as soon as he and Jill entered the restaurant. Dave was glad the MATS article had not been in the papers yet. When Dave called for Jill he brought her a beautiful corsage for her dress. "Beautiful flowers for a beautiful lady." "Oh Dave, you are so thoughtful!"

When they were seated, Dave gave Jill a beautiful necklace of Indian design he had bought in San Antonio. Jill said "It will go well with the bracelet you bought me in Seattle more than a year ago." "I remember." They had a good dinner followed by dancing in the lounge. Dave told Jill of some of his adventures during the summer training in Florida. They had some good laughs. Jill did seem a little distant to Dave. But maybe it was just the new surroundings, places she had never seen. Also, he realized for the first time that Jill was not interested in talking about current news and world events.

They stopped off at Dave's apartment for coffee and some romancing by Dave. He took Jill to her apartment soon after midnight.. "I'll be here soon after nine in the morning to take you to Sunday school." "I'll be ready."

North Presbyterian Church
25-33 154th Street
Queens, New York
9:30 AM September 3, 1950

Jill and Dave were attending the adult class today. Dave wanted to learn if the age of the class would be close to Jill's. There were a number of younger couples attending, but this was Labor Day weekend so attendance was down. The class was completing a study of the Parables. Next Sunday they would start a study of Acts.

Following the class Jill asked the teacher about the church membership classes. He said, "A new class would start on the 17th of September. The classes are held from 5:00 to 7:00 PM. Two Sunday's are required. They are repeated, so if you miss a Sunday you can make up." "That's great. I have to work some Sundays."

After taking Jill home, Dave with B.B drove to the stadium under threatening skies. "We may not play two games today," Dave said. "Yes, it doesn't look good."

B.B. said, "I received my draft physical notice yesterday from California. I will write back requesting they change my address so I can take the exam here. I'm sure my feet will make me 4F."

B.B., who only read the sports page of the newspaper, had not seen the MATS article about Dave. So Dave decided to tell him about it so he wouldn't be in the dark when the players hit Dave with it. And they did as soon as he walked into the clubhouse. A player started calling him "The General." Dave had left his apartment early to have breakfast so he wouldn't have to answer the phone and the questions of reporters.

On days that looked like there was any chance of rain, Dave brought reading material with him, something he had learned early in the season. Today was a long wait until 5:30 when both games were called.

Coral Gardens Apartments
7:00 PM September 3, 1950

Jill had invited Dave to dinner. She promised a great dining experience. Dave wasn't sure what that would mean, but he had looked forward to it. Jill had told Dave that Dorothy was assisting in the creation of this dinner and would add some of her Montana food to the dinner. Dave arrived with a chilled bottle of Chardonnay for Jill. Jill was ready for him! She had made up a big "HERO" badge out of colored paper. When he entered the apartment, she had Dorothy play a march on a record she had, and Jill proceeded to read part of the article from a morning newspaper. Then she said, "I now proclaim you to be hero of the day." She and Dorothy clapped and gave three cheers for the hero. Dave, going along with the spoof, had kept a straight face and now said, "I thank you, and all the members of my fan club for this honor. I am underwhelmed!"

Then he couldn't keep the straight face and burst out laughing, and the girls joined in. "See I told you Dorothy. He can laugh at himself, even though he IS a big hero. She wasn't so sure you wouldn't get mad. I think she has been reading too many of your sports page clippings." "I only started after Jill told me who you were and I heard so many people talking about you." "Jill has always kept me humble," Dave said.

The dinner was delicious. Dorothy had provided large rib steaks that were so tender and she had broiled them to a tee. Dave wanted to know where she got such good steaks. Dorothy said, "Its Montana beef from my family's ranch." "And how did you get it to New York?" "My younger brother is a co-pilot for Northwest Airlines. He fly's between Seattle and Montana cities. He has a friend who has a Seattle Chicago flight and he in turn has a friend who has a Chicago New York flight. They carried the steaks sealed in dry ice all the way by placing them in the cold baggage compartment. I picked them up at the airport. I get a package almost every month. On Northwest Airlines they call the package, steaks for Dot." "That's quite a story Dorothy."

Since both girls had flights in the morning, Dave went home early. He had told Jill he would take her to the airport in the morning.

Dukes Stadium
Philadelphia at New York, Doubleheader
2:00 PM September 4, 1950

Today was the Labor Day doubleheader. Dave was pitching the first game. The game was a surprising pitcher's Deuel for the first three innings, with no score. The Dukes scored a run in the fourth inning on B.B. Katcher's fifth home run of the season, a line drive over the left center field fence. Philadelphia tied it in the top of the sixth on a hit, sacrifice and a double down the first base line. The Dukes did not answer so at the end of six innings it was a 1-1 tie.

Both teams made threats, putting men on second, but no runs scored. It was still 1-1 as the ninth inning started. The Philadelphia lead off man beat out an infield single. A sacrifice put the runner on second with one out. The next batter struck out. Now there were two out and a man on second. On a 1-2 count the batter hit a ball to deep short stop. The ball tipped off Billy Duke's glove into left field. The runner rounded third and headed for the plate. The throw from left fielder Bill Wood bounced in front of Catcher J.B. Felton, it looked like it would be in time, but it must have hit a rock because it flew in the air out of Felton's reach and the runner was safe. Philadelphia 2-1. The next batter struck out to end the top half of the inning.

With one out J. B. Felton singled. But Larry Mann hit into a double play and the game was over. Dave had lost his second game of the season.

In the second game of the doubleheader, Doug Abbott pitched well and won 4-3. At the end of the day the Dukes had lost a half a game of their lead over the Tigers and were now 7 games ahead.

After the games, the writers wanted to talk to Dave about the MATS article not his loss. Dave said he wouldn't talk to them until they had talked to Doug Abbott about his pitching. He had pitched well today, something he hadn't been doing lately.

Dave and B.B. had dinner at Bob's, then went to Dave's apartment and watched the Fred Waring show on TV. The programs were improving.

The next morning Dave called Fred Duke, but learned he would not be in until after lunch. "Please have him call me. It's important."

Fred called back at 1:35. Dave explained the offer of OCS he had received and how it would affect his arrival at next year's spring training. Fred Duke said, "Do what ever you think best Dave. Being late for spring training will not be a big problem." "Thank you Mr. Duke. I will let you know what I decide." Dave now had until Saturday to decide. I'll will talk to dad and make my decision.

La Guardia Airport
1:35 PM September 5, 1950

On a day with no game scheduled, Dave had caught up on things that he couldn't do while he was on summer training.

Now he was picking Jill up following her return flight from Cleveland. Jill said, "I wasn't impressed with Cleveland. My supervisor said she would switch me to a Chicago flight as soon as she has more girls to take the Cleveland flights. United is really short of girls and I'm told they are recruiting in every city."

"How do your feel Dave after your loss yesterday?" "You know?" "Yes, I still read the sports page first." "Good for you Jill. Yes, I'm not too happy. Hopefully the kids at Turner Chevrolet will cheer me up tonight.

Dave had told Jill she could have his car while he was on the next road trip. He would be gone for ten days, return for MATS duty and be gone again for four days. It would give Jill transportation to the airport. "I'll bring the car to you some time after 9:00 tonight." "Thank you Dave, the car will be a big help."

Turner Chevrolet
7:00 PM September 5, 1950

The kids did cheer Dave up tonight. Not one mentioned his losing the game yesterday. This would be Dave's next to last appearance. He was going to miss these kids who were so excited about baseball. When the appearance was over he told Dick Chevrolet how much he was going to miss these evenings. "We are going to miss having you here Dave." "I'll see you on September 25th Dick."

Fenway Park
New York at Boston, Night
8:00 PM September 6, 1950

Lindsey Barrett was the starting pitcher in this night game. However, it was no contest. Barrett was racked for five runs in the first two innings and was followed by Ed Edgar and Ed Card. Only Card pitched well. The final score was 12-2. It cost the Dukes a game off their lead over Detroit, now 6-1/2 games.

Dave had written a post card to Sharon saying he would call her when the team came to Boston. Sharon had not sent many post cards recently. Dave thought she was probably dating some "hot shot" lawyers. Dave tried to call Sharon before the game but didn't reach her. He called again after the game even though it was late and Sharon answered. "Oh Dave I've been reading good things about you and I had reserved tonight for you. Then I realized you had a night game so we couldn't get together." "I'm sorry it didn't work out Sharon."

"Dad sent me the MATS article about you Dave. I was so surprised." "So was I Sharon. I wasn't told about it until it was written and about to be in the papers." "When will you be finished here in Boston and go home Sharon?" "I'm done her on September 15th. Mother will drive up to take me and my collection of stuff back to New York." "Please call me when you return to town Sharon. The team will be in town on the 15th and 16th, but we leave on a trip on the 16th." "I'll call and maybe I can get to a game." "That would be great Sharon. It's getting late so I'll let you get to bed. Good night Sharon." "Good night Dave."

Copley Square Hotel Room 920 10:00 AM September 7, 1950

Dave was on the phone talking to his dad. He said, "I have decided to accept the OCS opportunity and I wanted to let you know." "I think that's a good decision Dave. It will help you in the future, no matter what you do." "Thanks dad. How was the wedding?" "Everything went well. It was very hot during the reception in our backyard which added to the punch of the Champaign. The newlyweds are now honeymooning in Carmel and your mother is recovering nicely." "That sounds good. Goodbye dad." "Goodbye."

Dave then placed a call to Capt. Jergens at MATS. "I have decided to accept the OCS opportunity Sir." "That's good news Dave. We need to get the paper work done as soon as possible. How can we do that?" "I'm on a road trip and won't return until the 22nd, so I need to receive the papers while I'm gone. There is a way. Our traveling secretary didn't come to Boston with us, but he will meet us in New York on our way to Washington. If you can get the papers to Ray Arnold at the Dukes office today he can get them to me." "I'll do that."

Fenway Park New York at Boston 5:45 PM September 7, 1950

Again the Dukes' starting pitcher was knocked out of the game early. Today it was Louis Leon who lasted just two innings. He was followed by Bob Pennell and Tom Harris. Only Harris pitched well and the Red Sox won the game 10-7. It cost the Dukes another half game off their lead over Detroit. The Dukes lead was now 5 games.

Following the game manager Felton had a short team meeting. His words were right to the point. "You haven't won the pennant yet, so let's stop playing like we have. That's all I have to say!"

Chapter Twenty Nine

Capital Hilton Hotel

1001 16th Street NW

Washington, D.C.

8:30 PM September 9, 1950

THE GAME WITH Washington had been rained out. Dave was working on the OCS paperwork. He wanted to complete it so he could send it special delivery in the morning. The schedule for OCS class 4-50 might take Dave out of the World Series if the Dukes shaped up and won the American League Pennant. Trainees were required to report to Lackland AFB by 2400 hours 07 October 1950. Dave wasn't sure what the schedule for the series was, but he didn't think it would be over by October 7th. Only time would tell. Dave had told Randy White his intention about OCS. Randy thought it was a good move. "If you're going to be in the military it's best to be an officer."

Griffith Stadium
Washington, D.C.
New York at Washington, Doubleheader
6:35 PM September 10, 1950

Vic Carlisle pitched the Dukes to a 7-1 win in the first game. Then the rains came again and a long sit out until the second game was called. The Dukes lead was now 4-1/2 games. The team needed to get some games played and win them. There would be another doubleheader tomorrow.

New York at Washington, Doubleheader
2:00 PM September 11, 1950

The Dukes were hoping the rain would stay away so they could play and win a doubleheader today. Dave was pitching the first game. In the early innings it looked like Dave had shed his rustiness from his two weeks off. He breezed through the first four innings, allowing just one hit and no runs. The Dukes had a 2-0 lead. They added three runs in the sixth inning and Dave had a one hitter through seven innings. Washington got a run in the eighth on two hits and an error, but that was all Dave allowed. It was a 5-1 win for the Dukes. Dave allowed 5 hits, struck out 1 and issued no walks. It was Dave's 23rd win.

The Dukes won the second game behind the six hit pitching of Jake Filner. The two wins upped the Dukes lead over Detroit to 6-1/2 games.

Cleveland Municipal Stadium
New York at Cleveland
5:15 PM September 13, 1950

The Dukes had lost Tuesday's game 8 to 6, but won today's game 10-3 with good hitting and pitching. This gave them a split in the two games with Cleveland. It dropped the Dukes lead over Detroit to 4-1/2 games. The next three games would be head to head with Detroit.

Following the game Dave took a United Airlines flight back to New York so he could report to MATS for his duty weekend on Friday. Dave had called last night and talked to Dorothy, giving her his flight number and his 8:30 arrival time so Jill could pick him up.

Jill was waiting for him at the gate when he walked off the airplane. He got a big hug and a kiss from Jill, and they walked to the parking lot. They drove to Dave's apartment so Dave could tell Jill about OCS. He explained the opportunity, reminding her that he would have gone home when the season was over to continue his Master's degree study at Stanford. He would have had to come to New York once each month for his weekend of duty at MATS.

Jill said, "I've known ever since you came to New York that you would return home following the baseball season. But I wanted to be with you, even for a short time. And I needed to experience New York. I'm joining the church Dave. Now, what will happen next March after your training is completed?" "I'll go directly to spring training in late March. Jill thought about Dave's response… Then she said, "If I joined you in Florida for a week, do you think we could… get married?" "Would you really like to get married away from your family and friends, with no time off for a honeymoon?" "I know it's not the best plan, but give me an alternative." Dave was silent for a while. Then said, "When I ask you to marry me Jill it will be at a time when we can go back to California and have a wedding in a church of your choice with our families and friends participating. In addition, I want you to be sure of a life of seven months in New York and five in California."

"I'm sorry Dave. We've been together for almost five years now, and I see so many of my friends getting married, I wonder if I'll be an old maid." "I understand your frustration Jill, but we are still very young people. I think we have time to make the most important decision in our life and to make a good one. I want to be able to look back on a wedding as a celebration and a life changing occasion. One I would remember all my life." "As usual, you're right Dave. I'm here in a new city, you've been on the road, and I don't know anyone but Dorothy. I'm a country girl in the big city." Dave said,

"I'm sure it will get better as time goes on Jill. Now come, sit on my lap."

Dave's Apartment
8:00 AM September 15, 1950

Dave had finished his breakfast following his devotions. He was missing the Sunday school class at Fifth Avenue Presbyterian. He hadn't been able to attend for five weeks. The phone rang and it was Jill calling. "I just received a call to take a flight to Chicago for a stewardess who called in sick. So, I'll miss having lunch with you. Can you take me to the airport at ten o' clock?" "Sure. When will you return?" "I'll be back tomorrow afternoon. I can ride home with Dorothy. She will return about the same time." "Okay. I'll see you at 10:00." "Thanks Dave."

On the drive to the airport Dave said, "As I mentioned before, I'm going to leave the car with you while I'm gone. I'll write up a letter that will authorize you to have possession of the car and use it." "Oh thank you Dave. That will be a big help." After a good by kiss, Dave said, "I'll see you Sunday night after my duty weekend."

Briggs Stadium
New York at Detroit
2:30 PM September 15, 1950

Detroit had won the first game of the series 7-5. Louis Leon took the loss. The Dukes lead over Detroit was now down to 4-1/2 games. Vic Carlisle was the starting pitcher today. It was another game of lots of hitting. In the last half of the fifth inning the score was tied 4 to 4. Detroit scored three runs, knocking Carlisle out of the game. He was replaced by Ed Card who retired the Tigers with no further damage.

The Dukes tied the game again in the seventh inning at 7 to 7. Card had been lifted for a pinch hitter and Bob Pennell was now pitching. He held Detroit scoreless in the seventh and eighth innings, but the Dukes did not score. It was still a 7 to 7 tie going into the last of the ninth inning. Pennell walked the lead off batter. The clean up batter was coming to the plate. Manager Felton had him intentionally walked. Runners were now on first and second and the number five batter coming to the plate. After getting two strikes on the batter, Pennell made a mistake. A fast ball he intended to be outside, well off the plate, was located over the plate which allowed the batter to hit the ball on the fat of the bat for a three run home run giving the Tigers a 10 to 7 win.

The loss cost the Dukes another game off their lead in the pennant race. It was now down to 3-1/2 games

New York at Detroit
5:15 PM September 16, 1950

The team had a short meeting before the game called by Vic Marko and J.B. Felton, two of the veteran players. They asked every player to bear down, stop the losing and clinch the pennant so we can prepare for the series. A win today is important. "Let's do it." And they did, winning the game 8-2. Jake Filner pitched one of his better games, and got the win. So the Dukes departed Detroit with a 4-1/2 game lead. Now it was on to St. Louis where the team should win more games.

The team took a New York Central train at 10:40 PM for the overnight trip to St. Louis where the Dukes would play only a twilight/night doubleheader They arrived the St. Louis Union Station at 11:40 AM on Sunday morning. The first game would start at 5:00 PM.

Sportsman's Park
New York at St. Louis, Doubleheader
5:00 PM September 17, 1950

The Dukes were expecting to win two games today, but it didn't happen. In the first game Doug Abbott was relieved in the sixth inning by Ed Edgar who lost the game by a run in the ninth inning 6-5. The Dukes won the nightcap 6-1. Lindsey Barrett pitched a five hitter. The split gave the Dukes a 5 game lead in the pennant race. Detroit had lost a single game.

With no game on Monday, September 18, the team had plenty of time to travel to Chicago for the first of a three game series, starting Tuesday night.

Aboard United Airlines Flight 1615
1:30 AM September 18, 1950

It was Monday afternoon and Dave was flying to Chicago following his duty weekend at MATS. He would get a good night's sleep and be ready to pitch the opening game of the series. He was thinking about the weekend, his last duty prior to departing for OCS. Upon reporting for duty on Friday, all Dave's fellow airmen that saw him gave him a big welcome. Most had seen the article regarding his training experience. Few, if any knew about OCS. However it was announced at the show up formation on Friday evening. An evaluation of summer training by the officers was given by Capt. Jergens

For the first training session, the evaluation was good, but improvement was needed. The transfer of Lt. Funk and the appointment of Capt. Tracy as Acting Engineering and Maintenance Officer were announced. Dave's squad spent most of the weekend working on the C-54 systems. The age of the airplanes was requiring lots of parts replacements. During the briefing on the war, a report told of an air drop to a surrounded Marine unit. Two old C-47s were sent with supplies of food and ammunition. The aircraft returned full of shell holes, just able to limp back to base.

The DC-6 had started its' let down for the landing at Chicago's Midway airport. In a few years the airlines would be moving to a new larger airport out in the countryside near Des Plains, Illinois. How many years would it be? No one knew.

Comiskey Park
New York at Chicago
8:30 PM September 19, 1950

Dave allowed one hit in the first inning, but then retired fifteen batters in a row. However the Chicago pitcher was matching Dave's effort and it was a scoreless tie in the top of the sixth inning. Then the roof caved in on the Chicago pitcher. Duke, Hoff, Wood and Vic Marko singled. B.B. Katcher doubled, cleaning the bases, for a 4 to 0 lead.

That was the end of the scoring in the game. Dave scattered seven hits and won his 24th game 4 to 0. The win increased the Dukes' lead to 5-1/2 games over Detroit.

New York at Chicago
5:30 PM September 20, 1950

After two wins the Dukes wanted to make it three in a row. Louis Leon was hit hard and the Dukes lost 8 to 1. Could the Dukes be doing a "swoon" at the end of the season? The loss cut the New Yorker's lead over Detroit to 4-1/2 games.

In the evening Dave attended the Kiwanis Club of Archer Road for a make up. He hadn't been doing too well making up, so he had a happy dollar for the make up.

Dave hadn't taken the time to read the paper this morning so he started reading it when he returned to the hotel. He was reading an article about the draftees called for their pre-induction physicals. Of 1250 called, 502 were accepted, but 531 were rejected. 133 failed to show up. Dave wondered why so many failed.

New York at Chicago
5:45 PM September 21, 1950

Vic Carlisle had pitched well and the Dukes were in a 4 to 4 tie at the end of the sixth inning. In the top of the seventh Chicago banged out two singles and a double that produced two runs for a 6 to 4 lead. The Dukes threatened in their half of the sixth, seventh, and eighth, but produced no runs. In the ninth, Dave led off with a pinch hit double. But even with no outs, the Dukes could not get Dave home and produce any runs. Chicago won the game 6 to 4. Detroit won their game, so the Dukes lead shrunk to 3-1/2 games.

A very unhappy band of players took the Lake Shore Limited to New York, arriving Friday afternoon. Traveling Secretary, Ray Arnold pointed out to the players that they could have been home Thursday night if they had flown. He further stated, "I'm almost sure the 1951 schedule will be based on traveling by airplane." A few players would need to decide if they wanted to continue to play baseball if they had to fly. Some might retire because of the change from train to plane.

Jill was waiting for Dave when the team bus arrived at the stadium. They went to his apartment and talked. Jill reported she had completed the membership classes at North Presbyterian Church. She would be received during the next worship service she could attend. "That's great Jill. I'm proud of you." Then they decided to take in an early movie. It was A Lonely Place a Humphrey Bogart movie. They had dinner and Dave took Jill to her apartment. She was now on Chicago flights and had an early one in the morning.

Dave's Apartment
10:00 AM September 23, 1950

Dave's orders for OCS and travel vouchers were in his mail. He immediately made his airline reservation. There was no game yesterday but Dave was still catching up after his travels and tight schedule. He had made arrangements to vacate his apartment at the end of the month. The phone rang and it was Sharon calling. She said she knew he had been on a road trip, but had tried to call last night. "Will you be attending the Sunday school class tomorrow?" "Yes I will Sharon." "Great, I'll see you there." Dave still had things to do, but soon it was time to collect B.B. and get to the stadium.

On the way to the stadium, Dave asked B.B., "Would you be interested in renting a two bedroom apartment together next year? I think we could save money." "Sure Dave." Dave suggested they rent one in the Coral Gardens Apartments. "You wouldn't be influenced by the fact that Jill lives there, would you?" "It never crossed my mind B.B." They both laughed. Dave said, "We'll have to work out how we can get one rented before we return from spring training. I can have Jill do it for us if necessary." "Dave, I will drive my new car back here before going to spring training, so I can do it." "Okay, I'll talk to the manager at Coral Gardens and tell him what we want effective March first." "That sounds good Dave. It will sure give us more room." "Also, B.B the security is better at Coral, and I think we'll need that in the future." "You mean you will need it Dave." "Come on now B. B., I'm confident you will start attracting the girls next year." "That will be the day."

Dukes Stadium
Boston at New York, Night
8:00 PM September 23, 1950

Dave was pitching tonight with the intention of stopping the losing and starting a wining streak. In the first three innings Dave was at his best. He made only 18 pitches and retired nine batters. At the end of three innings there was no score.

The Dukes scratched out a run in the fourth inning on a single, a wild pitch and another single. It gave the Dukes a 1-0 lead. Dave continued to shut out the Red Sox and there was no further scoring until the seventh inning. Wood, Hoff, and Marko singled scoring a run. B.B. Katcher hit a three run home run over the left field fence. The ball was hit so high, it cleared the fence by 20 feet. The Dukes now led 5 to 0. Boston changed pitchers after a home run by B.B. bringing in a rookie just called up from triple A. Jim Essick met him with a double. Larry Mann beat out an infield hit to third. Essick had to hold at second. Dave was coming to bat. The Red Sox pitcher fired a fast ball that Dave hit into the seats in right field for another three run home run. The Dukes lead was now 8 to 0 and that was the end of the scoring.

Dave finished the last three innings on twenty pitches, maintaining the shut out and a final 8 to 0 win. It was his 13th shutout. He made a total of ninety pitches allowing just three hits. Detroit lost two games, so the Dukes' lead was back up to 5 games.

Fifth Avenue Presbyterian Church
9:30 AM September 24, 1950

Dave arrived early. He wanted to talk to teacher Steve Early and tell him this would be his last Sunday until next April. He explained about

OCS and his training schedule. Soon, Sharon arrived and took a seat next to Dave. They had little time to talk before the class started. Sharon said, "Please call me when you can." "It will be in a day or two, but I will." "Thanks Dave."

The class study had progressed to the second missionary journey of Paul. He had written his first epistle, the letter to the Thessalonians. He gave them fatherly advice, reminding them about his teaching.

Dukes Stadium
Boston at New York, Doubleheader
4:00 PM September 24, 1950

The two games today would give the team an opportunity to increase their league lead. Vic Carlisle was the starter in the first game. At the end of the seventh inning it was a 2 to 2 tie. In the eighth inning Boston scored two runs before Ed Edgar could get warmed up and into the game. He retired Boston without any more damage, but was lifted for a pinch hitter in the next inning. The Dukes did not score and Bob Pennell was the next pitcher. He allowed two more runs for a 6 to 2 Boston lead. The Dukes did not rally and the game ended 6-2.

In the second game, Jake Filner pitched well, got good run support, and the Dukes won 9 to 2. The Dukes had increased their lead by a half game so it was now 5-1/2 games.

When Dave and B.B. returned to the apartment house, Dave said he was going to church and asked B.B. to go with him. B.B. said, "All you did today is sit in the dugout and chart pitches. I played two games and I'm tired." They both laughed. "So I'm going to turn in early. I'll see you tomorrow."

Flushing Baptist Church
Flushing, New York
7:00 PM September 24, 1950

This would be Dave's last church service before departing for OCS in Texas. He looked forward to hearing a good sermon. The title sounded interesting. One Day in the Work of the Lord. The scripture was the 9th chapter of Matthew. The 9th chapter gives a detailed account of one day's work in the ministry of Jesus Christ. From his notes, Dave's wrote out this summary of the sermon.

The activity begins at sunrise. Jesus was a morning person. It allowed him to add another hour to his day. Soon a small boat is crossing the Sea of Galilee with Jesus and his disciples. It takes them to Capernaum, the favorite city of Jesus. Jesus and his disciples proceed to the house of a friend. But soon people discover he is in town. He heals a palsied man, telling him "Your sins are forgiven." However, some members of the crowd didn't approve. They asked, "Who authorized this man to exercise the functions of God?" Jesus asked, "What's the objection?" Then, he said, "Arise, take up thy bed and walk." The man stirred, got up, and walked away with shouts of joy. Jesus asked, "What was the difference?"

Matthew, a tax collector had been attracted by the commotion, departed and was hard at work when Jesus walked by. Jesus said, "I want you." Matthew promptly closed his office, prepared a feast for Jesus and his disciples, and announced that he was a disciple.

The feast was good natured and noisy. The doors had been flung open and no one was excluded. This brought protests from the Pharisees because it included the "riff raff" of the city. Jesus said, "Who needs the doctor most—those that are well or those that are sick"

As the meal grew to a close, a dramatic event occurred. A ruler of the city entered and stood at the head of the table. He said his daughter was dead, but if Jesus would come a lay his hand on her she will live. Jesus rose from his seat and started for the door. The ruler led the way up the street. But before their journey was over another interruption occurred.

A woman who had been sick for twelve years came through the crowd and touched the hem of Jesus' garment. Jesus turned and said, "Daughter be of good comfort, thy faith hath made thee whole."

When Jesus and the ruler entered the house, Jesus took the daughter's hand and she arose alive.

Before the day was over Jesus healed two blind men and cast

the devil out of a dumb man. The multitudes marveled, saying it had never been seen in Israel.

At the end of the day Jesus said to his disciples, "The harvest truly is plenteous, but the laborers are few."

Dukes Stadium
Washington at New York, Doubleheader
3:30 PM September 25, 1950

If the Dukes swept the two games today they would insure a tie for the pennant. Doug Abbott was pitching the first game. It was a typical game for him. He walked seven batters, but won the game 8 to 3.

In the second game the lead changed often. The Dukes led 2 to 0. Then it was tied. Washington went ahead in the fourth inning 4 to 2. The Dukes tied it in the fifth, 4 to 4. Barrett was still on the mound in the seventh inning when he gave up two runs, and he was relieved by Ed Edgar. Edgar got the Dukes out of trouble, but Washington led 6-4. Edgar allowed one more run and the Dukes could not generate any offense so the game ended 7 to 4 for Washington. There was no change in the Dukes lead over Detroit.

Turner Chevrolet
7:00 PM September 25, 1950

This was Dave's last appearance before departing for OCS. The usual crowd was waiting. Schools were back in session, so there was a big crowd including lots of high school age boys. The questions tonight were about the World Series. Dave could only speculate since it would be his first.

At 8:30 Dave thanked Dick Chevrolet for his help and support during the season. Dick said, "I hope we can do it again next year."

Dave went to a restaurant so he could call Sharon from a phone booth. She said her dad had ordered World Series tickets and she would attend one or more games. "I would like to see you pitch Dave." Dave said, "I guess you will know as soon as I do what the schedule will be."

Dave told Sharon about OCS. "That's great Dave. When do you have to be there?" I will leave on October 7. I hope I'll have an opportunity to pitch in the series. I'll call you Sharon when I return from Boston next Monday." "That's fine Dave."

Dukes Stadium
Washington at New York, Doubleheader
6:00 PM September 26, 1950

Another doubleheader was needed to make up for rain outs. In the first game the Dukes banged out a 10 to 7 win.

In the second game, the Dukes led 8 to 7 at the end of the eighth inning. In the ninth, Vic Carlisle gave up a two run home run that gave the Senators a 9 to 8 lead. The Dukes put two men on base in their half of the ninth, but did not score. Washington won the game 9 to 8. Detroit won their one game, so the Dukes lead dropped to 5 games, but they had clinched a tie for the pennant.

The team would end the season on the road with games in Philadelphia and Boston. Would they clinch the American League Championship tomorrow in Philadelphia? Dave would be the starting pitcher. They left the stadium after the game for Penn station and a train trip to Philadelphia.

Shibe Park
New York at Philadelphia
2:30 PM September 27, 1950

To Dave, this will be the most important game of the season. It was an opportunity to clinch the pennant and be in the World Series in his first year in the major leagues. He started off well, retiring the first nine batters, all on ground outs.

In the third inning something occurred that violated one of baseball's unwritten rules. For example if an umpire makes a mistake on a fly ball trapped and not caught in the outfield and calls an out the player does not correct the umpire even though the player knows he trapped the ball. The same goes for a tag not made or a pitch that did not hit a batter. With two outs in the third inning the batter hit a ball up the first base line about two feet fair. Dave ran to the ball picked it up, and while running beside the base runner swiped at his uniform as he ran to first base. The first base umpire standing behind and to the right of first base was slow in running to see the play. He called the runner out. Dave went to the umpire and talked to him. The umpire shook his head and Dave walked off the field while the Phillies protested to no avail. He told B.B. that he had missed the tag and that's what he told the ump. Dave had violated one of baseball's unwritten rules by being honest.

The Dukes scored a run in the fourth inning on Vic Marko's 39th home run. The score stayed 1 to 0 until the seventh inning when Randy White hit a two run home run. It gave the Dukes a 3 to 0 lead. Dave had allowed only three hits on few pitches. Dave pitched to the minimum six batters in the eighth and ninth innings, making just 15 pitches. The Dukes had won the game 3-0 and the American League pennant! The game had taken only one hour and forty-five minutes!

After the game some of the writers wanted to talk to Dave about what he had said to the umpire in the third inning. Dave said he wouldn't talk about it until they had talked to Vic and Randy. They hit the home runs that won the game.

Finally he told the writers and a few of the players standing around his locker what he had said to the umpire. That was all there was to it. Now, "gentlemen I would like to celebrate the win and our winning the pennant."

In his first year in the American League, Dave had won 26 games and lost two. He had pitched 28 complete games, 255-1/2 innings. His ERA was .74 and he had walked only 13 batters. To top it off, he had hit .326.

When Dave returned to the hotel he called his mother to tell her the good news. Dave described the game to her including all the little things that result in a win. She was happy for Dave and sorry she and George could not attend the World Series. The schedule of the games and Dave's OCS reporting date made it too indefinite to plan the trip.

New York City
New York
7:00 AM September 28, 1950

On the sports page of the New York Tribune under the byline of Dane Sullivan a column was headed Dave Mason Did Something I've Never Seen Before.

In yesterday's game that clinched the American League pennant for the New York Dukes Dave Mason did something I have never seen before during playing and watching hundreds of baseball games. In the third inning with two outs a Phillies batter hit a ball up the first baseline just fair by a couple of feet. Dave Mason chased the ball down, picked it up swiped at the runner with a tag. The first base umpire running a bit late to the play called the runner out. Dave went to the umpire and told him he did not tag the runner so he was safe at first. The umpire shook his head and did not change his call. The Phillies protested to no avail.

Later when I asked Dave what happened he said, "I missed tagging the runner and told the umpire. So my conscience was clear." Why did the umpire not change his call? Did he not want to be shown up to be wrong? Was he protecting that unwritten rule of baseball that a player never admits to the umpire that he didn't tag a runner catch a fly ball or wasn't hit by a pitch? Unless the supervisor of umpires of the American League make a public criticism of the umpire we'll never know.

New York at Philadelphia
5:15 PM September 28, 1950

Jake Filner pitched and the Dukes won 8 to 6. Soon after the game the team was on a train back to New York. There was no game tomorrow. The season would end with games on Saturday and Sunday in Boston.

Dave's Apartment
9:00 AM October 2, 1950

The team won on Saturday and lost on Sunday in Boston. Ed Card, Bob Pennell and Tom Harris had pitched. Ozzie Felton had rested the pitchers who would pitch in the World Series. Dave and B. B. had arrived home at midnight.

Dave had lots to do today. Flushing Transfer & Storage would pick up the items he was having stored tomorrow morning. Dave was calling Jill to tell her where they would go to dinner tonight. Dave had promised her a night out in Manhattan. "Good morning Jill." "Good morning Dave." "I'd like you to put on that beautiful I. Magnin red dress for our date tonight. We are going to dinner at the Astor Hotel on Times Square. Tommy Dorsey and his band are opening tonight." "Oh, that sounds exciting Dave. I only wish it wasn't another of our parting dates." "Yes Jill, it seems to be our fate. I'll come to the apartment at 6:30. We have an eight o'clock dinner reservation." "I'll see you then."

Dave took Don Frank and B.B. Katcher to lunch. He wanted to thank Don for charting and counting his pitches during the season. He was going to give him a bonus payment for the good work he did. Dave had helped B.B. buy a Chevrolet from Turner Chevrolet that he would pick at the assembly plant and drive home to Redwood City. Dave told B.B he was sorry the appearance at Turner had not worked out.

Late in the afternoon Dave called Sharon. Mrs. Knox answered. "Hello Mrs. Knox, this is Dave Mason" "Hello Dave, how are you?" "I couldn't be better." "Are you ready for the World Series?" "I sure am." "Here's Sharon." "Hello Dave I'll bet you are busy." "Yes I am Sharon." "But you're never too busy to do what you say you're going to do Dave. I like that." "I try to do what I promise. I'm moving out of my apartment tomorrow and will stay in the Flushing Hotel when we return from Philadelphia. Will you attend the games Friday and Saturday?" "I'll be there to watch you pitch on Friday Dave. Dad wants to take another customer to the game on Saturday, so I'm giving up my seat."

"Good for you Sharon."

"Can we exchange post cards while I'm in Texas?" "Sure Dave, just send me your address." "I'll do that Sharon. I'll try to stop by your box after the game on Friday if the writers don't keep me too long." "Oh, that would be great!" "Okay, hopefully I'll see you then. Goodbye Sharon." "Goodbye Dave."

The Astor Hotel
Times Square
New York City, New York
9:00 PM October 2, 1950

Jill and Dave were eating their desert when the strains of Marie, Tommy Dorsey's theme song filled the dinning room. As soon as they finished eating Dave said, "May I have this dance Miss. Garber?" "I don't know Mr. Mason, I hardly know you." They both laughed. Please hold me tight Dave. I don't want to lose you." Jill and Dave danced to a Dorsey favorite, I'm Getting Sentimental Over You. They danced the night away, staying until the last dance at midnight.

On the way home, Dave drove by Turner Chevrolet to show Jill where to bring the car for service and any problems. "I have advised Turner that you will be bringing the car in for service so they won't be surprised." "Thanks Dave."

Dave's Apartment
8:00 AM October 3, 1950

Dave had the storage boxes packed along with his furniture ready for pick up by Flushing Transfer. He was keeping only the clothes and items he needed for traveling.

Dave called Jill and said, "I'll need to pick you up at 6:30 Saturday morning. My flight departs at 8:15. What time do you return on Friday?" "I'm on a later flight that day, and arrival is scheduled for 5:15. "Okay, I'll call as soon as I can after the game, to get an ETA, but if I'm not there, I suggest you call the hotel and leave a message. In any case, let's plan to have dinner." "I'll look forward to that Dave. Win your games in Philadelphia." "Have a good flight Jill."

Shibe Park
Philadelphia, Pennsylvania
World Series Game One
New York at Philadelphia
2:00 PM October 4, 1950

The Dukes had taken a 3:00 PM train the day before, arriving in Philadelphia at 4:35. Manager Ozzie Felton had announced the pitchers for the first four games of the series. Doug Abbott was the starter today to be followed by Lindsey Barrett, Dave Mason and Vic Carlisle.

Felton said he favored veteran pitchers in World Series games. Mason would pitch the third game only because he must leave the next morning for Air Force Officer training in Texas. Felton said, "Louis Leon and Ed Card would be in the bullpen in addition to Ed Edgar.

The Philadelphia Phillies, winners of the National League Pennant was a veteran team with three young players who became stars this season. However one of the pitchers had been drafted into the army and wasn't available to pitch. It would leave the team short of starting pitchers. The starting pitcher for Philadelphia today would be Phil Bell, the Phillies leading pitcher with a record of 25 wins and 10 losses.

The game was a pitchers duel for the first four innings. In the top of the fifth inning, Billy Duke led off with a single. Passing up a sacrifice, manager Felton had Bill Wood try to move the runner and he did. He hit a ball hard between first and second for a long single that allowed Duke to run to third. Now there were runners on first and third and no outs. Cliff Nelson singled to centerfield, scoring Duke and moving Wood to second. Runners now on first and second and there were still no outs. With Vic Marko coming to bat and a base open, he would likely get a free pass.

The Phillies manager held a meeting on the mound with his pitcher. The discussion was whether to walk Marko and pitch to B.B. Katcher who had hit ten home runs since being called up from

Buffalo. The home plate umpire broke up the conference, and Marko was given an intentional walk.

The bases were loaded with no outs. The rookie, B.B. Katcher was coming to bat. B.B. worked the count to 2-2. The next pitch was a good fast ball on the inside of the plate but B.B. adjusted, backing away and getting enough wood on the pitch to hit a 360 foot grand slam home run. The Dukes now led 5 to 0. That was the end of the scoring. Doug Abbott held Philadelphia to two hits and only walked two batters. Dave was the first player out of the dugout to congratulate Abbott. Next he gave B.B. a big hug and said, "What did I tell you about the girls."

B.B. was the center of attention of the writers, radio and TV people. It was the most interviews B.B. had ever given.

Just watching a World Series game was a thrill for Dave. He did chart the game from the dugout so he would be prepared for Friday's game.

That evening Dave, Randy White and B.B. went to see the movie "Francis," the horse, staring Donald O'Connor, Patricia Medina and Zasu Pitts. It was hilarious.

Shibe Park
Philadelphia, Pennsylvania
New York at Philadelphia
World Series Game Two
2:00 PM October 5, 1950

Today it was Lindsey Barrett on the mound for the Dukes. Could he match the pitching of Doug Abbott in game one? Les Minor was the pitcher for the Phillies. He had been the team's third starter during the season.

The Dukes wasted no time today in producing runs. Wood and Hoff singled with one out in the first inning. With runners on first and second, Philadelphia pitched to Vic Marko. With a three ball, no strike count, Vic got the green light, and hit a home run over the centerfield fence, 393 feet away. The Dukes led 3-0. The Dukes added two runs in the fifth inning, making the score 5-0. Philadelphia scored one run in the seventh inning, but no more. The Dukes won the game 5 to 1 for a two to nothing lead in the series. Were the Dukes going to sweep the series?

The team took a Pennsylvania Railroad train to Penn Station, arriving in New York at 7:35 PM. Dave and B.B called a cab from Dukes Stadium that took B.B. to his apartment and Dave to the Flushing Hotel. Dave went to bed early.

Dukes Stadium
Queens, New York
Philadelphia at New York
World Series Game Three
1:00 PM October 6, 1950

Preparing for the biggest game he had ever pitched in, Dave was surprisingly calm. He thought he would be more "pumped up." He had stopped at the Knox box to see Sharon. He wasn't sure he would have time after the game. He had a good warm up and was ready to pitch as soon as the National Anthem was sung. Philadelphia was sending a part time starter and reliever to the mound today.

Dave started the game allowing the lead off batter to single to center field. Then he retired the side on five pitches, all ground balls to the infield. There was no score through four innings. In the top of the fifth inning, the Dukes put two runners on base with one out. B.B. Katcher singled to right field. J. B. Felton struck out, but Jim Essick singled to center field. Two runners were on base with one out. Larry Mann popped out to the catcher. With two outs Dave was coming to bat. He hit the first pitch down the third base line for a double scoring B.B. and Essick. It gave the Dukes a 2-0 lead. Billy Duke beat out a slow roller to third base and Dave had to hold at second. Bill Wood worked the count to 3 and 2 and hit a single over second base. Dave scored and the Dukes still had two men on base. With the score 3 to 0, all the scoring had come with two outs. Tommy Hoff fouled off six pitches with a 2-2 count, then hit a double in the left centerfield gap scoring Duke and Wood and the Dukes had a 5-0 lead. Vic Marko then flied out to deep centerfield, to end the inning.

With the big lead Dave worked with his usual speed and threw just fourteen pitches over the next three innings. He had allowed just two hits at the end of the seventh.

The Philadelphia lead off man singled in the eighth, but that was the last hit Dave allowed. He retired the next six batters on 13 pitches and the Dukes had won game three. When the last Philadelphia batter was thrown out at first base, the crowd gave Dave a standing ovation that was overwhelming. Many of the fans knew that Dave was pitching today because he was leaving for Texas tomorrow for Air Force officers training. Dave had pitched a three hit shut out in his first World Series game.

Dave had a long session with the baseball writers and radio broadcasters. During one interview B.B. was making faces at Dave in the background. It was all Dave could do to avoid laughing.

Even though the game lasted just a little over two hours, Dave could not call to check on Jill's flight until 5:15. He learned it was twenty minutes late, so he had time to get to the airport.

La Guardia Airport
5:45 PM October 6, 1950

Dave checked at the ticket counter to learn when Jill's flight had arrived. Advised it had been in for ten minutes, Dave started walking to the gate. He was getting close when he saw three stewardesses walking towards him. One of the girls said, "Here comes your hero Jill." "Hi hero," Jill said. One of the stewardess that Dave didn't know said the co-pilot embarrassed Jill by announcing the score of the game and saying the winning pitcher was Dave Mason and that will make one of our stewardess mighty happy. "Dave this is Marlina and this is Susan." "Hello girls." "Oh that Jim Wise has teased me ever since he learned that Dave was my boy friend. Jim's a big baseball fan."

"Well girls, other than being a little late was it a good flight?" Jill said, "Most of the businessmen were too tired to act up, so it was okay." "I'll get the car Jill and meet you in front. It was nice to meet you girls."

Golden Pheasant Restaurant
Westbury, New York
7:00 PM October 6, 1950

They had arrived for dinner and Jill was wearing a beautiful corsage Dave had bought while she changed her clothes. "Here we are Dave, another last dinner before we part again." "Yes Jill. If we make it through this separation, I think we will be good for life. We can be together again on January 13, 1951 if you accept my invitation to come to Texas to attend my graduation from OCS. I'll send you an airline ticket." "Oh Dave, if I can get off work, I'll be there." "Great. Now, let's enjoy our dinner and not think about the separation." And they did, eating a nice lobster dinner with piano and organ music in the background.

In Jill's apartment with Jill sitting on Dave's lap, they had their last kisses for three months. Dave departed at 10:30, saying he would pick Jill up at 6:30 in the morning.

Dave's flight departed at 8:15.

Chapter Thirty

Approaching San Antonio, Texas

American Airlines Flight 1340

4:20 PM October 7, 1950

DAVE HAD READ and slept during most of the trip today. He changed planes in Dallas for the short flight to San Antonio. The fourth game of the World Series should be over by now, but there had been no announcement from the cockpit. He would have to wait until he arrived in San Antonio.

After deplaning, he searched for the World Series game score while he waited for his luggage. He had asked a number of people, but none knew the score. Dave decided Texan's were not big baseball fans. Finally, he asked a porter who said, "I sure do, I had a bet on it and I won $10.00 because the Dukes won 5 to 1 and swept the series." Dave thanked him, gave him a tip and collected his luggage. Then he looked for transportation to Lackland AFB.

Dukes Stadium
4:35 PM October 7, 1950

The celebration was on. Champagne was being sprayed around the clubhouse. The Dukes had won their fourth World Series in a row. In the win today that gave the Dukes a sweep, Vic Carlisle pitched a six hitter and the Dukes won 6 to 1. Carlisle was the fourth of the

Dukes pitchers to go the route, pitching a complete game. In the four games, no relief pitcher even warmed up.

It was redemption for the pitching staff that had struggled at times during the season. Manager Ozzie Felton said, "I never lost faith in my pitching staff even though they did have some bad times during the season. I'm sorry Dave Mason is not here to enjoy our victory, because he covered for us when we had injuries and our pitchers were having problems. I'm just happy he'll be back with us next year."

The Dukes veteran catcher, J. B. Felton announced his retirement following the game. Felton has been the Dukes' regular catcher since the 1939 season, less three years out during the war. A 1938 Boston College graduate, Felton became the regular catcher after just one partial season in the Pacific Coast League playing for the Oakland Oaks. Felton 34, said, my oldest boy is eleven and with four other children, it's time to be a family man. Felton will again join Lorton & Company, the seafood firm he spent three years working for during the war. Felton's wife is a member of the Lorton family. Felton was one of the Dukes players who refused to fly. Asked if that was a consideration, Felton said, "I hadn't thought about the flying issue for next season. My focus was on my family's needs."

Felton's retirement will give B.B. Katcher the opportunity to move back to his regular position. Kattcher was called up from Buffalo in late June to supply some power the Dukes were lacking. He hit twelve home runs had 32 runs batted in and a batting average of .295. Katcher will need to improve his defensive catching and throwing to be the regular.

OCS Cadet Barracks
Lackland AFB
San Antonio, Texas
5:45 PM October 7, 1950

Dave was entering the two man room assigned to him when he reported in. He was greeted by a fellow with a "drawl." Dave said, "I'm Dave Mason. Are you a Texan?" "Guilty." And you are that pitching sensation of the New York Dukes." "I'm a pitcher for the Dukes, but I don't claim to be a sensation." They both laughed. "My name is Rex Reynolds. My home town is right here in San Antonio, but I went to Purdue to study airport management. It looked like it had a promising future and still does. But I didn't figure on another war." "When did you graduate Rex?" "Just last June. I had a starting job here at the airport lined up, being an all around flunky. It started a week after graduation. I had worked every summer here during college. Then, two weeks later this war starts and I knew I would be in it when the draft was started.

I was advised to check out the Air Force where I could get valuable experience while getting paid. I thought about the four year sign up for a while, but decided I should sign up instead of wasting two years in the army." "So you're on active duty?" "Yes sir, for four years, after the commission. Now I've been rambling away. I know you are a baseball player, but how'd you get here?"

"Yes I'm now a baseball player, but I was trained to be an aeronautical engineer with a heavy emphasis on maintenance engineering. Cal Poly in California is my college. By my senior year I had decided I didn't want to work in maintenance, but my instructors convinced me I should take the CAA tests for my Aircraft and Engine Licenses. I'm glad I did, because it helped get me into a MATS reserve outfit where I can use my education and training instead of two years in the army. Even though I had to sign up for the four year hitch it allows me to continue to play baseball." "So how did you get to OCS?" "Well, I started as a lowly Airman, last class mechanic. I didn't want any favoritism, and they didn't give me any."

"Then on our two weeks summer training I impressed the Colonel and he gave me the opportunity to attend. I was advised to accept for a number of reasons, the most important to me is management experience and when I would go home in the off season, I will have a higher priority to ride MATS flights to get to weekend duty. After OCS, I'm signed up for ten weeks of engineering officer training. That's my story." "You'll go back to the MATS reserve outfit after all this?" "Yes. I'll likely be an assistant maintenance officer, or they could give me something else if they have other needs." "It's after six Dave, no it's what, 1800, and they both laughed." They told me the mess would open at 1800, so lets go see how the food it." "That sounds good to me."

Dave and Rex joined a table of cadets and introduced themselves. The food was very good. Rex said, "At least the food will be good."

Office of the President
New York Dukes Baseball Club
Queens, New York
10:00 AM November 3, 1950

President Fred Duke had asked General Manager Don Newton to come to his office and bring a list of initial contract amounts to be included in the 1951 player contracts. Newton reported the total was under the budgeted amount by $20,000. Newton said, "I'm sure we will get some contracts returned with requests for increases." "The only contract I'm interested in is for Dave Mason, said Fred. How much have you increased him?" "I gave him a bit less than a 50 percent increase to $8,000. When we win the Series again in 1951 he'll make at least $15,000."

"I think we must consider that Dave is more than a baseball hero. Now he's a patriotic hero, and I'm sure the Air Force PR people will have the papers flooded with articles about his graduation from OCS in January. He didn't accept your first offer last year, as I remember." "That's true. He wanted $6,000, the $1,000 per month he was paid in the PCL. We settled for $5,500. With his Series money he made over 12,000, more than enough for a rookie." "I think we got our monies worth Don and I don't want any negative PR regarding Dave. He is a Dukes hero to New Yorkers and we must keep that image going. Increase him to $10,000. I think that will make Dave happy and we won't have a problem." "I think it's too much Fred but I understand the position we're in."

"Next week when Damon Minor (Director of Scouting) and all the scouts are here, I want you to tell Damon that our priority for 1951 is to sign Black baseball players. My fan surveys have convinced me they will be accepted. We are behind the other American League teams with the exception of Boston in developing Black players, and we must catch up. If we don't, I think the other teams will pass us up." "You know my feeling about it, but I'll do what you say" "Thank you Don."

Lackland Air Force Base
1630 13 November 1950

Dave had received a large mailing envelope at mail call from his dad. Enclosed was a letter and the 1951 Dukes contract. The contract was the first thing Dave looked at. He saw the amount of $10,000 and was amazed! He hadn't thought too much about it because he was just too busy with OCS. He had guessed it would be $7,500. It made him very happy. A new letter signed by manager Ozzie Felton covered Dave's batting practice with the position players. The Dukes must want to keep me happy. Dave signed the contract and mailed it the next day.

Then Dave read the letter from his dad. George Mason reported Dave's world series check in the amount of $6,700, had arrived. Per Dave's instructions, it had been deposited in Dave's savings account. Dave's dad wanted to know if Dave wanted any money from the check. Dave would write to his dad, requesting $670.00 so he could send his tithe to the Menlo Park Presbyterian Church. Since March, Dave had been mailing his monthly tithe to the church on all his income. In addition, he had been giving $25.00 per month to Fifth Avenue Presbyterian Church.

General Manager's Office
The Dukes Baseball Club
1:30 PM November 15, 1950

Donald Newton was talking to veteran catcher Bill Parks of the San Francisco Sea Lions via telephone. Parks had been a back up catcher for the Dukes after the war. He was an outstanding defensive catcher and a good handler of pitchers. His poor hitting sent him back to the Sea Lions where he had played before the war.

The purpose of Newton's call was to contract with Parks to instruct B.B Katcher in the catching skills. "He needs work in throwing to second base, catching pop ups and calling pitches. I'm offering you a contract for six weeks of work with Katcher starting in January. I'll make it worth your while Bill and named a figure" Bill said, "I agree." "Okay, I'll call Katcher and then let you know I've talked to him. Then you can call him and set up a schedule." Parks said, "I'll look forward to your call Don."

Aboard an Air Force B-29
30,000 feet over Eastern Texas
2115 28 November, 1950

Dave was sitting in the bombardier's seat in the nose of the bomber. The aircraft was on the trip back to Kelly AFB, next to Lackland in San Antonio. This was a familiarization flight for six officer cadets. They had taken off from Kelly early yesterday morning and flown to Brookley AFB in Mobile, Alabama. It was a base Dave had visited during the summer training of MATS. A tour was conducted of the big supply base. It was more extensive than that of his summer trip. Also, the base was much busier than in August. More supplies and equipment were being received for shipment to Korea.

The return flight had been planned for evening, so the cadets could experience night flying. Dave had a great seat in the nose of the bomber.

He thought back to the description of the dropping of the first atomic bomb over Japan in 1945, and the bombardier who released it. But now he was thinking about the past seven weeks of OCS.

The Sunday morning after reporting in, Dave was awake early because of the time change. He put on his uniform and went for a walk to look around the area. Returning to his room, he started his devotions with his Bible. Rex soon woke up, and seeing Dave's Bible, he said in a somewhat surprised voice, "You're a Christian Dave?" "I'm also guilty of that Rex." "Well shake, Brother, I'm a Baptist, Southern style." "I'm a member of the Presbyterian Church but I've attended Baptist evening services to hear sermons."

Following orientation they had studied Air Force organization and history, military law, leadership and tactics. They had daily physical training (PT) and twice a week they played basketball or volley ball. There had been no passes to town until Thanksgiving Day. Rex Reynolds had invited Dave and two other cadets to have Thanksgiving dinner with his family. Rex and Dave had become good friends and Dave accompanied Rex and his family to the Thanksgiving Eve service at the First Baptist Church. Dr. Fred Reynolds, a prominent San Antonio surgeon was the father of Rex, whose family included, mother Lucy, and a younger sister and brother.

Initially Dave was known only to the baseball fans among the cadets. Then articles in the local and base newspapers told of Dave being selected as the Rookie of the Year in the American League. This was followed by the articles on the vote for the most valuable player. The vote was split between Vic Marko and Dave that allowed Sam Nell, the Detroit third sacker to win the award. Instead of voting for one of the Dukes players, the baseball writers who covered the Dukes, split their vote.

Dave had written weekly postcards to Jill, his parents and Sharon. He had recently written letters to Jill and his mother and dad, inviting them to his graduation ceremony on January 13, 1951. Jill's post cards had become short ones on United Airlines cards. Sharon had written more and longer cards. Jill reported she and Dorothy had gone to Manhattan to shop. She said the stores were much larger than those in San Francisco. Dave was thinking more about his relationship with Jill.

The weekly briefing on the Korean War was the most interesting to Dave. Particularly the after action reports of the Air Force. When he arrived, it appeared the war would soon be over. Then on 25 October, Chinese troops who had hidden in North Korea, after crossing the Yalu River, attacked. Two ROK divisions were wiped out. The right flank of the eighth army was exposed and they had to retreat.

Captured Chinese soldiers reported 300,000 troops were in North Korea. In twenty degree weather, the First Marine division was soon retreating under enemy fire.

Air Force B-29s bombers, F-51 fighters and F-80s, the first Air Force jet fighters to fly in combat, bombed the twin main bridges over the Yalu that linked Autung and Simuiju.

On November 8th, the first all jet air dog fight had occurred between U.S. F-80s and Russian MIG-15s flown by Chinese pilots. The F-80, at least 120 miles per hour slower than the MIG, shot down one while we had lost no planes. The Red fighters would flee across the Yalu following their incursion into North Korea, a sanctuary where U. S. planes were ordered not to follow. If the MIGs continued to come across the border of the Yalu, it was expected the Air Force would rush F-86 fighters to Korea. It was a much improved fighter over the F-80.

The extensive deployment of F-51 aircraft was because many were stored in the Far East and were readily available. The Air Force knew the North Korean Air Force had no jets. Also, there were more ground crews with experience on propeller fighters than jets. However, the F-80s based in the Philippines, had been immediately sent to Korea.

An offensive by U.N. forces on 25 November had died when they were attacked by 180,000 Chinese supported by artillery.

A change from level flight to a decent, brought Dave out of his thoughts and he prepared for landing.

Lackland Air Force Base
1900 29 November 1950

Dave was writing another letter to Jill because he had not received an answer to his invitation to attend his graduation. He invited her to come for the weekend and repeated his offer to send her an airline ticket. He said his parents would be attending. George Mason had advised Dave he and Ann would attend, traveling by train.

1730 15 December 1950

Dave had received a letter from Jill. Before he opened the envelope he thought she's not coming to the graduation. Dave went for a walk before he opened the envelope. He would read it while he walked. He was right. She wasn't coming. She said she couldn't get the time off, even vacation time. She blamed it on the continuing shortage of stewardesses. Dave had to accept her reasons, but was skeptical. He had been doing more thinking about Jill and the differences in their interests.

After dinner he returned to his room and wrote a letter to Sharon, inviting her to the graduation. He made his offer to send her an airline ticket.

1635 22 December 1950

Dave had been called to the orderly room. He arrived, wondering what the call was about.

The Corporal on duty said "I have a special delivery registered letter for you." "Oh, that's a surprise." "Do you know a Miss. Sharon Knox?" "Oh, yes I do," Dave said in a surprised voice. "Sign here." Dave read the letter as he walked back to his room.

Wednesday
December 20, 1950

Dear Dave,

Thank you so much for your invitation to your graduation from OCS. I enthusiastically accept your invitation. I'm so proud of you Dave. My parents have approved my trip and you don't have to send me a ticket. Dad will pay for my trip. Please let me know when I should arrive and depart

As I have said before Dave, I support your service to our country.

Sincerely,
Sharon

It was 9:00 AM the next morning and Dave was in the telephone center to place a call to Sharon. "Operator" "Operator, I'd like to place a person to person call to Miss. Sharon Knox in New York City. The number is MU 3-2855 and this Dave Mason." "One moment please." The phone call was answered by Mrs. Knox. "This is the operator. I have a person to person call for Miss. Sharon Knox from Mr. Dave Mason." "Just a minute please." "Hello." "Is this Miss. Sharon Knox?" "Yes." "Go ahead sir." "Good morning Sharon, how are you?" "I'm fine Dave, did you get my letter?" "Yes I did and that's why I'm calling. I suggest you plan to arrive on Thursday afternoon, January 11th. I will have that day free to visit with friends and family. I will make a hotel reservation for you where my parents are staying. How does that sound?" "Oh, that's great Dave." "I would like you to stay through Sunday, if you can, returning Monday morning." "I'll talk to dad about that Dave, but I think that will be okay." I'm looking forward to seeing you for three full days Dave!" "I'm so glad you wanted to attend my graduation Sharon." "Thank you Dave." "Please let me know your schedule and flight numbers." "I will Dave, and thanks for calling." "You're welcome Sharon. Goodbye." "Goodbye Dave."

Dave was "Happy as a clam." I'll have to call home and explain why Sharon is coning instead of Jill.

Field House
Lackland Air Force Base
1400 23 December 1950

Dave was playing basketball in a pick up game. The Christmas leave of ten days had started at 1200. Dave decided not to go to New York. If he did, he wouldn't see Jill very much because she would be working during the busy holidays. He would soon see his parents. Rex had invited him to spend the Christmas weekend with his family. Dave had asked his dad if he could get tickets to the Cotton Bowl football game for them. George Mason said he would see what he could do. Dave also wanted to use the time during the week to study for the final examinations coming up in January.

George Mason was able to get two press box tickets for Dave. He advised Dave they should act like sports writers by bringing notebooks and taking notes. They planned to take the train to Dallas and return by American Airlines. The game was between Texas and Tennessee.

Dave and those in today's basketball game were all staying on base. They had agreed to play a game every afternoon at 1400 starting next Tuesday. They agreed it would keep them in better shape than those who were going home to eat big Christmas dinners. Dave thought he was in the best condition he had been in for some time. He had lost five pounds, so now weighed 185.

Kiwanis Club of San Antonio
San Antonio, Texas
12:00 noon December 29, 1950

Dave had come into town to get his first make up in weeks. There had been articles in the San Antonio newspaper about Dave Mason, baseball player who was in the OCS class at Lackland AFB. None of the articles mentioned that Dave was a member of Kiwanis so club members were surprised when Dave signed in as a member of the Kiwanis Club of San Francisco.

The club had a program to support children and families of service men who were away from their family. Dave had a happy $5.00 to support the program. A report was given on last week's Christmas meeting for children from these and other needy families.

When Dave sent his make up to San Francisco he included a note that explained why he was in Texas.

The Cotton Bowl Texas State Fairgrounds Dallas, Texas 5:15 PM January 1, 1951

The game, played before a crowd of more than 75,000 had just ended. Tennessee won an exciting game in the last three minutes, 20 to 14. Going into the game, each team had lost only one game during the regular season. However Texas was favored because of their outstanding defense. The Texas team out weighed Tennessee by ten pounds per man.

The score was 14 to 13 for Texas when Tennessee recovered a Texas fumble on the Texas 43 yard line with less than five minutes to go. A pass from tailback Hank Lauricella to Burt Rechichar took the ball to the Texas 17. Runs by Lauricella and fullback Andy Kozar set up the touchdown scored by Kozar on a blast through center. Only three minutes remained when the touchdown was scored.

It was a big comeback for Tennessee. Trailing 14 to 7 at half time, the Volunteers missed an opportunity to tie the game in the fourth quarter, when the conversion was missed. Dave and Rex had decided to divide up their recording of the game to look like sports writers. Rex, of course took Texas and Dave took Tennessee. They even had a small wager of a lunch on the outcome. So Rex was sad and Dave was happy, but they both enjoyed the exciting game. It was well worth the cost of flying to the game.

They had changed their plans and had flown to Dallas early this morning. It saved the cost of a motel and meals. They had come directly to the Cotton Bowl from the airport. They would return tonight on a 7:30 flight.

During the flight Rex took a nap. Dave thought about the last month of training. It had included budgeting and payroll, aircraft and equipment, tables of organization and equipment, and weapons firing. They also had a survival exercise, similar to the one Dave experienced during the MATS summer training. Since his record included his leadership of that exercise, he was not a team leader.

However their group had a good leader and had a high score. The daily physical training (PT) and frequent basketball and volleyball games was something Dave looked forward to. It also was a good release from studying.

Field house
Lackland Air Force Base
1400 13 January 1951

It was graduation day for OCS Class 04-50. Dave was seated with the 49 other candidates, soon to be Second Lieutenants in the Air Force Reserve. George and Anne Mason and Sharon Knox were seated in the section for family and friends.

As the speeches began, Dave thought about the last six weeks of Korean War briefings. The Chinese had come into to war in October. During the retreat from the Yalu, the Air Force had dropped tons of supplies to the retreating U.N forces. Air Force ground crews had been evacuated by stuffing them into B-26 bomb bays and any other airplane. It was a heroic retreat from the Yalu through the central mountains of North Korea. Those on the east flank, who were cut off, had to be evacuated by sea.

An Air Force C-119 Flying Boxcar had dropped an entire prefabricated bridge to the 1st Marine Division so they could bridge a 1500 foot deep gorge to allow retreat. The two sections of the bridge each weighed two tons.

To slow the Chinese offensive, the Air Force flew hundreds of missions. Using heavy Mark VIII flares, developed to light up wide areas of ocean for air-sea rescue, C-47 "Lightning Bugs" were deployed. The flares were dropped by parachute and were timed to light at 5000 feet. The flares illuminated several square miles of ground at near daylight intensity. This allowed aircraft to attack the hordes of Chinese troops with napalm bombs of jellied gasoline. An Air Force pilot had described the throngs of Chinese soldiers as an army of ants on the march or a scene from a Hollywood Biblical epic. Not since Valley Forge, had American troops suffered such appalling winter conditions of twenty below zero.

In early December the former capital of North Korea, Pyongyang, was abandoned by U.N forces. Thousands of civilians, sick of the oppression in North Korea, joined the throngs heading south with the armies.

On December 23, Lt. General John Walker, Commanding Officer of the 8th Army was killed in a jeep accident, in which the driver and two other passengers survived. The next morning Lt. General Matthew Ridgway was appointed to replace Walker. Dave reflected on how bad the war had turned since he arrived at Lackland, as he awaited the awarding of commissions to the men of class 04-50.

The speaker, the Air Force General in charge of training, was about to speak. In his opening remarks, he said, "I'm here because I place such a high priority on officer leadership in our Air Force. The innovative leadership being provided by Air Force officers in Korea as I speak has been critical to the successful retreat of our ground forces. So I want to impress upon you, how important your leadership role will be in your Air Force service."

At the conclusion of the general's remarks, it was announced that he would now present the award to the officer candidate with the highest grade of class 04-50.

The award was earned and will be presented to Airman David D. Mason. Airman Mason achieved the highest score of any officer candidate since Air Force OCS was initiated in 1947. Airman Mason, please come forward. Dave was presented with a beautiful plaque.

Then the commissions with the gold bars of a Second Lieutenant were awarded to each officer candidate.

The Antonio Hotel
San Antonio, Texas
7:00 PM January 13, 1951

Dave, his mother, father and Sharon were having dinner in the hotel dinning room. It had been an overwhelming day for Dave. While he was aware that he had been achieving a high grade during the training, no scores had been posted since December 22nd. Dave's practice of not having big expectations had made the award a surprise. It had made George Mason a beaming proud father. After his parents had given him big hugs, Sharon wrapped her arms around Dave's neck and gave him a big kiss. She was so excited she could hardly contain herself.

Dave had introduced Rex Reynolds to his parents and Sharon. Then Dr. and Mrs. Reynolds met Dave's parents.

Rex had received orders to report to Hamilton Air Force Base in California. He would serve as an assistant airport operations officer.

Following dinner the Masons and Sharon went to the Mason suite and visited. Soon Dave and Sharon went to her room. They talked about the next ten weeks of Dave's training and when he would return to New York. Dave said it would be in early April following spring training in Florida. The 1951 season starts in mid April.

Dave asked how her junior year was progressing at Columbia. Sharon said, "My subjects mean so much more to me now that I have experienced working in a law firm." "I was sure it would Sharon. You can't beat learn-by-doing. Have you thought about what you will do this coming summer?" "I haven't decided yet Dave, but dad has talked to me about working for the firm to learn about Wall Street." "Oh, that would be interesting. If you still want to be a Wall Street lawyer, the more you know about the street will be an advantage." "Yes, and I'd like to be in New York to see a certain baseball pitcher play the game." "Oh, you mean you have a crush on another baseball player?" They both laughed. "You like to laugh, don't you Dave?" "I sure do. Laughter is important in life."

Dave and Sharon watched an interesting TV program on San Antonio and the history of the Alamo. At midnight Dave departed Sharon's room after a goodnight kiss at the door. As he walked back to the Mason suite, he thought, I've tried to resist it, but I think I'm getting close to considering Sharon more than jus a good friend. I really don't know her yet, but I would like to know her better. Am I ready to end my relationship with Jill? That will require more thought. The next ten weeks will give me plenty of time to think about it.

Chapter Thirty One

Lackland Air Force Base

1330 15 January 1951

DAVE HAD MOVED out of his OCS room on Saturday afternoon, taking his bags to the hotel. This morning he reported in for the Engineering & Maintenance training school and was assigned a room in a different barracks building. He didn't have a roommate yet. The reporting in deadline was 2400 tonight. The training orientation was scheduled for the next day at 0800 hours.

Yesterday morning, Dave had accompanied Sharon to the airport and to her flight. They agreed to write a weekly post card to each other. Dave's parents would depart on the Sunset Limited today.

Dave's main concern now was to find a catcher who he could pitch to. Since he would be late reporting to spring training he needed to get his arm in shape. He had talked to Sergeant Jones who was in charge of physical training to learn if he knew of a catcher, either softball or baseball. Sgt. Jones said he would talk to a soft ball player he knew and let Dave know.

Dave walked to the field house to see Sgt. Jones. "Congratulations Dave. I heard you were the top OCS man. If it was basketball and volleyball, I knew you would be the top man." "Thanks, Sergeant." "Did you contact the softball player you talked about?" "Yes I did. He said his catcher of last season was transferred, but he knows one who is retired here in San Antonio and he will contact him. Check back with me in a week." "Okay, I will." "Are there any pick up games going on this afternoon?" "No one has been in for a ball, so I doubt it. How long is your next school?" Ten weeks." "Well, you should be in great shape for baseball when you leave here." "Yes, I'm in my best shape ever right now."

On the way back to his room, Dave stopped at the post library. He had heard about a baseball pitcher by the name of Cy Young who had won more games than any other in the history of baseball. Dave wanted to find out about this pitcher. Dave found a good book on baseball and learned that Cy was a nick name for Denton True Young. However his teammates had started calling him Cy, short for Cyrus, a name the author called a scornful one. Dave looked forward to reading about Denton T. Young.

Returning to his room, Dave met his roommate. To his surprise, he was Tom Sanderson, who had been a Cal Poly aero student a year behind Dave. They both decided it was a small world. Dave asked Tom, "How did you get here?" "Well, when I graduated in early June last year there were no jobs, so I decided to take a trip to Europe, buy a motorcycle and tour." "That's right you rode a cycle to college from your home in Arroyo Grande" "Yes, I've been a rider since I was 16. My dad is a motorcycle shop owner. So I toured Europe and while I was doing that the war started.

When I returned home, my dad said, "You're sure to be drafted into the army unless you can get some consideration from the Air Force." So, I went to L.A. to a big recruiting office and told them about my degree and education. The recruiting Sergeant fell all over himself with a sales talk about joining. The big kicker was the four year hitch, the Sergeant covered that by telling me I could go to OCS, get a commission in the reserve, and the war would likely be over before my hitch was up. Then the Air Force would take me off active duty. He said I could get a good job in the aircraft industry after my time in the Air Force.

So, I signed up, was sent here for OCS in July and was supposed to take this engineering course immediately after. But there was a screw up, and there was no slot in the class. So, they sent me over to Kelly AFB to work on the staff of the maintenance base. So I've been a flunky officer over there for the past four months. However, I probably got a real good Air Force education, so I'll know what to expect when I get my next assignment." "That's interesting Tom. You'll have to tell me what you learned."

"Everybody knows about your baseball, but how did you get here?" Dave told Tom the story.

Field House
Lackland Air Force Base
0730 17 January 1951

The members of E & M class 01-51 were taking their first PT in the field house. Sgt. Jones had selected Dave as one of the leaders because he knew Dave was in good shape. Some of the members of the class needed to lose some weight. When the PT time was up, Sgt. Jones told Dave he had a line on a catcher for him. "Come by my office when you can, and I'll give you the info." "Thank you Sergeant."

Later that day Dave visited Sgt. Jones and learned about a retired Air Force Sgt. who had played some semi-pro ball and lives here in San Antonio. Sgt. Jones said, "His name is Ben Brown" and gave Dave his phone number.

Later that day Dave received a post card from B.B. Katcher. He reported starting a program of catching instruction by Bill Parks the veteran catcher of the San Francisco Sea Lions. The Dukes had retained Parks to work with B.B. to improve his catching techniques. He also reported he had been attending church at Menlo Park Presbyterian and "I'm getting close to joining!" Dave was excited about that. If B.B. became a Christian he would be the second person he had led to accept the Lord.

Amphitheater Classroom
Lackland Air Force Base
1400 24 March 1951

It was graduation time for the officers who had completed the ten week Engineering & Maintenance Officers course. Dave was thinking about the past ten weeks. The course had been interesting. The major emphasis had been on managing the maintenance process. A good knowledgeable sergeant is critical. "If you get a bad one try to replace him. Remember the airmen and non-commissioned officers do the work."

The weekly briefings on the progress of the war continued. By February 12, the UN line ran from just south of Seoul in the west, through Chipyong in mid-peninsula and Kangnong on the east coast, well beflow the 38th Parallel.

An operation Dave found most interesting was a paratroop drop of the 187th Airborne Combat Team north of Chunchon to block the escape of the Communists (CCF) and North Korean troops in conjunction with operation Ripper. On March 23 at 0900, 80 C-119s and 55 C-46 aircraft transported the paratroops to the drop. At 1830 the 187th combat team linked up with an armor task force. However they did not trap the North Korean main force. It had withdrawn north of the Imjin River, leaving only a rear guard.

In the last days of March, the 8th Army had consolidated positions below or near the 38th Parallel. The 187th, dependent on air drops had received 264 tons of ammunition and food in 56 supply missions flown by the Air Force.

Just a week ago Dave had received a letter from Hank James, reporting that he had been awarded the advertising contract by Turner Chevrolet. It would mean much activity and a new source of income for Dave.

It was time for awarding of certificates of completion of the Officers Engineering & Maintenance course. After almost six months of school and training sessions, Dave was looking forward to playing baseball again.

Petersburg Hotel
Petersburg, Florida
10:00 AM March 26, 1951

Dave had finally arrived at 2:00 AM this morning after his travel from

San Antonio. He had departed San Antonio at 6:00 Saturday night on a flight to Dallas. His next flight was to Atlanta. He arrived there just in time to make his connection with a flight to Tampa. Then it was a taxi ride to the hotel. There was a room reservation for him so he was able to take a shower and fall into bed. Dave had advised traveling secretary Ray Arnold that he would arrive very early Monday morning and not to expect him to report for training until Tuesday. Arnold had reserved a room for him with no roommate, for which Dave was thankful.

Dave was about to go down for breakfast when the phone rang. It was Ray Arnold. "I understand you arrived in the middle of the night." "Yes it was a long trip. I'll have to sleep some more today to catch up. I'm about to go to breakfast." "Okay Dave, I'll see you at dinner tonight." "That's fine Ray."

After breakfast, Dave went to the front desk to confirm the reservation he had made for Jill. It was confirmed. The clerk said, "We will give her a room on the top floor away from the player's rooms." "Thank you."

Petersburg Hotel
5:35 PM March 28, 1951

Dave had entered the hotel after the bus ride from Knickerbockers' Field. He asked at the front desk if Miss Jill Garber had checked in. The clerk said she had and directed him to a house phone. "Hello Jill, this is Lieutenant Mason calling." "Oh, I don't know any Lieutenant Mason you must have the wrong room." "Oh, I'm sorry, please excuse the call and Dave hung up." Now we'll see what happens. Dave went to his room, and when he entered, the phone was ringing. "Lieutenant Mason, Sir." "I'm not a sir, and I'm looking for Dave Mason, the baseball player." "Please hold the line and I'll see if he's here." Dave held the phone away, and said in a loud voice, "Is there a baseball player here by the name of Dave Mason." "Oh Dave, you're carrying this too far." Dave started to laugh and couldn't stop. Finally Jill joined in. Finally, Dave said, "Where's your sense of humor

Jill?" There was no answer from Jill.

"Okay, Jill, if you won't recognize Lieutenant Mason, will you let just a regular fellow named Dave Mason buy you dinner?" "Oh, I would like that Mr. Mason." More laughs "Are you ready to be serious Dave." "Okay, I'll be serious. What time do you want to eat? "How about 6:30, but you can come to see me any time." "That sounds good. I'll be there in about twenty minutes."

When Dave entered Jill's room he picked Jill up and carried her to a chair and started kissing her on her lips, her face and neck. "Please Dave don't get carried away." "What kind of a greeting is that after six months?" "It's just not like you. If this is Lieutenant Mason, I wonder about him." Dave laughed again, but this time Jill didn't, and Dave noticed. "Okay, you can fix your lipstick and we'll go to dinner." "Fine Dave, as Jill got out of Dave's lap and went into the bathroom, he could tell she wasn't happy.

In the dining room many of the players came by to say hello to Dave, but the real reason was to "look over" Jill. B.B. Katcher had let the cat out of the bag by telling his teammates that Dave's girl friend of more than five years was coming to town. The players wanted to know what Dave's girl looked like. Jill soon said, "Let's finish our dinner, go to my room and order desert from room service. I don't want to be looked over anymore." Dave laughed and said, "You're getting more attention tonight than you get on a late Friday afternoon flight full of businessmen." "Yes, and I don't like it."

Later in Jill's room, they had finished their desert and Dave had taken the tray out to the hall. When he returned, Jill said, "It's time to talk Dave." "That's fine Jill."

"First, I don't like New York and living in the east because of the weather and the cities are too big. I'm a country girl and a city like San Francisco is as big as I can take. I would not look forward to living in New York for seven months and California for five. I couldn't hold a decent job after I stopped flying. I observe and talk to businessmen who fly regularly. Many are ambitious, go-go men who talk mainly about their work, not their wife and family. I think you Dave, are a go-go man. You play baseball, do personal appearances and in the future I'm sure you will be on radio and TV doing commercials. You will attend Stanford until you earn your master's degree and likely work for an engineering company at the same time. When you are in California you will have to travel to New York each month for your duty weekend if you're still in MATS. You are ambitious and have a great future Dave, but how much time will you have for a wife and family?"

"Since you left for Texas, I joined a Bible study at North Presbyterian Church. I've been learning about the husband being the head of the family in all areas including the spiritual head. Will you have time for all that Dave? Our study now is about the ministry of Jesus. The disciples had returned after Jesus sent them out. They told him all they had done. There were so many people coming and going that Jesus and his disciples had no time to eat so Jesus said, "Let's go off by ourselves to a place where we will be alone and you can rest. I immediately thought of you Dave. You could get so busy you won't have time to eat."

"This is my suggestion to you from a woman's perspective. Before you get married you retire from baseball. Then save some time for your wife and family"

"While I've had dates with two men since you left San Francisco, I haven't found anyone like you Dave. There is no other man affecting my decision to end our close relationship. I started it back in San Luis Obispo more than five years ago and I'm ending it. However I want to be your friend for life Dave because you are one of a kind."

"I'm going home tomorrow and I'll spend the rest of my vacation time at the ranch and visiting Jane, Woody and Sally. I plan to request a transfer back to San Francisco and bid on a Hawaii flight."

"I'm so glad you led me to become a Christian Dave. My life is so much better now. I'll always remember that."

"Well Jill I'm not surprised. Your UAL post cards instead of the penny cards told me you weren't devoting much time to writing to me. Then, when you didn't come to the graduation, I wondered." "Yes, I was having doubts and if I decided to end our relationship it wouldn't be fair for me to attend. Also, I'm sure you realize I'm not enthusiastic about the military." "Yes I've suspected that." "During the big war, my dad was initially exempted because he was raising cattle for the war effort. Then the army needed meat inspectors, so the draft board had my dad inducted and the army made him a Sergeant meat inspector. To manage the ranch, he had to pay a neighbor who was overage for service to do it in addition to running his own ranch. It wasn't working out because there just wasn't enough time in the day."

"Dad applied for a hardship discharge, but was turned down and they transferred him to England. All the meat inspectors were given a bad time when they turned down meat that was bad. Eventually, my mother had to take over managing the ranch."

"Much of what you've said to me is good advice Jill. I did want you to know what the life of a baseball player would be and that's why I explained it after I was sold to the Dukes. But you had to experience it."

"I agree with your decision. During the last six months I have thought a lot about our relationship Jill. Since I've had no other long time girl friend I've not experienced a comparison with others. I have come to the conclusion that we have very different interests. This could result in our future inability to have good conversations and not do a lot of talking together. That would reduce our interest in spending time together. I think you and I have come to a good decision."

"I do want to be your friend and I wish you the best in your future Jill. Please let me know your progress in getting back to California." "I will Dave. Now I should go to bed because my flight leaves at 8:30 in the morning. Oh, I left the keys to your car with the Coral Gables Apartment Manager. I thought he should have them in case the car had to be moved." "That was a good decision Jill. Okay, I'll give you a last big hug and I'll be gone." "Thank you for everything Dave." "Goodbye Jill." "Goodbye Dave."

As he walked to his room Dave thought I think Jill and I have made a fortunate decision that has avoided some future unhappiness. One big lesson I have learned is not to tell any girl that I love her until I'm sure I want to court her to be my wife and be the mother of my children. Since I had only three dates and the family dinner with Sharon before she came to San Antonio, I really don't know her. I must remember what I have learned as I get to know Sharon better.

ISBN 142515230-9

9 781425 152307